THE SILVER HAND

ALSO BY SHAWN CARPENTER

The Price of Redemption

THE SILVER HAND

The Tides of Magic:

Book 2

SHAWN CARPENTER

SAGA PRESS

LONDON **NEW YORK** TORONTO
AMSTERDAM/ANTWERP NEW DELHI SYDNEY/MELBOURNE

SAGA PRESS
AN IMPRINT OF SIMON & SCHUSTER, LLC
1230 AVENUE OF THE AMERICAS, NEW YORK, NEW YORK 10020

First Saga Press trade paperback edition August 2026

SAGA PRESS and colophon are trademarks of Simon & Schuster, LLC

Interior design by Erika R. Genova

Manufactured in the United States of America

1 3 5 7 9 10 8 6 4 2

Library of Congress Control Number: 2026938256

ISBN 978-1-6680-3375-3 (pbk)
ISBN 978-1-6680-3376-0 (ebook)

To Friends here and gone. I regret not spending enough time with all of you.

To my Wife, my Children, and my Children's Children, each a Pole Star.

To my Mother and the memory of my Father.

To my Brother and my old brothers at arms.

To all who struggle to steer our world off a lee shore.

To my heroes, one and all.

Speaking of heroes: Слава Україні! Слава героям!

(English translation: *Glory to Ukraine! Glory to the heroes!*)

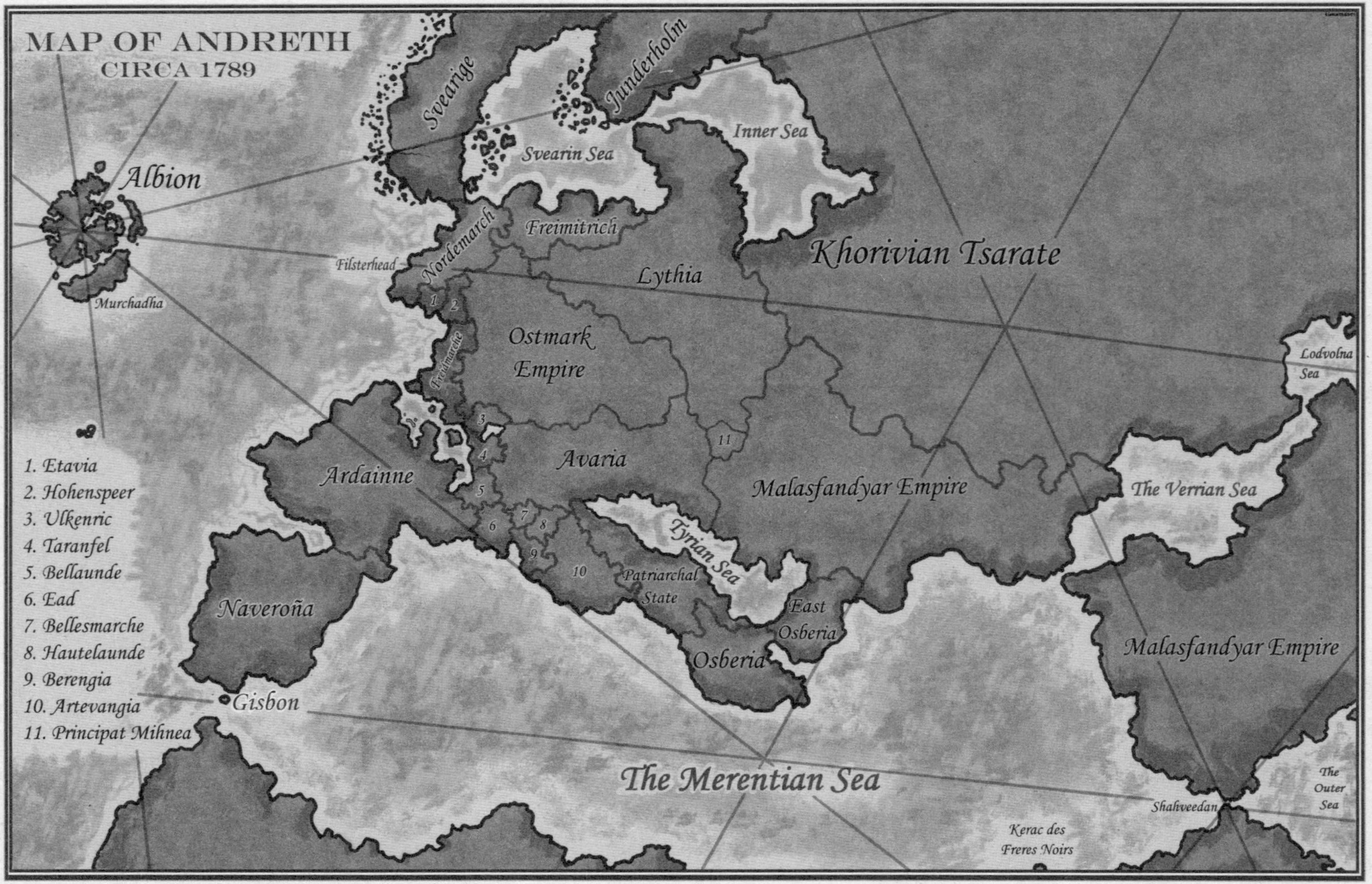
MAP OF ANDRETH
CIRCA 1789
Albion
Murchadha
Sveariqe
Svearin Sea
Junderholm
Inner Sea
Filsterhead
Nordemarch
Freimitrich
Lythia
Khorivian Tsarate
1
2
Freimarche
Ostmark
Empire
3
4
5
6
7
8
9
10
11
Avaria
Ardainne
Naveroña
Gisbon
Malasfandyar Empire
Tyrian Sea
Patriarchal
State
East
Osberia
Osberia
Lodvolna
Sea
The Verrian Sea
Malasfandyar Empire
The Merentian Sea
Shahveedan
The
Outer
Sea
Kerac des
Freres Noirs
1. Etavia
2. Hohenspeer
3. Ulkenric
4. Taranfel
5. Bellaunde
6. Ead
7. Bellesmarche
8. Hautelaunde
9. Berengia
10. Artevangia
11. Principat Mihnea

PART ONE

chapter 1

Rue Nath, newly minted post captain and temporary commander of the *Redemption*, 38 guns, stood at the taffrail and smiled as he watched the island fortress of Gisbon sink below the horizon astern. His countenance was in marked contrast to Enid d'Tancreville, the noble Ardain expatriate who now served as his ship's magister. While he wore a boyish grin which would do him no credit with the ship's crew if they could see it, Enid's lips were set in a grim line and her forehead was creased with worry.

Perhaps sorcerers as accomplished as Enid must adopt such a long view that they are robbed of the ability to live in the moment, Nath thought. Out loud, he said, "Come now, Enid, how can you frown at the spectacle of such a great tower of stone vanishing like lost Eressea beneath the waves? See how the old fortifications are pricked out in white under the forenoon sun? It reminds me of a passage from one of Maupin's plays—"

"Yes, yes," Enid said. "It is lovely. I am more concerned with the sea and sky before us, however. Mid Yeardly remarked that the hazy smudge on the horizon is likely to be heavy weather. I have yet to learn to revel in the crazed rocking of a vessel beset by storm, and I find the approach of a tempest daunting."

"The barometer is sinking," Nath admitted. "But not so rapidly as to indicate what I would call heavy weather. Simply weather. Certainly not a tempest. You should adopt a sailor's view of nature's capriciousness and enjoy the sun while it shines but prepare for the inevitable storms. Take the middle ground between the grasshopper and the ant."

"Your allusion escapes me."

"Oh, it regards a common fable praising ants who labor to the exclusion of pleasure to prepare for lean times and chastising grasshoppers for their short-sighted profligacy."

"It may surprise you to learn cautionary tales concerning carefree excess are not common among the more aristocratic circles to which my family belonged." There was a touch of dark humor in Enid's voice, but Nath was relieved her tone lost some of its gloom. "I will strive to take your advice to heart. I must say your serenity in the face of what awaits us at Middlesea surprises me."

"I am quite sensible of the potential ruin of my reputation a court-martial represents, Enid. But there is naught I can do about it now, save prepare to defend myself as well as I may." Nath's smile was vaguely apologetic. "I am satisfied my logs will speak for themselves. If they do not, my fate was predetermined by Lord Ambrose's friends in Admiralty, and any failing is in their character, not mine."

"Forgive me, but you sound as fatalistic as a Malasfandyari mystic."

"Not fatalistic, I assure you," Nath smiled. "I will fight tooth and nail to defend myself, but there are no foes before me now, only a bright day, an amiable breeze, and a fine sailing vessel beneath my feet."

"Again, I find your serenity admirable!"

"Admire it while you may," Nath said with a grin. "I reckon it will be a much rarer commodity once I've trod Admiral Morrin's carpet and received formal notice of my court-martial."

Enid mustered a thin smile for his jest and left him to his own company to conduct practical magic lessons for the young gentles. Alone on the quarterdeck, Nath loosed a long sigh. *Poor Enid,* he thought. *She may have pinned her fate on a falling star.*

He closed the door on the disheartening prospect with an effort and turned his face toward the warm sun and his mind toward ways to coax the best speed and handling from *Redemption*, even if he would not command her long enough to enact his theories.

The next three days gave Nath ample opportunity to make what changes to the rigging and displacement of cargo could be accomplished with the time and hands available to him. He was not at all pleased with the rake of *Redemption*'s masts, but there was nothing he could do about them at the moment. He could shift some things around the hold to throw her on a better strake for swift sailing, though, despite the remorseful expressions of some of the old *Alarum*s who had assumed they would be on something approaching a holiday on the voyage from Gisbon to Middlesea, regardless of what might await them there. *Let them grumble,* Nath thought. *They'll forget all about the sweat spilled correcting the Naveroñians' heedless packing of* Redemption*'s hold! We'll make port a day earlier without her listing starboard and settled to aft like a great cow, taking her ease!*

His understanding of his crew's moods was confirmed when, at the end of their efforts, the frigate lay over half a strake and added at least a knot to her running speed. Their spontaneous cheer at the joy of it warmed his heart, as did the overheard words of one of the topmen as she descended the ratlines to the deck, "That's our cap'n. He's a sailor's sailor, he is!"

Despite his short stature, he felt ten feet tall as he strode across the quarterdeck to check the current course at the binnacle. Satisfied, he called out to Yeardly, "I leave her to you, Mid Yeardly!"

The mid's sharp salute and joyous smile broke Nath's officerly reserve long enough for an answering wink to slip past, but it was firmly restored by the time he reached the taffrail. He stood next to one of a pair of brightly polished chase guns sited there. When he laid a hand on the grim, warlike visage of some Orthodox saint that adorned the gun, he found the metal warmed by the afternoon sun. He admired the gun frankly, and if he were the captain who received *Redemption*, he would fight the Board of Ordnance tooth and nail to keep it and its sibling aboard.

The Naveroñians weren't famed for the quality of their guns, but this pair had breech marks proclaiming them to be products from the famed Ouvrard foundry in Arleonne. He was mortally certain a fleeing foe would find their accuracy disconcerting in the hands of a crack team of gunners. *Perhaps I will sift out the best of the gunners aboard tomorrow and put these beauties through their paces.* The gods know they'd find it a relief from wrestling with those lumps of brutish iron with which the Dons replaced *Redemption*'s great guns. It irked him to think of her original armament gracing the gun deck of some pigsty frigate in the kingdom's notoriously lax "navy."

The bleak thought passed quickly under the warm sun and cool spray of an idyllic Merentian day. He sighed contentedly. The only improvement he could imagine to the day was the taste of smoke from one of Enid's sublime cigarillos. As appealing as he found the day's perfection, though, he couldn't help gazing ahead at the cloud-dulled horizon before them and speculating eagerly on how well *Redemption* would weather rough seas, wind, and rain.

Enid resumed the mids' sorcery lessons on the third day out of Gisbon. The ship was now running as smoothly as could be hoped, with such an imbalanced admixture of new hands and veteran *Alarum*s. Nath kept his mids busy drilling their divisions to blend the new hands into the ship's people, but was careful to leave time enough for Enid to continue the training routine she established aboard *Alarum*. In this, as in all things it seemed, he was filled with an unshakable optimism. As

Enid opened various basic instructional sorcery books to the pages pertinent to the day's lesson and laid them out on a table in her workspace on the orlop, her opinion of Nath's phlegmatic outlook on the future alternated between envy and irritation. His court-martial was entirely motivated by a personal grudge and political opportunism. It represented the malice of powerful enemies. Enemies who were now hers by way of association. If she were reduced to a persona non grata by Lord Ambrose Aixely's supporters in Admiralty, she was unlikely to find a Magister's berth again. Worse still, it seemed likely the black mark against her name would make finding a commission in an Albionic cavalry regiment just as unlikely, particularly considering Nath's admittedly biased characterization of those regiments as cliquish social clubs for the sons of Albion's most powerful noble families.

Her finances were not as bleak as her military prospects. She had substantial funds in Albion thanks to her father's investments there, as well as the prize money for *Redemption*. She could sail far more safely to the Spice Islands or Free Colonies from Albion. Once there, she could join an expatriate regiment or stand one up herself. Realistically, though, her chances of such a regiment playing a direct role in the liberation of her homeland were slim. Most Royalist regiments were composed of old aristocrats yearning to prove their military prowess undiminished by age or young fops fascinated by colorful uniforms and certain of an easy victory over mere common folk. The Albion Royal Navy had thus far demurred from providing transport for such questionable formations, viewing such an effort as a waste of time, treasure, and cargo space.

The young gentles filed in as she finished her preparation; Yeardly first with Dinwitty in tow, then Harlech, her fair cheeks blooming from the effort of a rapid descent from the dizzying heights of the mainmast where she'd been skylarking on the pretense of observing the topmen at their duties. It was more difficult than usual to keep the mids focused on her brief lecture and demonstration. She assumed they were too excited at the prospect of a new ship to explore. Only Yeardly was attentive, despite the material being far below his competence thanks to her individual mentoring. In the end, she surrendered and closed her book with a loud clap, which elicited a startled jerk from Dinwitty.

"That is all for today, and I pray you're never required to remember Van Dernan's ratio to account for the difference in powder charges during an equatorial solar eclipse, which, as I say it, seems likely. Have you any questions?"

She was already rising to leave when Dinwitty piped up, asking, "Can ghosts and spirits be commanded like elementals?"

Enid sat down and regarded the young man gravely. "Have you encountered a ghost or spirit recently?"

"No, Magister, leastwise not myself. But some of the people are saying they've seen shadows moving belowdecks and the sound of footsteps where there weren't nobody walking!"

"Some hands in my division say the same," Harlech chimed in, her eyes round as saucers.

Enid glanced at Yeardly. "Are the hands practicing on Dinwitty and Harlech?"

The pock-faced older mid shook his head. "I don't believe so. If they are, their tomfoolery extends to me as well. I've been approached with the same tales. Lieutenant Merryweather has been advised."

"Good. Now, Mid Dinwitty, the answer to your question is both yes and no. Ghosts and non-elemental spirits are not subject to the same basic formulations as elementals, but they can be negotiated with. Some advanced methods can make persuading them to your cause more efficacious."

"When do we learn those?" Dinwitty practically quivered with excitement at the prospect of commanding ghosts.

"Never." The certitude with which Enid imbued the single word wiped the excitement from Dinwitty's face. "None of you are prepared to treat with such powers, which are almost uniformly malefic and deceitful. You would likely lose your own soul in such an encounter. There is a reason necromancy is purely focused upon wardings, and banishment and other applications are illegal in all but the most backward and benighted societies. If you find yourself in the presence of a ghost or spirit, come to me posthaste so I can take the appropriate action."

Yeardly waited until the other mids had filed out of the workroom before asking, "Do you think *Redemption* might be haunted? Providence knows she's seen enough betrayal and murder for one of Kirutzov's tragedies."

Enid remembered her first impression of *Redemption* as a predatory beast, husbanding and redoubling its enmity until the opportunity arose to spring forth and spend its hatred in a welter of blood and fear. Her keen arcane senses had set her nose a-wrinkle with the smell of strange magic that hung over the ship as well, and the odor had not dissipated since Nath and the few remaining crew from *Alarum* took possession of her. She had no doubt something was amiss with *Redemption*, but she kept her tone light as she answered Yeardly.

"Referencing Kirutzov now, are you? Your interest in the great dramatists may expand past Captain Nath's at this rate. As to *Redemption* being haunted, oppressed by ghosts or malefic spirits, I prefer not to speculate. Instead, I'll make some inquiries of my own."

"It would be my pleasure to assist you with your investigation, Magister," Yeardly said, the depth of his longing to be involved betrayed by his formal manner.

"I'm sure I would profit from your involvement," Enid said, intending to demur, but a phantom intuition changed her mind mid-sentence. "Particularly if you were to devote yourself to a close study of the chapter on warding sigils and seals in the volume by Ceridwaith I lent you last week."

"I will make it my priority, Magister!" Yeardly touched the brim of his hat in salute and left with a satisfied spring in his step.

Not all ghosts are murderous, Lady d'Tancreville, Dunaughy drawled in the recesses of Enid's brain. His "voice" wavered and sounded distant.

Of course not, Enid replied mentally. *But I doubt we'll find any felicitous specters aboard, present company excepted, of course.*

It seems unlikely. There is undoubtedly something here, though. I cannot put a name to it. Perhaps older relicts can conceal themselves from the more recent dead, like me, or perhaps the presence is not a ghost at all, but an entity of some other sort. The violence the mutineers visited on their officers could easily have manifested a spirit of wrath or despair.

"I agree, but it seems likely this is a riddle *Redemption*'s next magister must solve. Nath tells me she will surely receive a new captain before the disposition of his court-martial. Let us put this haunting aside for a more pressing question: Why do you sound so distant and weak?"

Even though my axis mundi is now the silver ring on your right hand, my connection to Alarum *is still quite strong. I am struggling to break the connection completely, but it is difficult. It is almost as if the very vessel seeks to bar my entrance, but I can find no source for this subtle resistance. I fear you may find yourself alone from time to time, as my strength waxes and wanes.*

The memory of Dunaughy's words sprang up to startle her awake each time sleep made inroads until, finally, exhaustion reduced her to a fitful slumber from which she was inevitably startled to wakefulness by a recurring dream of a dark figure who contrived to spy on her from the darkest corners of *Redemption*'s hold. Thus, the third night out of Gisbon found her on deck as two bells of the middle watch rang. The fact that she could translate the infernal bells as an hour past midnight without consulting Dunaughy brought a wan smile to her face.

She found Merryweather and Yeardly taking hot coffee by the taffrail. Enid accepted her own cup from the cook's mate, whose open, gap-toothed smile of hospitality melted her usual urbane distance. Enid raised the steaming mug in a casual salute to the fellow before he hobbled off on a clubfoot, which brought to mind Archbishop

Archambault-Deodat, the Theocratic *le diable* Bordeaux. She noticed Merry's expression was troubled and shared a brief glance with Yeardly, whose mien also betrayed more than a touch of worry.

"What is amiss?" Enid asked, and Merryweather answered in a voice so low it was barely discernible to her over the hissing song of the sea as *Redemption* slid swiftly through its foamy embrace.

"Suspicions that *Redemption* is beset by some form of a Naveroñian curse are spreading among the ship's people. There have been half a dozen reports of a shadowy figure of a man in the hold."

Gooseflesh prickled to life on Enid's forearms, but she succeeded in banishing all trace of alarm from her voice when she replied, "Well, the hold is a darksome place, particularly on a vessel with such a troubled history as *Redemption*. Are the reports from individuals of a serious mindset who are not prone to morbid fancy?"

Her words elicited sheepish smiles from both Yeardly and Merryweather, the latter of whom said, "In truth, you describe few, if any, of our friends from before the mast. Sailors are possessed of remarkable deep wells of superstition and dread of the uncanny."

"Unlike their scrupulously skeptical officers," Enid remarked dryly. Merryweather and Yeardly accepted the jibe with smiles tinged with embarrassment.

"I'll warrant you'll find ghosts and goblins in the ship's shadows less ridiculous when you've been at sea as long as we," Merryweather chuckled. "But tell us true, Magister, have you not perceived a—how can I say it?—a weight has settled over the ship? A blanket sodden with night sweats born of sinking cheer and rising dread?"

Enid lit a cigarillo to gain time to consider her answer. It would be rude and ill-advised to openly share her thoughts with Merryweather and Yeardly until she revealed them to Captain Nath. She slowly drew and exhaled a deep lungful of smoke and said, "I have experienced something along those lines, but I assume it is the product of the dread with which I hold the court-martial awaiting Captain Nath in

Middlesea. Certainly, the ship's people began the voyage with light hearts. Why should they not, leaving the threat of being stranded in Gisbon behind and delaying the dissolution of the heroic *Alarum*s for a last cruise together? But each day we speed closer to Albion and a future which is uncertain for us all, from the lowest powder monkey to Captain Nath himself. It is bound to produce a slowly building melancholy, think you not?"

Her fellow officers seemed dissatisfied with her rationalization but were reluctant to appear credulously superstitious. Yeardly chewed his lip for a moment and then asked, "So you do not believe the ship's increasing dolor is eldritch in nature?"

Enid shrugged and exhaled a stream of smoke, which made three circuits around her head before darting skyward. To Yeardly and Merryweather, it was the very image of Lady Chum-Chum in miniature. "As for that, I cannot say for certain. *Redemption* has a tragic history and has been in enemy hands for many years. She may be laden with the evil spiritual residue left behind by bloody betrayals or dozens of minor malevolent charms which activate gradually and serially the further we sail from Neveroña. Such nefarious practices are common, according to Herbstrom's invaluable text."

"You cannot detect such charms?" Merryweather asked, arching a brow.

"A skilled mage will camouflage such workings behind or within beneficial dweomers, such as the one that prevents *Redemption*'s hull from becoming too befouled by weeds and moss. It is for this reason captured ships are stripped of all their native enchantments, which are then replaced with new, trustworthy ensorcellment."

"That is so," Merryweather said. "I had always assumed the practice is intended to make the maintenance of a former prize's enchantments easier for our Navy's magisters. Now I see there are deeper reasons as well."

chapter 2

The strange frigate was hull-up on the horizon, a creamy curl of froth flying before her prow like the wild mane of a river horse. She'd been spotted before dawn when the glitter of sunlight lit up her t'gallants while darkness still shrouded the rest of the visible world. A long, coy dance followed, with the stranger obviously as intent on closing with *Redemption* as she was on avoiding his unwanted attention. The stranger was long, clean-bottomed, and stiff, however, and she would not be denied her discourse. As Enid watched, a series of colorful flags were hauled up the ship's mainmast and unfurled with undeniable martial precision and vigor.

"I perceive they are signaling us," Enid observed. "But I am ignorant of this language of flags. What do they signify?"

"She is making her number," Nath answered with a schoolmaster's patience. He was used to his new ship's sorcerer's wildly inconsistent grasp of naval lore. At one moment she would speak with the authority of an old salt; the next she'd ask questions lubberly enough to shame the meanest landsman. Her eccentricities were well worth bearing, though, considering her vast skill with the sorcerous arts. Her moments of ignorance hardly stood notice compared with the amount of knowledge she'd absorbed after only a few months at sea. Half smiling,

Nath turned to the young girl standing nervously a few feet down the rail, a heavy, leather-bound signal book clutched in her hands.

"Mid Harlech, what number is that?"

Harlech's fingers flashed down a page bearing depictions of flags and the numbers they stood for. Once she'd interpreted the numbers, she flipped through the book's thick pages to find what ship bore them.

"*Dutiful*, 40, sir! Home Fleet, Captain Dorning commanding!"

"Thankee, Mid Harlech." Nath's curt nod of approval elicited a very non-officerly grin of pleasure from the young girl. Enid shook her head. Eventually, Harlech would master the intricacies of military bearing and present the same stern, blank face expected of officers, whether they were announcing a victory or surrendering their sword to the enemy. On that day Albion would have a better sea officer, but another bit of brightness would be banished from a world that tended increasingly to the drab and colorless.

"Well, sir, what d'you think?" This from Nath to Oxley, an aging lieutenant whose slumped shoulders and lumbering manner seemed to be dissolving as he resolved into a taut, brisk officer.

"She's the right lines for *Dutiful*, and it would not be surprising to find her cruising these waters. We'll likely have the Albion in sight tomorrow next, after all. Or she could be bearing orders and dispatches for the Gisbon fleet."

"True enough," Nath granted, raising a come-hither glass to his eye and studying the rapidly growing vessel intently. "But does she *feel* like *Dutiful* to you?"

With any other officer under whom he'd served during the last decade or more, Oxley would have believed the question to be a trap to make him look foolish or an invitation to toady by guessing at his commander's opinion and then playing the obedient parrot. With Nath, Oxley knew, this was not the case. He thought for a moment, allowing his instincts free play, and then shook his head gravely.

"No, sir. She don't. Sure, and she got the private signal right, but she don't smell right. Look at her rigging—it's a might sloppy, ain't it?

She's got Albion canvas hung on her, but she don't quite look Middle-sea-fashion, do she?"

Before Nath could answer, a pock-faced, straw-haired mid hurried up, a squat, bald-headed sailor in tow. The mid knuckled his brow in courtesy to his captain.

"Your pardon, sir, but Borrel has something to report."

"Thank you, Mid Yeardly. Let us hear it and sharply, Borrel."

Borrel, an acting carpenter's mate, stiffened to something resembling attention as he addressed his captain and twisted his greasy cap in his tar-stained hands as he spoke. "Well, sir, word is she flew the *Dutiful*'s number?"

Nath's eyes lit with amusement. News traveled from stem to stern of a man-of-war faster than a beam of sunlight. Such was the magic of the common sailor. He nodded for Borrel to continue.

"Well, sir, yonder frigate may be showin' *Dutiful*'s number, but that's the *Ambition*, sure as I'm standin' here."

"How can you be so sure?"

Borrel's fretful expression was transformed by beaming pride. "I reco'nize 'er figgerhead, sir. Helped carve 'er meself. Caught a sharp set o' remarks from 'er blue-lighter of a first luff fer makin' its pillars—err—its berzooms too big." The sailor cast a chary glance at Enid, whose aloof expression remained unchanged. Reassured he was not about to be transformed into some creature ill-suited for survival on the deck of a frigate, he nodded firmly and announced loudly, "I'd reco'nize them berzooms anywhere, sir! Them's *Ambition*'s berzooms!"

"It's fortunate for us you have a keen eye for such things, Borrel! An extra tot for this man, Yeardly!" The pock-faced mid shared a fierce grin with the sailor and clapped him on the back as they returned to their duty stations.

"He'd have been better served by 'pillars' if his intent was to speak circumspectly in the presence of a lady. I hadn't the vaguest idea of what the word meant."

"Pillows, Enid. Pillows."

"Oh. Of course." Enid paused a moment. "While I appreciate your concern for my nautical education, sir, there are areas of jargon that I am not likely to find applicable to my duties aboard ship. Please do not exert yourself explaining every colloquialism we might encounter while in company."

Nath gave a brief snort of amusement and turned his glass back to the *Dutiful/Ambition*. Enid watched his placid face and knew that he was performing a myriad of calculations that, while rooted in such mundane matters as wind, tide, and the sailing qualities of his ship and the stranger, were every bit as complex as any magical formulation she'd ever attempted. She and Oxley stood silently, ready to give their advice should Nath request it, but fully aware that the decision, any decision, would be his.

"*Ambition* may have been captured by the Rats." Nath used the disparaging term for the Theocratic Republic, which currently ruled Ardainne without reservation. He knew that Enid, although an Ardain expatriate, lost no love for the brutal regime that ruled her homeland from behind mountains of headless noble corpses. "She could have been refitted in Ourest and turned around as quick as Mid Yeardly's head when a pretty girl walks by. She is longer than us, I perceive, and in far better sailing trim than the Naveroñians left our poor *Redemption*. I wish we'd had a few weeks to make the barky ship-shape, but time and tide are relentless."

Nath chewed the corner of his mouth a moment and then closed his come-hither glass with a snap.

"Barring Magister d'Tancreville summoning up a kraken to devour *Ambition*, pillows and all, or a team of monstrous undines to pull us over the horizon as fast as I can say 'knife,' it seems an engagement is inevitable." Here he glanced at Enid with a theatrically hopeful expression. She shook her head, a shadow of a smile lurking at the corners of her lips. Nath heaved a stage-worthy sigh and shrugged at Oxley. "Well, if there are to be no krakens or Sea King's stallions, I suppose we must do this the old-fashioned way."

"They're signaling rendezvous for dispatches, sir!" Harlech's voice rang with girlish indignation.

"The rascals!" Nath exclaimed for the little mid's benefit, along with a wink for Enid and Oxley. "We'll put a round turn to their capers!"

"Shall I call the crew to quarters, sir?"

"No, Lieutenant. Let us pretend to be taken in by their ruse. Send a quiet word to Lieutenant Merryweather to prepare the gun deck for action as quietly as may be. Let the mids instruct the hands to move slowly to their positions and make every effort to appear as if they expect nothing more than a friendly conversation between two of the king's ships. What is more, I desire them to look as lubberly as they might—let *Ambition* take them for a lot of slipshod idlers making the best of a lax captain who won't know the difference or else don't care. Let her think we're taken in by her sheep's clothing—then, Providence permitting, we'll show her our fangs."

The *Redemption*s, most of whom were former *Alarum*s who'd been put ashore in Gisbon as a demonstration of Lord Aixely's spite, took great pleasure in practicing upon the Rats' credulity. After making a show of sloppily taking in sail to allow *Ambition* to catch them up, the sailors loitered about quite disreputably. With a sure knowledge of exactly what actions and poses would excite instant and savage rebuke from a hard-driving captain or his officers, they arrayed themselves about the ship in a manner calculated to warm the heart of any predator. In a world filled with lions, *Redemption* presented the image of a plump, limping gazelle.

From a position reserved for her on the less exalted side of the quarterdeck, Enid watched with interest as the sailors above deck lolled about or sauntered to and fro, their hands thrust deeply and heretically into the pockets of their slop pants. Her vantage point allowed her a narrow glimpse into the gun deck below. What a contrast! There

*Redemption*s stood in tense knots by the guns they served, each man and woman of the larboard watch ready at a moment's notice to shatter the illusion of peace and complacency above under the roaring hammer of a broadside. Lieutenant Merryweather, her face scarred from the wound she received in cutting *Redemption* out, stalked from gun to gun, encouraging their crews to speed and accuracy. Enid marveled at her way with the sailors, one moment stern and confident, the next laughing at a bloodthirsty jest. Like Nath, she seemed to have a muse whispering in her ear with exactly what words would encourage each salt to put forth their maximum effort.

Enid's attention was drawn back above deck by a thin but clear call from *Ambition*, which was now gliding smoothly up on the larboard side, a little more than a cable's length off the aft quarter. "Halloo the ship! We could not make your number! What ship are you?"

"The rascal means to pull us into a conversation—hopefully draw the captain to the near rail and then blast as many of us as he may to hell," Nath observed gravely from the side of his mouth, speaking in a stage whisper as if his words might be audible over the distance separating the two ships. "Give him a taste of his own medicine, Magister!"

Enid nodded curtly and raised the brass speaking horn to her lips as Nath had instructed. In perfectly Ardenois-accented Ardain, she cried out, "We are the *Belligerence*, en route to Ourest! What ship are you?"

She saw the officers on the opposite quarterdeck stiffen in momentary surprise. They'd expected an answer in Albion, not Ardain, nor one that identified their prey as a Theocratic naval vessel bound for an Ardain port. As one, they turned their faces toward a whip-thin woman who wore no coat and whose shirtsleeves were carelessly pushed up past her elbows. *There is* Ambition*'s captain,* Enid thought. *She has cast her uniform coat away because it would be red or gold rather than the blue worn by an Albion officer.* Enid saw the woman snatch the speaking trumpet from her lieutenant and lift it to her lips, but whatever she might have said was lost as Nath shouted the command to fire and the guns of the larboard side cleared their throats in a roar calculated to rend heaven from earth.

The guns, which could not be run full out and preserve the illusion of credulity demanded to secure surprise, were snugged up so that their muzzles pressed into the wood of the still-secured firing ports. Enid saw one of the ports blasted loose by the initial volley and sail off to skip several times before scything into the face of a following wave. That splash was soon joined by others as *Redemption*'s broadside slammed home, tearing wood, guns, and people into mangled splinters and flying debris. Nath had timed the broadside well, so that it erupted just as *Ambition* slid nearly abreast of *Redemption*. Only the front two or three guns missed their targets entirely, sending their iron balls scorching through the air just forward of the enemy frigate's bow.

Ambition staggered visibly under the simultaneous impact of so much heavy iron, but when the shudder had passed, Enid saw that she'd suffered no crippling damage. All her masts still stood, and there was no indication her helm would not answer as needed.

From the corner of her eye Enid saw the few red-coated "lobsters" not allocated to the prize crew scurry up the ratlines to take up their positions in the fighting tops and rain death on the enemy deck far below, but she could not tear her eyes away from the dully gleaming muzzles that seemed to grow miraculously from Ambition's gun ports. *How many were there?* she wondered. *Twenty-five? A hundred?* Even as the question entered her mind, the answer was obscured by a blinding flash of cyan smoke and flame and the ululating warble of iron balls tearing a path through the heavens to wreak vengeance upon *Redemption*.

Enid stood stoically, the hailing horn clutched absently in her left hand. She recalled Nath's admonition never to flinch from fire in front of the other officers and crew and stood her ground even as the more pragmatic part of her brain screamed for her to take cover behind the bulwarks. She saw one of the enemy balls punch a star-shaped hole through the scantlings before her and carry away the legs of a marine rushing to his place at the rail. The sight at once horrified and comforted her. Even the thick oak of the ship's outer hull would provide no protection from great guns fired at such close range, so ducking below the rails would serve no purpose. Better to stand gamely and let Providence's hand move as it would.

Spell-lock balls began smacking into the surrounding deck, and she bent her will toward Nath. Here, at least, was a circumstance where the mortal caprices of Fortune could be opposed. She handed the speaking trumpet to Mid Harlech, who stood pale and shaking at her side, and quickly wove a ward of protection around the little Albion captain designed to throw astray the flight of any but the most carefully enchanted balls. For herself, she relied upon the dweomers woven into her uniform coat and breeches. The cloth, thick and sturdy as it was, didn't provide as much protection as her hunting leathers, but Nath was punctilious about "proper" uniforms. As the volume of fire increased, Enid sought and found a sylph to thicken the air around her, making her figure less distinct to enemy marksmen in *Ambition*'s tops. As she pulled the sylph around her like a cloak, the unsettling chill of another mage's attention crawled up her spine.

Great guns boomed and roared, and spell-lock balls and jagged splinters shrieked past Enid as she allowed the range of her awareness to widen in search of the other sorcerer's will. In an instant, the chaos of noise and destruction faded until all that remained was an abstract impression of the intangible forces that always crowded the borders of the physical world, even more so where men met in violent contention. Here, the forces of nature and un-nature met and mixed in swirling patterns and vortices that could leave even the most disciplined sorcerer dazzled and overawed. Against this continually shifting backdrop of power and potential, Enid located the tracks of her opponent aboard *Ambition*.

The man was no hedge-witch or fumbling apprentice. That much was clear from the methodical manner with which he marshaled his power. Here was no frantic clawing for whatever weapons might fall to hand, but rather an astute gathering of the most useful entities and forces that could be bent to his will. If he had any obvious shortcoming, it was his apparent lack of concern over covering his efforts behind anything more than the most diaphanous veil of misdirection. Enid wondered at that. Did her opponent deem himself so powerful that feints could be utterly dispensed with in favor of a series of blunt, direct coup de main? Or was he merely a talented journeyman, strong in basic technique but lacking in finesse? The next few moments would tell.

A part of her consciousness continued to register the thunderous exclamations of the great guns and the sharper crackle of spell-lock musketry, but most of her attention was devoted to raising her own sorcerous levies. Sylphs sped to her call, as did undines and certain creatures whose sole glee lay in bending the course of Fortune's wheel to send it careening off in unexpected directions. Raw power responded to her call as well, seeping and surging around her, an amorphous mass of potential awaiting only the caress of her will to give it shape. Unlike her opponent, she did not spurn misdirection and laid down a screen of obfuscatory feints and passes designed to confuse and deceive her enemy.

He sends his sylphs to slow Redemption, a faint, hollow voice inside her ear warned. The silver ring on her left hand chilled noticeably. *His captain wishes to slow us enough that he can gain enough way on us to cross our bow and rake us. Ware the winds!*

Dunaughy! Enid exclaimed silently. *You have been so quiet I had begun to fear—I am with you yet, my lady.* The relict's ghostly voice seemed tired and weak. Tenuous. *And shall be for some time. Have no fear on that account. I've been forced to steward my strength carefully of late, however. There is a force within this ship, a force that oppresses. We'll speak of it more later, when I have the energy. For now, though*—Enid gave a nod and sent her own sylphs to impede *Ambition*. It seemed wiser to her to counter her opponent's efforts in this way rather than sending her sylphs to contend with his. Such a confrontation might result in contrary gusts of wind that did *Redemption* more harm than good. Her concentration faltered momentarily as a great crash sounded nearby and shouts of alarm registered dimly in her mind. With a blink of her eye, she was more fully grounded in the material world again. She stared blankly at a heavy piece of wood that lay amid a litter of slightly smaller debris not three feet from her. Something shook her, and she realized that Nath held her arm near the elbow and was shouting urgently in her ear.

"I have never seen the like of it! I glanced up in time to see the splinter netting writhe! It twisted this way and that and distorted enough to allow that chunk of spar to fall through. We were both nearly brained! I think this is the work of the Rat Magister!"

Enid's expression turned positively feral. Through her bared teeth she hissed, "Brilliantly deduced. If the sea hadn't called you, what a thief-taker you'd have made. Leave me to my work!"

Nath frowned at her answer, but did not pursue the matter. She noticed he was bleeding from a ragged gash across his left cheek and put a finger to the wound, the familiar formulation for a healing cantrip instantly filling her mind. He shook his head vehemently and stepped out of her reach.

"This pinking don't signify against the pounding that Rat bastard is giving us. She has us outgunned and would dearly love to dismast us for a rake and a quick capture. That I cannot allow. If you have something horrible you've been saving for a rainy day, it won't get much wetter than this. You have my word on't!"

Enid glanced around her and saw that *Redemption* had indeed been severely beaten about in the brief time her attention was elsewhere. A lengthy portion of the waist rail was missing, and loose hammock rolls littered the deck. She saw at least one dismounted gun framed by a welter of blood on the deck and could see that Dr. Rondelle's loblolly boys were busy bearing the wounded below. The crew's spirits seemed to remain high, though, and she relished the malicious joy she saw on the face of one of the gun captains as she yanked the lanyard to discharge the great gun under her command. If Nath wanted horrible, she thought, he need only contrive to put that woman aboard *Ambition* with a cutlass in hand.

"I have nothing stored up," Enid said with a frown. "But I will see what I can do. Do you wish to board her?"

"Ashes, no!" Nath snapped, almost recoiling at the thought. "She's either a privateer or a national ship. Either way, you can bet she has three or four times the crew we have. Mine's only a prize crew, and a thin 'un at that. If she closes us, we're done for!"

"Then she will not. Please have Harlech there give me a shove if I appear to be in danger of another braining. I will be indisposed for a few moments."

Without waiting for Nath's reply, Enid once more released herself to study the situation from the far quieter vantage of the Elsewhere, the abstract space between the corporal and preternatural world in which sorcerers treat with the elemental energies they wield. She immediately drove all the undines at her command between the two vessels and planted in their dim, formless minds a fierce loathing of the prospect of these two wooden interlopers in their watery realm ever touching. The density of water between the two ships shifted, like a tide flowing with equal force from a point someplace in the shot-torn margin between them. Without great effort from the Rat Magister, there would be no boarding action today.

A cold victory should *Redemption* be pounded to flinders by the more powerful Rat frigate, though, and that seemed sure to happen if she could not contrive some powerful working to prevent it. She sought Dunaughy's phantom counsel but found him unresponsive. With an inward grimace, she returned a part of her awareness to the tossing, hell-swept deck and her pathetically vulnerable body.

Something pressed against her waist, and she looked down to find Harlech standing before her, both small hands pressed against her.

"What, pray tell, are you about, Mid Harlech?"

"I'm standing by to give you a shove if you look about to be brained, Magister," the little girl answered earnestly. "The captain's orders!"

"Hmm. Well, I'll answer for my own brains for the moment."

"I'll stay near at hand just in case, Magister."

Any reply Enid might have voiced was swallowed up by a caterwauling howl that culminated in a sharp crack somewhere to her left. A spray of splinters filled the air, and Enid stepped protectively in front of Harlech. Whether by fortune or the dweomers surrounding Enid's coat, the little mid was spared any harm. Enid looked up in time to see Nath stagger, however, and rushed to his side as he regained his feet.

"It's nothing, Enid," he reassured her. "Although I wouldn't refuse a bit of aid. The blood is likely to prove distracting."

Nath's hat was missing, no doubt borne overboard by the passing splinter that laid open a neat slice that traced a line from his right brow, across his forehead, and a few inches above past his hairline. The wound bled freely but did not seem to cause Nath any real inconvenience otherwise. She removed a handkerchief from her sleeve and staunched the blood flow with a few quick cantrips and a bit of pressure.

"That will stop the bleeding, but you'll want Rondelle to—"

"Later," Nath snapped, and then nearly fell again. Enid's first fearful thought was that a spell-lock ball had defeated the wards she'd placed on him, but then realized he'd only misstepped, nearly tripping on a spent ball that rolled back and forth on the deck between two pieces of shattered railing. Unconsumed alchemical powder still smoked and hissed in bright blue arcs across the ball's dull black surface. Nath righted himself with a growl and strode forward, shouting arcane orders, and Enid could feel the ship's resolve strengthen as her fighting captain took direct command once more.

"And there is the insult to give the injury its sting," Lieutenant Oxley snarled near Enid's elbow, pointing an accusatory finger at the smoldering ball. "To be butchered by our own good powder and iron!"

"What do you mean?"

"See the color the powder burns there? That's Albion powder. You see enough of it; you get an eye for it. *Ambition* must've had a good supply of powder on her when the Rats took her." It was clear Oxley would have spat but for the sanctity of the quarterdeck, even when reduced to such a chaotic condition.

"You're sure of this?" Enid demanded, the kernel of an idea forming in her mind.

"As sure as perdition, Magister."

Enid seized Harlech by the shoulder and shouted over the fading roar of a cannonade, "Take me to the gunner!"

"I'm only acting gunner, Magister," Anse Loren groused. "And while I'm gratified in your sudden interest in my trade, I find myself a bit indisposed at the instant!"

Loren was from a mercantile family, apparently a spell-lock smith's failed apprentice. Her magical ability, albeit minimal and entirely focused on the intricacies of the mechanical dweomers and alchemical lore necessary to maintain the great guns and the stores of powder that fed their destructive appetites, made her ideal for the role of ship's gunner. Her height, which topped Enid's by at least a head, made her an uncomfortable choice for the gunner's position, however. Loren seemed to have developed extra joints to crouch within the incredibly cramped, low confines of the antechamber to *Redemption*'s suspended magazine and directly oversee the recharging and changing of spell-locks while her mate directed the powder monkeys as they filled powder bags on the other side of a heavily enchanted leather curtain plated with lead. Enid ignored her sour disposition and pressed her again.

"I understand that this room is dampened by enchantment, so powder bags borne through may not be ignited through mischance with a nearby lock, but what of the powder room itself?"

"This is the powder room itself, Magister," Loren snapped, slamming a hopelessly bent lock onto the scarred surface of her abbreviated workbench. "Nartin! Tell those thumbless fumblers on Number

Seven that if they mangle another lock, I'll blow the bastards up myself and save the Rats the trouble!"

"Yes," Enid continued patiently, a heroic effort considering her detestation of the mariner's tendency toward overweening niceness regarding nomenclature. "But the part of the powder room where the powder is actually kept—is that area dampened as well?"

"The magazine. It is called the magazine, and no, it ain't dampened. You keep powder too long under enchantments designed to keep it from firing, and when you need it to fire, it won't. Loses its charge. Now, if you don't mind, Magister . . ."

"A moment more of your time. Will the formula for a spell-lock work to ignite powder for a great gun?"

Loren didn't deign to look up from her work. "Of course. Powder is powder."

The gunner, busy calibrating a stubborn lock, didn't spare Enid a parting glance as she rushed from the powder room, a grim smile barely subdued at the corners of her lips.

"Number Six is the most accurate, Magister," Harlech answered, proud to show off her knowledge while assisting Enid. "The men have written 'Old Bone-Crusher' on her carriage, but they have spelled it wrong. We mustn't judge 'em, though, as they are common sailors and prone to igerr—igra—"

"Ignorance," Enid finished for the stuttering mid as she followed her through the battle-choked gun deck to reach the named gun. Wreckage was thick on the deck, much of it stained a far brighter crimson than the walls and floors it lay on. Twice Enid stopped as Harlech put a hand out, and twice she marveled at the terrifying power the great guns' recoil reflected as they leapt backward like mythical beasts, barely kept in rein by their stout snubbing cables.

The crew of Number Six had indeed misspelled the gun's name when they painted it on its carriage. Enid suspected Harlech had misread as well, however. She doubted that "Old Bunnecrusher" had anything to do with powdering bones.

"It is pronounced ignorance and does indeed beg forbearance from the wise. Now, pray fetch me one of Bonecrusher's iron balls and ask the sergeant in charge of the gun to hold his fire after discharging the next round."

Harlech patiently informed Enid that the man in question was a captain, not a sergeant, and implored her not to stir an inch from the spot she stood lest she be "crushed like a bowl of eggs." A moment later, she returned and thrust a heavy iron ball into Enid's long-fingered hands. Enid produced a scribe from her coat pocket and engraved a lock sigil deep in the ball's surface in no more time than it took the captain of Number Six to shout, "Come along, then, if you please, Spells! T'other guns is gettin' 'em off while we stand here warmin' our thumbs in our arses waitin' to cop it!"

Enid glanced at the waiting gun crew and found them all crouching uneasily around their gun, flinching, and cursing as the guns around them roared their defiance at the heavier Ardain frigate. It was clear to her that these men and women believed that the rapid firing of their gun provided some supernatural protection from the Ardain iron that sought to penetrate *Redemption* and stir her guts into a slush of blood and powdered bone. She put the matter from her mind for future examination—along with Harlech's assertion that a captain commanded each of the guns—and bent her will to the matter at hand.

First, her opposite aboard *Ambition* must be distracted and if that distraction slackened the fire against *Redemption*, so much the better. She extended herself across the waters and sensed the stubborn resolution of the undines beneath her to keep the two frigates apart. The vague outline of the enemy frigate became visible, dull patches of glow along her sides indicating the magical potential of the spell-locks affixed to each of her great guns. Enid's awareness seeped into the Ardain ship's gun deck and she allowed her perceptions to sharpen, but not enough to attract the attention of *Ambition*'s magister. Smoke, shadows, and blood greeted her, but it was clear *Ambition* had suffered less from the engagement than *Redemption*.

Enid's will fought for purchase and found a tenuous toehold among the enemy gun deck's stark, black shadows. Deep in the heart of her foe's domain, she lacked the force of presence to command, but persuasion was well within her means. She purred, wheedled, and coaxed the shadows to do mischief upon the weak, light-loving creatures of the gun deck, an effort that was made all the easier by the malicious nature of the minor Umbra and the Veil thinning effect of the *Ambition*'s numerous and mechanically regular volleys of magical artillery. When enough of the petty creatures of darkness were whipped up into a sufficient lather, she withdrew to leave them to their fun. As her consciousness reeled in across the smoky verge between the two ships, she registered the howls of horror rising from the Ardain ship and smiled.

She was still smiling when her eyes snapped open just in time to witness another broadside slam into poor *Redemption*. The broadside seemed to take the frigate in its teeth and shake her, sending men, guns, and horrifyingly sharp splinters flying through the air like dander from a stricken hare. As horrible as the volley was, however, even Enid could tell it was more ragged than the one that preceded it. The lesser Umbra had done their work and disconcerted the enemy gunners. Even without exerting herself, the efforts of the Ardain sorcerer were clear to her as he struggled to banish the marauding darkness to whatever fastnesses it normally called home.

A subdued cry sounded near her feet. She glanced down to find Harlech staring in wide-eyed horror at a severed hand on the deck. She lifted the girl's face by its quivering chin and stared calmly into her tear-dewed eyes.

"You are an officer, Mid Harlech, and you have a duty to perform. I am about to work my magic and it is your job to keep me safe. You must push me aside if I am about to be injured while unawares."

Harlech nodded dumbly and placed her balled fists against Enid's hip. Enid nodded her approval and turned her attention to the iron ball in her hands. She took a bit of unburned powder residue recovered from the Ardain ball above deck and muttered a short, sharp formulation. Number Six, Old Bunnecrusher, stood smoking before her, the rise of the swell rolling it back to strain against the thick strands of rope that prevented it from crashing through the opposite bulwark while in the throes of recoil. She handed the shot to the gun's captain, who took it with a quizzical expression on his scarred and powder-darkened face.

"Load that one. Ignore the other guns firing around you. Fire only when I touch your shoulder. You attend me? Fire the instant you feel my hand on your shoulder, and only then."

The gun captain nodded grimly and passed the ball to the loader, who dropped it into the great gun's hungry maw. A wad followed, rammed home by a sailor with a nasty, unheeded gash across her left shoulder. Other evolutions, arcane to Enid, followed, but they were lost to her. Her mind was on the ball, the powder smeared into the sigil carved into its surface—and in the same instant it was probing the dark belly of *Ambition*.

Everyone and everything longs to return home. Poets know this and play upon it in their verses. Mothers know this and pray the longing will seize their children turned adult and pull them inexorably to their lonesome arms. Sorcerers know this and use it to reunite those things which have been parted. Enid grasped the powder's faint, inchoate longing to return whence it came and exerted her will to make the path home clear and easy. She left a brilliant trail of encouragement for the powder to follow and planted in its lifeless heart the sure knowledge that home could be regained and that its destiny lay there and not here, in the dark and foreign confines of a great gun's barrel.

She strengthened the relationship between the Ardain powder and the ball upon which it rode. The powder could never leave the ball now. To do so would be to defy the preordained. No, where the powder went, the ball must follow—and if the way was impeded, the ball must use its kinetic persuasion to clear a path. Half a dozen heartbeats and two eternities passed before Enid's work was done and her slim hand closed with surprising strength on the gun captain's shoulder. He started at her touch and then roared the long-awaited command: "Fire!"

The cannon's spell-lock whirled home with a dull click, but the gun remained silent. The gun captain shrugged in answer to Enid's alarmed expression.

"Soddin' lock failed!"

Enid spared a fraction of her focus to examine the lock. The cantrip was intact and well formulated. It should have fulfilled its purpose and ignited the great gun's alchemical powder charge. Something external must have interfered with its operation, yet she'd had no inkling of another sorcerer's attentions in her vicinity—besides, she was confident that her foe was busy with the problem with which she'd beset him. She dismissed the question with a snarl and hastily cast a protective aura about the lock.

"Reset the lock and fire when you feel my touch on your shoulder!"

"Lock's bad, Spells! We should—"

"Do as I say! Fire at my touch!" As she loosened the bonds that tied her to the material world the stuttering thunder of *Redemption*'s guns battered her ears when they belched forth a ragged broadside. She knew that *Ambition* would unleash a murderous reply at any moment. She bent her will to clearing the enchanted ball's path and found it easier the second time.

Her hand closed on the gun captain's shoulder an instant before she perceived the sudden pressure of the Ardain Magister's attention upon her. There was a vast roar, and she was pummeled by a great gush of wind as some huge and enormously powerful beast leaped past, but her attention remained locked on the ball as it soared in a slight arc across the water. She rode it through a weak spot in *Ambition*'s hull and sent it knifing into the big ship's belly. The powder that rode the ball with her suddenly quivered and rang like a tuning fork resonating with a tone of the same pitch and in that instant, she mouthed the final word of the ignition cantrip she'd started—how long ago? Ages it, it seemed. Mortal ages.

chapter 3

Someone near at hand wept in great fluttering sobs of the sort one is reduced to when the force of grief has robbed them of their voice and breath. The sound troubled her. Her last memory was of a flush of victory, although the circumstances of the triumph eluded her now. It was hard to reconcile the glow of success that still warmed her heart with this noisy demonstration of utter disconsolation. The more she tried to ignore the sound and slip more deeply into the gauzy comfort of unconsciousness, the more it pricked her curiosity. Cursing inwardly, she opened an eye to see what the matter was.

The first sight that met her eyes was her bare feet framed by a gaping hole that had once been at least two gun ports and perhaps three. She turned her head slightly and saw an overturned gun near at hand, a white numeral six standing starkly against the ominous black paint of its barrel. An arm and a leg protruded from beneath the great gun, and she was mortally certain they did not belong to the same man. There was certainly enough blood on the deck to mark the passing of at least two of Olde Bunnecrusher's caretakers. It occurred to her that some of the blood might even be her own. *Ambition*'s Magister might not be a subtle man, she thought, but he was not one to be trifled with. The lingering weight of his formulation still hung in the air, deadening it. As she'd ridden a ball into his ship's vitals, he'd ridden one straight for her. She wondered if she'd been more successful in her undertaking than he had and strained to look past her bare toes and through the great gap blasted in *Redemption*'s gunnel for a glimpse of the Ardain frigate, but she was once more distracted by a sobbing voice at her elbow.

"I didn't do my duty, Magister!" Harlech declared in a tear-stained moan. "I swear I didn't see what hit you or I would have pushed you away! I swear it!"

Enid turned her head to offer the girl a reassuring smile just as Dr. Rondelle pushed the mid roughly away.

"Enough of that sniveling, Mid Harlech," the surgeon huffed. "You are an officer, not a goose girl! Fetch a pair of hands to assist me with the magister here!"

As the girl rushed off, tears still streaming from her eyes, Rondelle cast a searching gaze over Enid's recumbent form. "I see no injury. Where are you pained? Can you sit up without assistance?"

"My head and my right ear. And everything sounds faint, as if perceived from a distance." Enid answered the surgeon's second question by groggily levering herself off the deck.

The surgeon leaned into Enid and examined her head with surprisingly firm but gentle hands. She was also amazed to see the set of genuine concern to his features, which were usually locked into a stolid expression of superiority and contempt.

"There's no obvious injury. The faintness of your hearing is no doubt due to the gun going off next to you and the clamor of it being overset by enemy shot—or even from the horrendous concussion of *Ambition*'s disintegration. My ears are still ringing from it."

Enid struggled more upright and peered through the gap in *Redemption*'s hull. At first, nothing but drifting smoke, low waves, and a darkening sky were to be seen. As her vision sharpened, she saw floating wreckage and, as she watched, one of *Redemption*'s boats rowed past, Mid Yeardly in its bow carefully scanning the waters ahead of it.

"Disintegration?"

"Exploded. Blown sky high. Not two flinders left together. The boats are out, but I doubt they'll find any survivors."

Rondelle finished Enid's examination and nodded with satisfaction. "Nothing seriously wrong, I think. Certainly nothing a night's rest won't set to right. Do you have any other complaints other than your head and ears?"

"Yes. Someone seems to have stolen my shoes while I was unconscious."

Rondelle barked a short, brassy laugh. "Ha! A sailor has little use for shoes of any nature, let alone those you wear, Magister! Let me look about here. Ah! Here they are, right where your feet left them." He pressed the shoes into her hands just as a pair of burly sailors arrived and ever-so-carefully shifted her onto a stretcher.

"To her cabin, if you please," Rondelle directed. "And be gentle. By all appearances, the dear has just been blown right out of her shoes by a passing ball!"

The sailor by her head stared down at the shoes Enid clutched to her stomach and exclaimed, "'Orrible bad luck, Spells!"

"Horrible grand luck, rather," Rondelle sniffed. "The same ball blew the crew of Number Six right out of their mortal shells. Now, get her to her berth and settled into her cot. I'll bring something for your head later, Enid. Sleep if you can."

She could not. Instead, she lay in her swinging cot and listened to the shouted orders, running feet, and the bang and rasp of carpentry from above decks and was plagued by a dread whose provenance she found both surprising and disconcerting: What if Nath had been injured, even killed in the action? Though she strained her ears for the familiar sound, his voice was not among the chorus of shouts above. Surely, he would be in the midst of organizing his ship's repairs. Only the direst eventuality would keep him from giving his every attention to his beloved prize, taken at such cost from Naveroña.

Still, someone would have mentioned it if he were dead or mortally wounded, she assured herself. Rondelle would have said something, if no one else. She chewed her lip and stared at the ceiling so intently that her eyes burned. When had she developed such a fondness for the little Albion officer, she wondered? She respected him, of course. Nath was a brave and dutiful officer that would not have been out of place among Achardemagne's gallant Immortals. He obviously cared for the welfare of the crew, particularly the young mids, and took every step to keep them well and safe from unnecessary harm. He was also possessed of a fine, if somewhat uneven appreciation of theater, a gentle wit and when seen in the right light, a handsome set of features despite his somewhat diminutive frame.

Her thoughts came up short as she realized that Nath had made the transition from a useful acquaintance to an actual friend, whose potential loss stoked dread in her heart. She'd had few enough friends that truly merited the title before the ravishing of Ardainne filled her core with cold hatred and hardened it with an implacable resolve for revenge. It seemed doubtful she'd ever have such a surplus that the loss of even one might not prove the final blow to her beleaguered will to live.

And what of Merryweather, whom she also held in high esteem—and more, if she were honest with herself? Their amiable exchanges had developed into a tender relationship. She despaired of ever knowing again, as the warm parts of her soul seemed frozen.

Perhaps, she thought, *I can be of two hearts: One coursing cold blood for vengeance against my nation's defilers and one pumping warmer stuff to fuel what remains of my humanity. Dichotomy is an element of sorcery, after all, and what is more sorcerous than the mortal soul?*

Tired of introspection and harrowed by worry, she was about to struggle out of her hanging cot when there was a sharp knock on her cabin door, followed by Nath's strong voice inquiring if she was fit to receive visitors. She sat up in the cot and bade him enter.

Nath stepped into the narrow berth with Harlech in tow. The

young girl's eyes were still red with tears and her expression was one of such raw remorse that Enid longed to take her up and comfort her as a mother might. Warm stuff, indeed.

"You see, Mid Harlech, Magister d'Tancreville is as sound as a copper bottom! You did your duty and I commend you for it. Is it not so, Magister?"

"Even so, sir," Enid answered seriously. "The surgeon has said it himself: I was not struck by so much as a shaving from a splinter. It was only the rush of wind accompanying a passing ball that knocked me down. There was nothing for Mid Harlech to see, let alone push me away from."

Harlech's grief seemed to lift, but she studied Enid's face carefully, wary of deceit, however comforting. "Is that true, Magister?"

"Of course it is," Enid answered firmly. "You may ask Dr. Rondelle if my word isn't sufficient for you."

"Oh, no!" Harlech gasped. "You'd never lie!"

"Then there's an end to that, isn't there, Mid Harlech?" Nath's voice was firm and gruff, but anyone more seasoned than a young mid would not fail to see the warmth in his eyes.

"Aye, aye, sir," Harlech answered with relief. "I'm sorry about the wind, Magister! I would have pushed you down if I'd heard it coming!"

Enid nodded. "Of course you would have. Harlech is a name well known for the dutiful protection of others."

"Is it?" Harlech asked, her eyes widening in wonder.

Before Enid could answer, Nath informed the little mid that hers would be a name known for misery if she weren't on deck in time to assume her watch. As the girl scurried topside, Nath pulled the chair from Enid's writing desk with his foot and lowered himself into it with a tired sigh.

"Warm work today, Enid. Almost intolerable warm. Ten dead, at least twice that wounded. We'll barely have enough hale hands to win Middlesea if the weather holds. If it turns dirty, well, then I can make you no promises."

“Ten dead.” Enid said flatly.

“Nine sailors. One marine corporal. Most of the wounded are also ship’s people. The officers were fortunate today. Oxley and I were the worst wounded, and neither of us has more than a scratch, really. Merryweather emerged from the scrap without so much as a powder stain on her stockings.”

“Hmm.” Enid noted the stitches in Nath’s scalp and a dressing around his left wrist but decided to let the “scratch” pass. “Do you think it will turn dirty, as you say?”

“I wouldn’t provoke Fortune by venturing an opinion,” Nath answered, and lightly tapped the wooden top of the writing desk. In a slightly hushed tone, as from one conspirator to another, he said, “But I doubt it. There are no signs of it, at least.”

“That is a relief. Hopefully, we won’t encounter anymore Ardain warships, either.”

“The Kraken was spotted while you were recovering, Enid, so—”

Nath held out a calming hand as Enid sat bolt upright in her cot, nearly over-setting it.

“No, no! Calmly now! The Kraken is a landmark, a barren lump of a rock that marks the nearness of Albion. Sighting it means that we will most likely make Middlesea in three days, four at most, if the wind stays true.”

As he mentioned the wind, Nath unconsciously tapped the desktop again. *So superstitious for a well-bred gentle,* she thought. *Surely he knows the winds must be summoned before they can be treated with. They do not loiter about waiting to overhear some casual remark about their behavior, then to react with malevolent contrariness. He is an intelligent man of some education, so these fanciful notions must be the result of living in such proximity with common sailors.*

They spoke for some moments more of such inconsequential things as the foul taste and questionable value of Rondelle’s concoctions (she held they were worthless, he swore by them) and the reason for the Kraken’s name (Nath said it looked nothing like a kraken, so he guessed one might have lived there in a submarine cave ages ago) before Enid found the nerve to ask the question that had troubled her almost as much as her worries over his safety as she lay "resting" at the doctor's order.

"Rondelle said *Ambition* disintegrated. Surely, he exaggerates?"

Nath shook his head, and his expression became grim. "No, he does not. She exploded with such force much of our standing rigging was knocked all a-hoo. We very nearly caught fire, as well, as pieces of her rained down on deck. When you turn your mind to bloodshed, you certainly do not do it by halves."

"Were there any survivors? I thought I saw Yeardly searching the waters for them in a boat, but I was still somewhat addled."

"There were none," Nath answered stonily.

Enid stared at her feet for a long, silent moment before asking how many officers and crew such a ship would carry.

"Nearly three hundred," Nath answered. "And may the Redeemer have mercy on them."

"And on me," Enid said softly. Nath must have sensed her need for solitude and withdrew after giving her hand a soft, un-officerly squeeze. She lay in silence, thinking of the men of number six who had died while the executioner of "three hundreds and more" remained among the living. Troubled, she sought Dunaughy's company. She could not find him, though, and was left in the company of *Ambition*'s hundreds and the men and women of gun six, Olde Bunnecrusher.

chapter 4

Enid found she could not sleep. The phantoms of the folk she'd slain in Arden, many of whom were guiltless in her uncle's death, and of the officers and crew of the *Ambition* gathered around her bed and she wilted under their accusatory gaze. *Ashes! How many had she slain now?* Her total must equal or exceed the count of many small Ardain town's Roget's Device. The best she could accomplish was a sort of staring trance in which her thoughts ran freely through the haunted causeways of her mind.

She was in just such a state when her desultory revery was interrupted by a sudden warning hissed near her ear. She sat upright in the swaying bed and stared into the darkness. She was alone in her berth and the air smelled of unwashed sailors, mildew, and weathered wood. The discordant smell banished the shaky conviction that she slept in her familiar rooms in her uncle's hotel in Arden. She was on the *Redemption*; she was alone—against what had she been warned? And by whom?

Outside, a bell chimed six times and the last veil slipped from her senses. She threw a long leg over the edge of her cot and called up a hovering orb of light, the words of its summoning voiced in a tone more suitable to profanity than a simple cantrip. She sat at her tiny writing desk and rubbed her eyes as she struggled to translate the bells. The middle watch—which made it approximately three o'clock in the morning. *Ashes! What a barbarous hour!*

What had roused her? The ship seemed to be sailing easily enough despite the battering it had received from the guns of *Ambition*. There was no untoward noise from above decks. She laid her fingers on a half-empty cup of coffee, and in a few heartbeats, it was bracingly hot, if somewhat foul and thick. The bitter, rewarmed draught cleared the last cobwebs of sleep and she struggled to wrest a memory from that murky zone between sleep and wakefulness. She stared at the shadow-deepened details of the wood grain of the stout oak planking that made one wall of her berth, curving away from the low ceiling to trace the arc of the ship's outer hull—the back of her neck prickled as she suddenly recalled the earnestly whispered words that had jarred her from sleep.

"Do not meddle in the affairs of your betters, upstart! Leave my ship and return no more!"

She remembered the voice that spoke those words. It comprised the creak of heavy boughs and rustling of dry leaves in the wind, the recollection of which stood the fine hairs on the back of her neck on end.

Instinctively, she focused her mind to contact Dunaughy. Her efforts were met with silence, and the silver on her finger remained warm and uncommunicative.

Enid frowned. Unfortunately, this silence was not an unusual phenomenon. Since boarding the *Redemption*, it was increasingly difficult to establish a lengthy, meaningful conversation with Dunaughy. Only rarely did she find the scent of licorice floating in the close air of her berth, and then only faintly. She feared the binding she'd created between his ghost and her silver ring had not been strong enough and now, beyond the familiar *axis mundi* of his beloved *Alarum*, Dunaughy was drawn inexorably to his reward, willing or no.

Dunaughy's sudden silence contributed to her growing sense of isolation, as had the frantic preparations for the voyage, which had monopolized the attention of both Captain Nath and Lieutenant Merryweather. She knew her own mind well enough to understand the true roots of her loneliness were not found in her current situation, but instead lay at the end of her journey: When she debarked in Middlesea, her exile from Ardainne would begin in earnest. She had fled her homeland, fallen in with its enemies, and taken up arms against it. Only a few days past, she destroyed one of its ships and slew every officer and sailor aboard. The Theocratic Republic would never forgive her. If she returned openly to Ardainne, it would be to slake the bloodlust of Roget's Device. Only the destruction of the murderous, criminal regime would restore her to her homeland.

But would even that restore Ardainne to itself? She had known men and women of impeccable breeding who had suffered so cruelly that even after Providence restored them to good fortune, they remained changed, bitter, and reduced in character; mean, miserable, and broken. Perhaps entire nations could be brought so low. And perhaps the people of some nations *deserved* to be so stricken if they could be so distracted by their entertainments that they ignored a threat to their way of life, too self-interested and self-absorbed to raise their voices until the executioner fed them to Roget's Device.

The porcelain handle of the coffee cup snapped under the force of her grasp. Muttered curses mixed with a quietly uttered cantrip to staunch the flow of blood from a minor cut in the meaty part of her thumb. Part of her attention turned to the broken cup, coaxing the snapped-off handle to resume its former state of harmonious and utilitarian union with the cup's side. The progress of this elementary task was retarded by a distracting thought, a dolorous seed that took root at the back of her mind and threatened to fill her conscious with a tangle of black, thorny vines: She might live to see the Theocracy destroyed yet never see her homeland restored to its former glory. The Ardainne she sought to save might be dead, the life crushed from it by the weight of its own failures, its own excesses. When she considered the shameful way her people had allowed their country to spiral into chaos virtually unopposed, she wondered if the Theocracy was a sufficient container for her hatred. When the Republic was crushed, and she had no doubt that an institution founded on self-hatred and the blood of kin would someday be crushed, she feared where she might find the stains of spite that might remain beyond its destruction.

The handle adhered to the cup, its newfound urge to be separate overcome by her will—but not completely. A part of the handle remained corrupted by a desire to deny its rightful place in the order of things, even though this rebellious bent might doom both it and the cup to the dustbin. She doubted the handle would support a cup full of hot coffee again and was on the verge of a bitter if obvious analogy when a polite knock on the lath door of her berth interrupted her reverie.

"Magister d'Tancreville." The voice was that of Mid Yeardly, pitched softly enough to avoid awakening nearby sleepers, but hopefully insistent enough to rouse the officer he'd been sent to fetch. "Magister d'Tancreville! Your pardon, but Captain Nath requires you on deck. Magister?"

"Yes, Mid Yeardly. Cease your hissing like a snake. I will join the captain immediately."

Enid stepped through the narrow door to her berth into the night-vacant gun room. A chill draft from the companionway compelled her to button her lounging coat closed at the throat, only to find she still held the damned cup in her left hand. She pushed it into Yeardly's hands without a word, ignoring his baffled expression, and turned to go on deck.

"Pardon me, Magister, but . . ."

"Do what you will with the damned cup, sir. Throw it overboard. Fix a mast to it and sail it round the world. Bail out the Ocean Sea to plunder the Sea Lord's trove. It really doesn't signify to me at this hour."

"No, Magister, not the cup. Your light there—best put it out afore going above decks. The captain . . ."

"Yes, yes, the captain and his primitive aesthetics. Redeemer save us from the paltriest comfort! Far better to stumble in the dark and break a leg than resort to perfectly natural magical light . . ."

She lurched up the companionway muttering under her breath, annoyed beyond reason at the mid's innocent and legitimate reminder of light discipline aboard a running ship. Her unfounded ire shamed her, which fueled it into a brighter flame.

Yeardly watched her go, his faint smile barely visible in the fading light of the dissipating orb.

Enid found Nath on the weather side of the quarterdeck, Lieutenants Oxley and Merryweather standing close at hand. Nath glanced in her direction and nodded, giving her permission to enter the captain's hallowed sanctum. The gesture aggravated her for some reason, rankling her dignity like a calculated affront. If Nath noticed her petulant expression, he ignored it and greeted her cordially, his voice warm with apology and concern for her comfort.

"Magister d'Tancreville, you really must wear your ship's cloak in the middle watch. I know the calendar indicates otherwise, but I assure you the Strait cares as little for the dictates of seasons as it does the curses of sailors. I would not call you from the warmth of your cot at such a chilly hour, but—"

"I was awake, so do not trouble yourself, sir. I perceive, however, that you have the entire crew at your disposal should you find yourself in need of conversation. I assume you had something more productive in mind than criticizing my attire when you sent that smirking jackanapes of a mid to rattle my door?"

Lieutenant Merryweather looked down to hide an un-officerly grin and Lieutenant Oxley took a step back, his horror-widened eyes tracking back and forth between his commanding officer and the apparently suicidal ship's magister. To his amazement, Captain Nath only chuckled and shook his head.

"I'm fortunate conversation was not on my mind, Enid, as it's quite clear you'd rather bite off my head than bend my ear. Look to larboard there, no, Enid, to larboard. Yes, there. See the lights? That is Middlesea. We are almost home."

Enid stiffened slightly at the word "home," and her irascibility deepened. "I have seen lights before. The morning light would have revealed more unfamiliar vistas, I'm sure."

Nath laughed, his jubilant mood proof against her waspishness. "And I'm sure it still will, but a cutter has come out with word from the Lord Mayor that there will be a demonstration to greet us that is best seen at night."

Enid made a noncommittal noise in the back of her throat and accepted a warm cup of fresh coffee from an elderly sailor standing in for poor old Alston, Nath's recently departed steward. The coffee helped, but the sight of Harlech in the waist reminded her of a conversation earlier in the day and rekindled her sharp mood.

"I recollect, sir, that you once asserted there is but one captain aboard any man-of-war, however large she might be?"

"It is true," Nath answered blithely, his eyes patiently scanning the skies above Middlesea. "No ship may have more than one captain, any more than any of the Redeemed may have more than one God."

"Is it true, then?" Enid turned on Nath with sudden vehemence. "I ask because this very day Harlech represented to me that each of *Redemption*'s guns has its own captain and, when I pressed her on the matter later, she assured me that there also exists some mysterious cabal of captains whose domain is some region she referred to only as 'the tops.' I left the matter where it lay, but I assure you, sir, that I do not relish being practiced upon. If either you or Harlech are making me the butt of some sort of nautical joke, some sort of maritime merriment, you will not find me a forgiving target for your whimsy!"

Nath shook his head, but was wise enough to contain his chuckle. "You are not being practiced upon, Enid. I assure you that neither Harlech nor myself would find any pleasure in confusing you with regard to naval organization. It is important that you clearly understand our hierarchy so that you might fully understand your place in it."

"Well, then?"

"It seems more complicated than it is," Nath began slowly. "There is only one *real* captain aboard any man-of-war, and he is her commanding officer. But Harlech is right, there are also some men who are responsible for key positions or tasks who are also called 'captains,' such as the gun captains and the captains of the tops. They are not to be confused with the actual captain, though, and are not officers at all, neither commissions nor warrants."

Enid frowned. "Then why in the Redeemer's name—"

"Tradition, Enid, tradition. Now look! The sky is lit up with flowers, flocks of flaming birds, and winged dragons of gold and green! They welcome us home with fireworks, Enid! Fireworks! Now *there's* courtesy for you!"

Merryweather contrived to stand close to her as the sky was lit with pyrotechnics that rivaled anything she'd seen in Ardainne. As the other officers were distracted by an enormous explosion that blossomed into a stooping flock of red, gold, and green ospreys, she leaned close to Enid while pointing toward the fireworks.

"I will be as busy as the devil in a convent making *Redemption* ready for her new captain," she said in a low tone, barely audible over the crackles and booms echoing over the water. "But if you wish, I will call on you at my first opportunity and show you what I know of Middlesea, Enid."

"I would be most pleased for your company, Augusta."

PART
TWO

chapter 5

Despite Nath's efforts to will the flags bearing *Redemption*'s number to the peak of Admiralty Tower, they refused to materialize. Instead, around ten o'clock of the morning, a navy gig bearing a lieutenant forced its way through the flotilla of civilian boats that now surrounded the frigate and glided across the open water between the ragtag fleet and *Redemption*, a space demanded by navigational law and enforced by the Master of the Middlesea Basin.

Now he stood on the quarterdeck and watched the gig pulling hard for shore. The whip-thin Lieutenant who delivered Seal Lord Morrin's venomous orders with a thin, spiteful smile sat stiffly upright in her stern sheets. Nath imagined they still wore that damnable smile.

He took a deep breath and turned to Lieutenant Merryweather, who stood at his side, making a brave effort to hide her anger behind an officerly reserve. "Well, you heard them, Lieutenant Merryweather. We have our orders. Pray spread the word while I put my papers in order and prepare myself to call upon the Sea Lord. I leave it to you and Oxley to organize the crew for departure and pick a gang to await the arrival of the yard crew from Ordwych. Make haste, please."

Summoned by three sharp raps, Enid opened the door to her cabin and found Merry standing without, her expression as dark she'd ever seen.

"Merry! I have been absorbed in a thin volume on Murchadhan history from my predecessor's small hoard of books. I found it quite distracting and only just noticed the racket above decks and below. What is afoot?"

"Give me your full attention, Enid, and set aside any questions, as I have no time for answers that will generate a dozen more each. Captain Nath has been relieved of command. You, I, and all the rest of *Redemption*'screw are relieved of duty. We must vacate the barky as quick as we may. Pack your things and stack them there, by the back of the cuddy. Trusted hands will bear them aloft to be whipped to one of the boats, along with your dunnage stored below."

Enid nodded once, sharply. "At once. And Rue?"

"He is in his cabin, signing out of the log and such. Leave him be for now—we will all be reunited above shortly, where he will see to the people's orderly departure for shore."

The *Redemption*s, who were mostly former *Alarum*s, had recent experience in shifting all a ship's people's earthly belongings from ship to shore at short notice. They, their officers, and their belongings stood in a throng on the Reaver's Steps far more quickly than seemed reasonable. During her quick passage to shore, Enid could clearly see the legion of Middlesea townsfolk who crowded those same steps in their hundreds, no, in their *thousands*.

Now, she and Nath stood ashore, surrounded by multitudes of humanity, only held at bay by a thin line of Marines and former *Redemptions*, all armed with bayonetted muskets or belaying pins according to their employment. He took in the crowd before them with a dramatic sweep of his arm and quoted a verse from the Apotheotica, the central holy book of the Church of the Redeemer, proclaiming, *"Lo, they came in their multitudes and prayed for his deliverance or, should he prove false, the spectacle of his living flesh burned away by flames of fire."*

Enid arched a brow; she'd never seen Nath evince a shred of religiosity in the time they'd been together. Perhaps he learned the verse from the lips of a character in a play, as she could not imagine he had much in the way of youthful religious study, considering the tender age at which he went to sea. She, on the other hand, had suffered through the endless hours of the catechesis expected of a young Ardain noble. With a little effort, she was able to bring a suitably uplifting passage to the forefront of her mind.

"Though he was surrounded by enemies who armed themselves to do him harm, he passed among them without hurt, for the flame of his heart burned bright and pure," she counter quoted. "And so shall you. I have learned many unpleasant lessons regarding the strength of the commons speaking as one and the resolve of a self-serving aristocracy. I will put what I have learned to use in your favor and may the gods pity those who stand against you."

Nath regarded her from the corner of his eye, and she was hard put to tell whether the gleam she saw in it was born of good humor or incredulity. They stood next to each other and pursued personal musings in companionable silence for a moment as the other *Redemption*s stood in an uncomfortable knot surrounded by cheering citizens of Middlesea. Enid was inexplicably pleased to see the bright flash of Lady Chum-Chum circling over their heads.

"It doesn't appear that any assistance is forthcoming from the constables of St. Ygraine," Lieutenant Harcourt observed. "They seem satisfied to stand at the verge of this horde and make a dumb show of stopping its growth."

Nath nodded and scowled.

"Yeardly," he shouted. "Shake a leg, lad! I have instructions for you!"

The mid stood at attention as Nath gave him his orders. When he was finished, he dropped a purse of coins into the young man's coat pocket and said, "Remember, ask the advice of the Master of the

Landing for a warehouse that suits our needs; clean, dry, and as far from the temptations of spirits and bodies as may be."

"Aye, sir!" Yeardly's sharp salute did not hide his doubtful expression. "But will the tars abide such captivity?

"Remind them that the press is hot as a don's blood and all but the most thickheaded of the lot will, and they're no great loss to us."

Enid made to ask what Nath was about, but he shook his head. "It can wait and no harm will come from your ignorance, Enid. The Sea Lord, on the other hand, does not like to be kept waiting and holds our fate in his hands."

So saying, he straightened his coat and stock, and barked, "Lieutenant Harcourt! Gather a detachment of your lobsters to accompany me to Admiralty, lest I be trampled beneath the mob before reaching it. Assign a like number under your corporal to provide the same service to Lieutenant Merryweather and Magister d'Tancreville to the Best Bower."

"Yes, sir!" Harcourt called back and snapped a sharp salute.

Harcourt's lobsters, reinforced by the *Redemption*s, pushed back the crowd to form a cordon around the officers. The din was of such volume that said officers were forced to put their heads close together in a huddle and shout to be heard.

"I will depart for Admiralty now," Nath said. "Wait a bit while I make my passage. With any luck, the mob will focus on me and make your escape easier."

They nodded in an exaggerated fashion to signal their understanding.

"Yeardly, take ship's people to the warehouse district and see if you can let enough space to accommodate them for a month or more. See to it they are fed! Use the card from my prize agent as a pledge against the cost.

"Lieutenant Merryweather! Guide Magister d'Tancreville to the Best Bower Inn and secure her and I a suite of rooms. See to it that she is safely settled in. I cannot say how long my ordeal at Admiralty will last and she is a stranger to our country and this city. I would admire it if you would keep her company until I am able to join you."

Merryweather's nod was so gravely obedient that Enid nearly laughed at the sight of it.

Ascending the Reaver's Steps required Nath and his party of marines to pierce a veritable wall of humanity, all apparently intent on demonstrating their admiration by trampling their hero to death beneath their feet. He was thankful that Lieutenant Amiable Harcourt was in personal command of the lobsters that ringed him in and that worthy would brook no nonsense from mere civilians no matter their love for his captain. Despite the kind set of his features at rest, Harcourt went about soldiering with a cold efficiency that left several members of the crowd who snatched at Nath's uniform in hopes of securing a swatch of cloth to cherish or sell with cracked heads or broken wrists instead. Once the marines and their ward broke through the crowd and came within earshot of the constables trying to contain the crowd, Harcourt hailed them.

"You there! This is Captain Nath, and he has business at Admiralty. Stop mooning around and do you earn your pay! Close your ranks and don't allow any of this rabble to pursue him past this point!"

His voice was so commanding that the constables practically tripped over one another to obey him, despite his complete lack of authority over them.

"Well done, Lieutenant Harcourt," Nath said as the distance between themselves and the racket of the raucous crowd diminished sufficiently to allow normal speech. "I'd admire it if you and your marines would keep my company until I secure a coach to Admiralty before returning to *Redemption*."

Harcourt saluted briskly and said, "It would be our pleasure, sir!"

Barely a quarter of an hour passed before Nath sat in a moderately priced coach bound for Admiralty Tower. It seemed a monumental waste of his dwindling "fortune" to pay to ride such a short distance, but the anonymity the coach offered was worth the price. The driver congratulated Nath on his victory over the Dons as he stepped out of the coach, and he found himself momentarily at a loss for words and could only answer with a jerky nod and the ghost of a smile. The polite admiration of the woman drove home the fact that he was no longer an anonymous lieutenant or commander, nor even a nondescript post captain. He was, at least for the moment, a national hero.

As he robotically accepted the semi-worshipful salutations of the officers that crowded the tower's walled courtyard, he wrestled with the portentousness of his newfound fame. It seemed to him that it could just as easily work against him as for him in this farcical conflict with Lord Ambrose Aixely and his Old Charter supporters. They were just as likely to redouble their efforts against him as to relent in the face of Middlesea's popular acclaim.

Gods of old, he thought as he approached the great doors that led to the Sea Lord's sanctum, *my only ambition has ever been to serve Albion as a frigate captain, and now I'm mired in a political quag. I was better off as the commander of a little sloop-of-war, which is a damned sight better than being drummed out of the navy by a court-martial!*

Nath schooled his voice and expression to ape the bored confidence that marked a post captain and approached the lobsters standing watch outside the door to the Sea Lord's office and apartments.

"Captain Rue Nath, *Alarum—Redemption*, to see the Sea Lord at his command."

Neither of the marines' faces betrayed the slightest recognition of his name, but snapped to attention and held the door open for him to pass. He crossed a small anteroom toward the Seal Lord's clerk and her wide, paper and log-strewn desk with as much assurance as the gait of a sailor so recently returned to shore could muster.

The room was darkly paneled and decorated with huge, heavy-framed pictures depicting naval victories that were famous a century or two ago but defied his half-hearted effort to identify. The clerk was a lovely young woman, less than a year or two his junior. She was clad in a short blue jacket and a spotless white blouse. Her long, blue-black hair was drawn back into a clubbed tail. Her skin was a deep brown that spoke of Malasfandyari blood. She also possessed the refined beauty of those people, which was a great improvement over the desiccated, sour-faced wight that served Admiral Weymouth's clerk. She shared the devil's cool disregard for the value of an officer's time weighed against her own. After a brief, irritated glance up at him from beneath her long lashes, she returned to scratching rapidly in a logbook with an ink-stained, ivory pen. He opened his mouth to introduce himself, but she interrupted him with a voice that, though sweet and smooth as honey, was every bit as dismissive and contemptuous as Weymouth's horrid clerk.

"Yes, yes. Captain Rue Nath. *Redemption*. Despite their thickness and solid oak construction, the doors did nothing to muffle your barking at the marines. They are not deaf, you know."

He began to argue that he addressed the marines in a perfectly moderate tone but caught himself. That was exactly the weakness that the wicked race of clerks thrived on.

"Excellent. A person blessed with your keen senses is no doubt aware of my purpose here. I will not waste your time further by describing it or its urgency."

So saying, he briskly stacked his logs and ledgers on her desk.

Rather than fix him with a chimerical gaze, the clerk looked up from the logbook, set aside her pen, and regarded him with an amused and appraising eye. "Hmm. You have some fire in you, sir. I suppose there may be some substance to your reputation after all. We shall see how long you are able to keep it fueled."

"I suppose we shall."

"Well, there is no better way to test your mettle than under fire." She winked at him and rose to limp to the door, leaning on a cane topped by a silver dolphin's head in her right hand. She rapped three times on the polished brass plate on the door before opening it to lead Nath into the Sea Lord's office.

"Your Lordship, Lieutenant Commander Rue Nath, late of the *Redemption*, 38, and the *Alarum*, 32, before her."

Nath made a leg and doffed his hat. "Your Lordship."

"Nath," Sea Lord Morrin said in plain distaste, purposefully omitting the courtesy of stating his rank. As Nath straightened to attention, Morrin glanced at the other man seated in a claw-footed chair beside his desk and spoke to him as if Nath were a purely notional creature, not a flesh-and-blood person physically present in the room. "Duke Aixely, Nath is that young officer I spoke to you of, whose shortcomings your son Ambrose was so wise in reporting to the Service."

"I am familiar with him, sir," Duke Aixely drawled. "I would recognize him anywhere based on my son's description and those in the papers and pamphlets that seem so intent on heaping glory on any callow youth Fortune turns her smile on, no matter how briefly."

Nath stood at attention and forced his features to a passivity that was very much at odds with his throbbing heart and the wrathful fire burning in his veins.

The Sea Lord leaned back in his chair and refocused his attention on Nath. Morrin carried on without allowing Nath to stand easy.

"Well, Mr. Nath, you'll be happy to hear that I have examined the charges against you, and while I found them valid on many, many points, I also believe that holding officers responsible for the fate of prizes before they've been inspected and accepted into the navy is a bad precedent to set. With that in mind, the court-martial has been dismissed. What do you say to that, sir?"

"I'm gratified to hear it, your lordship."

"And well you should be," interrupted the Duke of Aixely, in whose face Nath recognized Lord Ambrose, albeit cast with a narrower brow and sharper features. "For you would surely have been drummed out of the service. You are fortunate that the Sea Lord has such long vision that he prefers to risk the damage you may do to the Sea Service in your lifetime rather than establish a precedent that might injure the King's Navy for generations to come."

Nah felt a bead of sweat begin a southern peregrination from betwixt his shoulder blades. Aixely's words added kindling to his anger, but a sloop engaged with two First[t] Class men-of-war stood a better chance of escaping unscathed than he did of leaving this room with his commission intact if he responded intemperately. Instead, he stared straight ahead and limited his response to saying, "As you say, Your Lordship."

"You are obviously relieved of your command of *Redemption*," Morrin continued. "It is too much ship for a captain with as little experience as you can claim and will be doubly so once it has been refitted. A portion of your crew will remain aboard to assist in that effort, but your officers and most of your warrants will have to make do ashore until they can be reassigned. You at least will be fortunate enough to draw half-pay, thanks to Admiral Weymouth's precipitous decision to make you post."

This was exactly what Nath expected, but to hear the words spoken out loud in such a callus tone constricted his heart as if the Sea Lord's bony fingers were crushing the life from it.

"Yes, sir," he said, still standing at attention. "May I ask if another command might be in the offing?"

"You may ask, but I have no answer for you. You are no pampered favorite here, man! You are of a kind with dozens of captains who spend each day praying to receive a commission of any kind, and most of them with far more seniority than you. I suggest you husband your prize money carefully and secure modest accommodations. Your wait for a new command is likely to be a long one."

That said, the Sea Lord turned to Duke Aixely and said in a warm, convivial tone, "Will you join me at my table tonight, Lord Uthred? We can share a bottle of wine and discuss your son Ambrose's career. I've a mind to transfer him to the St. Mahaute station, perhaps under the command of a vessel more suitable for an officer of his standing."

Aixely said nothing, but glanced significantly at Nath who continued to stand at rigid attention as he had neither been dismissed nor allowed to stand easy. Morrin followed his glance theatrically, and then bellowed, "Well what are you still doing here, man? I have no more use for you! You are dismissed."

"As you will, sir," Nath said and turned on his heel. As he stepped through the door into Sea Lord's outer office, he heard Morrin shout after him.

"Lieutenant Holyoke! Give Mr. Nath his orders and see to it he leaves the premises without causing a disturbance!"

Nath reseated his hat upon his head and shot his cuffs before approaching the Sea Lord's secretary. She studied his face as he approached and said, "The fire has not been snuffed out, I see."

A hot retort was forming on his lips before he noticed her genuine expression of sympathy. Instead, he smiled half-heartedly and said, "Not extinguished, but somewhat banked, I'd say."

Holyoke held out a fat envelope of papers to Nath, who arched a brow at its girth. He was surprised the Admiral used so much paper and ink to say, *This is Captain Nath. Extend him no favor or your career will be as fucked as his.*

As if reading his mind, the clerk shrugged apologetically and said in a low voice, "Robbed of the pleasure of humiliating you in a court-martial adjudicated by his most loyal toadies, the Sea Lord saw fit to detail every shortcoming he could imagine or fabricate in your orders, all for the reading pleasure of Ambrose Aixely and his asp of a father."

Nath shook his head. "Lord Ambrose must number clairvoyance among his accomplishments to compile such a thorough accounting of my deficiencies after spending less than half a day in my company, eked half an hour to an hour at a time."

The clerk smothered a chuckle behind her hand and glanced toward the door to the Sea Lord's office.

"He is a powerful seer, indeed," she said with a mischievous gleam in her eyes that nearly made Nath forget his woeful position. "Those are preliminary orders. The final packet will be half again as thick—which reminds me, where are you lodging? I must know where to send your official orders and your first month of half-pay."

"I've taken rooms for myself and Magister d'Tancreville at the Best Bower. I assume you know the place?"

"I do," she said, as she scribbled the information next to his name in one of the logbooks from her desk. Without looking up, she asked, "Are you and Magister d'Tancreville *avoir une liaison*?"

"No, I flatter myself to think we are friends, though. We share several interests and our conversations are—" The question was asked so matter-of-factly that Nath answered before realizing Holyoke had overstepped the bounds of conversation between a lieutenant and a captain. He stiffened and said, "How are such private matters any of your affair, lieutenant?"

Holyoke was unfazed by his sharper tone and shrugged as she looked from the log and into his eyes. "It is the question on everyone's mind. You are a national hero now, you understand? I believe you'll find your definition of 'privacy' will require an overhaul from the keel up."

Nath frowned at the thought, but her words rang true. Besides, it would be disingenuous to pretend he was not flattered to hear her praise for his military prowess. Still, he didn't savor the idea of his personal life receiving the same level of attention from strangers.

"Since you are already set up at the Best Bower and have no ship to command, it would seem you are at loose ends for the rest of the day. Perhaps we could continue our conversation in more privacy at the Red Hare? The food and drink there is excellent, and the proprietor would happily reserve a private corner for us."

"I doubt the Sea Lord would commend you for making such advances to the black sheep of the entire Sea Service," Nath replied, intrigued by the lady's unabashed forwardness.

"Advances?" Holyoke said with a merry chuckle. "How confident you are in your allure, sir!"

"Well," Nath drawled, "that quality, like my spark, is best put the test in action, don't you agree?"

"It might be entertaining to make further character observations of the man who is either Albion's greatest naval hero or the Navy's most incompetent officer. Perhaps we could indulge ourselves in such a study at the Red Hare?"

The offer was tempting. Nath's stomach churned at the thought of breaking the miserable news to Enid. The prospect of that conversation was only slightly less daunting than his audience with the Sea Lord had been, owing to how his own bitter fortune would impact her. *Perhaps,* he thought, *it would not hurt to lighten my spirits a bit before dealing Enid such a crushing blow. I may find better words to express my regret and promise my support if I am not full to the scuppers with melancholy. What harm could there be in saying, "I would be happy to dine with you this afternoon?"*

Instead, he said, "It would be my pleasure to dine with you, Ms. Holyoke, but I have commitments I cannot neglect. Perhaps later this week, if you are still inclined."

"Ah. I understand completely," she replied with a sad moue. "You can expect to hear from me. But for now, you'd best scarper before Their Lordships notice you have not fled with your tail between your legs and conspire further mischief against you."

Nath could not contain his smile, despite his dark mood and the clerk's utter disregard for decorum. "I will hasten to follow your advice! You know these waters better than I, Ms. Holyoke."

"Emley Holyoke. It only seems fair to share my given name since I know yours."

"I hope you'll forgive me my impertinence, but you are a far cry from what I expected of the Sea Lord's clerk."

"I am the Sea Lord's *interim* clerk. I fear he finds my personality to be too human for his tastes, preferring a desiccated, monosyllabic carcass for the role." She shrugged and rolled her eyes.

Nath stifled a laugh with some effort, which seemed to please Holyoke greatly. "And you are no stick-in-the-mud like most of the officers that call on his Lordship. Truly, you are a diamond among shards of glass, sir."

The Sea Lord's voice came faintly from his inner office, calling for the most recent dispatches from the Shards. Ms. Holyoke rolled her eyes and said, "But hark, the beast is stirring, so perhaps you'd best make haste. I'm sure we'll speak again. Now, shoo!"

Enid's party struck out for the Best Bower, and though the distance covered was negligible, it took a great toll on her equanimity. The mass of passionate faces and sour smells around her recalled the horrors of her escape from Arden. It took six Marines to eventually clear a path through the cheering mob, whose members would trample their idol to death in order to lay eyes on him. Merryweather ordered the *Redemption*s to brandish their belaying pins freely, and the determined display of which proved sufficient to part the crowd. Still, the journey up the Reaver's Steps disturbed Enid to her core.

At the offing, Enid thought the crowd's only interest in their party was its origin, the brave *Redemption* from which they had debarked marked this knot of sailors and officers as heroes who took part in the frigate's restoration to the bosom of Albion. She soon found that a more personal interest attracted the attention of the throng, though. More than a few in the crowd recognized her by her description in the dispatches: An Ardain woman with raven black hair who towered over most folks around her. No sooner had the *Redemption*s braved the front ranks of the crowd than its members took up chanting her name and resolutely focused their attention on her. They surged forward, waving little Albion flags and forgetting, for the moment at least, that she was a native of their kingdom's most implacable rival throughout history. Some reached out to pluck at her clothes until the *Redemption*s in her company wrapped a few of them on the wrist or elbow with a heavy oaken belaying pin.

Thus contested, their march uphill forced its way through the press of humanity until it finally broke free of the mob, who were held back from blocking the thoroughfares leading to the Steps by a group of burly constables.

"Ashes, your Albion common folks are a demonstrative lot," Enid groused, setting her hat straight and noticing that its cockade was missing, no doubt a relic that would be worshipfully displayed on some family hearth for generations to come.

"They are," Merryweather agreed. "But there were more than a few gentlefolk in that crowd as well. The loss of *Redemption* was a hard blow to our pride and confidence in our Sea Service. Her restoration has an almost religious aspect for my fellow Albions. I'm proud to have had a hand in it."

"I'm happy to have survived it," Enid said.

"I'm happy that both of us did," Merryweather said and gave her shoulder a surreptitious squeeze as they wended their way through Nath's throng of admirers.

Enid was not impressed by the portion of Middlesea they passed through en route to The Best Bower. The buildings that crowded the street on either hand were of moderate height, with two or three stories being the norm. The upper floors of some overhung the street in the old style. They were all utilitarian in design, with few decorative flourishes and none of the fine proportions that graced all but the plainest structures in Arden. The streets themselves were cobbled and foot traffic contended for passage with horse-carts, hansoms, and the occasional ox-drawn wain. Still, it did have the advantage that she could walk openly without fear of being taken up by a mob for beheading in the nearest square.

Merryweather noticed her wrinkled nose and said, "We are not in the finest of neighborhoods, Magister, but the lodgings hereabout are of passable quality and can be obtained at a cost a poor naval officer's budget will support. All Middlesea is not so squalid, though much of it is more so."

"Arden is no better in that regard, I suppose. It is only its familiarity that makes such neighborhoods there seem less dire," Enid lied. It was the natural style and grace with which the meanest Ardain mason imbued their work that made the difference. She was a guest here, though, and she was determined to be graceful.

The Best Bower was easily identified by its sign in the shape of an anchor. Its ground floor was a public room offering food and drink served in a sizable room whose arched beams gave a nautical impression. The inn's mistress, one Mrs. Rangle, was nearly of a height with Enid and thin as a whip. Her resemblance to a lash was not restricted to her physique, for her manner was quick and snappish. She made her disapproval of two ladies reserving a room with two bedchambers for a man who couldn't be bothered to present himself quite clear.

"Mind you, your dissipations are your own and as long as you keep them quietly to yourself and do not disturb the other guests," she said as she unlocked the door to a suitable room on the third floor. "And you pay your rents on time."

"It is good to hear that we are under the roof of a woman of such strong moral values," Enid said, brushing past the woman to survey the room. Before her was a small, comfortably appointed, if somewhat shabby, sitting room. Its back wall consisted of tall, narrow windows that looked over the heads of lower buildings that marched down toward the Middlesea Basin. Squinting her eyes as she gazed toward the harbor, she was presented with a vista of softly intimated mastheads through the haze and smoke that hung over the intervening rooftops.

She dropped gracefully into an easy chair situated between the windows and the small iron stove that provided the room with warmth and watched as Merryweather directed the bosun's mate and his gang of *Redemption*s in stowing their dunnage. Mrs. Rangle clucked in the background, admonishing the hands not to batter her furniture, scuff her floors, or tear the carpet. The room filled with the racket of brisk activity in an enclosed space, but Enid didn't notice it. A comforting globe of tranquility seemed to envelope her as she watched Merryweather impose order upon chaos. She admired her composure and the graceful arch of her neck, the mobility of her expression, and the flash of her white, even teeth when she noticed Enid looked on.

When the work was done, Enid dismissed the *Redemption*sand pressed a week's worth of coin into Mrs. Rangle's hands. She shooed her off with an ease that the woman clearly found disconcerting. Once the door was locked behind her new landlady, she turned to Merryweather and said, "Tell me Augusta, how long do you estimate it will take Nath to navigate the halls of naval power, face the treacherous potentates controlling his fate, and find his way back to a safe harbor here?"

Merryweather pursed her lips in thought, then said, "Not before the evening meal at the earliest."

"Excellent," Enid said, closing the space between them in a stride. She looked down into the lieutenant's eyes and stroked her cheek with the back of her hand. "That leaves us ample time to fulfill Mrs. Rangle's lascivious expectations."

Merryweather signaled her agreement with Enid's plan by immediately seizing her in a powerful embrace and smothering her lips and neck with forceful kisses. When Enid was able to draw enough breath to speak, she said, "Come, let us retire to my room. The bed will be more . . ."

Enid found she was unable to finish her suggestion as another deep kiss silenced her and Merryweather's strong, deft fingers set about freeing her from her Magister's uniform.

Nath arrived well before the evening meal, but after Enid and Merryweather had restored their persons to order. When they became aware of his approach, they were sitting shoulder-to-shoulder and hand-in-hand on a padded bench before the windows. The last of the sunlight that initially drew them there had long faded away. Reluctantly, they put a little space between themselves at the sound of Mrs. Rangle's penetrating voice fawning over Nath in the hall, followed by the rattle of her key in the lock. A moment later, she ushered an obviously exhausted Nath into the room.

"Yes, yes," he said as he extricated his arm from Mrs. Rangle's overly felicitous grasp. "I'm sure the accommodations will do, even if you weren't aware for whom they were reserved."

Enid came to his rescue and helped steer Mrs. Rangle back into the hall with patient smiles and a mixture of Albion and Ardain pleasantries that put the woman on her back foot. Rangle safely wrangled, she turned in time to see Nath divesting himself of his coat and hat, which Merryweather hung carefully near the door. He let out a long breath of air through pursed lips and lowered himself into the easy chair near the stove.

"I don't suppose we have any wine set by yet?"

"As it happens, we do," Enid said. "I sent that termagant of an innkeeper out to secure us some bottles of a decent vintage."

"Lieutenant Merryweather, may I impose upon you to do the honors?"

Enid studied Nath's face carefully as he drank off the top third of his glass. What she saw there wasn't encouraging. The set of his brow left no doubt of the storm brewing there. She glanced at Merryweather, who returned her frown of concern.

Nath set his glass on the table at his elbow and stood.

"I can see you're both with child for news of my reception at Admiralty," he said, and paced unevenly to the window, his gait still not adjusted to solid ground. "The Sea Lord has stripped me of *Redemption*'s command and insinuated I shall spend the rest of my life ashore, on half-pay."

Merryweather's face turned grim at Nath's news, but Enid only nodded and said, "This was not unexpected, and we have our basic strategy in place. Judging from the crowds in the street, it is well founded."

"Damn politics," Merryweather cursed.

"Indeed," Nath said with a wan smile. "Learn from my mistake, Lieutenant, and do not foul the hawse of the Great Powers."

"Mistake," Enid snapped. "Mistake? Diligent service and heroic action are never mistakes. The only error I see is in your king's inaction in the face of such blatant pursuit of a personal grudge to the detriment of his kingdom's interest!"

"The King, bless him, leaves the work of his ministers to his ministers," Nath raised a hand when he saw a hot retort forming on Enid's lips. "No. Speaking ill of the monarch to whom I've sworn my loyalty will only make me more low."

Enid's jaw closed with a snap and she held her peace.

Nath settled tiredly onto the couch and Enid took her place at its opposite end. He took the lit cigarillo she offered him with a grateful nod. A moment later, he slowly exhaled a cloud of smoke that hung heavily about his head. "Perhaps it would be best if I simply resigned. My father has offered me a place in his business affairs, though I doubt the position would happily serve either of us. I could parlay my current fame into investments to outfit a privateer, though, and then serve my king without regard to whatever political faction held the high ground in Middlesea at a given time. I would not be the first wronged officer to do so. Braithwaite was knighted for his actions during the last war, and set himself up a great fortune, besides."

"Sir! I beg you to put such thoughts from your mind," Merryweather gasped. "Do not give these, these *politicians* a victory that two enemy frigates failed to achieve! I implore you to stay the course! Let the magister untangle the political knot before it strangles you!"

Nath, clearly moved, looked up into Merryweather's eyes and said, "I will take your counsel into consideration, Lieutenant, and I shall give it the same weight as I would in the heat of battle or the heart of a storm. But it is my responsibility to make the final decision and do what I believe is in the best interest of the ship and her people."

"I understand, sir," Merryweather said. "If you will excuse me, I should check on those people and ensure Mid Yeardly hasn't allowed them to turn their quarters into a knocking shop."

"Fine idea, Lieutenant," Nath said. "But you do not require my permission. My command over you and the rest of our folk ended the moment Lieutenant Calver set foot on *Redemption*."

"You may find that opinions differ on that, sir," Merryweather said with a brisk salute and took her leave.

"Will you resign, then?" Enid asked, leaning across the space between them to top off his glass.

Nath shrugged. "It is the only way I can see to do good by the officers and warrants, such as you and Merryweather."

"Spare any thoughts for me. I will not serve beside any captain but you. I have sufficient funds to support me for the foreseeable future and would find no pleasure in serving an institution that treats its best officer in such a deplorable manner."

Nath coughed smoke as he laughed. "I think personal affection may color your assessment."

Enid shrugged. "Perhaps. Still."

"I appreciate your friendship and loyalty, Enid," Nath said. "But I must also consider the futures of young Yeardly and Harlech. Not to mention poor Oxley. He might make lieutenant without the black mark of his association with me by his name. The longer I wait, the more indelible that mark will become."

"I understand what you say," Enid said. "But understand me: this is no time for rash decisions. I'm a political veteran of both noble courts and the *Institut*. Please take no action until I understand the situation more clearly. Allow me to help you navigate these hazardous waters, just as you have helped me."

Nath stared at the burning end of his cigarillo for a time and then nodded his silent assent.

One of Mrs. Rangle's maids, a pleasant young lady named Joy, appeared at the door to their apartment at a decent morning hour, bearing a tray loaded with a traditional Albion breakfast. She bore the platter to the small table that dominated the sitting area, craning her head this way and that, apparently on the off-chance *Redemption*'s famed savior lurked behind an easy chair or the drawn curtains. She left the room disappointed but richer by a few pennies from Enid, as Nath was still in his bedchamber making his morning ablutions.

Enid ignored the horrifying breakfast staples of a culinarily benighted nation and made do with a bit of buttered toast, sharp cheese, and a cup of strong, black coffee.

While Nath readied himself for the day, she perused the stack of broadsheets Joy thoughtfully delivered with the morning slop. News of

Redemption's arrival in Middlesea under the command of the "Rising Star of the Royal Navy" dominated the first page of the paper. There were several images of Redemption and fanciful imaginings of Nath's appearance. None resembled him in the least. She was grateful that they had relegated her to the story's cast of supporting characters since it spared her a similar artistic treatment.

"What is the news of the day, Enid?"

She glanced up to see Nath emerging from his room, clad in his best uniform. His face had a haggard cast that spoke of a poor night's sleep.

"You are the author of it all, so you would find it tiresome for me to repeat it," Enid said. "You may find it amusing to know that several journalistic wags have dubbed you Rue-Naught."

Nath sat across from her at the table and began filling his plate. She was relieved to see that he reached for the carafe of coffee rather than the bottle of wine on the platter.

He snorted. "Would it were so."

"Come now," Enid said firmly. "I have never seen you so glum in the face of overwhelming odds at sea. You must remind yourself this is but another form of battle. Steel yourself for the action and victory will be yours. Where is the sanguinity that you commanded on the cruise from Gisbon?"

"Abandoned on the *Redemption*, as I predicted, you may recall," Nath said. "But you are right, of course. Even so, a newly made Post Captain going against the Sea Lord is a bit like a cutter rounding up at a cable's length from a ship of the line."

"Nonsense." Enid flipped the broadsheet with her finger. "This sort of public acclaim is powerful. Bold headlines replete with exclamation marks brought down the King of Ardainne. Your Sea Lord will suffer the people's displeasure and find it necessary to placate them or alienate them entirely, either of which works to your advantage."

"Perhaps. But the working folk of Albion have a short attention span. They will forget me quickly once a newer, more urgent story supplants me from the front page."

Enid's smile would have done a wolf credit. "Then we must not allow you to be supplanted. We must seize and hold the weather gauge, as you would say. I have some ideas to that end but must learn more of the Middlesea *ton* to carry them to fruition. Once your belly is full, you must share all you know of capital society."

They passed the morning discussing the terrain upon which Enid's war for Nath's career would be waged. Fortunately, Nath was no stranger to the gossip of court and upper society. He knew even more of how the luminaries of the civil world were connected with the Sea Service. Indeed, his knowledge of the intricate network of interest that helped shape the Royal Navy was exhaustive and, at times, exhausting. Their discussion was frequently interrupted by one of several maids, each carrying invitations for Rue to attend a party, dinner, or more discreet assignation.

"Lord," Nath sighed and waved an envelope. "Here's another, stinking of perfume and containing a lock of shining gold hair."

"Place it in this pile, then."

"Best to discard it, don't you think? Many of these are from married men and women."

"And that is precisely why they should be saved. It may prove that the spouses of the star-struck admirers are more valuable than they."

The pair spent the remainder of the morning sorting through the bag of mail, which was delivered courtesy of Admiralty, to whom the missives were addressed, and Miss Emley Holyoake, who redirected them to the Best Bower. Within, they discovered enough perfumed and cologned envelopes to fill the air of their rooms with the conflicting scents of a florist's shop and a tobacconist's shop with a sideline in fine saddlery. They sorted these lusty letters into one of several piles on the table, while segregating more respectable correspondence into their own stacks. Here, by the lukewarm pot of thin, brown swill Mrs. Rangle called coffee, was a heap of business offers, there, hard by a tame but tasty bottle of table wine purchased by Enid, were congratulations from Rue's friends, friends of the extensive Nath line, and a multitude of well-wishers who only knew of him by the newspaper accounts of the captures of *Artagny* and *Redemption*. Finally, gathered safely in one of Enids upturned hats, were squadron after squadron of dinner and ball invitations, which she arranged in order of their political influence.

Out of this sea of paper, Enid was able to pluck a few items of potential value in her efforts on Nath's part, including an introductory letter from one Verity Hicks, an artist of some repute in Middlesea, who offered a share of the sale of any resulting engravings in exchange for posing for her exclusively. Nath objected to the idea as vainglorious, but he relented when she pointed out the travesties purporting to be "the true and accurate image of the heroic savior of HMS *Redemption*" on the pages of several papers and pamphlets.

"Ashes! I believe that is an image of old Admiral Oulart with no changes save the epaulets being exchanged for the single brush of a newly made post captain. I am not half-so old, nor do I resemble a walrus in the least!"

"Then we will accept her invitation to call upon her for a preliminary sitting later in the week."

There was also a letter from a person employed by the Middlesea Informer, which requested an interview with Nath at a rude and ill-considered time; this would doubtless interfere with their supper, which they continued to practice as if they were at sea, rather than transmission to dinner, as it was called ashore, and its later hour. What is more, its author's tone was impertinent and shockingly familiar, with its use of Nath's given name and a few flings at humor that bordered on actionable insult. The hand which wrote this was strong, confident, and clearly feminine. She waved the letter at Rue to draw his attention, and asked, "Is a person named Muirean Alderbow familiar to you, or perhaps with you?"

Nath opened his mouth to answer and then twigged to Enid's entendre and laughed, the full, merry sound of which she had not heard since stepping ashore in Middlesea. He snatched the letter from her fingers and skimmed it, his lips moving, sometimes pursed, sometimes curving into a grin as he read. Enid stared at him as she awaited the answer to her question, which, to her ears, had been quite direct.

"Muirean, that is to say, Miss Alderbow, is my cousin, Enid." He returned the letter to her with a grin. "Not an old lover. She is my dearest friend from childhood. Our parents' estates were situated next to one another and we were inseparable."

"Your cousin, nay, your book companion as a youth is a journalist?" Enid's irritation should have been as obvious as a squall line, but Rue was too transported by fond recollection to notice his peril. "Indeed," he proclaimed proudly. "And more than a mere scribbler! She is an editor of some sort, and gauging the last letters I had from her, she is to the paper's owner what first lieutenant is to a captain."

"You may recall that I asked you for a list of friends, relations, and such-like who would be of use in winning the public fully to your side?"

"Certainly," Nath said. "As if it were yesterday, and I—failed to mention Muirean. Damme for a fool, Enid. Still, no serious harm is done. You will meet her at supper tonight and I'm mortally certain you will find she is a willing partisan in our cause!"

Enid regarded him silently for a moment before shaking her head and saying, "Make ready to go out. If you 'shake your legs,' we can call on this artist, Miss Hicks, and return home in time to sup with your cousin. And what half-formed thought lies hidden behind your simpleton smile?"

After Nath took leave of Enid and Miss Hicks, he called upon a few young officers of his acquaintance who resolutely and unanimously deplored his treatment at the hands of the Sea Lord. Their words of encouragement and consolation were a balm to his battered ego. More than a little pleased by their copious outpouring of support, he splurged on a pair of large, well-aged hens for Ms. Rangle's cook to prepare for them special and a brace of expensive bottles of Ardain wine with which to wash them down. He hoped the vintage would please Enid.

As an afterthought, he ducked into a shop specializing in spices and momentarily dumbfounded the clerk by asking for "spices of the like a fine Ardain lady might find pleasing and some of a more rustic nature, too, as might be used by a country housewife of the same nation." His mind filled with rather lecherous conclusions regarding Nath's living situation, the clerk gathered several parcels of useful Ardain herbs and, out of jealousy, overcharged the little naval captain by half-again for them.

There was a brisk rap at the door of Enid and Nath's rooms at the Best Bower. When Nath opened it, he found Joy, who had only just finished setting their table with three places, the two hens under a pewter cover that had seen better days, and an abundance of side dishes. She appeared flustered. "Beg pardon, sir, but the young lady was quite insistent. I tol' you was about to have your supper, but—"

"It's quite all right, Joy, you did well," Nath replied absently, studying the message written on the obverse of the card in a firm but feminine hand. It read, *Care to negotiate? Your Friend in Admiralty.*

"Holyoke," he said.

"What is that you said?" Enid lowered a week-old paper from Arden.

"Holyoke," Nath repeated. "The young lady from Admiralty I spoke to you about. She wishes to call on me, in the instant."

"The secretary?" Enid shrugged. "I have no objection. If her company is tiresome or I perceive I'm impeding a more intimate conversation, I'll take my leave. I'm to meet Merryweather soon in any case. There's a clothiers' shop that trades in the more intimate underlayment of a lady's costume that she thinks will meet my admittedly exacting needs."

Nath blushed a little despite himself, which, he suspected, was precisely the reaction Enid set out to achieve. He turned to Joy and said, "Please show the young lady up."

Joy sketched a curtsy, cast a quick glance at Enid as if to reassure herself that the wild leopard Nath kept in his rooms was still on its chains, and retreated in all haste.

"I have no idea what I have done to instill such loathing in that girl," Enid said, faintly amused by the maid's display. "I swear to all the Powers that I have never had a harsh word with her."

"You're a wizard. Wizards turn young girls to toads."

"Only if we're rankled. I can't think of anything that sweet wisp has done to rankle me. I don't hold her responsible for your nation's gustatory crimes. She is but the messenger from the kitchen to our table, after all."

"Damme. I should have had her clear the breakfast table before—" He was interrupted by a tentative rap on the door followed by Joy's voice beyond it, announcing the arrival of the "Young Miss."

Nath was surprised, and a little puzzled to find Holyoke clad in her clerk's togs with a courier's satchel slung over her shoulder. The brief message on her card had nothing of Admiralty business in it and promised a more social, even intimate purpose to her visit. Still, he ushered her into the room with a smile and introduced her to Enid, who deigned to set aside her paper, rise, and accept Holyoke's smoothly delivered recognition of her elevated, if hollow title. Introductions dispensed with, Nath bade her sit on one side of the sitting room's long couch and took his place at the other end, as Enid had reclaimed the easy chair whose ownership was a constant bone of contention between them.

Holyoke leaned her cane against the arm of the couch and retrieved a bundle of papers from her satchel before taking a seat. Nath accepted them from her with the same enthusiasm he would have shown had she offered him a furious viper.

"These are your copies of the official orders removing you from command of *Revenant* and assigning you to the half-pay list."

Nath held them in his lap and stared down at the twine that bound them as if it truly were a venomous serpent.

"*Revenant*?" Nath asked. "She has been renamed?"

Holyoke nodded. "And she has been sent to the Gorwich yards to be refitted. She is long enough and sufficiently broad of beam to be safely rigged out as a modern 40-gun frigate. She'll be fitted with the new smashers."

"Properly done, she should do well as a 40. I doubt she'll lose much in the way of handling or speed."

"I agree," Holyoke said. "And Borelane is the ship's architect assigned, so I trust she'll use the ship's innate lines to her best advantage."

"If I may interrupt," Enid did not wait for their assent before doing just that. "Is it common practice for the Sea Lord's personal clerk and private secretary to deliver his orders in person? I would think your Admiralty would be aswim with mids to serve as his runners."

Holyoke smiled and shook her head. "It is not common at all, but I contrived a reason to make this exception."

"Why?" Enid asked.

"For two very sound reasons, I believe. I wished to ensure that Captain Nath understands what unwritten messages lurk between the lines of his orders and it is far easier to explain this visit away as the Sea Lord's business if I'm clad in his livery."

Enid nodded her satisfaction. "Sound reasons, indeed. Pray, forgive my intrusion in your conversation. My curiosity overwhelms my courtesy at times, I fear."

"I find no fault in your question to forgive, Lady d'Tancreville. In fact, I find it reassuring. I assume that a lady of your stature is familiar with the sort of spiteful politics that consumes so much of the nobility's time, the more so the more exalted their rank?"

Enid replied with a silent nod, apparently unaware or unstung by the criticism of her strata of nobility couched in the question. Nath doubted the former was true, and hoped the latter explained Enid's unreadable expression.

"Good," Holyoke said with a genuine smile of relief. "For our poor captain is ringed around with jealous plots and I suspect he is not adequately equipped to recognize, let alone counter, them all."

"Your assumption is astute."

Nath let out an exasperated sigh. "Ladies, I sit here in the same room with you, if you've forgotten the fact."

Holyoke chuckled but Enid fixed him with a hard stare and said, "I've said nothing you have not admitted yourself. You know I have only your best interests at heart. Ms. Holyoke seems to share my concern for your well-being."

Before he could reply, she turned her penetrating eyes on the clerk and asked, "Why do you take such an interest in Captain Nath? He cannot be the first officer you've seen ground between the gears of the Sea Lord's political machine."

Unfazed by the interrogative turn the conversation lurched down, Holyoke answered, "He is not, though I pray he may be the last. I assume we may speak openly, each confident of the discretion of the other?"

"You have my word on it," Enid said, beating Nath to the proclamation by a half-second or so.

"Then I will be frank. I hate the Sea Lord and all he stands for. My brief time in his service has been a preview of hell if ever there was one. My days of servility to the snake are nearly at an end now, and it is my dearest desire to undo at least one of the evils he has done and leave him grinding his teeth and tearing his hair as I take my leave."

"How did you come to find yourself in his service?" Nath asked. "I understand you were forced to abandon your lieutenant's commission due to injuries received in battle, but it seems like a long step from that to the Sea Lord's private offices."

"Battle is too strong a word, I fear. I received this wound from Captain Arum Hovarth, then in command of Osprey, 32. Through a combination of savage drink-driven discipline and indecisive leadership he transformed her people from a competent and sedate crew into a brewing pot of resentment on the verge of boiling over into mutiny."

"One night I found him in a besotted sleep on the quarterdeck, and fearing for his safety, sought to wake him and assist him to his bed. Alas, he was unresponsive to my words, so I made to lift him to his feet. At this point he awoke with a violent start and, convinced that he was about to be thrown overboard by mutineers, produced his pistol and fired blindly. I was able to knock the barrel away from my face, but still took the ball in my knee."

"Ashes," growled Nath, while Enid was content to allow her horrified expression speak for itself.

"Our doctor was one of those sawbones who expended all his discipline and vigor in collecting the coin to purchase her warrant, but he did all he could. Without his efforts I'm sure I would have lost my leg altogether."

"A horrible tale," Nath said. "But how—"

"Hovarth was—is—one of Earl Morrin's creatures. Through his efforts the event never saw the light of day. He received no censure, let alone a court-martial. My father was incensed that I lost my career and the officer who robbed me of it suffered no consequences whatsoever. Like Morrin, he is a member of the Old Charter Party, but blood is thicker than ink. Morrin was faced with the very real possibility that Hovarth's incompetency and his support for it would become public despite his best efforts."

"Your father is a man of some standing, I take it?" Enid asked.

"Yes. He was a very successful frigate captain during the last war with Naveroña and just as successful as an investor. He established the Mariner's Bank and saw his fortune grow to rival that of many of Albion's wealthiest old families."

"A formidable person, indeed," Nath said. "I've read of some of his actions. He was a fine, gallant officer while commanding frigates, too."

"Morrin couldn't ignore him. He and my father agreed that I would be consoled for my loss by becoming Morrin's private secretary. I would wield tremendous power by controlling access to the Sea Lord and work closely with him to 'reform' the Sea Service. Instead, I have been employed as a doorman and wine bearer. I received a short respite when Devil Aryl resumed office, but alas, he passed and Morrin resumed office."

"You could resign," Enid suggested. "Surely there is no dishonor in that."

"I was about to do so when this business between the Aixelys and Captain Nath arose. It is an opportunity to poke Morrin in the eye and save yet another good officer from his overweening spite."

"Admirable," Enid said.

"I'm glad you approve," Holyoke said, the trace of a hidden smile lurking at the corner of her mouth. "It is my intent to share information you might find useful, so long as there is no potential for it to provide comfort to our enemies, the Theocrats."

"Thank you, Miss Holyoke," Nath said earnestly. "I need all the allies I can marshal. Have you intelligence to share today?"

"Very little, I fear—and please, call me Emley." Once Nath agreed and extended the same liberty with his given name to her, she continued, "The file in which your orders and records are kept bears the infamous black mark, indicating you are never to be given another command of any kind. That cannot be a surprise to you, considering the odor you are in with the Sea Lord. It is interesting to note, however, that the Sea Lord is so determined that you never command *Revenant* that he has given her to Captain Chastin, even though she will be in the yards for at least a month."

Nath gave his head a sad shake. "Even if the cloud of Aixely's vendetta were not hanging over my head, I would never expect to be given a 40-gun frigate as my first post ship. I would hope for a 32 and be happy for a 28. How grasping and vainglorious he must think me!"

"He assumes that everyone is cut from the same cloth as the selfish villains with whom he surrounds himself," Enid said.

"The marquise has the right of it," Holyoke agreed. "He overestimates the greed of everyone around him, while underestimating their wit and cunning. He and men like him view themselves as a singular island of genius in a sea of simple-minded, self-centered wretches whose only reason for existence is to serve as a consumable resource by which the furnace of their ambition is fueled."

"Providence willing," Nath said. "And with your help and Enid's, he'll find me to be a stick of firewood so combustible that it leaves his furnace thoroughly exploded."

They spoke of issues that affected Nath's future, such as Morrin's contempt for the opinion of the masses, until they began crossing the same ground. At that point Holyoke abruptly announced, "I hope you will forgive me for being so forward in your company, Enid, but my available time is limited, and I hope to spend some of it in private discourse with the good captain. Would you be so kind as to—"

"Leave you to it?" Enid asked. "Of course! I have an assignation with a friend, and it would be amusing to see her expression if she found me waiting for her, rather than the other way round."

The instant the door closed behind Enid, Holyoke crawled across the couch and wrapped her arms around his neck.

"Now, Captain Nath," she breathed into his ear. "Let us negotiate a mutual surrender."

Enid returned to the Best Bower and found Emley Holyoke was gone, leaving behind a faint but pleasant scent of honeysuckle and a sated and self-satisfied Rue Nath.

"Banish that imbecilic expression from your face immediately," she scolded him. "Else your cousin will form the wrong impression of our relationship. And freshen up, for the Redeemers sake! You smell of . . . perfume."

And so Nath's expression was more officerly and his clothing fresh when Ms. Muirean Alderbow arrived. She was a quarter of an hour early for their appointment, a shocking display of punctuality for a member of a society that viewed five minutes late to be an inconveniently early arrival. She obviously flouted that norm with the same casual contempt in which she held most of polite society's rules of behavior. Mrs. Rangle presented her at Enid and Nath's door, her disapproval of the young lady's modern attire and hairstyle all but palpable. Muirean accepted the unspoken censure with a *bon ami* that rankled the innkeep all the more.

After dismissing the rancorous Mrs. Rangle, Enid paused a moment to take in an impression of this, the only other member of the sprawling

Nath clan she'd had the opportunity to meet. Nath was accepting his cousin's continental kisses on the cheek, his face a study in flustered joy. Enid judged the young woman to be her within a year or two of her own. The Nath bloodline was painted on her features, albeit with a soft brush. Her eyes were sharp, active, and intelligent. Enid thought her features lay somewhere on the nebulous border between pretty and beautiful. She shared her cousin's admirable auburn hair (though hers tended more toward red and his toward brown) and overtopped him by several inches, as most folk did. Her clothing and accoutrement were simple, modern, and attractive, although the loose bodice and deep neckline of her blouse might have been more acceptable on the *Rue de Sanctuaire* than on Midhill Street, upon which the Best Bower was situated.

"And this must be the famous Marquess d'Tancreville," Muirean said. Her voice was another mark of the Nath bloodline, being of the same warm timbre as her cousin's. "I've read about your exploits with Rue here, which were quite impressive, but I wonder if your greatest adventure remains untold."

Enid arched a brow. "My greatest adventure? And what might that be?"

"Why, your escape from the clutches of the Theocratic tyrants. It must have been a peril fraught ordeal!"

Enid nodded. "It was not a pleasant outing, nor did it fail to collect a terrible cost."

"I should love to hear all about it! I would admire your leave to share the story with my readers and disabuse them of their fallacious impression that winning free of the Theocracy is as easy as changing into a servant's costume or being swept to safety by a domino masked adventurer."

"It would be a pleasure to share the tale for the edification of your readers," Enid lied, for she would never find any pleasure in reliving her last night in Arden. "But there are doubtless émigrés with more affecting stories than mine. Captain Nath tells me you are employed as an exalted editor of one of Middlesea's larger newspapers?"

Muirean cast an amused look at Nath. "I'm surprised he

remembered, as my post has nothing to do with ships or sailing! I am the senior editor of the *Middlesea Informer.* The publication's other editors answer to me and present the stories I assign them in the manner of my liking. I am only answerable to the paper's owner, Lady Leodora Dorenshire. The *Informer* is not in the kingdom's three largest papers, but it is certainly among the top five."

Joy tiptoed into the room and furtively set the table for tea with an extra place provided for Muirean. Enid rolled her eyes when she saw the girl's fingers crossed behind her back as she practically fled the room. Muirean's alert gaze took in the girl's warding sign and Enid's exasperated expression.

"The common person views practitioners of magic with suspicion and fear, regardless of the spellcaster's national origin," Muirean observed.

"I suppose that is true," Enid said. "But I have been naught but kind and generous to that sprig of a girl, so her fear of me is, I must admit, wounding."

"How would you contrast the Albion townsperson's attitudes toward mages against those of the same class in Ardain?"

"You are a skilled interrogator, Ms. Alderbow." Enid smiled. "Excelling at one's profession seems to be a common virtue in your family. But come, let us share some tea and speak of lighter matters."

"Different matters, at least," Nath said, looking somewhat absurd carefully holding a delicate teacup and saucer with all the structural strength of a hummingbird in his weathered and scarred hands. "I apologize for my selfishness, but I invited you here in order to beg a favor from you."

"You need beg for nothing from me, Rue!" Muirean smiled ear-to-ear and patted Nath on the knee. "Of all my kinfolk—even my parents—only you supported my ambition to be a writer, a wringer of stories from the wronged. I have never forgotten your encouraging words or the fortune you gave me—No! Do not demure, for it was a fortune to us both at that time. Without your largesse, I would never have been able to make my own way in Middlesea, unencumbered as I was by a husband or particular friend. Besides, I've already performed your favor, as evidenced by the front page of today's *Informer*, and I will continue to do so until justice is done for you!"

Muirean whipped a folded paper from beneath her arm, unfurled it with a practice snap of her wrist, and held it up for Nath and Enid to behold. It was emblazoned with a bold, heavy lettered headline that shouted, "SPURS FOR RUE-NAUGHT!" In smaller, narrower letters below it asked, "WHO POISONS the KING'S EARS AGAINST HIM?"

Enid read the words and nodded her appreciation of their message. Common folk would read them and think, *The King, may the Redeemer keep him, is not Rue Naught's enemy. He is merely deceived by the same cunning men of wealth for whom we labor tirelessly for little reward and no recognition!*

"You knew what I would ask of you before we ever set foot in Middlesea?" Nath grinned and shook his head. "You've always been a canny one, Muirean!"

She bowed her head with exaggerated courtesy and continued. "I began stirring up support for you among the public at large the moment word of the ridiculous charges that scrub Ambrose Aixely leveled against you. Anyone with a passing familiarity of your nature would know in an instant the last failing one could ascribe to you is dereliction of your responsibilities. It's unthinkable."

A quick smile flashed across Enid's face at Muirean's pronouncement. "You Naths are a proactive lot," she said. "Of that there can be no doubt!"

"Along those lines, I acquainted the Duchess of Esdivere with my assessment of your character and value as an officer, Rue. She and I share many opinions on the state of affairs in Albion and she frequently reaches out to me to express hers with my pen to maintain the illusion of neutrality she maintains regarding any alliance with the Old Charter or Young Briar parties."

"Ashes," Nath said. "You have friends from rarified heights of society, Muirean!"

She offered him a playful scowl and said, "You needn't look so amazed by that, Rue. I'm not always the wild she-cat with inky claws bared for combat, you know!"

"Now, as I was saying," she said. "I shared my opinion of your *bona fides* with the Duchess, and it corroborated the reports she'd already gathered on you—Her Grace has an extensive intelligence network, you see, of which most of its members are totally unaware. Thus informed, she bade me give you this."

Muirean produced a large, stiff envelope with a red wax seal from the scuffed and battered leather satchel at her feet.

"It is an invitation to a private dinner at Lady Esdivere's townhome tomorrow night. Her guests will all be people of substantial influence who are interested in your fate. I suggest you attend, as they will form their plans for your destiny with or without you. It would be better to have a hand in shaping it as well, don't you think?"

Nath reached for the envelope, but Enid's hand darted out like a snake and snatched it before his gesture was half-complete. She studied the seal for a moment, nodded her approval, and snapped it to unfold the invitation.

"By the Redeemer and whatever old gods remain," Enid said in a calm voice that belied her predatory posture as she read the invitation. "The Duchess was at the apex of the aristocrats I hoped to woo into Rue's support. I thought weeks of effort would be required, and here you have handed it to me in as prettily worded invitation as I've yet to see!"

"I am only happy I could help in some small way, Lady d'Tancreville." Muirean's smile was wide and genuine, apparently another family trait she shared with Nath.

"There is nothing small about this," Enid said, waving the invitation at Nath's cousin just as he reached for it to read himself. "Please, you may call me Enid after the great service you've done us, unbidden and all of your own accord!"

"Enid it is, then! What else might I do to help you and my dear cousin out of your current predicament?"

The three conspirators spent another hour huddled around the table, formalizing Enid's planned campaign in the newspapers with Muirean's insightful input. By the time they closed their war council and hied themselves to a nearby chop shot Muirean swore by for supper, a fully developed strategy to keep Nath's name and face in the newspapers was carefully outlined in Enid and Muirean's personal journals and Enid's war with the Sea Lord was launched in earnest.

Nath sat across from Enid and worried his hat as their hired coach bounced over the cobblestoned road, bound for the Duchess of Esdivere's hotel—or townhouse as the Albions preferred. Enid clucked at him and her eyes glittered with amusement to see him start.

She gave him a stern look and said, "Enough of that, Rue, or you will ruin your new hat. Do you want the duchess to think the older boys tipped it off you in the schoolyard?"

He carefully placed his hat in the seat next to him and shot her a glare that was only partially playful. Despite that, he grinned and shook his head in self-reproach.

"I confess my nerves are getting the better of me, Enid." Nath tossed the stub of his cigarillo out the partially open coach window with no regard for the foot traffic crowding the street.

"It amazes me to see you so beset by doubt before a simple meal in the wilds of society when I have seen you pass the hours before a battle in perfect equanimity."

"It is different, Enid. Surely you can see that!"

"No," she replied firmly. "I cannot. All battles are won by maneuver, and naval battles often involve subterfuge, deceit, and taking whatever advantage is offered. The goal we pursue at dinner tonight will be won through the same means. Slow your heart and clear your mind and follow my lead. All will be well."

Nath took a deep breath and nodded. "I shall. These are your home waters. You have my utmost trust in steering a course through them."

Nath handed Enid down from the coach. The Duchess's townhome rose three stories aboveground and was faced with great slabs of pale granite, polished to a high sheen. Two footmen stood on either side of the manse's wide doors, clad in vermilion uniform coats with parchment-colored silk. As Enid and Nath approached, one of the footmen threw open the door and the other marched through it to announce them.

They followed the fellow deeper into the Duchess's home until they reached an ornate double door flanked by another pair of footmen. They briskly opened the door at their guide's nod. He stepped through and announced them before stepping to the left with celerity to clear the doorway for his wards to enter.

"Captain Rue Nath, RN, late of HMS *Alarum* and *Redemption* and Magister Enid d'Tancreville, RN, Marquise of Tancreville."

Enid and Nath entered a large dining room, sumptuously decorated by the hand of a master fabulist. Overhead, ospreys and gulls performed an aerial ballet, weaving gracefully between artfully arranged beams of light emanating from breaks in the scudding clouds that obscured the room's tall ceiling. Errant, cooling breezes ruffled their clothing, bearing with it the smell of fresh sea air, captured somewhere far, far from land. A mellow chorus comprising the creak of timber and squeak of ropes in blocks, transformed by the art of a virtuoso of atmospheric magic, greeted their ears and contrived to simultaneously transport Enid back to serene moments on *Alarum*'sdeck and to the orchestral performances she loved as a youth, before the study of the High Arts reduced music to mere mathematics.

The display brought a smile of boyish joy to Nath, but struck Enid's heart a bittersweet blow. Would Arden's halls ever see such sublime displays of spirit lifting sorcery again? Or would that once celestial city continue its decline into purely quotidian workings rendered in tones of browns and gray?

The Duchess Esdivere arose from where she sat on one of several elegant but comfortable-looking chairs surrounding a small table. This little lounge in miniature was tucked away in a corner a discreet distance from the larger, formal dining table that dominated the room. A shockingly handsome man stood with her and followed in her trail as she strode smiling across the room to greet her guests in person.

She was dressed in a lovely gown whose every hue accented the deep, warm tone of her skin. She was of a height with Enid and used it to her advantage in the same way to affect a regal air. Her features were dominated by large, hazel eyes and full lips whose expressive mobility Enid found delightful. Even barring the subtle glamour of her cosmetics, her complexion of warm, burnished mahogany was striking in its flawlessness. In Albion, she was proclaimed one of the great beauties of the world and, upon firsthand observation, Enid could find no arguments against that claim. She was pleased to see that Ardainne's current, puritanical distaste for magic in fashion had not spread to Albion, as evidenced by the Duchess's gown, which swirled evocatively about her form like surges of foam-topped, emerald waves. The ruby choker about the lady's throat and rubies and garnets that floated and danced in the slowly pulsating umbral halo of her hair glowed with an unnatural fire. She was a lovely vision, which would not have gone unnoticed in any environment, even that of the jaded court of Achard XIX, let alone here, in a relatively small chamber of her own design.

The Duchess offered her gloved hand to Nath, who bowed courteously and held it near his lips. When he straightened, she leaned down and kissed his cheek. Enid was amused to see his face flush from her attention.

"Thank you for gracing my home so soon after your triumphant return to Middlesea, Captain Nath."

The Duchess greeted Enid just as warmly, who wondered if the impact of the lady's soft lips and gentle floral scent were enhanced by some dweomer or another. She did not blush, as Nath had, but her eyes lingered warmly for a moment on the Duchess's lips. The lady noticed the reaction and her smile widened as she spoke.

"I confess that I find you fascinating, Lady d'Tancreville. I have read of your significant contribution to the action in Naveroña and believe it was integral to its success. I've also heard of your beauty, but the writers failed to capture more than its shadow."

Enid bowed her head in acknowledgment of the Duchess's compliment, and replied, "You are too kind, Duchess. Whatever meager beauty I possess is a pale shadow against your own."

The Duchess laughed. "Nowhere are tongues more honeyed than Ardainne! We must find time for private conversation so I can savor the sweetness of yours. But for now, allow me to introduce you and Captain Nath to Viscount Uthred, Lord Reinard."

Enid recognized Lord Reinard's name from the pile of papers she'd consumed that morning. He was the current face of the Young Briar party and, according to rumor, the object of the Crown Princess's adoration. *The future ruler of Albion has rather pedestrian taste in men,* Enid thought, as she observed Reinard's appearance, which was that of a storybook prince—hair of unpowdered gold, glittering blue eyes, strong features that lacked any threatening angles or proportions. Lean but obviously well-muscled by the fit of his coat and, more revealingly, his hose. *I might have been drawn in by his non-threatening good looks myself, when I was thirteen, but now—Oh! Here is what she sees in him!*

Upon being presented to Enid by the Duchess, Lord Reinard flashed her a smile that seemed unerringly aimed at her heart. She saw an amiable friend, a keen intellect, and a broad streak of adventure in the gleam of his icy-blue eyes and instantly reconsidered her opinion of the Crown Princess's opinion of men.

"Lady d'Tancreville," Lord Uthred said, pausing for her nod of permission before pressing a firm kiss against the back of her hand. "It is my honor to meet you and my sincere pleasure to congratulate you on your successful escape from the monstrous regime that holds your nation in bloody servitude. Would that more Ardain lords and ladies would lend their strength and talent to the Albion cause of liberating Ardainne and restoring an Ardain king to your people."

"That worthy prospect would be more likely, were the Albion military not so costly a club to enter." She kept as much heat out of the remark as she could manage but still expected an offended reply. Instead, Reinard's features remained set in the same cast of genuine interest they'd worn before.

"I cannot argue your point, my lady," he said, and gently squeezed her hand, which she only then noticed was still caught up in his. "And indeed, I have raised this very matter in the High House and have imposed on the Right Honorable Cian Ylfarland to do the same in the Low. My aim is to waive commission fees for former Ardain officers in the ranks in which we are most lacking or in parts of the organization that would best benefit from an influx of fresh blood and the fresh ideas that flow with it."

With introductions disposed of, Lady Esdivere led her guests to table. They were instantly surrounded by servants who filled their glasses, and, after a short time, their plates. Enid could find no fault with the Duchess's chef or wine cellar and the conversation was both clever and convivial. The topics allowed at table seemed somewhat constrained, however, as any thread promised to lead to the current state of Ardainne or Nath's troubles was quickly cut short. Enid assumed her host's reticence to allow such subjects at her table was intended in some part to allow her and Nath to enjoy the evening without reminders of the cloud that hung over them. There was another motive at work, though. She was certain of that.

Her suspicions were confirmed when the last course was carted away and the Duchess led them to a semicircle of chairs arranged in the corner for the purpose of conversation. When they were all seated with a self-chilling glass in their hand, Lady Esdivere said, "Captain Nath, Lady d'Tancreville, it is our desire to assist in extricating you from your current troubles. The viscount and I find your situation abominable and have agreed it cannot be allowed to stand, either from fairness to a national hero or for the good of Albion."

"That is most kind of you both, Lady Esdivere," Nath said.

"It is also self-serving," Reinard said with a wan, self-deprecating smile. "Your triumph over the Sea Lord's enmity is a tide that will raise more ships than your own."

"How so?" Enid asked.

"The fate of Captain Nath's naval career is a matter of contention between the Young Briar and Old Charter parties, and its disposition will announce which faction holds the greater share of political power in Albion," Reinard explained. "If you are not commissioned for another command, it is most likely that the Old Charter Party will shape Albion's destiny. Should you receive the recognition and reward you so richly deserve, however, the Young Briars will begin the Crown Princess's lifelong ambition to reform the kingdom before she is ever crowned its queen."

"While my fate is eminently portentous to me, I do not flatter my value to Albion to be so great as you pretend," Nath said with a cavalier smile.

Reinard laughed. "Do not doubt the heights of my admiration for you and your heroic accomplishments when I say that you are correct. The destiny of Albion does not turn on the axis of a single frigate captain. The political balance of the kingdom, however, does."

"How so?" Enid asked.

"Forgive us, Lady d'Tancreville, but before explaining the situation, we must have your word and that of Captain Nath that whatever is said tonight is spoken under an unbreakable oath of confidence."

"You have my word, within which resides all the honor left to my line," Enid averred. "And I believe Captain Nath's reputation is unassailable."

Satisfied, the Duchess nodded to Reinard, who launched into a description of the royal court's current state that left Nath disconcerted and Enid dumbfounded.

King Ruadric III was ill. He suffered from a malady of the mind that left him forgetful and easily distracted. A hard-nosed ruler with a firm finger on the political pulse of his kingdom in the past, now only the histories of Albion's past glories held his interest. In the last few years, he had increasingly abdicated his authority in specific areas of the royal government to whatever lord or lady seized his confidence at the moment. Questioning the wisdom of his choice was to court his ire and, perhaps, banishment from royal office. It was in just such a manner that Admiral Weymouth doomed his chances of sitting behind the Sea Lord's desk when he warned the king of Morrin's extreme nepotism, corruption, and factional intransigence. His decline became more precipitous in the last month or so, to such a degree that his daughter approached him and suggested gently that she take on a portion of his responsibilities to ease the strain under which he labored.

Her father did not welcome her solicitousness, which he interpreted as an unseemly eagerness to take his throne, a sentiment that members of the Old Charter Party took pains to encourage. Sadly, according to Reinard, Aixely and his cronies were so successful in their efforts that Ruadric had all but disowned his daughter and viewed her supporters in the Young Briar Party as radical social levelers. While he did not act directly against the crown's various ministers, sinecures, and government officials with loyalties to the Young Briars, he did take every opportunity to relieve them for the flimsiest of causes. The resulting vacancies were quickly filled with Old Charter members or their loyal cronies.

"So, a gradual retrenchment is in progress," Enid mused. "Why does the king, or, more to the point, those who fill his ears with poison, move at such a measured pace? Fear of goading your Parliament into action?"

"In part, yes," Reinard said. "Although the Upper House, wherein lies the institution's real power, is deadlocked between both parties. Surprisingly, though, the opinion of Middlesea's common throng is the main factor restraining His Majesty from an outright purge of the Young Briars. Our king, Redeemer bless him, is under the sway of public opinion—or at least what he believes their opinion to be, fed as it is to him by Old Charter partisans who surround him in nearly every waking moment. His Majesty's dread of losing the affection of the common folk can be used as a lever to shift his support to your favor and discomfit that misbegotten whelp, Ambrose Aixely."

Reinard savored Ambrose's name in his mouth with the same delectation the taste of a live, scabrous rat might evince. *There is more than politics behind Lord Uthred's distaste for Ambrose,* Enid thought.

"So you believe, as do I, that a sufficient weight of adoration and support from the commons for Rue would shift the scales sufficiently to counter the grumblers that surround the king?"

"We do," Reinard said. "And if we can prove that theory with your case, the Old Charter's monopoly on the king will be broken. They may have his ear, but we will hold his heart, and they will know it from that day forward."

Nath glanced at Enid, who nodded and said, "It is a sound plan and one which will be beneficial to us both should it succeed."

Duchess Esdivere raised a speculative brow. "Lady d'Tancreville is your *conseillère de guerre*, I take it?"

Nath nodded. "She is. Her experience in political matters far outstrips my own."

"I applaud the wisdom of recognizing another's skill is ascendant over your own," Reinard said. "It is difficult relinquish control of one's fate to another, particularly for once so used to command as yourself. Now, perhaps we should discuss how best to move forward?"

The balance of the evening passed in exploring various gambits to further brighten Nath's star in the eyes of the people of Middlesea and outlining a comprehensive set of actions to pursue. When he and Enid finally departed for home in one of the Duchess's coaches, her mind was running with the speed and precision of one of the new undine-driven looms that were rising to prominence in Nordmarche. Nath, seeing the deep, thought-filled lines between her eyes reckoned that conversation was not on the agenda and leaned back into the coach's soft, padded seat and instantly fell asleep.

The next few days were as exhilarating for Enid as those spent setting the *Redemption* to right had been for Rue. Unfortunately, the days and nights spent courting the interest of the social elite were as trying for him as the constant hammering, sawing, and mum gun drills were for her. To his credit, he showed the same dogged determination in adhering to the stratagem she'd concocted with the Duchess Esdivere and

Viscount Uthred as he would have shown in pursuit of a prize. There were dinners to attend, appearances to be made at fetes in his honor, and dinners with trade associations, bankers, and tradesmen groups to be endured. He found the latter to be the most trying, but he understood the masters of his master's money could be more persuasive than a dozen parades in his honor.

Not all of their tasks were onerous, though, and some were quite enjoyable, such as their visit to the studio of Miss Verity Hicks, the artist and engraver who wished to establish a business relationship with Nath based on the authorized sale of his image. Her rooms were situated in a boardinghouse of good quality located directly across Waltham Road from Mandleby's, an inn that catered to the wealthier class of military officer, a situation Enid supposed the artist found profitable. Her living quarters and sitting room took a sizable portion of the ground floor, while her studio dominated the second floor and was blessed with windows on three sides that allowed the sunlight in throughout most of the day. Enid and Nath were now bathed in that sunlight, she seated in a worn but comfortable chair, her sword across her knees and her hat in the crook of her left arm, he behind her, hip cocked and hand resting on the hilt of his sword and his hat firmly planted on his head. These poses were necessitated by the difference in their heights: Miss Hicks had initially desired them to pose standing side by side, gazing earnestly out a window, which would be transformed into some more nautical structure by the magic of her art, but Enid towered above Nath to such a degree that his heroic image must suffer by contrast. The artist seemed disappointed, but Enid was frankly grateful. She'd posed for portraits before and infinitely preferred to be at her ease in a chair rather than frozen standing like a statue for torturous hours as her muscles cramped and her nose prickled from the smell of linseed oil.

"You are frowning again, Lady d'Tancreville," Miss Hicks protested. "A stern look is acceptable, but a frown will never do!"

Enid coaxed her face to a neutral set, which the artist apparently found stern, and apologized. "I'm sorry. It seems to be my natural expression these days."

"I understand, poor dear," the common woman's commiseration came with a familiarity that might have earned her a whipping in Ardainne, talented artist or no. Enid found her easy manner charming, though, and took no offense.

Miss Hicks was quite short and waifish in build. She gave Enid the impression that she was in the company of some miniature homunculus conjured up for the entertainment of children. The woman's solemn, thoughtful eyes and kind but assertive manner gave her an authority that belied her stature, though, as did her appearance, which was unusually comely despite her low birth. No pockmarks marred her skin, which was as pale and near translucent as any noble woman could hope for, and her long, brown hair, tied back to avoid a dipping in paint, was thick and lustrous. If she were not involved with Merryweather, Enid believed she would have pursued Miss Hicks, assuming she was not spoken for.

"Frowning, my lady," Miss Hicks sighed. "You're as grim a flower of society as I've ever laid eyes on! I suppose the news of Redemption's new captain would be sobering. Did you know her well?"

"Captain Chastin?" Nath spoke through clenched teeth, so his words were only just intelligible. "I have met her socially. A prodigious large woman and a good officer. I doubt she will have command of *Revenant* any longer than it takes to see her moved to the yards and refitted. She has read herself in aboard her, I take it?"

"Sadly, no. When she went aboard to do so, one of ship's battens gave way beneath her and she fell, bearing one of her lieutenants with her as she did. They were both drowned before they could be pulled from the water."

"That is . . ." Nath searched for a word that would serve, but any escaped him. He settled on ". . . madness. I've never heard of such a thing!"

"Ashes," Miss Hicks cursed. "Now you're both frowning."

Miss Hicks worked diligently for another hour or so until Nath produced his pocket watch to check the time. The little artist put her brush down and drew a sharp breath, which she held for a moment before saying, "Let us stop here for the day, shall we?"

"That would be grand," Nath said, and restowed his watch. "I fear I'd be forced to leave shortly at any gate. My prize agent expects me today to discuss how best to extend what is left of my savings. Enid, do you wish to come along, or—"

"Or. As fascinating as watching you and your agent juggle numbers and shift decimal points, I believe I will part company with you for the day."

"That is probably for the best," Nath said. "I do wish to delve into the state of the coffee trade. I have it on good authority that the coming harvest will be greatly diminished, so investing now could result in great profits when the price of beans skyrockets."

"Well, I wish you joy of it. I'll take the opportunity to catch up on my journal back in our rooms."

"I am at loose ends for an hour or more," Miss Hicks said. "You are welcome to tarry here over a glass, if your journaling doesn't require your immediate attention."

"I'd be obliged for the companionship," Enid said. "Frankly, I've no burning desire to attend to my journal at all."

Once Nath was seen to the door, Miss Hicks ushered Enid into her sitting room, which was small but elegantly appointed. A number of portraits crowded the walls, giving Enid a momentary feeling of being onstage before a small and remarkably remote audience. Miss Hicks directed her to a padded bench large enough for two and sat down beside her. She regarded Enid closely for a moment, the hint of a frown creasing her forehead, and then asked directly, "Do you have a particular attachment to Captain Nath, Lady d'Tancreville? Forgive my forwardness in asking, but the gossips paint you and him as warrior beaus, but your manner with one another seems more comradely than passionate."

Enid chuckled and shook her head. "No, Miss Hicks. You are

correct. The captain and I have developed a bond of friendship. I greatly admire his skills as a captain and find him a gentleman of wit and taste, but our friendship lacks any romantic impediments."

"Please, call me Verity. Considering the liberties I'll be taking with your image, I owe you at least that much familiarity. You find romance to be an impediment to friendship?"

"Then you must call me Enid—and yes, that has been my experience. Where Romance enters, Amity flees. True friendship, to my lights, is based on the free exchange of honest thoughts and feelings—such an exchange cannot survive the rigors of romance."

Verity rose and produced a pair of glasses and a bottle of wine from a cabinet hidden cunningly within the pedestal of a frowning patriarchal bust that Enid recognized as some classical Ettolian sculptor or another. As Verity filled the glass, she asked why Enid saw romance as an enemy of both honesty and friendship. Enid accepted the wine, a sip of which revealed it to be a cordial vintage well suited to free conversation, and explained.

"The object of romantic conversation is not truth; rather, to use the sorcerous term, its object is glamour. A would-be lover wishes the object of his affections to believe that he is the same ideal creature he believes her to be. If she returns his attentions, she will have the same goal. In the end, both parties will present themselves as near as possible to each other's ideals—worse, since their deception is reciprocal, they will be forced to pretend to be the ideals held by the other's ideal. They become not just actors, but actors playing the parts of actors. In such falsity there is no purchase for either truth or true friendship."

Verity sipped her wine, obviously lost in thought. After a moment she came to herself and said, "If romance is bound hand and foot to falsity, how can any marriage hope to prosper?"

Enid shrugged. "Perhaps such hopes are forlorn. There are still those that hold that arranged marriages are the best, and it is true that I can point to several such unions where neither party would dream of straying from perfect commitment to their spouse. On the other hand, if marriage is as inimical to romance as I have heard, perhaps truth wins out and illusions are set aside even as vows are exchanged."

"If that is the case, all marriages must be doomed. How can love survive without romance?"

Enid shook her head. "What does romance have to do with love? Witness the love between a mother and her child. Between brother and his sister? None can doubt either its presence or potency, and yet there is not a jot of romance between them."

Verity chuckled slyly. "Among Albions of the high blood? You might be surprised—but depravity aside, I take your point. Still, I'd say that familial love is different from that between lovers."

"True enough—but still, I cannot see that romance is in any way required for the sustenance of love. Honesty, understanding, compassion, and an objective understanding and acceptance of a lover's true nature, foibles and all, seem infinitely more valuable than carefully marshaled words and gestures designed to deceive and enchant."

"Still, there is something to be said for the romantic gesture—this wine and the flowers you may have noticed in the foyer as you entered are both the product of the deceptive tactics you decry."

"Oh," Enid said, taking another sip of the truly wonderful wine, "as to the gestures, you'll receive no complaints from me. I love flattery and gifts as much as anyone—I simply do not believe they reflect the true nature of the person giving them. They are an artifice. A pleasurable and rewarding artifice, but an artifice nonetheless."

Verity smiled merrily and raised her glass. "Well then, here's to artifice!"

And so they drained their glasses.

They finished the bottle of wine as Verity showed her all her finished and near-finished pieces. Enid was quite impressed by her skill and by the eloquence with which she commented on each portrait. It was an enlightening experience—Verity's talk of "finding the image the subject unknowingly wished to project" reminded her of her own art, which relied heavily on recognizing the desired potentiality in the forces she manipulated. Verity's paintings, which never failed to make her subjects seem interesting despite their strikingly unnatural poses and lack of flattery—here was a dueling scar plainly visible on a viscount's forehead and here was the girlish gap between the front teeth of a baroness—led Enid to the conclusion that, had sorcery been the artist's medium of choice, her grasp of hidden potential would have made her an archimagus of the old school.

Verity frowned at the length of the shadow an Ettolian bust cast across the floor.

"How the day has escaped me! Such is the peril of pleasant company! I hope you will feel free to call upon me whenever you wish, Lady d'Tancreville. I have enjoyed our conversation immensely. The people whose portraits I paint rarely find talk of their painting interesting."

"Surely you have friends among Albion's artistic tribe?"

"I do, but I find most creative folks to be infinitely tiresome. Most are too concerned with self-aggrandizement to indulge in an open discussion. Truthfully, I would rather spend eternity chained to a baker than an artist. At least the baker would smell of warm bread."

Enid laughed. "You can count on my company in the future, Verity! Perhaps I'll come calling with a couple of freshly baked loaves in my pockets!"

chapter 6

Weeks accumulated into a month and a half as Enid and the rest of Nath's cabal worked tirelessly to loosen Admiralty's grasp on a command for the Hero of *Redemption*. With the aid of Lord Reinard Uthred and Lady Esdivere, Enid infiltrated the less conservative branch of Albion's aristocracy and wooed them into the support of "poor Rue Naught" and, to her gratification, support for a more active Albion hand in removing the Theocratic stain from Ardainne. Nor did she spare the fence-sitters her attention. As they were identified, Lady Esdivere ensured they were invited to affairs where Nath would be present, and his natural charm could be counted on to bring them to his side.

Still, it was a pleasant time for both Enid and Nath, despite the doom that hung over their heads. Nath suspected that the very real threat of failure increased the intensity of each day's or night's experience. Enid called regularly upon the delightful Miss Hicks, and he joined them at times to suggest corrections to details of the engravings. Enid and Merryweather had become fast friends, true shipmates it seemed, and he wished them joy. They were both possessed of forceful, self-assured personalities, qualities that made it difficult to find and nurture genuine friendships. He regretted that their camaraderie robbed him of time with Enid, whose company was a delight and often a challenge, but he was not without interesting people with whom to socialize. He played cards with Lady Esdivere at her club regularly and had enjoyed several days fowling with Lord Reinard on his estate just outside Middlesea. And, finally, there was Emley Holyoke, with whom he met in disguise once or twice a week at an inn famed for its discretion and the jealousy with which it protected the identities of the wealthy and high placed for whom it was the preferred destination for trysts they wished to hide from their spouses, peers, or what-have-you. There she was briefed on news from the Sea Lord's own office and, afterward, they engaged in further intimate negotiations.

It was after one such vigorous give-and-take that Emley said, "Your confederates have done their jobs so well that we may be forced to contrive some other excuse for our liaisons soon. Morrin frets to Aixely that the king may soon take matters out of his hands if the 'unwashed masses' continue to cry out so loudly and persistently for you to receive another command."

"From your lips to the ears of Providence," Nath sighed. "But, as you know, the Sea Lord has more than one arrow in his quiver. There are commands and then there are commands—a sheer hulk has a captain, as does a prison ship."

"True," she said and pressed herself more tightly to his side. After a moment she rose on her elbow and gazed fiercely into his eyes. "Rue, you have my word that should our efforts to extricate you from Morrin and Aixely's deceitful web be unsuccessful, you will sail again, if I have to lay down the keel of a privateer to make it so."

He was mortally confident that she meant what she said, but he would only turn privateer as a last resort. Better to take up a commission from the King of Svearige, who was always eager to take on Albion officers. He kept his opinion to himself, though, and pulled her gently down atop him. "I'm prepared to sail again now, if you are."

Emley laughed. "You are as incorrigible as your reputation suggests!"

Now, alone in his room at the Best Bower, Nath took advantage of Enid and Merryweather's absence and seated himself at the room's battered but serviceable writing desk and opened the new leather-bound journal centered upon its top. Muirean suggested that he take up the habit of recording his personal thoughts, which, at some point in the future, she might edit and beat into an autobiography to their mutual enrichment. The idea repelled him at first—he was already half a clerk maintaining all the required logs and ledgers while at sea—why should he look for more opportunities to stain his cramped fingers with ink? But, he admitted to himself, he was not at sea and was possessed of a surfeit of time, so he reluctantly took up the practice. After a week or so, he found he enjoyed his time spent with his pen, ink, and blank pages he could fill however he wished.

He dipped his quill into the ink and wrote the date atop a fresh page, as was his practice, began filling it with his thoughts, written in a surprisingly elegant and assured hand.

19th Ralifrimon 1798—The Best Bower, Middlesea

I am fortunate above all else in my friends and family. Their efforts on my behalf have been energetic and unstinting. It sometimes seems that I have no role to play in my own "rehabilitation," but Enid, Providence bless her, reminds me that I do myself the most good by making the social rounds. In her words, it is my task to "put a person behind the name and engravings, because it is far more difficult to watch a person suffer unfairly than a mere name." She worded it more elegantly, of course, as she has a greater facility with words than I, even when she is handicapped by the use of a second language. Lady Esdivere has ensured that I have entrée to any events that serve our purpose and has kindly introduced me to many influential members of her circle of society, all of whom have promised their support. Should my career survive this gust front stirred up by

Morrin and Aixely's incessant whistling, I may find myself with a surfeit of interest.

My dear cousin, Muirean, has exceeded herself maintaining a steady stream of articles in the Informer, pamphlets, and broadsides presenting my character in such excess as would embarrass a saint's hagiographer. My every action aboard Alarum and Redemption are cast as decisive engagements that delivered Albion from immediate destruction. Worse yet, she has used her familial knowledge to present my youth as a series of morality tales or humorous tales of the "great man as a mischievous boy" model. She assures me that while these exaggerations are persuasive, no one but the most credulous believe they are literal accounts. This may be so, but I suspect they will be quoted as jeers by my fellow officers, should I be so fortunate to remain in their company.

Enid's intuition regarding Verity Hicks's value was prophetic. Her engravings of the Alarum and Redemption's actions are stirring while accurately reflecting the many notes I provided. While she improved my looks with an artist's magic, Enid's portrait required no improvement. Our images are accurate enough that we are no longer anonymous, which is a damned nuisance.

Perhaps the greatest argument for my cause came from an unsuspected quarter: fabulism entitled Redemption Redeemed, which was staged at the Old Royal Theatre a few weeks ago, and there are some who say it is the most stirring play of the last half century. I suspect that is the voice of enthusiasm, but I do find it surpassingly gratifying to be a character in such a well-received production. I have not had the opportunity to view it, and, in truth, I'm in no passion to do so. There are limits to my self-indulgence, though it must seem otherwise at times.

I am pleased to hear Emley report that, thanks to the activities above, the Sea Lord is in a greater stage of frustration than I. The Old Charter Party has gained little ground in countering Muirean's campaign in the Informer, *which, thanks to the avidity with which the common folk consume it, has spread to other periodicals. The best he and his lackeys in the press can do is toddle out the accusations that* Artagny, *Lieutenant Bascombe, and her prize crew were captured due to my laxity. While this is accepted as truth by the Old Charter's supporters, the majority of the public find it to be quite exploded, at least according to Muirean, who swears she would not give me false hope through falsehoods.*

Indeed, by Enid's estimation, there is likely division among ranks of the Old Charter regarding my fate, as the Redemption*'s cutting out is one of the few bright moments in what has been a woeful year for the Royal Navy. Your average landsman in Albion does not see glory in the success of our blockading squadrons. Only victories in great fleet battles, hard-fought frigate duels, or impetuous deeds of valor would signify for them. Aixely's attacks against me cast a pall over the heartening glow of* Redemption*'s repatriation, a glimmer of hope that is sorely needed in the face of recent troubles at the Ainsley Bottoms yards, where the crews of all the vessels moored there for repair, replenishment, and so forth have risen in mutiny against Admiralty.*

The mutiny's leadership, who appear to be a lettered lot of covers for foremast tars, go to great pains in the sheafs of letters they pour forth to papers (including your own, Muirean) and the Crown government to emphasize that they are not in mutiny against the King, *but against Admiralty for the ill treatment they've received at their hands, ill treatment that has redoubled in the short time since the commencement of hostilities between Albion and Ardainne. They vow to be ready to return to the war the instant their demands for better pay received more regularly, regulations intended to limit the punishments a cat-happy captain might visit upon them, more liberty ashore, and so forth, are met.*

While I would never condone mutiny of any stripe, I must say that I'm impressed by the orderly nature of this one. While they raised arms against their officers, they did not brutalize them. In fact the whole affair was prosecuted neatly and bloodlessly. Many representatives from individual vessels have included in their outpouring of declarations and pleas to the public and the king that they do not hold their officers at fault for the shortcomings of Admiralty. The crews continue to perform their duties in maintaining their ships and allow yard workers aboard to complete repairs and refitting. Their leaders have ensured that the spirit locker remains secure and give the tars no more grog than they would normally receive. They are well-disciplined and will brook no rough antics from their mates, several of whom have been surrendered to officials ashore to be tried for serious affronts, such as assault, theft, or, tellingly, the mouthing of Theocratic Revolutionary cant or seditious remarks against the king.

While I condemn the mutineers' rebellion against their officers, I recognize that many of their complaints are valid and that the Sea Service would benefit from alleviating them. It is a sad fact that many a tar's family must starve while their breadwinner's salary goes further and further in arrears. Too, all but the most heartless of officers would agree that too many good sailors have been transformed from cheerful hands to sullen brutes by the over-application of the cat. I pray that reason will prevail and this affair is ended without bloodshed or mass-hangings, which would only deepen the blot it has left upon the Service's legacy.

So, all of this is recorded for posterity, or at least for you, dear cousin Muirean. I pray she finds it as useful as she hopes and implore her to show discretion when choosing which of my remarks to share with the public. My fellow officers and every official in Admiralty are numbered among the public's ranks, after all, and should they see some of my private thoughts, my career, Redeemer grant I still possess such a thing, could be ended in a trice. That would be a sad outcome for all the labor and toil she has spent on my behalf.

I believe all has been done that can be done. I have shown my flag in all the societal ports of call Lady Esdivere suggested and Lord Reinard has run an extensive whisper campaign among her peers. Enid has been my ambassador to the more politically speculative members of the Duchess's set, and you, bless you, have seen to it that I have seen more ink spilled in my cause than those of the king, parliament, and the war altogether. Now it is only a matter of waiting to see from which quarter the wind comes and pray it does not take us aback. I hope for the best, but I am prepared for the worst, which, despite the monumental efforts of my partisans, still seems the most likely outcome to me. I cannot recall a single instance in which a Sea Lord's ban on an officer who displeased them has ended before that Sea Lord's last breath. I often consider telling my dear friends and family to drop the matter before my misfortune becomes their own. I'm certain that Enid would not cease her efforts, though, and as long as she does not strike her colors, neither will my other champions.

And, Redeemer forgive me, I cling to the hope that they will succeed, and I will once again revel at the roll of a frigate's deck beneath my feet, be she the most disreputable jackass frigate in the fleet. I am a selfish brute, of that there can be no doubt.

The quiet of the Best Bower's weekend morning was shattered by a messenger in the livery of Viscount Uthred delivering a large wicker basket and a letter, both addressed to Captain Rue Nath. Mrs. Rangle, convinced the basket contained a baby, would not let it pass and howled at the persistent messenger that hers was a respectable establishment that wouldn't receive any goddamned foundlings or unacknowledged bastards. When the contents of the basket were revealed to her, the volume of her diatribe increased, although its theme changed to "Captain Nath may be used to having sailors jump to his every whim, but he's another think coming if he is mad enough to believe either me or my staff will clean up after those . . . creatures!"

The basket now sat in the middle of the sitting room shared by Enid and Nath's private rooms, with a pair of Parson Riordan puppies, one black and white and the other brown and white, struggling in and out of it. Their efforts frequently overturned it and, as often as not, themselves as well. They were small dogs with bright, intelligent eyes, docked tails in constant movement, and erect clipped ears. They were all pink belly and stubby, kicking legs now, but Enid knew they would grow into athletic, broad-chested little dogs ideally suited for worrying foxes gone to ground back into the chase without slaying them.

"You know, this is most handsome! I only mentioned my intention to acquire a pair of these pups once, and yet he recalled it! What a handsome gift! What a handsome sentiment! And to recall a minor desire voiced but once from a virtual stranger, why, that is—"

"Handsome?"

"Yes," Nath drawled with a sideways glance at Enid. "Most handsome. Now, what shall I name these lads?"

"You should name one of them Marbury. You'll probably have the same unreasoning fondness for the beast as you do for your nation's most overrated plagiarist."

Nath laughed heartily and picked up one of the fat-bellied pups. "That's your name then, lad: Marbury. And if we're to name you after an overrated plagiarist, we may as well name your brother here Maubin, after Ardainne's most famous word-thief."

"Is the content of the letter equally handsome?"

Nath carefully placed Marbury back in the basket alongside Maubin. They fell asleep almost instantly, exhausted from their exploration and sated on small scraps of meat Enid secured for them despite Mrs. Rangle's voluble disapproval. He scanned the letter and nodded.

"His lordship's sources verify the reports I've received from Emlin—Ms. Holyoke, that is. Viscount Morrin is increasingly vexed that the public continues to sing my praises. To further goad the old devil, he and Lady Esdivere have gone so far as to start a whisper campaign to advance a rumor that His Majesty is considering granting me a baronetcy."

"And he should, too," Enid said. "Such gifts cost little, grant no real power to their recipient, and move the commons to praise the generosity of their king when they are granted to a war hero rather than some fat, jewelry-draped shopkeeper whose sight sends every lad or lass of less than twelve summers fleeing in terror or a rail-thin, syphilis-raddled courtier who earned some peer's eternal gratitude for being handy with their shirttail in their moment of royal incontinence."

Nath stared at her in silent, wide-eyed horror. "Those are remarkably specific examples, Enid!"

"They are remarkably apt, as well," she said with a shrug.

"In any case," Nath said, "the tidings are good. You may be pleased to hear that he commends your tireless efforts in my favor, as do I, and characterizes you as an 'angel descended from heaven.'"

"This Enid d'Tancreville is a devil," Sea Lord Morrin hissed. "A devil from the very depths of the Malasfandyari's deepest hell! Beyond her sorcerous skills, she is a rabble-rouser of the first stripe. Half the papers in Albion revile me for failing to give Nath"—he fairly spat the name—"command of the *Revenant* and most of them contrive to link that 'failing' to the troubles in Ainsley Bottoms!"

Earl Aixely could not help but agree. Placating his hot-blooded son by ruining a post captain who had yet to make a full cruise in that rank should have required less effort than choosing his costume in the morning; instead, it became a grueling war of attrition waged on the front pages of the kingdom's papers for weeks. Worse yet, the skirmishing soon leaked over into general discussion among Middlesea's politically active, filling every coffee shop, inn, and private club with discussions of Nath's merits, critiques of Morrin's glacial progress in securing him a new command, and speculation on how long His Majesty would permit the farce to continue. Worse, his heavy-handed mistreatment of a heroic captain deepened public sympathy for the mutineers at Ainsley Bottoms.

"Let the matter drop," Aixely suggested gently. "The Ainsley Bottom Mutiny does enough damage to our cause in the naval department. Give Nath a 38, which is far more ship than most captains receive when they first make a post. Then sweeten the proposition and make it clear that *Revenant* is reserved for him once he has accrued a few years of seniority as a post captain—a promise that you can forget when the public has moved on to their next hero of the hour."

"And what of my vow to see this rascal pay for the harm he has done to you and your son? I should 'drop' that as well? Oh, and while I'm at it, I'll abandon the authority of my office to the will of the mob. Perhaps we can import some of these Roget's Devices from Ardainne that one reads about. The ones so clever at lopping off heads such as ours? That will save the common folk the trouble of building their own!"

Fuming, the Sea Lord shoveled a prodigious amount of Ulewe into one nostril, sealed the other with his thumb, and inhaled with a sound not unlike a bull's snort. Aixely's sources told him Morrin consumed an astounding amount of the stuff, despite his doctor's direct prescription of stimulants until his humors were restored to their proper balance.

"I do not believe that the Theocratic Revolution is of a kind with this situation with Nath," Aixely drawled, resisting the urge to belabor his point with sharp, sarcastic remarks. Morrin might still be of use to him and the Party if he could be convinced to abandon his obsession with this vendetta, which was not even his own. "I've already spoken to Ambrose of this possibility. He understands the realities of politics and is willing to put his feud with Nath aside to further the Old Charter Party and our plans for the succession. Do not expose yourself on his account or mine. Let this drop. We can unsheathe our daggers for Nath at some more propitious time."

"I will consider your counsel, of course," Morrin said. His words were not snarled, but neither were they in any wise genial. "Now, if you will excuse me, Lord Aixely, I have work that requires my immediate attention."

"Of course," Aixely said, as if the Sea Lord had addressed him in a normal tone. He was intrigued as to the nature of Morrin's plan, but the man clearly had no intention of sharing it now. "I will leave you to your work and pass your regards to Ambrose."

So saying, Aixely departed. As he closed the door, he saw Morrin hunched over his desk, reading the topmost newspaper from a pile he had apparently produced from a drawer in his desk. He saw the Sea Lord's face darken perceptibly as he read and, after watching for a heartbeat or two, Aixely closed the door quietly behind him.

It may be time for a change, Aixely mused to himself as he strode past Holyoke at her desk. She made some polite nicety to which Aixely offered a disinterested grunt before walking briskly out of Admiralty and to his coach, which bore him away in a clatter of hooves and the snap of a whip.

chapter 7

The sun was setting and although Enid had walked two miles or more, she still seemed no closer to the Best Bower. She suspected she'd taken one or more wrong turns, but the street was so closed in by the tall buildings on either hand that she couldn't espy a landmark that might put her back on track. The buildings' upper stories, which hung out over the street until little more than a sliver of sky could be seen overhead, gave her the impression that she was in a tunnel—and reminded her of the mazelike alleys near Arden's Dolorous Gate, the alleys in which her uncle had died in her arms.

She pushed the dark thoughts to the back of her mind. They wouldn't serve her in finding her way back to her rooms, which she had abandoned to be free of the racket Nath made with his new puppies and the odors they produced periodically. She looked about for someone to request directions from but saw nobody she was comfortable approaching. The people she saw all had a dark, speculative cast to their eyes that spoke of criminal intent. She had obviously stumbled into one of Middlesea's less wholesome areas.

If she retraced her steps, she might find the turn she'd missed—or she might find herself somewhere worse. Any of the four streets might take her to a better part of the city and from there she could hail a coach that would take her home. Of course, any one of them would be just as likely to lead her deeper into Middlesea's most disreputable districts. She wore a small sword at her side and there was a spell-lock hidden beneath the tails of her coat—and as long as she had the strength to call upon her sorcerous arts, she would never be truly unarmed. Still, she had no desire to tempt disaster. A stone dropped on her head from an overhanging window would render her weapons and arts useless and leave her defenseless to the depredations of the resentful gangs of bandits found in the worst parts of every city in the world. Indeed, a stealthy local could come up behind her with a lead-weighted sap and—

"I'm sorry, Magister Tancreville! I didn't mean to startle you! It is me, Mid Yeardly!"

"So it is," Enid snapped, re-clipping her pistol to her belt. "Very nearly the *late* Mid Yeardly! Dangerously gamesome to approach me stealthily from behind. It was very nearly sad jape for both of us!?"

"No game, Magister!" Yeardly's pockmarked face was drawn up in an expression of extreme concern. "I called your name several times as I approached and only took you by the elbow at the last moment. It seemed to me you might be lost and so distracted as to fall prey to some of the bad elements here about. I only had your interests in mind, m'lady!"

A sour remark formed on Enid's lips but died there. Yeardly was right. She had been utterly distracted and the mid's arrival had probably saved her from being robbed or worse. There was no point taking her frustration at her own foolishness out on a young man whose only crime was benevolence toward her.

"Mid Yeardly, I'll mince no words to spare my dignity—I'm lost. I've been walking for hours trying to find the Best Bower and I fear I may be farther from it than when I started. I'm also parched with thirst. Your assistance would be *most* welcome."

Her admission brought a broad smile to Yeardly's face, and she marveled at his resemblance to the late Mid Cullen when he smiled. The unfortunate scarring on his face had distracted her from its otherwise handsome cast. Certainly, his nose was rather long and his face somewhat narrow, but he was also young, and those deficiencies might vanish in the full blossom of manhood.

"You aren't so far from the Best Bower as all that, Magister, and we can kill your thirst within a hundred yards if you're not too particular about the company it passes in."

"I would sup with a marsh hag if she'd give me a glass of warm vinegar!"

Yeardly's smile broadened further. "We can do much better than that. But let's get off this block, milady. I recognize some bad faces nearby and this is never a place for respectable folks at any gate."

"What brings you here, then, Mid Yeardly?"

His smile vanished, replaced by an embarrassed frown. "I was just on my way from somewhere else. Now, let's make steerage way, shall we?"

The King's Crown Tavern was a low, wedge-shaped establishment that sat on a corner formed where Halyard and Old Rendell streets contrived to cross one another at an acute angle. The place had a checkered reputation. Loose women and men frequented it in the pursuit of their livelihoods, and it was not uncommon for fists to fly or knives to be drawn when rum made slights of any proportion too burdensome to bear without recourse to violence. Still, it was not an evil place, like your true bed-'em and bury 'em hellholes found deep in the Middlesea's Maze. What it lacked in outright peril, though, it made up for in squalor and cheapness. Add to this its proximity to the Reaver's Steps, a happy situation that guaranteed even the lowest, crawling species of drunk could find his way to a hired boat and thence to his berth aboard-ship, and the reasons for the place's popularity with sailors and mids were laid bare.

Enid knew nothing of this, of course. To her the low-ceilinged, dimly lit taproom looked like any of the dozen dives she'd toured in

Arden during her youth. The sport of slumming had been popular there since the age of Achardemagne XIV, when the ownership of gambling houses and brothels was restricted to the low-born. She noticed the great number of prostitutes of all sexes but was untroubled by their presence. She saw no more shame in offering such services than in seeking them. The place seemed to be frequented almost entirely by sailors, a fact that no doubt explained the abundance of "brutes," as she'd learned those who took coin for sex were called by those in the sea service. Fortunately, she wore a uniform coat and hat, so no one would mistake the nature of her presence at Mr. Yeardly's side.

Yeardly ordered them each a glass of stout beer. "It's potent stuff, Magister, and coarser than you're used to, but you'll find it slakes the thirst quicker than you can say *knife*."

She took a drink and found the assertion true. After two more deep drinks she turned to Yeardly and asked earnestly, "Tell me, Mr. Yeardly, what is this fascination you Albions have with how fast the word *knife* trips off the tongue? Why not faster than you can say *fork*? Surely it, and any number of other words, can be said just as quickly as 'knife'?"

Yeardly pulled his long jaw thoughtfully and finally gave a shrug. "I can't say with any authority, Magister. If I were forced to guess, I'd say it's because we like knives. What's handier than a good knife, after all?"

Enid nodded. "I find your argument convincing, Mr. Yeardly. In Ardainne we have a saying that translates to something like *as welcome as a good—*"

"I knew rats could be found underfoot in the Crown, but I never knew them to sit upright at a table and drink beer like a human! How the war has brought us low!"

Enid turned slowly on her bench at the sound of the familiar voice that boomed out behind her. Isembard Harde stood there, flanked on either side by a pair of scowling sailors. She watched as they sat at the table behind her and then turned back to Yeardly, who found her expression to be inhumanly calm.

"*Alarum*'s in port. Lord Aixely is running the despatches from Gisbon." He paused to glance over her shoulder at Harde. "We can leave if you want, Magister. I know you and Master Harde—"

"No, I'm perfectly happy where I am, Mid Yeardly. Thank you for your concern. I was aware *Alarum* was in port. I'm told her arrival constituted a boom in the sale of the peculiar cats used by the Navy for flogging. What other news have you?" Enid smiled, but Yeardly noticed it did not reach her eyes.

"Have you read that *Redemption* was renamed *Revenant*?"

"I have heard. The name seems to suit her."

"And you know that two captains came to a strange end in as many days, and this after Captain Chastin and her first luff, fell off the battens and drowned?"

"I didn't know. Are you aware of the circumstances of their passing?"

"Captain Wandell tripped and fell from the weather deck to the gun deck and snapped his neck like a twig. The cutter bearing Captain Heofeld was struck by a rogue wave and capsized as it pulled for *Revenant*. Every man and woman aboard was lost."

"Ashes!" Enid said softly. "Are such waves common in the Basin? It seems as sheltered as a babe in her nurse's arms!"

Yeardly shook his head. "Not in the least. None has been reported for as long as far back as the Sea Service records reach. Some hands are saying *Revenant* will only suffer the command of the man that delivered her from Naveroña."

"And why not? When his witch-woman of a ghost-talker has raised all of hell to get her lover a command! I've seen her at work, and summoning a wave to drown poor Cap'n Heofeld would be as easy as that!" Harde's finger-snap took two tries, owing to his drunkenness and the greasy state of his thumb.

Enid stood, and the sailors seated with Harde urged him to silence, but he was deep in his cups before setting foot in the Crown and refused to hear reason. When she approached his table, he continued just as loudly, "And shame on you, Yeardly, for sharing naval secrets so freely with a Rat spy! Yes, I see you there, Lady Rat, but you got no captain twisted around your finger to shut me up now, do you? A Theocratic spy you are and a Theocratic spy I name you and there ain't nothing—"

Enid's fist caught Harde in the temple and lifted him out of his chair to deposit him on his seat on a floor sticky with spilled wine and worse. The blow filled the Crown with a sound like a butcher's mallet on a cow's skull. To Harde's credit he was able to pull his rolling eyes from gazing at the back of his skull and return Enid's glare as she stood over him.

"Rise, you bastard, and I will seat you again! You natural son of a gentle-born woman who may as well have coupled with an ape for the honor you've brought her. It was Captain Nath who protected you the last time you uttered your slanderous lies about my character, but as you say, he is not here today, and I am under no form of naval discipline. I gave my word in the hearing of witnesses that I would kill you at the first opportunity and here it is delivered to me on your own sour breath! If you are too low to understand the nature of this challenge or the forms that must be followed, consult with your master for guidance between administering his tongue baths and fondling his ego."

Enid's cold glare froze Harde in place and his voice in his throat. She stepped away from Harde and transferred her inimical gaze to his associates. "If either of you has the wits to do so, recall this: I keep lodgings at the Best Bower. Mid Yeardly and my other seconds can be found there, should Mr. Harde find the nerve to meet me with weapons more tangible than the lies and boast that flow from his gullet like a fountain of filth."

Harde rose shakily to his feet, leaning so heavily on a table that he nearly overset it. His gaze at Enid's back was murderous as she strolled out of the Crown with Yeardly in her wake.

"Bitch." He blustered loudly, rubbing the side of his head. "She's spent so much time with ghosts she thinks she can't die. Well, she likes 'em so much, we'll see how she likes bein' one!"

An uneasy laughter filled the Crown and within moments wagers were being made on who would be a ghost first, Harde or the beautiful Ardain woman with eyes like ice.

Enid and Yeardly found Merryweather in the Best Bower's public room, where she nursed an ale with one eye on the latest edition of the *Naval Chronicle* and the other on the door. She waved them over with a polite smile that faded as she saw the dark set of their faces.

"What is amiss? You both look grim as a funeral!"

"There has been an unpleasant incident," Enid said, slipping into a chair gallantly proffered by Yeardly.

Yeardly took the seat next to her and said, "Unpleasant for Master Harde!"

"Sailor Harde," Enid corrected.

Merryweather regarded Enid through narrowed eyes. "How unpleasant, Enid?"

"Mildly so for me, beyond some bruised knuckles. The churl dared soil my name with his filthy tongue, denigrating my honor and falsely proclaiming me a devotee of the Theocratic cause. After knocking him to the ground for his insolence, I challenged him to a duel. His seconds will call on mine in the morn."

"And I am to be one of her Seconds," Yeardly announced with an enthusiasm that exploded his attempt at gravity.

"A duel? Oh, Enid." Merryweather reached across the table and laid her hand over hers. "Why would you hazard yourself against such a coarse example of Albion's worst?"

Yeardly, who had no doubt that Enid would serve the bastard a round turn in a finger snap, shot Merryweather a curious look. There was something in the lieutenant's voice that was new to his experience with her. It was not fear, because Providence knew she was fearless, but something deeper than natural concern for a shipmate.

"You may not believe it, Enid, but Harde is a dangerous man: large, strong, and faster than you'd credit," Merryweather continued. "You must be cautious with him. I cannot bear the—"

Enid silenced her with a slight tilt of her head in Yeardly's direction. Merryweather withdrew her hand and straightened her shoulders.

"Well, then," Merry said. "If it is to be a duel, I should share what I know of the practice of Duello local to Middlesea. It will differ from what you are accustomed to in Ardainne. Mid Yeardly, if you are to serve the magister as a second, you must get your rest."

Enid produced a few heavy silver coins from her purse and pressed them into Yeardly's hand. "Give these to Madame Rangle with my compliments and inquire after a room here. It would be good to know my seconds are near me."

Yeardly accepted the specie with a speculative nod and departed. A few moments later, Mrs. Rangle's voice rose above the chatter of the public room exclaiming that soon she would have all the *Alarum*'s officers, who would crowd out her other customers, but she could make room for one more, as lean and half-starved as he looked.

"Enid," Merryweather said in a low voice. "I worry for you, and it makes my blood run cold. I would be crushed to lose you to a man-ape like Harde. Absolutely crushed."

"I would be devastated to lose you under any circumstance, Merry," Enid replied just as quietly. "But we both pursue a perilous profession. You must learn to bear your fears with an officerly complaisance."

"Oh, I would mourn you fiercely if you were carried away by ball, shot, or sword in battle, but the prospect is bearable in the same way as losing my friends and subordinates in action is bearable: I assume you are all immortal until our martial calling proves otherwise."

Enid frowned. "Then why are you fearful of this *petite affaire* with Harde? He is less of a danger to me than a broadside or even fierce storm at sea!"

"Death in action serves a purpose. The fallen have done so while weakening the Theocracy that threatens to crush us under the weight of its ignorance and hatred. Such a death serves the common good. But to die fighting a rascal like Harde? That serves no one but yourself and robs me of my dearest friend."

Enid was surprised to see Merryweather's eyes glisten with tears as she spoke.

"Come," she said. "Let us go to my room, where we can speak more on this in privacy—but I promise you, Merry, Harde is as good as dead."

It was nearing midnight when Nath breezed into their sitting room, dressed to the nines and smelling strongly of wine, cigarillos, and Emley Holyoke's perfume. He smiled at Enid and scooped up Maubin, whom he couched on her back in the crook of his arm and rubbed her round, hairless belly with playful affection.

The grin he flashed Enid was a bit wine-soaked but far from drunken.

"You missed a wonderful evening, Enid," he enthused. "Captain Althing, a friend of mine from the mid's berth, dropped by unannounced and invited me to wet the swab of his cousin, Emilia Althing, on the occasion of her promotion. It was a jolly affair! I may never tire of being treated like a hero out of legend, Enid! I know it is a shortcoming in my character, but it is great fun. I left when the drinking turned serious, for I have no desire to be caught drunk and muzzy-minded should opportunity knock—"

"I have been contemplating the Code Duello as it is practiced in Albion," Enid interrupted. "I believe you have some expertise in the subject. I recall you mentioned stepping out in the past, so I would fain benefit from your counsel on differences between its practice here and on the continent. I pray you will not find it presumptuous of me to request your service as one of my Seconds?"

"Seconds?" Nath was taken aback. "Seconds for what?"

"An affair of honor, of course. A duel. What else would it be?"

"A duel? Do you not recall that Lord Reinard advised us against involving ourselves in any controversy?"

Enid shrugged. "There should be nothing controversial about dueling with a man who slanders your honor in public. I would think it would only be controversial if I let his falsities stand."

"With whom will you step out, then?"

"Isembarde Harde, formerly Master of HMS *Alarum*."

"I know who he is better than you," Nath groaned and eased himself into a chair across from her. "The challenge has been issued?"

"I struck him in the head with my fist and told him to send his seconds to our rooms in the morn. Will that suffice?"

"You truly are an irascible creature at times, Enid."

She shrugged. "Be that as it may, do the basic forms here differ much from those practiced on the continent? Other than your barbarous use of pistols?"

"These are gifts from the Lord Mayor of Somewhere-or-Another-on-Rys. They're quite good." Nath chewed his lip thoughtfully as he produced a pair of cigarillos for each of them. "Well. You've already mentioned pistols. I think that is the only real difference. You'll need at least one person of gentle blood to act as your Second. Two is better. As the challenger, you'll be expected to supply the surgeon. As the challenged, Harde will have the choice of weapons. I would imagine he'll choose pistols. He'll know he's no match for you with a hanger or small sword."

"Mid Yeardly, who witnessed the affront, has already agreed to stand with me. As I said, I would be honored and gratified if you would join him at my side. Your deeper knowledge of the forms would be most helpful."

Nath frowned around his cigarillo. "The honor would be mine, Enid. I have gone out more than I find pleasing to recall. You might find it surprising, but as a younger man my temper was extremely volatile. I assume Merryweather will be joining us as well?"

"No. I thought it best to expose her career as little as possible to any fallout from my personal controversies." Enid thanked the stars that Nath's acute perception was dulled by a haze of wine fumes, else he would have surely noticed her words' hollow ring.

"Very thoughtful of you! I wonder who Harde will find to Second him, the bum-nuzzling swine?"

Captain Hefflin called on them the following morning. She was dressed in a severely austere uniform and wore an expression of grave contempt. She was accompanied by a handsome young lieutenant who looked vaguely familiar to Nath. Mrs. Rangle ushered the pair into the sitting room and made a hurried exit. Gossip held that one of her boarders was involved in a duel and she wanted no part of it. When aristocrats took to dueling, they could be free and arbitrary with their enmity. She didn't want any of it splashed on her or her establishment for no better reason than proximity.

As the door closed, Hefflin bowed stiffly to Nath and said, "Captain Nath, Mid Yeardly, allow me to present Lieutenant Leonid Bascombe."

Nath stiffened at the last name. *So that's why the strange lieutenant looked so familiar! He is the spitting image of his sister, cast in a masculine mold.*

"Lieutenant Bascombe, it is an honor to meet you. Your sister Cierina is one of the finest officers I've served with. I hope the Ardain parole her soon."

Bascombe's only response was a deepening of the frown lines at the corners of his mouth.

"We have not come to socialize, Captain Nath," Hefflin observed in a ridiculously piping voice. "We have come on a matter of honor. Since a blow cannot be withdrawn, I assume you are prepared to discuss terms for the affair?"

"Your principal barely qualifies to meet the Marquise d'Tancreville, natural son that he is." Yeardly shocked Nath with the cool disdain with which he spoke. "As such, he can apologize without loss of honor. It is well recognized within the Code Duello that a blow delivered to a gentle's common bastard is not irrevocable, as opposed to one delivered to another gentle. In fact, by custom, your principal's failure to apologize immediately borders on pretension!"

"Unless you come bearing an apology?" Nath interjected diplomatically.

"Preposterous!" Hefflin squeaked. "Apologize to a—a *foreigner*? I think you'll find we're not all as easy with our standards as you are, Captain Nath!"

"We are not here to examine our respective standards, Captain Heflin. We are here to avoid unnecessary bloodshed and death if it is within our means to do so. Now, your principal is the child of a commonborn man and an aristocratic woman. He may, and *should*, withdraw from the duel honorably despite the blow he received. I implore you to dissuade him from false vanity that will surely result in harm to his person and repute."

"Damn tradition! He will have none of it! Master Harde is no coward!" This from Bascombe, in a dangerous-sounding snarl.

"So be it," Nath said with a shrug. "What weapon does your principal choose to face ours with?"

"Pistol, I'll wager," Yeardly scoffed.

"Wager and lose, then," Bascombe fairly spat. "The duel will be fought with naval cutlasses."

"Cutlasses? I've never heard of such a thing," Yeardly said, clearly astonished at the idea.

"What you've heard of don't signify, which leaves precious little that does," Hefflin smirked. "A cutlass is a sword, and the challenged party may select whatever type of *sword* with which he wishes to defend his honor. I'm sure you can find someone to loan the—lady—a serviceable pair."

"Doubtless," Nath said. "But the cutlass is the implement of a common sailor. It is not the gentle weapon tradition requires—"

"Damn tradition, I say again!" Bascombe barked. "It is not tradition for a gentle woman to brawl and bandy about challenges in a taproom either, yet here we are!"

"By God, you will remember you are addressing a superior in their own home," Nath thundered and everyone in the room, Hefflin included, took half a step back. "You may come at the traditions of the Duello with a bitter tongue, but you forget the regulations of the Sea Service at your own peril!"

He turned a ferocious gaze on all assembled and said in a marginally more moderate tone, "This is a serious business and I expect all gathered here to treat it with the gravity it deserves. Remember that you are gentles *and* officers of His Majesty's Navy and will behave accordingly! Now, let us get back to business. Captain Hefflin, what has yet to be resolved?"

Hefflin, having recovered some bluster, if not aplomb, snapped, "Where shall our parties meet and who will act as surgeon?"

"Herry's Keep should serve our needs. It is tucked away private-like, and the paved area before the gate should make an adequate dueling salle. We shall meet the day after tomorrow if that suits your principal. Dr. Rondelle will attend upon the duelists, along with whatever assistants he deems necessary."

Harde's Seconds stared at Nath in horror for a long moment. Finally, Bascombe exclaimed, "That place is haunted! Everyone knows of Old Herry!"

"Everyone knows of the bogeyman, too, but it don't stop 'em putting their shoes under the bed at night," Yeardly drawled.

"Enough," Nath said. "No more of that nonsense! Now, as to Old Herry, he may or not haunt the place, but he troubled none of the half-dozen affairs of honor I have undertaken there."

"It will suffice," Hefflin snapped waspishly, and turned for the door. "But there will be no trickery, neither! If I sniff the faintest hint of sorcery, and I have a keen nose for such things, I will—"

"Watch your step there!" Nath interrupted sharply.

"No, you watch *yours*! All this vulgar public acclaim has made you half-again too large for your britches, you—"

"No," Nath sighed, pointing at Hefflin's foot. "I meant watch your *step*! Maubin, that stealthy devil, has soiled the carpet and now you've put your foot in it."

Hefflin looked down in horror at her befouled shoe, cast a final murderous gaze at Nath, and stormed out. Bascombe stepped gingerly over the spot on the carpet and closed the door behind him with some force.

Three heartbeats later, Nath and Yeardly dissolved in laughter.

"She has a keen nose for such things," Nath gasped and, despite the disparity between their ranks and the grim business at hand, they sat together on the couch and laughed till they wept.

When Enid had only been walking a year or two, she sat a horse beside her father and watched a stream of disconsolate prisoners of war trudge by on their way home to Naveroña, their banners lost in defeat, their once gallant uniforms stained with mud, and their weapons stacked in great piles on the field of their defeat.

"Father, there are more prisoners here than soldiers in your entire army!"

Her father nodded grimly. "And as many more of them lay dead on the field, picked over by the crows and peasant women."

"How did you defeat them? Are our soldiers so much fiercer than theirs?"

He shook his head. "No, the Naveroñian are as skilled at war as any nation on earth. They are an equal to our warriors and may, in some ways, exceed them."

"Then how did you best them, Father?"

"I allowed them to beat themselves—and here is the lesson I brought you here to learn: Never face a foe on ground he knows better than you! To do so is to lose whatever advantage you might have held and to magnify his strengths tenfold!"

With that in mind, Enid hired a horse for the day and got directions to Herry's Keep from the ostler. She rode up to the keep alone. This seemed a task best accomplished by herself, and she'd frankly grown tired of Nath and Yeardly's endless assurances that she'd "settle that dog Harde on his heels." The entire ordeal made it clear to her why contestants in judicial combat were required to spend the time before battle in solitary meditation.

The keep stood on a vaguely loaf-shaped prominence that overlooked the entrance to the Middlesea Roads. She supposed it had witnessed many a brave flotilla of Reaver ships setting forth after receiving the blessing of the High King. The tower itself was built in an antique style and was wider than it was tall. Trees, many over-topping the tower, pressed in on three sides, leaving only the fourth an unobstructed view of the Roads and the Ocean Sea beyond. The track she rode up the hill's side was wide enough for a cart or coach to use and was not too overgrown or cluttered with detritus to prevent the passage of such vehicles. When Enid reached the top of the prominence, she found the ground at the foot of the keep choked with brush and tall grass. The trail led through this miniature jungle to a paved landing in front of the tower's gate, which gaped open like the toothless maw of some blockheaded beast.

Enid dismounted and hobbled her horse with its reins. She surveyed the paved landing with satisfaction. It was roughly rectangular and more than commodious enough for the purpose at hand. The stone slabs of which it was constructed were worn smooth by ages of wind and rain and, when she knelt to run her hand across their surfaces, were finely pitted. Footing would be sure, she thought, even if there should be a morning mist or, Providence forbid, rain. She stood and stretched with her hands pressed to the small of her back. The weather was fine and the view magnificent, so she took her lunch from a large purse hung over the horn of her saddle and sat down to eat.

A fine breeze blew out to sea, and she watched as several ships took advantage of it to make their offing. It struck her how sedate their evolutions looked from a distance, with the hurly-burly of setting sails rendered smooth and balletic by the lack of squealing bosun's pipes and the bone-rattling shouts of officers. She supposed most things looked easier from a distance. The devil, after all, was well known to reside in the details.

She finished her lunch, packed her things, and turned to remount her horse for the long ride down to Middlesea, but stopped in her tracks. There in the black maw of the ancient tower stood a young girl clad in a white mantle. A spray of flowers and, incongruously, what appeared to be the skeletal remains of birds and mice crowned her head and her long, golden hair hung in a gleaming unbound cascade to her knees. The girl's eyes were so dark that they gave the disconcerting impression of standing on the edge of a two-fold abyss.

"Lady Enid," the girl said with a smile and curtsied. Her voice was at once melodic and as dry as old bones and dry leaves.

"Who are you?" Enid asked, her hand edging cautiously toward the hilt of her small sword.

"I've been called many things. Most recently they call me Old Herry, which seems unnecessarily hurtful. Many names have I, but only one truly names me. It is much the same with you, isn't it, Lady Enid?" The girl skipped down the few, low steps at the mouth of the gate and paused to pick a flower, which she offered to Enid.

"No thank you, Lady Herry," Enid said, taking a step back. "We do not know each other well enough to exchange gifts and, besides, I have nothing so grand to give you in return."

The girl laughed and the faint call of crows answered in the distance. There was a tingling buzz in her chest, as if her heart were home to a hive of wasps. "You will, though, Lady Enid! Crowns will fall from your fingers and your touch will be silver more valuable than gold. You will perform wonders before emerald skies press you down to your death. Shall I tell it to you?"

Enid shuddered, her mind suddenly filled with a waking dream in which she sank deeper and deeper into the cool green waters of some nameless sea.

"No," she stuttered. "I'd rather you didn't, really."

"Surprises are better." The little girl nodded gravely and was suddenly at her side, her small hand in hers—her flesh unnaturally smooth and cold to the touch.

"You think you know who you are, Enid, but you are a secret unto yourself. Do not frown so, pretty Enid. Old lessons are new to the ignorant! Shall I teach you?"

"I am not worthy to learn," Enid said, the bones in her right hand growing more chill with each passing moment that the girl's hand nestled in it.

The girl laughed again, and a bird fell from the sky, stiff and dead, and struck the ground nearby.

"You are courteous! I believe you have stolen my heart. There is a power in you that is older than the world. Shall I speak to you of that?"

"Surprises are better," Enid answered between chattering teeth. Her breath left a shredded shawl of frost on the warm summer breeze.

"Surely you are as wise as you are beautiful, dearest, but still foolish beyond belief! I will watch over you whether you wish it or not, and, when you need it most, I will lend you a hand."

The little girl reached up and placed a searing hot finger over Enid's lips before she could speak. "Do not answer me now, precious child. Hold your clever tongue until I speak to you next. Run along now, little Enid. Pretty Enid. My heart rides with you."

The child released her hand and skipped back into the tower, singing merrily in a voice of dead birds and mice. Enid did not spare her mount the spurs until they gained Middlesea's gate, and the poor beast was almost dead. The ostler that had let it to her was beside himself, but a handful of coins Enid snatched blindly from her purse and thrust into his hands silenced his complaints.

Back at the Best Bower, Enid locked herself in her room and flung herself on the bed. She fell asleep in an instant and dreamed she sat on a plain of skulls discussing the state of the human soul with one of Nath's dogs. She could not be sure if it was Maubin or Marbury and that, strangely, bothered her the most when she awoke the next day.

Mrs. Rangle prepared a hearty breakfast for them the morning of the duel and had the goodwill to serve it in silence and then withdraw. Enid ate eggs, bacon, a thick slice of pork steak, and almost half a loaf of fresh bread slathered in butter and honey, all under the disapproving eye of Dr. Rondelle.

"If you are wounded in the belly, it were better that it was not stuffed to bursting like a peddler's pack," he sniffed.

"It were better that I not wounded in the belly at all," Enid replied complaisantly. "But such things are beyond my control. If I fight on a full stomach, I might suffer for it. If I fight on an empty stomach, I am equally at risk if the fight is a long one and I have insufficient energy to strike the winning blow when the opportunity arises. If I must suffer, I prefer to suffer from my wounds rather than hunger."

"A very glib argument that will taste sour on your lips if your bowel is pierced. Still, it is your body to hazard as you will."

Merryweather, who joined them for breakfast, said, "I do not recall you speaking out against the practice of feeding the ship's people before battle, Dr. Rondelle."

"Of course not. They require a hardy meal to provide the reserves of strength necessary to withstand the rigors of the gun deck."

"Enid has a rigorous morning ahead of her, Doctor. Leave her to enjoy her meal in peace." Merryweather's expression was resolutely insouciant, but Enid knew her well enough now to detect the apprehension in her voice.

Nath nodded his head in agreement on the subject of bellicose nutrition but insisted that Enid wear a loose blouse of white silk and stockings of the same material.

“The silk is easier to draw out, you see, and the voluminous blouse makes it more difficult for your opponent to determine where your vitals are.”

Enid glanced down at herself and frowned. “That may be true of a male duelist, but I believe the silk will probably leave little doubt where *my* vitals lie.”

“Perhaps. I hadn’t considered the difference in, well, in our builds. Ah, well. It’s still worth wearing because it’s easier to draw the silk from a wound. Less chance for infection.”

Enid hefted one of the cutlasses lying on the table speculatively. “I believe, should I receive a serious wound from this great cleaver, infection will be the least of my concerns.”

Dr. Rondelle nodded. “That is one of the advantages of your clean amputation.”

They rode up to Herry’s Keep in a coach on loan from the Duchess of Esdivere. Enid was relieved the Duchess respected the privacy of the affair and did not ask to come along. Such discretion made the loan of the coach that much grander a gesture. She sat by the window with Nath on the same bench by the opposite window. To her annoyance, the space between them was taken up by a basket containing the restless forms of Maubin and Marbury. Yeardly and Dr. Rondelle sat on the opposite bench. They traveled in grave silence for a while until Enid broke it.

“I suppose it would be an unsupportable breach of form to move the duel to another site at this late a date?”

Under different circumstances the simultaneous drop of every human jaw in the coach might have struck her as humorous. Nath was the first to find his voice.

“I’m afraid so, Enid. If nothing else, it might give the impression of shyness on your part—a desire to postpone the moment of decision through pretense. Did you not examine the site yesterday?”

"I did." Enid turned her face to the window. She found herself deeply reluctant to discuss her experience at Herry's Keep.

"If you didn't find the ground acceptable, why didn't you—"

"There is nothing wrong with the ground," Enid interrupted.

"Are you concerned that Harde might be up to some mischief? Hidden sharpshooters or the like? Set your heart to ease! The dueling master will put any such pranks to rest before we arrive. He is a devilish thorough man. I wouldn't be surprised to learn he spent the night there last night!"

Enid stiffened at the thought and hoped for the dueling master's sake that he'd done nothing of the sort. If the girl was what she suspected her to be, Enid could think of few more perilous companions with whom to spend an evening. She saw nothing to gain in further conversation and let the matter drop. They rode on in a silence that each attributed to unease—but only Enid could accurately ascribe its source. It pained her to think her comrades might think she was concerned about her conduct in the duel, but she could think of no remedy for it and so sat in outwardly glum consideration of the scenery outside the gently rocking coach's window.

When the keep came into view, Enid's right hand grew chill just as it had when the girl held it. A dark foreboding threatened to overwhelm her, but she staved it off with thoughts about the mechanics of the duel. The cutlass wasn't much different from the dueling sabers so beloved by her oldest brother. Hero worship induced her to practice with him as often as time and his patience would permit. She thought she remembered enough to make a credible showing and perhaps even best Harde at his own game. After all, the man's only training had been a few hours a week drilling with some Master-at-arms who, according to Nath, probably resented the necessity and made a half-hearted effort at best. Nath also pointed out that the prize record of *Alarum* under Aixely and Harde hardly left one with the impression that either were particularly warlike.

When the coach finally ground to a halt on the opposite side of the paved area before the keep, the sun was well above the horizon and the morning mist was all but burned away. Another coach stood at the other side of the impromptu arena, an escutcheon on its side bearing an ornately rendered letter *A* which Enid assumed stood for *Aixely.* She saw Harde standing near it, sharing a jest with Heflin and Bascombe. Enid leaned against the Duchess's coach as Nath and Yeardly crossed the ancient stone flags to remonstrate with Harde and his Seconds a final time, imploring him to apologize for his ill-considered words and thus avoid the unnecessary death or injury of either or both participants.

Harde refused, of course, so Nath presented him with a choice of four cutlasses. The half-blood tried a practice swing with each of them and then selected one with a heavy blade and a plain, wire-wrapped hilt. The seconds then crossed over to Enid and, under Heflin's contemptuous gaze, she selected a cutlass that seemed the most saber-like in its balance. Bascombe, now that the matter was at hand, seemed more withdrawn, as if the gravity of the situation demanded a level of detached decorum that Enid believed was beyond the abilities of someone as petty as Heflin to achieve.

The dueling master, whose large gray mare was tethered to a stump well away from the dueling ground, beckoned Harde and Enid to approach. He was an extremely tall gentleman whose advancing age was evidenced by his slight stoop and the abundance of silver gleaming in his jet hair. He fixed both combatants with a disapproving uncle's stare and asked in an astonishingly deep voice if they would consider abandoning this course and let soft words and open hearts take the place of cold steel and blood on the ground. Enid and Harde each stood mute.

"I see that the challenged party has set upon the affair continuing until one party is unable to fight," the dueling master continued matter-of-factly. "Allow me to implore you to reconsider and pursue the engagement no further than first blood. What say you, Master Harde?"

"I say I ain't here for no pinkin'," Harde answered in a surly growl, glaring at Enid. "This Rat spy laid hands on my person and my dignity will not allow that to stand!"

The dueling master shrugged. "Very well. The duel will continue until the surgeons at hand agree that one or both parties are unfit to continue. Note that I will not countenance any unmannerly conduct. If either of you attempts to strike your opponent after they are rendered defenseless, I will shoot you between the eyes. You may trust that I have not gained my current position in society without some skill with a pistol. Now, take your positions. Lady d'Tancreville, this spot will suit you, I believe? Master Harde, you shall be here."

He placed them a step outside of each other's reach with practiced ease and a recognizable degree of bored disinterest.

"Can you both see me here? Very good." He raised his arm above his head. "When I let my arm fall, engage. And may the Redeemer protect you both."

The dueling master's arm fell and Harde was on her like a stamping, cursing whirlwind. He drove forward relentlessly, his attacks coming with metronomic regularity and amazing force, scything in from first this angle and then that, and drove Enid backward across the stone flags. This was more like fighting a bloodthirsty automaton than dueling an opponent of flesh and blood, and for a moment Enid's heart nearly seized with the cold certainty that she was about to die. Then she saw the smug and bloody-minded expression on Harde's face and redoubled her efforts. She might well die, she thought, but she'd certainly leave marks on this cur's body by which to remember her.

She slowed her retreat and timed Harde's cycle of stamp, slash, and thrust. She knew this was what he intended her to do, then tire her until she was too slow and weak to react quickly enough when he finally broke the martial rhythm to deliver a killing blow. There were few options available to her, though, as she'd be just as dead if one of his blows landed according to count or out of the blue. Her only hope was to break his timing and take the initiative herself. In the meantime, she must rely on what she remembered of her brother's lessons with the saber and her advantage over Harde in the articles of speed and grace.

The fight ground on and on. The clang of their blades clashing echoed off the keep's thick walls, occasionally eliciting a fit of barking from Maubin and Marbury. Some peripheral part of her awareness noted the dogs' bright eyes and wagging tails. She wondered if they were simply excited by the noise and action or if they understood the nature of what they saw and were eager for its bloody outcome. In that instant she developed a deep sympathy for all the little terriers she'd wagered on in various contests against rats and badgers over the years.

And in that instant, she nearly died.

She barely recognized the gleaming arc of Harde's cutlass blade as it whistled toward her eyes. Their prolonged dance had exhausted her, both physically and mentally, to such a degree that when the long-expected "surprise" blow came, it truly caught her off guard. She flung herself backward and struggled valiantly to bring her own blade up in a desperate parry, but it was too heavy and slow to answer. Her heel caught between two flags and as she stumbled backward, she instinctively threw up her empty right hand to protect her face.

The pain was so intense and generalized that Enid believed herself slain for a moment. It seemed impossible that such excruciation could be survived. Her vision narrowed until the dueling ground was reduced to a glimmering disk of dim light wavering at the far end of a long black tunnel. She nearly sank into that dark hole but was drawn back from its brink by a voice—Harde's voice.

"Not so goddamned high and mighty now, are you, you Rat bitch?"

The disk of her vision expanded and filled with Harde's vicious, gloating face. His grin broadened as he stepped toward her, revealing a missing tooth and compressing his eyes into glittering black slits of malevolence. She saw his right arm rise and was dimly aware the motion was laden with peril and, were her mind not crushed beneath an avalanche of pain, would have elicited an urgent defensive reaction.

Where self-preservation failed to goad her into action, his evil, self-satisfied sneer lit a cold fire of spite deep in her belly, a fire that seized her so suddenly and with such ferocity that she was not aware of it until her legs had uncoiled, releasing their energy in an explosion of violent action that hurled her forward, her left arm describing an arc through the air whose power was multiplied by her sudden velocity. She was vaguely aware of a shock to her wrist and then the ancient flags of Herry's Keep rose up to present her with an aching darkness full of brilliant, pain-filled stars.

Enid awoke to see Rondelle's face framed against a pale, cloud-streaked sky. The scent of the sea was in the air, and, for a moment, she thought she was back aboard *Alarum* or *Redemption* and wondered what sort of nautical mishap accounted for her loss of consciousness and the agonizing pain in her right wrist. Perhaps she had finally plummeted down a companionway as she'd been endlessly warned she must if she failed to "clap on like a good'un."

No, there was far too much blood on the sour-faced surgeon's shirt-front for a simple fall to answer. There must have been a battle. As the focus of her eyes slowly expanded to encompass some wind-twisted scrub-oaks and a high-up view of the sea between her feet (she was strangely relieved to see they were both demurely clad in *shoes*), she had a vague recollection of a struggle. There were sabers, she thought, though great clumsy ones, and she'd been fighting someone named—

"Harde!" She tried to thrust herself into a more upright position, but Rondelle refused to release her right arm and Nath's hands pressed down on her shoulders from behind.

She followed the direction of the surgeon's gaze and saw several people, drawn from both her party and Harde's, searching about through the surrounding underbrush with sticks, canes, or the tips of their swords. Most wore expressions that betrayed a clear reluctance for the task.

Enid's eyes narrowed as a dark presentiment tickled the back of her mind. "What are they looking for, Dr. Rondelle?"

"Your right hand, of course. You didn't happen to notice where it landed when Harde lopped it off, did you? It will be a sight easier to reattach if we have it in hand, so to speak."

"My right hand?" Enid struggled to raise her right hand into view, clearly feeling her fingers wriggling just as she willed them to, but Rondelle kept her arm pinned between his own and his side. He cursed as she fought his grip.

"Damn it all, Magister! If you do not hold still, you will finish the work Harde started! Do you wish to bleed out your last drop here in the shadow of a haunted keep? No? Then be still and quit your wriggling and writhing!"

"Calm yourself, Enid. They'll find it."

She glanced up at Nath and found his expression gravely solicitous and more than a little sad. Her stomach knotted as shame and realization hit her.

"I am unable to continue," she hissed up at him. "Harde has won. I must present my apologies at once . . ."

"Let's hope you won't be in any position to present them to him for another several score years," Rondelle snorted. "He's certainly in no condition to receive your courtesies at the moment."

"He's finished, Enid," Nath said comfortingly. "He's lost the number of his mess."

"And made quite a mess in the process," Rondelle groused. "Any luck over there?"

Nath leaned and whispered near her ear, "His great block of a head proved far easier to find than your elegant little hand—now it and his corpse are on the way down the hill on the back of the dueling master's horse. Here! Rondelle! Her eyes are rolling in a most unnatural way!"

A chill, fluttering wind that recalled the flapping of a great number of wings brought her around to find herself in the same position under a rapidly darkening sky. A rolled cloak had been thrust under head and another draped over her body. Her right arm, she found, was bound tightly to her side and across her middle. She looked up at Rondelle and asked, "Were there crows just now?"

"Crows?" His eyes rolled in tired contempt. "Oh, the injured and the pretensions of tragedy! No crows, buzzards, or vultures have come near you, brimming with life as you are. I'm alarmed that you think so little of my skills as to believe that something as trivial as the amputation of a hand might bring on an audience of crows! I am a naval surgeon, Lady d'Tancreville, and to your naval surgeon this sort of nonsense is of little more concern and of no more hazard than a stubbed toe!"

"No, that is not—never mind. Have they found my hand?"

"I'm afraid not. It must have gone over the cliff. It is far too late to reattach it now in any case. The sympathy between living and necrotic tissue is far too compromised at this point for any hope of—"

"You must find it! You must find my hand!"

"My lady." Yeardly had taken Nath's place and his hands patted forlornly on her shoulders. "Dr. Rondelle has said is no hope of re-attaching it now and even if there were, finding it on the cliff face is impracticable. It is too steep and covered in scree for anyone to safely search. You wouldn't want Captain Nath sliding to his death on the rocks below, would you?"

"I don't give too damns for my hand! It's the ring on it! I must have the ring from it!"

"That plain silver ring?" Yeardly's firm but gentle hands on her shoulders prevented her from sitting up. "We'll buy you another, Magister, a better one—"

"It is not just any silver ring, damn you!"

The thought of poor, diminished Dunaughy trapped in a silver prison wrapped around the rotting ruin of her lost hand desolated her. All his sacrifices for his beloved Sea Service deserved better repayment! She struggled to extend her will and discover some lingering sympathetic bond between herself and the severed limb, but her efforts produced nothing but a fit of dizziness that almost claimed her consciousness again. Her eyes filled with tears of frustrated loss and Dunaughy's name escaped her lips in a quiet sob.

"Did she say Dunaughy?" Yeardly asked Rondelle.

"Who can say?" the doctor answered sharply. "She's injured and a little feverish despite the physic of my magic. She might call out the king's name next. The ground is too cold. Clap on and help me shift her into the Duchess's coach."

Enid allowed herself to be lifted gently and carried by her shoulders and heels to the coach. Merryweather and Yeardly were forced to prop her in place with spare seat cushions supplied by the coachman. She was too forlorn to bear even the small effort of sitting upright. To Enid, the word *loss* seemed to summarize her entire being. In one short year she'd lost her family, her home, the society she'd claimed as her own, her hand, and, finally, the quiet, lilting voice in the back of her mind that she now realized was often the only buffer between herself and utter despair.

Like her uncle, Dunaughy had lent her his wisdom and knowledge, and as with her uncle she had failed him: one mentor left behind to burn in the filth-choked alleys of Arden's worst quarter and another left to dwindle into oblivion in a ring on her putrefying, worm-eaten hand. If this was to be the lot of all her friends, she would have no more of them. Merryweather must be warned off, she thought, and Nath and Yeardly as well.

"Where is Captain Nath?" she asked weakly.

"Listen. Hear that whistling?" Rondelle asked. "He's trying to call his dogs back in. Apparently, they got out of the basket while he was searching for your hand. They're no doubt halfway to the Westlands, following their irksome little natures to chase, nip, and bark at anything that comes under their pointed little noses. I'm sure they'll take every opportunity along their way to gnaw the toes out of whatever shoes are lying about and befoul any carpets that might be handy. He's well rid of them. The worst book is better than the best beast any day of the week. He should read more."

Enid smiled weakly. "Not a friend to dogs are you, Dr. Rondelle."

"My father said that houses were built to keep animals out, not in. I cannot find fault in his logic."

At just that moment the door to the coach opened and Nath climbed in, the panting form of Maubin clasped firmly under his arm. His downcast features lit up when he saw Enid was conscious and handed the struggling pup out the window to the coachman with instructions to "secure this lubberly rascal" before he knelt by Enid's side and took up her hand.

"I give you joy of your victory, Enid, however painfully bought. It was a race to see who would kill Harde first, the dueling master, Yeardly, or me—but you beat us all to the prize."

"A race? What do you mean?"

"It is a second's privilege to intervene if the forms are not followed. A wound as grave as yours obviously called for the attending surgeons to determine if you were fit to proceed, but that cowardly dog was about to strike you down before anyone could intervene."

Rondelle showed his disapproval with a sniff. "I have long said that your common folk have half the virtue demanded by the Code. Without meaning offense to Lady d'Tancreville, I believe one is demeaned by such uneven contests of honor."

"If the contest had been any more even, I don't believe there'd be any question of offending me. I'd be dead." Enid's voice was bitter. "But his behavior proved my point—regardless of his birth he was a man without honor and thus his accusations can carry no weight among those who value that commodity."

Yeardly, his eyes rimmed in red, said, "The dog deserved a longer death for his crimes against you. May he be damned and rot in hell!"

Enid gave the mid a weak smile, but any further discussion was forestalled by the coachman, who leaned over the side and asked Captain Nath if he was ready to return to Middlesea.

"I suppose," Nath sighed glumly. "It appears Marbury has returned to the state of nature, and we must abandon the poor lad to his fate."

Enid thought of poor Dunaughy, trapped for all eternity in a silver ring, year following formless year until all trace of his identity was lost, and removed her hand from beneath Nath's and transferred it to his shoulder in order steady herself as she attempted to sit up. She heard Rondelle muttering darkly under his breath at the prospect, but, abandoning dignity, pled with Nath, "If you love me, if any of you love me, pray linger here a bit longer and attempt a final search."

Nath glanced doubtfully from Rondelle, who was clearly unmoved by Enid's plea, and back to her. "Enid, I fear—"

The rest of Nath's words were lost in the dull roar of the fluttering of a vast murder of crows that swept through the coach window to circle its interior in a chaos of beating wings and clutching talons. Their night-dark feathers seemed to be carved volcanic glass, their sharp edges had an oily gleam and their curved beaks were polished brass. Their myriad eyes glowed with the sick, yellow-green light of burning swamp gases. She turned to look at Nath to confirm that he saw the circling cloud of corvids, but found Old Herry seated in his place, her cold, dry hands clasped around Enid's.

"Should I lend you a hand now, dear Enid? Or are you still too cruel to accept my mercies?"

"Yes!" Enid answered immediately. The loss of her hand troubled her not at all. She was not one of those sorcerers that required a flourish of finger and hand gestures to make her will be felt, but she refused to allow poor, loyal Dunaughy to be imprisoned for all eternity in a cold, silver oubliette affixed to her decomposing hand! "By the Redeemer, yes."

"The Redeemer? He has little to do with this, though I did share many lovely evenings with him during the siege of Ulthessar. It has been an age since I saw him last. Some say he is dead, while others hold that—" She glanced at Enid and smiled gently at her forlorn expression. "Do not be so morose, my lovely, my dearest of girls, my good left hand! It is my pleasure to grant you this small boon, and I expect very little from you in return save for your felicity."

"—we cannot tarry any longer. Dr. Rondelle assures me that every moment you spend out of a clean, comfortable bed steals a year of your life."

"No!" Enid interrupted. "Surely we can stay here for a bit longer. I'm under a naval surgeon's care, after all, who asserts wounds such as mine amount to little more than a stubbed toe. Yeardly will help you find him, won't you, Yeardly?"

"Of course!" Yeardly gave a gallant if somewhat confused smile and opened the coach door while Nath and Rondelle presented Enid with arguments against risking her health to find a lost dog—and not a very bright one, Nath sadly admitted. No sooner was the door opened a crack than the animal in question sprang through it to land on the floor between Enid's and Yeardly's feet, where, with the supernatural leaping ability of its kind, it bounded into Nath's lap, eyes aglow and tail wagging furiously.

Clamped in the little dog's maw was the gray and tattered wreck of Enid's right hand, the silver ring on its middle finger gleaming faintly orange in the light of the setting sun. Enid was struck by the intelligent sparkle in the little creature's glittering black eyes even as her consciousness abandoned her for the third time in a day. As the rational part of her sank into darkness, a voice of dry leaves and bones whispered in her ear, *It is as I promised, dearling: when you most needed it, I lent you a hand.*

Nath was surprised at Merryweather's reaction when Enid's unconscious form was borne into the Best Bower by Dr. Rondelle and his loblolly boy. He expected her to be concerned, of course, but not as stricken as she proved to be. She rushed across the public room like a madwoman and let out a grief-hollowed gasp as she grasped Enid's left hand.

"Her flesh is cold! Does she live? I warned her against this madness!"

"She is fine," Rondelle snapped and attempted fruitlessly to push the younger, more active lieutenant away from his patient. "And she will continue to be so if you do not undo my hard work by jostling her about so!"

Merryweather noticed the large dark stain on the right side of the thin blanket covering Enid. "So much blood! How badly is she hurt?"

"Lieutenant Merryweather," Nath barked. "Compose yourself and behave properly for an officer of your rank! This display only delays the doctor from settling her into a comfortable bed!"

The lieutenant stiffened under her captain's rebuke and stepped aside. She followed the train as they mounted the stairs to Nath's rooms. There, she helped settle Enid into her bed and, while the men waited in the sitting room, dressed her in a sleeping gown. She paled at the sight of Enid's right arm, which ended in a blunt, bandage-wrapped stump. When she stepped back into the sitting room, she found that only Nath, Rondelle, and Yeardly remained. She stepped aside as Rondelle and Nath entered Enid's room and closed the door behind them.

"Lieutenant Merryweather, may I speak plainly?"

Merryweather nodded.

"I suspected that a romantic relationship had taken root between you and the magister, and your behavior today has confirmed it."

"What of it," Merryweather said, rankled by the mid's sad, solemn tone. "We are ashore and not under ship's discipline."

Yeardly held up a hand and continued quietly, "No censure is intended, Lieutenant. Your behavior is a model for us all."

"But?"

"But Captain Nath seemed quite surprised by your obvious affection for the magister, so I suspect you have not shared news of your relationship with him."

"I have not."

"Then tread carefully with him when he returns. I fear he may feel betrayed by both you and Magister d'Tancreville. Remember that he is as concerned for her well-being as you."

Merryweather took a deep breath and nodded. "Wise advice, Mid Yeardly, and gratefully accepted."

At that moment, the door to Enid's sleeping room opened as Nath and Rondelle emerged.

"I have given her something to help her sleep," Rondelle said. "For that is the best medicine for her at the moment. She is best served by resting and avoiding any unnecessary movement. She has lost a significant volume of blood and sleep will help replenish that, as well. The concoction I gave her is strong, so she may sleep for several days. I will call on her regularly, though, to ensure her progress."

"Is there aught else I should do?"

"Provide her with peace and quiet and check on her frequently. Time will do the rest."

"Thank you for your good services, Dr. Rondelle," Nath said, opening the door to the hall. "And for yours as well, Mid Yeardly. Should I ever require seconds again, I will call on you, sir!"

Yeardly beamed and followed Dr. Rondelle out. When Merryweather made to follow suit, Nath held up a hand to halt her and closed the door behind Yeardly.

"Lieutenant Merryweather, I believe you have something to tell me regarding the nature of your friendship with Magister de Tancreville."

Merryweather stood to attention and responded with a brisk nod. "Yes, sir. It has progressed beyond a simple friendship."

"And was it your intent to keep this a secret?"

"No, sir. Enid and I intended to inform you, but this affair with Harde intervened."

Nath studied her for a long moment, and then let out a sigh.

"Augusta, I hope you know that I have no interest in meddling in your personal affairs or, powers protect me, Lady d'Tancreville's. You are adults and I have seen nothing to indicate that you have behaved in any way other than in accord with regulation and good sense."

Merryweather nodded and relaxed her stance.

"I understand that you have a policy against shipboard relationships, sir," she said. "If you wish to rescind your invitation for me to serve as your First when you receive a command, I fully understand and would bear no resentment at your choice."

"It would be a hard choice between you and Magister d'Tancreville,"

Nath grumbled. "But my policy doesn't prevent you from having a relationship aboard ship, only from being blatant about it or—ahem—taking advantage of it in ways that the rest of the crew are forbidden."

"I understand, sir."

"Understand this as well: If your shared felicity interferes with the swift and decisive actions expected from either of you, neither of you will sail with me again."

"I understand completely, sir."

"Good," Nath said, collapsing on the couch next to the basket containing the whining Maubin and Marbury. "Then perhaps you won't object to taking the first watch with Enid? I must walk these ruffians before they make a midden of the place."

Enid awoke to find Merryweather holding her left hand. She was dressed in comfortable civilian garb and her hair hung in loose strands that framed her concerned face. Domestic sounds drifted to her from the sitting room as did the aroma of fresh bread which set her stomach growling.

Merry squeezed her hand gently and said, "So, you have rejoined us at last! I was worried despite Dr. Rondelle's assurances!"

It took two tries for Enid to croak out the words, "How long?"

"A day and a half," Merry said, carefully lifting Enid by the shoulders and propping her into a sitting position. "Here is some cool water, dear. Sip it slowly or it may make you ill."

The water trickled luxuriously down her parched throat. When the glass was empty, her voice sounded less like two tombstones rubbing together.

"Nearly two days! I left poor Rue to face the consequences of my actions alone. What a lamentable friend I am."

Merry squeezed her hand and gently stroked her forearm. "Don't berate yourself, Enid. Harde's infamous attempt to kill you where you lay has cast a greater pall over his supporters than yours. Even Lord Ambrose has publicly repudiated Harde."

"That is good to hear," Enid said, genuinely relieved that Nath hadn't suffered visibly from her affair of honor.

"What has become of my hand?"

Merry nodded toward a plain pine box resting on the room's battered vanity table. "There it is. Dr. Rondelle troubled a magister friend of his to place a spell on the box to retard the decay of its contents."

"Good on him. And my ring?"

"It is here, Enid." Merry plucked it off a small table by the bed and dropped it in Enid's left hand.

Enid stared at it for a moment and then said in a voice more plaintive than Merry would have believed the steel-willed woman could produce, "I wish to wear it, but I fear I will require your assistance putting it on."

Tears welled up unbidden in Enid's eyes as she gently eased the ring over the knuckle of Enid's left ring finger. Seeing them, Merry took her face between her hands and gently kissed them away. She climbed into bed next to Enid and bore the shuddering strength of her embrace until her sobs ceased and she slumbered at last. Merry didn't leave her side that night and Nath was sensible enough not to intrude.

Enid was confined to her bed for the next few days, slowly regaining her physical strength and, more critical to her purpose, her sorcerous energy. Merryweather was by her side day and night, tending to her wound as Rondelle instructed and assisting her with tasks she was not yet capable of performing with a single hand. She did her best to conceal her annoyance at Enid's stubborn refusal to practice performing those tasks, warning her that she would not always be present to help, but failed. Enid did not have the heart to tell Merry that, one way or another, she wouldn't require her assistance much longer.

One night, while Nath was sunk in the deep, heedless slumber that characterized his sleep ashore, Enid bade Joy fetch her a carafe of strong coffee. The girl, who Nath had paid extra to look after Enid until she adjusted to her injury, balked at the idea, arguing that it was against Dr. Rondelle's direction that she take her rest and avoid all stimulants until the balance of her humors were restored. Her arguments shattered against Enid's obdurate resolve; she withdrew in an ill temper. Enid supposed Joy would wait in the sitting room until she saw the orb light fade beneath her bedroom door, despite her orders to the contrary. She shrugged and set about the coffee. The headstrong goose was in for a long night.

Her wound was an overflowing pool of fatigue in the evening, but the coffee helped. When her wits were as sharp as possible, she placed the silver ring in the middle of her writing desk. She took a deep breath and reached out for Dunaughy. There was no response. Her heart chilled with dread at the thought that he was beyond her reach, but, at last, the scent of licorice tickled her nose, and she followed the scent to its source: a rapidly diminishing spark of consciousness which was all that remained of Dunaughy's relict. Without pausing for thought, she poured her essence into Dunaughy in the same manner as she would have bolstered a flagging sylph or undine. She allowed the energy to flow unfettered, ignoring Dunaughy's increasingly stronger admonitions until the strength of his presence seemed sufficiently restored to maintain itself.

"What have you done?" Dunaughy demanded. He spoke aloud, a clear indication of the depth of his irritation with her. "Foolish girl! You'll make a ghost of yourself to save one!"

Enid smiled and reclined weakly in her chair. She was relieved and uncommonly pleased to hear the relict's familiar burr, even so stridently pitched.

"I need your aid, Dunaughy. You are the only mage of sufficient knowledge I would ask to assist me in the formulation I have in mind. Moreso, I would not dream of undertaking it without your consent and cooperation. Without our combined efforts, I fear you will not last a fortnight longer."

"Agreed," the ghost replied with a fatalistic calm. "The vigor you lent me is already dissipating—do not look so concerned! I'm sure I'll be hardy as a spectral oak for a fortnight or more. Still, I will eventually dissipate, and I doubt that even your augmented constitution will support too many efforts on tonight's scale."

Lamentably, she could not argue his conclusion. While her spent energies were gradually reconstituting, something in the process seemed strained, as if some esoteric muscle had been stretched to the point of tearing and further stress might leave her permanently lame.

"If I were to feed you energy more often in smaller doses, the effort might be less telling."

"Perhaps," Dunaughy answered doubtfully. "But I suspect the end result of repeated small shocks would be as detrimental as another large jolt. A continual trickle might answer, but you cannot spend the rest of your life in a half-trance to sustain me."

"We could alter the enchantment on my ring," Enid ventured thoughtfully.

"The sympathy would not be sufficient to support such a subtle operation. A more intimate connection would be required."

"My thought as well. That is exactly the nature of the project I propose we undertake together, since we have a powerfully intimate sympathy at hand."

Enid laughed giddily for a few moments and then explained her idea to Dunaughy, who found it flawless.

In the sitting room, Joy curled up tighter in her chair and kept a wide-eyed watch on her mistress's door. She caught snatches of conversation through the room's substantial door, a conversation that included Enid's voice and that of a man she knew had never passed by her and therefore *couldn't* be there. Something about the mysterious voice filled her with dread, but when it changed to laughter that mingled ominously with that of her mistress, she nearly wept with fear. Mamma was right, she thought. Serving a wizard was harrowing work!

chapter 8

Merryweather was positively jubilant to share an early-morning coach ride with Enid to Hafferty Square, home of Middlesea's traders in precious metals. She wasn't even put off by the contents of the large carpetbag in her lap, but chatted happily with her on topics as wide afield as the conduct of the naval war to the best place to buy the most provocative lingerie without fear of embarrassment. Enid was impressed by the depth of her knowledge on both topics.

"I cannot tell you how relieved I am to see you so recovered in a few days," Merry enthused. "Your color has returned—"

"Such as I have," Enid interrupted with a wry smile.

"Shush," Merry chided. "There are men and women in Middlesea who treat the skin of their faces with the same concoctions used to murder rats to attain the fine porcelain you deride! How the wealthy curse their riches!"

"Hmm . . ." Enid smiled and traced the curve of Merry's jaw with the tip of her finger. "Or fail to recognize those riches at all."

Merryweather laughed as the coach clattered to a halt outside a prosperous silver-monger's shop. Rather than spoil her friend's mood, Enid allowed herself to be helped from the coach. This nonsense would end soon enough, she thought, so why sour a lovely morning?

Her business with the silver-monger was quickly disposed of once the beetle-browed tradesperson was convinced that she was not practicing upon his credulity. Merry concealed the small chest under a fold of her jacket as she carried it to the coach.

"I don't mean to pry, Enid, but that is a sizable investment. I know there were problems with the banking houses in Ardainne toward the end, but I assure you that the Albion establishments may be trusted!"

Enid shrugged and smiled. "I think you'll find the investment worthwhile when it comes to fruition."

Their next stop was Verity's studio, where they arrived as she was about to sit down for her afternoon meal. Enid accepted her invitation to share it with honest pleasure. During the time she and Nath spent several days sitting for figure studies and sketches of their faces set in various expressions, Enid developed a deep affection for the little artist and her gentle ways, an affection that she shared with Nath. The meal itself was plain but filling, impeccably prepared and served by an elderly woman that Enid had learned earlier was the artist's aunt. Enid watched her as she scurried about, refilling plates and glasses with an energy that was only slightly impaired by the occasional but obviously painful complaint from joints pressed to greater action than their state of deterioration could comfortably sustain. She thought of Dunaughy, laboring away on the tossing deck of the old *Alarum* and following his captain into mortal danger aboard *Artagny* and was suddenly moved near the point of tears.

She turned her gaze back to the table to find Verity frowning at her in concern. "You seem suddenly sad, Enid. Have we reminded you of something best forgotten?"

She banished her dark reverie with the brightest smile she could conjure. "Not at all! I was merely lost in thought, struggling to find a way to ask a favor of you."

"Ask and it will be yours," Verity declared, slapping the table with her dainty palm. "The engravings from the portrait of you and Nath have proven so profitable that I could take the next year off if I wished! There is nothing you could ask that would be too much."

Enid chuckled sharply. "You Albions are too quick with your answers. If generosity can be a flaw, your people are deeply afflicted. Fortunately for you it is not in my nature to take advantage of a friend's hastiness. Tell me, Verity, do you know the method by which a death mask is cast?"

Verity nodded, unperturbed by the question. "Yes, it is quite simple. Far simpler than taking a mask from a living person who must breathe. It is only a matter of applying the proper plaster . . . but I will not bore you with details." She frowned with sudden concern. "Has someone close to you passed away?"

"Something close to me has," Enid answered with a mordant moue. "Would the plaster work as well on my severed hand as on a corpse's face?"

The little artist recoiled slightly as Enid placed the heavy carpet bag on her dining table but answered gamely enough. "It would require some extra effort, but I'm sure it could be done. But wouldn't your hand be too . . . ?" She sought a polite word for "decayed" or "corrupted," but could find none and let the question settle into silence.

"No. I have maintained it through certain methods. I will return your courtesy and not bore *you* with details. It is much the same as it was when Harde had it from me. The skin is supple, if somewhat drawn, and the fingers have not curled with rigor." Enid realized that both Merry and Verity were disturbed by her dispassionate description of her own lost hand and ended it with a cough. "In any case, it is nearly as good as new. Could you create a mold from it of the sort used to cast a bronze mask? More precisely, *would* you?"

"Of course! I would even cast it for you—but, if you will excuse my rude curiosity, why would you want such a thing? It seems a rather morbid keepsake."

"You must humor me my secrecy," Enid said. "And I have some very specific instructions for you that must be followed to the letter. You see, I may ask your assistance in casting this keepsake, as you call it, but I must have a hand in it myself."

She laughed at her own unintentional pun and once the laughter began, she could only stop it with some effort. Decorum is the first victim of madness she thought, as she wiped her eyes and waved away Verity's troubled expression.

"I am fine. Your wine struck truer and swifter than usual, that is all. The doctors have warned me to be careful of it during the day. Forgive my foolishness. No, Merry, please sit! I am fine! I have said it."

"I will be happy to assist you in whatever way I may, Enid," Verity said calmly and stood. "Now, let us have one more look at the completed painting before I have it delivered to Captain Nath." She raised her hand to silence her protests. "No, the engravings are complete, and their value far exceeds that of the portrait. It would be grasping of me to keep it, so I will gift it to him and wish you both joy of it with all my heart!"

"You are as gracious as you are talented," Enid said, before steering the conversation back to the subject that concerned her most. "But before we view the wonder you conjured from paint and canvas, pray tell me if this is enough silver to cast my hand once the mold is complete? Merry, if you please."

Merryweather nodded and placed the small chest of silver ingots on the table before Verity. She gave Enid a curious look as she did so.

"Why, yes," Verity said. "With some left over, I would say."

"Could I trouble you to begin the process today? I am eager to have the casting completed as soon as possible. I will happily pay the fees of any other clients my eagerness discommodes."

"No, I have the afternoon free. The windfall from the engravings has allowed me to cut my customers by half so that I may spend time on projects of my own. I should have a supply of everything required in my workshop. We can begin immediately, if you wish."

"I would be beholden to you if we can."

It took some time for Verity to prepare the plaster and the boxes for the mold, time that the three spent in conversation about fashion, gossip both social and naval, and discussion on the merits of different artists. It was all disconcertingly banal in light of the task in which they were engaged. Enid interrupted her efforts from time to time to trace sorcerous sigils in the air above the plaster or sprinkle it with pinches of preparations she drew from pouches in her pocket. When the plaster reached a consistency that pleased Verity, she asked Merryweather for the hand, then she secured it inside the mold box, which in turn was slowly filled with plaster.

"It is strange, but I would swear that I feel the plaster growing warm around my hand." Enid rubbed her maimed arm and frowned thoughtfully. "There is a great sympathetic connection here, even so long after the corporal bonds were severed."

After shaking the box carefully to ensure that the plaster settled firmly and all air bubbles were disposed of, Verity straightened with the air of a well-satisfied craftsman.

"There. It is done. It will take some time to prepare a mold from the cast and more to pour the final cast. Still, I should have it completed for you in a few days. Will that suffice?"

"It will, indeed. If the process requires more time to ensure the perfection of its outcome, do not hesitate to take it!"

"Perfection will be my goal and I will take every care to attain it," Verity assured her with a warm smile.

Enid gestured to the box of silver perched heavily on one corner of Verity's workbench. "Will that be silver enough?"

Verity cleaned the plaster from her hands in a basin by the window and nodded. "More than enough. Half again more than the project will require, as I reckon it."

"Whatever is left is yours in addition to your fee." Enid spoke firmly and Verity allowed herself to be compliant. Though she was flush with coin from the recent sales of Enid and Nath's portrait, no prosperity was without bounds.

"Can you melt this down and ensure it is included in the final cast?"

Verity looked down at the plain silver ring in her palm. "Of course, but there is no need. You have already provided more than enough silver."

Enid nodded. "I understand, but mark me well: all the silver from that ring *must* be included in the cast of my hand. Do not fail me in this, dear Verity! It is vital to me that you do not."

"Then it will be as you say."

"You are a dear, Verity. Now, please set aside enough of the silver thus prepared for a second, far smaller project. You may not be able to accomplish it yourself, for it may not lie within the limits of your artifice." She handed the artist a folded sketch with a few neatly written notes in the margin, careful to avoid revealing its content to Merry.

"I trust you to find an artisan to do the work, should that prove to be the case. Here is a sketch of what I seek."

Verity unfolded the paper and, immediately realizing the nature of the commission, refolded it and placed it carefully in a drawer of one of the many cabinets that lined her studio walls. "You have a talent for sketching, Enid. You should develop it. The instructions are quite clear. The size seems slightly large, though, are you certain it is correct?"

"Quite," Enid said with an enigmatic smile. "Now, let us gaze upon this interpretation of Nath and me so I can marvel again at your facility for transforming the physical shortcomings of my appearance to my advantage through the magic of your brush."

Without the distraction of other patrons, Verity finished the silver casting of Enid's severed hand in two days. When word came that it was completed, Enid sent Yeardly, whose half pay left him with no other affordable way to pass his time ashore than loitering about the inn, to fetch it. His share of the various prizes had apparently evaporated in a frenzy of debauchery, although Enid suspected that the greatest part of it had gone to restore his family's failing fortune. He returned a few hours later and placed a heavy, velvet-wrapped package on the small table beside her chair in the sitting room. She unwrapped it gingerly and gave a small gasp as her fingers brushed against the silver's unnatural chill.

"It must be uncommonly cold outside," Enid observed, removing the rest of the velvet wrapping with her good hand to reveal the graceful, icy sculpture. It was heavier than she'd expected.

Yeardly eyed the gleaming artifact with obvious curiosity and imperfectly concealed distaste. Despite a heroic effort, he could not resist asking, "What do you mean to *do* with that thing?"

Enid only smiled and pressed too many coins into his hands for his troubles. She withdrew wordlessly to her room, leaving a smoking cigarillo burning on the arm of her abandoned chair. Yeardly shrugged, thrust the coins into his coat pocket, and picked up the cigarillo. He fancied he tasted the Magister's perfume on it and smiled languorously, savoring a lascivious thought with the tobacco as he took his leave.

Enid laid the silver hand on a sturdy worktable she'd directed Joy to manhandle into her room when word came from Verity that Enid's commission was completed. Once the bench was in place, she'd given the girl the rest of the day off, firmly dispatching her to her mother's house, where she would remain till morning. There was no point in disturbing the poor girl unnecessarily.

The silver hand lay palm-up on the table, the fingers curled naturally as if in sleep. When she draped her fingers across the silver digits, she half-expected them to spasm in surprise. The cold metal remained inert, however, though it seemed to noticeably chill to the touch. She resisted an urge to recoil and tightened her grip on the thing. Eyes closed tight against distraction; Enid let her awareness expand.

The room was alive with power and potential. Elemental forces were present in abundance, but they were forced into the room's corners and narrow spaces by less familiar entities that packed the room so tightly that its walls seemed to bulge slightly outward. Iron bands of claustrophobia tightened about her chest and her breath came in halting gasps that left frost hanging in the deathly still air.

Dunaughy put a comforting hand on her shoulder while laying the other over hers on the simulacrum. The front of his blue coat was purple with blood from the gaping bullet hole in his chest. Enid tore her eyes away from the wound and met his calm eyes. A strong odor of licorice hung in the air.

Verity has indeed wrought truly, Dunaughy said, the words in Enid's head oddly out of sync with the movement of his spectral lips. *I believe she was unnaturally inspired in this work—do you sense the fey in it as I do?*

She nodded silently as the silver beneath her fingers felt for a moment like dry twigs and autumn leaves. She gathered her resolve with some effort and forced herself to answer. *There are forms and powers in this room that I do not recognize, Dunaughy. I fear it may cost my sanity to negotiate with them.*

The chill in her shoulder thickened as he tightened his ghostly grip there.

If you could but remember the first time a sylph revealed itself to you, you would recall facing the same fear, Dunaughy told her earnestly. *But you cannot. Just as the body cannot remember the true sensation of pain, neither can the mind hold the memory of the moment it ascends to a new level of awareness.*

Then I will not go mad?

Dunaughy shrugged. *If you do, you won't know it. Your mind will hide its broken edges and your new awareness will render them meaningless.*

Enid nodded stoically. Somewhere she was a woman weeping, and she loathed her for her weakness. *I am ready, then. How do I proceed?*

Reach out to them as you would to an elemental. Make your intentions known to them and they will guide you.

Enid nodded again, the tears on her cheek so cold they burned. She opened her mind and was aware of the powers peering into her as she peered out at them. At first, she tried to take charge of them as she would an elemental, but they were unmoved by even the most imperious effort of will. She could not bring herself to cajole them, fearing that utter dissolution lay down that path, so she simply laid out her plan before them. They seemed drawn to the idea, and she sensed their willingness to make her vision real. With that willingness came power.

Nath and Yeardly were sharing a bottle of wine when Enid's scream pierced the late-evening quiet. Joy, engaged in assiduously ignoring Yeardly's blunt, spirit-fueled attentions, froze in place, her eyes wide and mouth agape. Nath surged to his feet but his headlong charge to Enid's aid was brought up short by a wall of propriety: It would be unseemly to charge into a lady's chambers as if he were accustomed to such freedom. He rounded on Joy and barked in his quarterdeck voice, "Stop your gawping like a statue and convey us to your mistress! She is in distress!"

"I dursn't! She is a wizard and may have summoned a demon that will eat me if I open the door!" The girl shook with dread, but Nath was unmoved.

"I am no wizard, but I will summon a cat to lick the skin from your bony back if you do not let us into Enid's room immediately!"

Nath shoved past the nearly fainting girl the instant she opened the door and barged into a scene of horror. The smell of blood and blood-wet timber struck him; all that was missing was the reek of burnt alchemical powder and overturned cannons to re-create a familiar scene of carnage between decks. Enid's still form lay slumped across her makeshift workbench and Nath was appalled to see the wall beyond her dripping with great smears of blood.

"Redeemer!" Yeardly gasped. "What butcher's work is this?"

"Lend me a hand turning her! We must find her wound and stop it before she bleeds out entire!"

Together they lifted her from the workbench and lowered her to the floor on her back. The front of her blouse was washed in blood and her eyes stared fixedly ahead from a bloodless white face. His heart frozen with dread, Nath gave her shoulders a rough shake and was rewarded with a weak cough. Sentience returned to her eyes, and she struggled to sit up. Nath pressed her shoulders gently to the floor. "Stay put, Enid. Moving about may aggravate your wound. Where are you hurt?"

"Nonsense! I am not hurt at all." She pushed weakly against his chest in protest and Nath was horrified at the chill of its touch. She must not have more than a drop of blood left in her, he thought, her flesh is as cold as a corpse's. He sat back and took her hand in his to chafe some warmth into it and then recoiled as realization sank in: He held her right hand and it was made of metal. Metal that moved and flexed within his grasp as if it were flesh and bone rather than icy silver.

"What have you done?" Nath gasped involuntarily.

"I've replaced my missing hand." Enid's voice was weak but matter-of-fact. "I find it more useful to have one at the end of each arm, don't you?"

Nath was vaguely aware of Yeardly catching Joy as she fainted, the tableau playing out predictably in his peripheral vision. His full attention was captured by the cold silver hand clutched between his own. It looked like a perfect simulacrum for Enid's missing hand, perfect in detail down to the fine lace of veins across its back, and its fingers moved naturally as he squeezed them. Other than its smooth, cool texture and unnatural color, there was little to indicate it was not the hand Enid was born with.

"How—" he began to ask, but then thought better of it. "You have lost a tremendous amount of blood. Yeardly! Drag that lubber of a maid out of here and fetch Rondelle. Tell him the magister requires his attention immediately!"

"More stuff. All I require is a heaping plate of the beef you Albions pride yourself on and a steady supply of red wine. Red wine fortifies the blood admirably, you know."

So saying, she lapsed into unconsciousness.

Nath set her hand down carefully; its fingertips gave a hard clatter against the wooden floor as he released them. He removed a handkerchief from his coat pocket and carefully dabbed rapidly drying blood from his friend's face; a face that was, perhaps, more lovely in repose than when alert. He glanced up at the blood-spattered wall and the hopelessly gore-soaked rug beneath Enid's workbench. *It will take some work to clean this mess up,* he thought. *And what has she spilled that smells so strongly of licorice?*

chapter 9

A day had passed since the Sea Lord savagely squashed the Ainsley Bottoms mutiny by taking advantage of a parlay between the mutineers' top leaders and Admiral Larlock with the purported purpose of meeting their most pressing demands and sent in Infantry borrowed from the Ainsley Guard to cow the sailors and round up the rest of their leadership. Some fighting ensued, but the great majority of mutineers surrendered, bitterly certain that a man who would betray a flag of truce wouldn't hesitate to order their wholesale slaughter. While the Sea Lord's stratagem certainly met the King's widely publicized call for "quick and decisive action" to end the mutiny, it was wildly at odds with His Majesty's intent, which had been to defuse the situation peacefully by relenting to some of the mutineer's demands whilc insisting that the uprising cease immediately. His Majesty was not pleased to see Viscount Morrin throw fuel on the fire of resentment that the Sea Lord's own policies and grossly public feud with a new-made post captain had kindled.

Nath folded the paper he was reading over breakfast and passed it to Enid.

"A damned poor showing, no matter how much it may advance my cause. Now, I'm not a coddler of mutineers, but those tars at Ainsley Bottoms treated their officers with respect and saw them safely to shore with all their belongings. They kept their discipline and only wished to have their grievances addressed. Now half a dozen of 'em are marked D in their ship rolls and another dozen sport broken bones and cracked heads. A damned poor showing, and one that your real levelers and rabble-rousers will capitalize on."

"What will become of the mutineers? A wholesale slaughter, I presume."

Nath shook his head. "No doubt their more exalted leaders will be flogged and hung, and a few of the most visible troublemakers flogged and sent to one of the prison hulks, but the majority will be disrated and lose most of their back pay to fines before being distributed throughout the fleet."

Enid shook her head, the gloom of her expression deepened by her gaunt face and hollow cheeks. It was taking more than a few rare steaks and flagons of strong red wine to restore her health, it seemed. Nath was originally wracked with worry at the sight of her, but, poorly as she looked now, he'd seen her improve noticeably with each passing day.

"Will they be accepted by the captains and crew of the ships they are foisted upon? Or will they be spurned for their disloyalty?" she asked.

"Oh, they'll be accepted. It is rare for a captain to turn their nose up at sailors who can haul, reef, and steer, regardless of their provenance." Nath chuckled. "So long as their heads are unadorned by antlers and they stand less than eight feet in height. Some of them will be hard bargains, of course, made more obdurate by the Sea Lord's rough handling, but any sea officer with their salt can deal handily with such importunities."

"The ships from which the mutineers are taken must suffer immensely. Judging by your frequent and morose observations on what a rare commodity experienced sailors are."

"Shouldn't be as bad as all that. Only the worst of the troublemakers will be reassigned, according to the papers. And speaking of papers, have you seen how many papers have taken up Muirean's call for me to be knighted? Even one of the more moderate publications in league with the Old Charter Party!"

"Do not buy a pair of gold spurs just yet," Enid said. "Her campaign to see you ennobled is nothing more than a provocation we concocted. Still, it is good to see that the spark found such dry tinder."

"I take nothing for granted, Enid." Nath sat his paper aside and leaned back, his expression grave. "We are thoroughly outgunned. Our broadsides raise a cacophony, but our shot has little effect. Our opponent, on the other hand, have yet to engage us in earnest, and when they do, it will take no more than one or two of their rounds to stave us in completely. No matter how gallantly we fight, absolute victory is unlikely."

"It is well that you do not delude yourself with fantasies of certain victory," Enid said. "But do not delude yourself that it is impossible, either. I only warn you against overconfidence in light of a troubling report I've had from Lord Reinard."

Nath leaned forward and the depth of the creases upon his brow deepened. "Troubling how?"

"The First Lord was called before the king yesterday to report on the disturbance at Ainsley Bottoms. You were mentioned during the discussion and the king was heard to say there were more important matters afoot and that he would ignore the ruin of a half-dozen post captains if Morrin could bring one mutiny to a satisfactory conclusion."

Nath nodded and shrugged. "Well, there you have it. Morrin has His Majesty's leave to break me. There is nothing to do for it but stand straight as the shot pours in and thank the Redeemer for what we are about to receive."

The pair set aside further conversation and perused the various papers and pamphlets that were delivered to their rooms each morning until Joy's signature trio of soft raps on the door interrupted their reading. Nath stood and brushed the crumbs from his coat. Upon answering the door, he found Joy standing in the hall in the company of a young lieutenant whose otherwise pleasant features were marred by permanent frown lines that seemed altogether too deep to have been carved by the concerns of one of so few years.

The fellow saluted formally and asked, "Are you Captain Rue Nath, sir, formerly of His Majesty's ships *Alarum* and *Redemption*?"

Nath sketched a return salute and replied, "I am, sir. And who might you be?"

"Lieutenant Fellows, sir. From the Office of the Sea Lord. I am here to advise you that his lordship requires your presence and to bear you to him with all speed. A coach awaits us below."

Nath glanced over his shoulder at Enid, who arched a speculative brow. He shrugged and plucked his hat from the rack near the door and twisted it into place to rest at just the right angle across his brow. "Lead on, Lieutenant Fellows. Lead on."

The carriage ride to Admiralty passed in uncomfortable silence. Nath resisted every urge to straighten his stock or brush the errant dog hair from his coat sleeve, determined not to give the punctilious Lieutenant Fellows the satisfaction of seeing him fidget. No. He was determined to face whatever fate Providence placed in his path with the dignity with which the grand seigneurs of Ardainne were said to show while they awaited their turn to demonstrate how efficiently Roget's Device could deposit a still-blinking head into a basket. They were greeted by the First Lord's own footmen, who briskly ushered them past the long line of officers awaiting an audience with Viscount Morrin or one of his officers. This produced a murmur of complaint until they recognized Nath, at which point the murmuring was replaced by a susurration of speculation. Nath held his head high through it all.

In the Sea Lord's outer office, Lieutenant Fellows transferred his responsibility for Nath to Ms. Holyoke and briskly took his leave. The door to the inner office was ajar, so Nath restricted his interactions with her to a searching look. Her expression in response made it clear that she was as much in the dark as he. After she announced his presence to Lord Morrin with an admirable display of apparent disinterest, Nath entered the great man's sanctum and presented himself with a brisk salute. He could have stumbled in drunk and naked, and the obvious disapproval and animosity in Lord Morrin's slit eyes would have been no deeper.

"I will be forthright with you, Captain Nath," Morrin said in a hoarse voice. "I had hoped your last appearance before my desk would be the final time I would have to endure your presence."

Nath said nothing. To respond would only extend the proceedings and further inflame the Sea Lord's hatred for him if that were even possible. He resolved to stare at a spot over his oppressor's right shoulder until required to speak.

"It is good that you keep your peace. There is nothing you can say or do that would change my opinion of you in light of the rabble-rousing campaign you and Viscount Uthred have prosecuted against your superiors in both rank and breeding. Yes, I'm aware that you number him among your list of patrons and that he has the ear of the Crown Princess, among the other claims he makes upon her body. Not to mention your Ardain harlot's assassination of a good man whose career you and Earl Weymouth conspired to destroy. What is next, a duel with Lord Ambrose? Or perhaps his father?"

Morrin rose to his full significant height and seemed to loom over Nath despite the massive desk that separated them. "That chicanery is at an end! I have ordered Captain Ambrose to refrain from calling you or Harde's murderess out, although he fairly quivers to do so. Nor will you or your murderous magister goad him as she did poor Harde! There will be no more deaths to serve your overweening pride! Do I make myself clear, sir, or must my orders be tattooed upon the back of your sword hand as a reminder?"

"Your orders are clear, your lordship. Dueling between Captain Aixely and Magister d'Tancreville or myself is forbidden. Nor are the magister or I to attempt to goad Captain Aixely into violating that prohibition."

"Godamme, Captain Nath, against all previous evidence to the contrary you *can* apprehend an order! It has yet to be determined if you can obey one as well, though, so I warn you—if you ignore this ban, I will see to it that you are drummed from the service and flogged around the fleet! Doubt my determination and you will learn the same lesson as those mutinous fools at Ainsley Bottoms!"

Nath began to reply but, the Sea Lord shouted him into silence.

"Say nothing! I have no stomach for your false oaths of obedience. I've already borne your presence longer than my gorge will comfortably allow! You are the most self-serving manipulator of the ale-soaked populace I've ever had the displeasure of meeting. You should learn the lesson of the headless fops in Ardainne who courted the riffraff to the destruction of their titles. Instead, the King, Providence bless him even in this rash error, has been deceived into intervening on your behalf by your cousin's empty rhetoric—yes, I am aware of her part in your conspiracy."

He snatched a thick oilskin packet from his desk and threw it at Nath's feet.

"Take that and be damned! Know that I am set against you, as are all right-minded officers in the King's service!"

Nath retrieved it and gave Morrin a puzzled look.

"Oh, do not play the surprised innocent with me, you duplicitous rascal! You seem to have ears everywhere, so I have no doubt you expected this. I will not waste my breath explicating what you already know. Those are your orders. If you truly are ignorant of their nature, read them at your leisure anywhere but here. I will not have the air of this august office tainted further by the stench of your perfidy. You are dismissed! Begone! I pray that you are taking your ease in a gibbet the next time I clap eyes on you."

Nath turned on his heel and departed, closing the massive door behind him as he did. He paused in front of Holyoke's desk and shrugged when she pointed at the packet under his arm.

He mouthed the words *meet me tonight* and waited for a nod of understanding. Then he retraced his path out of Admiralty, with the packet under his left elbow and his head held high. His passage was followed by the eyes of the queued officers, who watched him pass in respectful and, for the most part, empathetic silence. They all knew that they, too, could run afoul of the Sea Lord's arbitrary passion at any time.

Outside, Nath made his way to the nearest coffeehouse and secured a table in a dark cubby where no one could peer over his shoulder. He carefully untied the oilskin wrapping and swallowed as he skipped the honorifics and read a line written in bolder ink. It took a second reading for him to be sure he understood the words:

". . . take command of HMS *Revenant*, of forty guns, she being refitted and to arrive on the 16th Lughfest, instant. Fail to do so at your peril."

He stared at the passage, filled with a strange combination of elation and doom. His wish had been granted, but he felt like the hapless mortal in a fey tale warning of the perils of making ill-considered wishes. He took a long pull of stout ale and transferred his commission to his inner coat pocket. His smile held all the unadulterated joy of a child looking upon their mother after a long absence.

Earl Aixely stepped out from the hiding place behind a decorative screen in the far corner of the room, from whence he had observed the exchange between the Sea Lord and Captain Nath, his expression carefully neutral.

"I applaud the frankness in which you addressed that cur, sir," he said. "You flayed the pride from his bones and locked his jaws in fear. I must admit, I was a bit overawed by the strength of your rebuke, and I was in no way its target!"

"I can bellow and curse with the best," the Sea Lord said and slouched into his chair. He seemed to visibly deflate before Aixely's eyes. "I understand your plan, and I do not doubt the wisdom of it, but

I must own that giving Nath those orders struck my pride as fierce a blow as I imagine surrendering my sword in battle might."

"Do not think of it as a surrender," Aixely cajoled. "We have not admitted defeat! We are employing a *ruse de guerre*. We have not struck. We are simply flying false colors!"

Morrin nodded doubtfully, his face still set in an expression of defeat. Aixely sighed inwardly. This Nath affair and his abominable handling of the Ainsley crisis seemed to have robbed him of all his confidence and drive. The earl was as sympathetic as his meager store of human sentiment would allow. Morrin had been a useful ally while his nerve lasted, but it appeared he had no more grit left in reserve. Aixely resolved that it was time to begin grooming a new Sea Lord.

"You need not torture yourself, Lord Morrin. Our plan is foolproof. Remember its tenets: Four loyal officers have died before they could read themselves in as *Revenant*'s captain. Despite the prattle in the radical press, we have no reason to believe Nath won't suffer the same fate. Should he be struck down by whatever curse afflicts the frigate, you will have both mollified the public and rid us of Nath. It also gives you ample reason to send *Revenant* to the breakers as an ungovernable ship, all on the grounds of avenging the intrepid Rue-Naught."

Morrin nodded but said nothing.

"Second, should Nath survive where four of his betters have perished, the mission to the des Fantômes will certainly end his credibility with the public if not lead to his outright death. Our spies in Ardainne could not have delivered the location of Bascombe's place of imprisonment at a better time, particularly coupled with the revelation regarding the related developments in the area from my private agents—and since only the two of us are aware of those developments, you will not be faulted for the paucity of resources assigned to Nath's mission!"

"You are right, of course," Morrin said flatly. "This course of action seems divinely inspired. I look forward to celebrating putting this matter behind by shifting Captain Ambrose into a command more suitable to his ambitions."

They spoke for a while of less momentous matters, but the flames Morrin breathed on Nath had clearly consumed the entirety of his energy. After an appropriate interlude, Aixely excused himself and left the Sea Lord hunched at his desk and staring at a shipyard model of his favorite old command, *Invictus*, 74 guns. Aixely closed the door behind him and when he turned, he found Holyoke down on one knee, picking up spilled papers nearby. Her brass-headed walking stick lay near at hand.

"Pardon me, your lordship, but please take care where you step. These are urgent papers awaiting the Sea Lord's signature."

The Earl started to step clear of the mess without comment, but there was something about the confident manner in which he had been addressed that gave him pause.

"Of course, Miss—?"

"Holyoke," she answered, meeting his eyes without hesitation. "Your lordship."

Aixely admired her appearance, but her frank, intelligent expression intrigued him more. Her face would leave most who looked upon it sure that she was an open, workmanly young woman who lived a life whose concerns were constrained to the scope of the demands made upon her in her profession. He saw something different, though. Those eyes saw everything and forgot nothing, and the mind behind her unblemished brow was quick and analytical.

"During our conversation, the Sea Lord lauded you for your tireless efficiency, Ms. Holyoke," Morrin said, and leaned down to present her with his card. "I was most impressed. If you should find yourself seeking the same position in a different office for better recompense than the Crown will ever offer, please make an appointment to discuss it."

"Thank you, your lordship," she said and placed his card in a silver case she produced from her jacket pocket. "I will."

Another point for her, he thought. Her response was neither fawning nor self-deprecating. This Holyoke had far more potential than it seemed Morrin appreciated. He gave her a small but courteous nod, stepped over the scattered papers, and took his leave.

Before leaving the tavern Nath hired a runner to find Enid at the Best Bower and advise her he would not return tonight, but he requested she and Merryweather attend him in their quarters for breakfast on the morn. That task accomplished, he spent a few hours wandering aimlessly and making the odd purchase at various shops, some items for himself but most as gifts for folk ranging from Yeardly to Lord Reinard. His first stop was at Brockwithe & Sons to purchase an item that caught his eye when he bought the new sword for dinner with Duchess Esdivere. As the sun was beginning to dip, he hired a coach to the inn at which he and Emley Holyoke routinely met to exchange news and enjoy each other's company.

He had wine and a selection of cheese, breads, and cold meats brought up to the room and resisted the urge to pillage it before Emley arrived. The weight that his commission and orders lifted from his shoulders left him with a superabundance of energy that made the wait trying. He sat down in one of the room's easy chairs and attempted to distract himself with a freshly printed pocket folio of Albert Thorogood's fabulism entitled *Redemption Delivered*.

He snapped into wakefulness at the sound of the door being latched. Emley stood smiling before it, leaning on her walking stick and smiling down on him with a look of affection he had not seen on a woman's face since awakening in his mother's arms as a child. It pierced his heart and he thought, *Surely this is the best day that has ever dawned in the history of the world.*

He noticed that there was no trace of disguise or glamour about her and, alarmed, sat up straight in the chair.

"I hope you didn't think our meeting was so urgent that you must risk discovery and exposure to the First Lord's wrath!"

"Not in the least," she said, and the tenderness of her smile transformed to mischief. "The Sea Lord can be hanged. I resigned from his service today."

"Resigned? Wish you joy, Emley, but why today?"

Her smile transformed again, from mischief to wolfish satisfaction. "Because today may well be the lowest day that wretch will ever experience, and it was eminently gratifying to make it even a hair's breadth worse!"

Nath allowed her to pull him to his feet and chuckled. "Enid may have met her match in the article of unalloyed spite."

She drew him to the bed and began pulling his stock loose.

"Requited spite is wondrously satisfying. I wonder if achieving it leaves Enid with the same urgent desire for another type of satisfaction?"

"I couldn't say." Nath grinned. "Our friendship isn't that—"

The rest of his remark was smothered by Emley's kiss and Enid was banished from their conversation until it culminated to their mutual satisfaction.

They sat naked and cross-legged on the room's brocade couch. The tray of food was on the cushion between them, and a bottle of wine sat on the floor within easy reach. Without discussion, they resolved to dispense with glasses and drink wine from the bottle.

"You look a different man," Holyoke said and reached across the tray to stroke his forehead with her fingertips. "There were lines here that I thought were permanent, but they have vanished."

"I am transformed! I worried for myself, of course; I'm a human, not a saint. But the proposition of seeing all my loyal officers, warrants, and people left with no means to support themselves because I had the misfortune to fall into Ambrose Aixely's orbit was like an anchor around my neck. I feel half a century younger than I did yesterday."

She looked down and frowned in silence at the slice of bread slathered with Malasfandyari cheese and thick green olive slices.

"The food isn't to your liking?" Nath asked. "I can send for more, or we can dress and dine at the chophouse you so admire since we can walk about together openly again, if you prefer."

"It is not that." She smiled ruefully. "The food is excellent and perfect for a meal taken after such vigorous exertion."

Nath held his tongue and gave her time to find the words for which she obviously searched. At last, she looked up, wearing a resolute expression.

"It is so pleasing to see you relieved of most of your troubles that I hate to burden you with more," she said. "But you must know that Earl Aixely and the Sea Lord contrived your commission and orders to do you harm. They hope *Revenant* will murder you just as she has the four captains before you."

Nath waved the statement away. "It is a risk I'm willing to take. If she wished to see me dead, she could have accomplished that easily enough at any point in the voyage from Gisbon to Middlesea."

"That is true, but there is also the matter of your orders. I do not know the details, other than they involve someplace called the *des Fantômes*. I know that the Sea Lord had them drawn up to specifically to see you dead, however."

"How do you know this?"

"I pressed my ear to the door as they spoke together after you left. Aixely is absolutely certain that your next cruise will be your last, either from the curse or whatever awaits you at the *des Fantômes*. Morrin is less sure, but he is an idiot. Aixely is not."

Nath was surprised to see tears forming in Emley's eyes and he set the tray on the floor to embrace her. As always, she smelled intoxicatingly clean. He hoped she didn't notice his body's reaction to holding her so close and feeling her breath against his neck and shoulder.

"You borrow trouble where there is none, Emley. They are both fools if they think some unexpected challenge will set me on my heels. I am a frigate captain. The unexpected is my stock in trade!"

The remark succeeded in coaxing a sad chuckle from her. He hugged her closer and said earnestly, "I know my trade better than most, and Enid—why, Enid has no business on a frigate. She should be in charge of a whole section of magisters aboard a first-rate ship of the

Line. Merryweather, Oxley, and the others are all solid officers with buckets of experience at war. We all know when to fight and when to run. Aixely is a lubber and doesn't understand that the power of a frigate extends far beyond the number of guns she carries or the number of people to serve them. A genius ashore is often a simpleton at sea, dearest. You were a first luff; you know what I say is true."

"The same is true of a sailor fighting ashore, as your orders require."

Nath scoffed. "That is what Harcourt and his lobsters are for! What other reason would we have for suffering the great louts aboard?"

She laughed and the dolorous spell was broken.

They finished the food and wine, rollicked a bit more, and then slept through the night entangled in each other's arms. Nath was mortally certain he had never experienced such a perfect night. He pressed his forehead softly between her shoulder blades and whispered, "I think I love you, Ms. Holyoke."

"I know you do." Her whispered reply was so soft that it was nearly imperceptible. "And I you."

A few moments later found them snoring lightly without the shadow of a care on the separate horizons of their dreams.

Despite the early hour, Nath found Enid, Merryweather, and the ever-present Yeardly awaiting him at his breakfast table. They greeted him warmly enough, but he was aware of the intensity with which all three sets of eyes studied his features, posture, and movements for the slightest clue to ease their anxiety over the nature of the tidings he bore.

"Please," he said, "stop staring at me as if I were like to sprout a second head. The news is good, overall. Let me shed my coat and join you at table and I will share it!"

Merryweather and Yeardly both developed a sudden interest in the texture of their toast, but Enid watched him until he sat next to her, a slight smile on her face all the while. Once he was settled, she leaned close to him and said, "You smell of verbena."

"What of it?" he asked.

"Nothing. I merely made an observation."

"Do you wish to hear the news or not?"

"We are all with child to do just that," Enid said. "Please, what was the outcome of your audience with the Sea Lord?"

Nath had composed his words on the coach ride to the Best Bower and his audience was sufficiently composed to refrain from interrupting his tale with questions, despite the unquestionable impact his answers would have on their future. When his tale was told, he was not surprised to see the joy of his revelation alloyed with obvious concern.

"I expected exultant shouts from you all and perhaps a merry jig from Yeardly," he said. "But I see a cloud hanging over your good cheer. I know the source of the fly in your ointment, though, and I assure you I will not suffer the same fate as the *Revenant*'s captains. I've survived reading myself in once, and I shall do so again, the gods willing and with Enid's assistance."

"And if you do not?" Merryweather asked gravely.

"Then I shall be most disappointed in the protective powers of the gods and our magister," he said, his grin and wink provoking subdued smiles from Merryweather and Yeardly and a stage-worthy eye roll from Enid.

"Ms. Holyoke truly pressed her ear to the door?" Enid asked. "She is irrefutably interested in your welfare to resort to such a precarious act. Someone might have entered the outer office and seen her. How would she have explained herself?"

"She planned to resign her position today, so perhaps she believed the reward outweighed the risk," Nath said.

"Perhaps," Enid said, the ghost of a smile on her lips. She pressed on more seriously, though, and asked, "You truly know nothing of the nature of these murderous orders?"

"Nothing," Nath lied. "Other than Aixely and the Sea Lord believe it is so perilous I shall not survive it."

"That's heartening," Merryweather said without a trace of sarcasm.

"How so?" Enid asked.

"Orders that hazardous are certainly not consigning us to blockade duty," Merryweather explained. "The endless, dismal horrors that you will never understand until you are unfortunate enough to experience them."

"There's your silver lining, Enid." Nath laughed. "And truth to tell, all orders of the type a frigate captain longs for are fraught. And these orders, however malevolent their intent, set my heart racing in anticipation."

"Blockade duty would quicken my pulse, sir," Yeardly said with a grin. "I'll just be happy to walk the deck of a ship again and stand a watch at sea!"

"I would be overjoyed to eat some of the breakfast Mrs. Rangle has so graciously prepared for us," Enid said, and began filling her plate with eggs, sausages, and buttered bread. The others, Nath included, looked on in awe, having never seen her take more than half portions, which she rarely reduced below a quarter.

"You have an unusually hearty appetite this morning, Magister," Merryweather commented, glancing speculatively from Enid's face to her silver hand and back again.

"My exertions to accomplish this were quite draining." She held up her right hand and wriggled its silver fingers as naturally as if they were flesh. "I have not been better since the duel and my body insists that I recoup all the lost and curtailed meals during my recovery."

Merryweather nodded. Enid had lost a noticeable amount of weight following the amputation of her hand.

"You believe you will be recovered enough to resume your duties aboard *Revenant* in three days' time?" Nath asked, watching in thinly veiled amusement as she shoved half a hunk of buttered bread smeared with honey into her mouth.

After chewing a moment, she swallowed with some difficulty and said, "I am well as houses, as you Albions say."

"We do not say that," Nath said. "But I take your meaning. A thought occurs to me, though. Perhaps you should wear gloves for a time. I would not have the ship's people distracted by your, well, your—"

"Hand, Rue," Enid said wryly. "It is simply my hand in another form. I will conceal it for the nonce, but I cannot walk around wearing gloves forever."

"Could you paint it in a fleshy tone? I'm sure Verity could whip you up a pot of just the right hue."

Enid's only response was a cold stare.

Nath cleared his voice. "Well, leave that aside for now."

"Or for good and all," Enid said and took a gulp of Mrs. Rangle's abysmal coffee.

"At any gate," Nath continued, "we mustn't waste a breath today. *Revenant* leaves the yards tonight and will arrive in the Basin tomorrow afternoon with a crew from Gorwich yard. I intend to read myself in as captain no more than an hour after she drops anchor. Enid, be so kind as to present yourself to Duchess Esdivere with my compliments and request she release as many of our *Alarum*s and *Redemption*s as she can part with to Merryweather. Lieutenant Merryweather, accompany the magister and take our people in hand. Find whatever lodging you can for them tonight. Here is a purse that should cover the expense."

"Yes, sir," Merryweather said and departed with a covert wink at Enid, who responded with a jaunty salute with her fork, upon which the last piece of sausage was skewered.

"Mr. Yeardly," Nath continued. "I believe you have remained apprised of the lodgings of our warrants and mids? Good on you, lad! Make the rounds and advise all who have managed to avoid the grasp of rival captains to meet with me at the steps opposite *Revenant*'s anchorage in the morning."

Yeardly knuckled his brow in salute and was nearly out the door before Merryweather brought him up short. "Don your uniform before setting out, Mr. Yeardly. You are under your commanding officer's orders now and would not want to bring shame to him by way of your scurrilous appearance. Perhaps apply a razor to your chin, as well."

When the door slammed and Yeardly's galloping footsteps faded, Nath turned to Enid and Merryweather and said, "Now, with unwelcome ears departed from the room, I must speak with you both regarding the relationship you have developed ashore."

Enid's eyes narrowed dangerously, and Nath held up a hand and said, "Pray, let me speak before lashing out. The course charted by your hearts is none of my affair and, frankly, I wish you both joy of it. Nor is there any cause to berate you, as your actions are all within accordance with naval regulations. However, I must make one thing clear: Your feelings for one another cannot interfere with your duties or be displayed in any way that might compromise the discipline of my command. Do either of you foresee being unable to abide by those limitations?"

"Are we children?" Enid's tone was affronted but not combative, which was more than Nath had hoped for.

"No, nor I your parent. I speak to you as the captain of the HMS *Revenant* and as your friend."

"More captain than friend, I'd say."

"Say what you will but answer my question." Nath's voice was firm and his gaze steady and unblinking. Merryweather sat to attention despite herself.

"I believe I can speak for Merryweather as well as myself: We are adults and are aware of your precious regulations, none of which we will violate in the least."

He glanced at Merryweather for confirmation, and she responded with a firm "Aye, sir."

"Good," Nath said as he leaned back in his chair. "With that disposed of, I have a number of things for you to attend to before the two of you call on the duchess. First, take this letter to Atherby's print shop on Old Quayside and have several dozen broadsides printed per its instructions. This pouch of silver should be enough to cover the expense. Offer him a bonus if he has them printed today and directs some of the urchins under his employ to post them anywhere a good salt might clap eyes on 'em."

"As you will, sir."

"That done, report to *Revenant* and perform a summary survey of powder, stores, and the state of the people. I will make my own once I read myself in, but I'd admire your opinion to set against my own."

"Yes, sir." Merryweather saluted briskly and took her leave.

"And what other orders do you have for me?" Enid asked, her tone unreadable to Nath.

"Only that you see to laying in any arcane or alchemical supplies or instruments you might require while they are easily at hand." At the utterance of the word, his eyes slipped instantly to her unearthly right hand.

Enid noticed his glance and sighed. "You will not be rid of your trepidation until you are acquainted with the object of your discomfort. Here, take each of my hands in yours and tell me what you feel."

Nath concealed his reluctance to touch her artificial right hand but let out a sharp gasp at its warm, giving touch.

"You see? It does not differ from my left hand other than in appearance. It is not cold, hard, or threatening. I have simply imparted my body's memory of the lost article into this perfectly cast simulacrum. It is magic based on the simplest principle, that of sympathy between likes."

"I take you at your word, Enid. It is just odd to me that I've never encountered anything like this outside the old stories and myths. If attaching an artificial limb is so easily done, why is it not common practice?"

"Well, as to that, silver is practically a required element, it being the preeminent sorcerous metal. My little hand cost a fortune, so you can imagine the expense of an arm or leg. Besides, all but the most demolished can be reattached by modern medicine augmented by healing magic. Such tattered flesh and shattered bones would not benefit from the formulation that replaced my right hand."

"I suppose not."

Her words seemed entirely sensible but failed to dismiss his instinctual misgivings. Still, he forbore arguing with her. She was the expert in this circumstance, and he trusted her not to endanger him or his people with perilous, unsanctioned magic. He must put the same trust in her knowledge of the sorcerous arts as she did in his grasp of the nautical variety.

Their errands run, Enid, Merryweather, and Yeardly reunited in the common room of the Best Bower. Mrs. Rangle orbited the table at a distance, anxiously rubbing her hands together. Enid deduced that she was aware of their impending departure and was undecided on how to address them about receiving the money owed to her for their accommodation.

Finding the otherwise forceful woman's reticence to conduct her business and leave them in peace unsettling, Enid called her to the table and said, "As you may be aware, Captain Nath has received command of *Revenant* and we will be relocating to her when she arrives from the yards in three days. Adding those days to our current obligation, what do we owe you?"

"I regret losing such upstanding and reliable lodgers, but I wish him joy of his new command. Your patience, please, milady, while I work my calculations," Mrs. Rangle said, and produced a small, gum-spined notebook and a pencil stub from her apron pocket. After a few moments of rapid scribbling, she announced a number that sounded quite fair to Enid, who counted out coins from her purse and poured them into the older woman's cupped hands.

"I have included extra coin to cover any overages that might occur," Enid said.

Mrs. Rangle's eyes widened as she noticed the gleaming gold coins among the silver. "I believe you may have miscounted, Lady Enid!"

"I did not. I perceive you are a woman with a keen sense of order. I am cut from the same cloth, so I recognize the disruption we imposed upon you and your establishment. Whatever surplus remains after you settle our account is for you, as a token of my appreciation of your flexibility in the face of our frequent and peculiar demands."

The innkeeper gave a deep curtsy and when she straightened, she wore a soft, amiable expression Enid had never seen grace her face before.

"You are wondrous generous," she said. "And I will share a portion of it with Joy, of course!"

"You need not," Enid said. "We will show our appreciation to her as well. The poor girl seemed terrified of me, but she never failed me when I had a need for her."

Once Mrs. Rangle departed, her coins clutched protectively to her bosom, she and her companions returned to their conversation.

"Tell me, Magister," Yeardly said in a tone that wouldn't carry to the surrounding tables. "If *Revenant* is indeed under a curse, why do you suppose Captain Nath didn't run afoul of it on our cruise from Gisbon?"

"I cannot say," Enid answered in the same low tone. "It could be a Naveroñian curse that was triggered upon the ship returning to Albion. Or . . ."

"Or?" Merryweather asked.

"Or she was cursed after her arrival here, in Middlesea."

Yeardly was thunderstruck by the idea. "Ashes! By whom? Ardain agents?"

Enid shrugged. "It seems likely, but who can say?"

"Cursed or no," Yeardly said, "she has a darksome air about her."

Enid nodded in grave agreement. Yeardly had more sorcerous talent than he suspected, but even a fool without a spark of sorcery in their body would have come to the same conclusion as the young mid.

"Well, Captain Nath has given me a list of tasks as long as my arm that I must attend to tomorrow," Yeardly sighed. "So, I'm off for a caulk. We only have a few more nights to enjoy a soft bed, so I'd best get as much joy of it as I can!"

After Yeardly's departure, Merryweather stealthily slid her chair a little closer to Enid and all but whispered, "Please do not take offense, Enid, but my deep affection for you demands that I ask you some questions that may seem impertinent."

Enid's frown would have been imperceptible to anyone who knew her less well than Merryweather, but it was there. "I cannot promise not to be offended by your question, but I promise I will balance any offense you cause against the affection we share."

"Are you well, Enid? Physically, you seem much recovered, but you seem disturbed by your experience. You are more snappish than usual, and your mannerisms are subtly different. Occasionally there is something to your posture when you stand that reminds me of someone else, though I cannot put my finger on whom."

A "snappish" response formed on her tongue, but she swallowed it. Merry was an observant officer and an attentive friend. It would be churlish to lash out at her for her concern. Instead, she covertly pressed her knee against hers and said, "I am well, but troubled. The workings I did to restore my hand were successful but may not be without consequence. I find that my ability in some matters has been greatly reduced. I can still perform my duties at a level that exceeds most of your navy's 'magisters' but I am noticeably diminished nonetheless. The problem occupies my mind and erodes my amity, what little I possess."

Her answer was true as far as it went. Her personal ability remained unchanged, but her *capability* was indeed diminished. Dunaughy was utterly silent for the first day or so after they completed the process of restoring her hand. It was early this very morning that she first found his thoughts intruding weakly on her own. His part of the task had left him all but depleted. Only the sorcerous safeguards they had in place kept him from vanishing into eternity's cold grasp. Who knew how long it would take for him to recover sufficiently to be of aid again?

For the nonce, at least, Enid was on her own, with no mentor a mere thought away to help her fulfill her duties.

Merryweather nodded and seemed relieved. "I surmised something of that nature might be at the roots of your, if you'll forgive the word, waspishness. I am much relieved to hear it from your lips, though, dear. I thought . . ."

"You thought what?"

"That you'd grown weary of our liaison," Merryweather said, and lowered her eyes.

"I must make a note of this in my private journal," Enid said. "I believe this is the first time you've uttered something so . . . well, *silly* seems to be the only word that will serve."

Merry returned her soft smile. "I would kiss you, but it would be an unacceptable breach of regulation to be seen showing such open affection, the both of us holding responsible positions in the Sea Service."

"Then perhaps we should follow Yeardly's example," Enid said. "As he said, we have only a few more nights to enjoy a soft bed. We should take as much joy of ours as we can."

chapter 10

Three days after Nath's orders were flung at him by the Sea Lord, *Revenant* returned to Middlesea Basin from Ordwych Yards, completely refitted and, other than the matter of a crew and victualing, ready to sail. Those days had not passed in indolent ease for Nath and his small core of officers and warrants, as the crowd of sailors and other ratings who stood in a loose formation behind him proved. Nearly a third of his *Alarum*s and *Redemption*s contrived to rejoin him after eluding press gangs that prowled Middlesea like packs of hungry wolves. They were joined by a mixed bag of lubbers and salts drawn to *Revenant* by the broadsheets posted wherever sailors were likely to gather, which promised glory and wealth to those bold enough to join her.

Further evidence of his energy and diligence took the form of a line of drays loaded with all the stores required to keep *Revenant*'s people fed for the duration of a long cruise. Gathering such a bounty required the greasing of many palms at a tremendous cost, but Nath didn't begrudge the expense. It was good to set sail with a full hold and, truth to tell, he could afford it. In the first month ashore, he was the recipient of a stream of recognition, often in a material form, from such worthies as the mayors of Middlesea and several other larger cities, various military orders, civic organizations, and wealthy aristocrats.

Nath had three gold- and jewel-encrusted swords, the sale of which would have supported him ashore for a year or more. He'd also been presented with several golden medals, a plethora of fine jewelry, and a half dozen or more ornate boxes filled with gold crowns. Enid had received her share of admiration as largesse, too, but she converted most of hers into hard specie and deposited it in the bank account her family maintained in Albion prior to the war, while Nath placed many of his trophies in the care of his newly hired man-of-business, Morlin Athern, of Athern, Athern, and Wycke, who also represented Admiral Weymouth and Nath's father.

"Why do we loiter so?" Enid asked, fidgeting with the gloves she'd taken to wearing since discovering her new hand transformed any otherwise reasonably well-mannered person within eyesight into a gawking, slack-jawed boor.

"She has barely run out to the end of her hawser, Enid," Nath said with a wry smile. "Besides, have you not taught me that haste is unseemly while so many look on?"

"You have a deplorable habit of only recalling my advice when it's useful to you as a weapon against me," Enid said, without a trace of heat. Nath and his little army of sailors (she was sure he'd suffer an actual pang of pain if she spoke such an ill-begotten phrase out loud) were indeed the subject of intense curiosity. Word spread quickly that he was on the Reaver's Steps and intended to read himself aboard *Revenant*, and, Enid believed, the gathering crowd might surpass the size of the one that had greeted his arrival in Middlesea.

Seeing her frown, Nath said, "I am a brute, Enid! You are recovering so swiftly from"—he gave his hand a loose-wristed waggle rather than mention her silver hand and the self-mutilation that preceded its attachment—"that I forget only a short time has passed since. It is fine for me to stand here on these damnably hard steps, but you should be seated! Look, there is a bollard yonder upon which you can take your ease until we depart."

"No," Enid said, simultaneously amused and offended by his

obvious distaste for her new hand, which was, she now knew, superior to her old, fleshy hand in all ways. Still, there were more magically learned people who would react with far more aversion, if not outright condemnation, than Nath, so she forbore confronting him on the subject. Instead, she sighed and said, "It is not that. I am as strong as ever. Besides, I lopped off a hand, not one of my feet. No, it is not the standing that discommodes me, it is the crowd. Close-packed people bring back memories of the mobs and riots I witnessed in Arden."

Nath nodded and leaned closer to Enid so he could speak without being overheard, "I understand. Some things attach themselves and will not lose their grip. While we slept in the Best Bower, the signal guns woke me at night. I would lay sleepless for as much as an hour at a time, seeing things behind my eyelids that I'd rather not recall or describe, but all things I'd seen—or done—in battle."

Enid nodded and answered in the same low tone, "My father had dreams that would wake him from a sound sleep shouting orders as if he were a general again, back in the wars with the Naveroña. Hearing a trumpet sounded as a signal or the cry of a horse in distress would drain the blood from his face."

Nath nodded. "Some things remain with us. I give you my word, I'll see us aboard as soon as can be. We are only waiting for the Fencibles to deliver the rest of our hands, with the Sea Lord's compliments."

"Why would Morrin do you a kindness?"

"He hasn't. The hands are all from Ainsley Bottom, probably dredged from the very worst of the mutineers."

Nath was as good as his word. Upon the arrival of the Fencibles, who were as coarse a looking bunch of ruffians as Enid had ever seen in the uniform of a king, Nath signed for the hands from Ainsley Bottom, placed them under the care of the master's mate with the able assistance of the Marine Corporal and most of Lieutenant Harcourt's lobsters, and then herded Enid, Lieutenant Merryweather, and Mid

Yeardly into a boat bound for the *Revenant*. When they were within shouting range, the yard hand hailed them, and Nath's coxswain raised one finger and shouted back, "Starboard!" as Nath ordered to avoid the necessity of a side party.

Lieutenant Dalroyd, commander of the yard party, welcomed them aboard with genuine pleasure. After exchanging salutes, Dalroyd held out his hand and said, "Lieutenant Bierce Dalroyd, Captain Nath, sir, and I beg your pardon, sir, but it would be my honor to shake your hand!"

"The pleasure is mine," Nath said and shook the young officer's hand vigorously. "Ashes, but don't the smell of fresh sawdust, paint, and tar make a morning bright? Our fine lady looks fit for the royal ball, Lieutenant! Pass my compliments on to your commander, sir, and pray grant your men a tot of rum before you depart!"

Dalroyd's grin was one of unalloyed pride. "Thank you, sir! I am gratified beyond reason that you are pleased with our work! Should I show you the major changes and improvements, or are you eager to formally take command of her?"

"Nothing would please me more, Lieutenant," Nath said, still smiling. "Who knows? It may be my last mortal pleasure!"

"Providence forfend, sir!" Dalroyd said. "You have already lived longer than any of your predecessors, though, so that is promising!"

Nath put Merryweather in charge of the ship's people before inspecting his command. Those who were not old *Alarum*s or *Redemption*s had been drawn by Nath's recruiting posters or were dragooned mutineers from the Bottom. Her orders were to survey the new *Redemption*s to ascertain their sailing skills and identify any promising candidates for vacant warrant or petty officer positions and place a mark by the names of any that were obviously hard bargains. Enid left Merry to her task and accompanied Nath on his tour of the rejuvenated *Revenant*.

Enid kept her otherworldly senses alert as she followed Nath and Lieutenant Dalroyd on a tour of the *Revenant* that meandered through her length, width, and depth. The young lieutenant's desire to present a detailed report of all the repairs and improvements he and his crew had made to the frigate provided Enid with ample opportunity to scour the vessel for the source of the darkness that hung over her like a cloud of doom.

She intensely regretted that the ordeal of creating her right hand had left Dunaughy so drained he dared not exert himself for fear of dissipating, despite the powerful new dweomers maintaining his spirit on the living side of mortality's veil. She had not realized how much his senses contributed to her ability to recognize presences or other anomalies in the non-corporeal realm. It was as if a blindfold covered one of her eyes when she peered into the invisible world. She was confident in her own astuteness, but it would have been comforting for Dunaughy to confirm he felt nothing out of the ordinary anywhere aboard *Revenant*.

As Enid searched *Revenant*'s invisible nooks and crannies for unwelcome and uncanny intruders, her mind registered most of the information Lieutenant Dalroyd had imparted to Nath, although the more esoteric portions of their conversation were beyond her ken. The changes to her armament, for instance, were impenetrable to her. She gathered *Revenant* had two new gun ports, raising her number of great guns to forty, all of which were heavier than those they replaced. She comprehended this readily, but the new, squat guns that graced the quarterdeck were a mystery to her.

They were ugly, stubby barreled beasts that hulked on equally unattractive carriages. She understood they were more powerful than the great guns but lacked their range. They were intended to savage an enemy vessel a couple of cables distant, not hundreds of yards away as the great guns could. It was hoped they would wreak such great havoc that the enemy would be forced to strike without the dangerous necessity of harrying them by sword, hatchet, and pistol. There were technical details that she was sure escaped her full comprehension, but on the whole, she understood the benefit of adding these new weapons, which both Nath and Dalroyd referred to as "smashers," to *Revenant*'s arsenal. She could not grasp, however, why they didn't signify for her gun count.

"So, *Revenant* is now a fifty-gun frigate?" she had asked Nath after Dalroyd had introduced them to the new guns.

"No," Nath said, looking as if she'd asked him if *Revenant* could fly. "She's only had two great guns added, which tots her up from a thirty-eight to a forty. It might not sound like so much of a difference, but—"

"Excuse me," she interrupted. "By my count, between the two new long guns and the ten 'smashers,' we've added twelve new guns. This brings her from thirty-eight to fifty guns."

Dalroyd had the temerity to chuckle and earned a mark of enmity from her, but Nath carefully and courteously explained that only the so-called great guns were counted toward a ship's rating. When Enid asked why this was the case, both he and Dalroyd stuttered out conflicting answers that they obviously found as unconvincing as she did. How the Albion navy could be so formidably consistent, fraught as it was with such inconsistencies, Enid knew not. She raised a hand as the two officers continued to grapple with a satisfactory reason for this strange custom and silenced them.

"It is not important. Pray, let us continue our stroll."

Despite her ongoing efforts to detect any curses or bane magic at work on *Redemption*, Nath's gratification that so notable a naval architect as Borelane agreed with his notes in the log regarding the proper rake of the masts was obvious. He volubly praised the new and improved pumps and capstans. She tuned out an apparently interminable conversation on the obvious wisdom of making some change or another to something called "the false keel" and similar technical gabble and was relieved that the next stop would be the tour's last.

When they reached prow of the ship, Dalroyd said, "Behold! A figurehead that suits a *Revenant* intent on vengeance!"

A pair of yard sailors heaved on ropes that lifted the canvas cover that concealed *Revenant*'s figurehead from view. Gone was the kind-faced, open-armed angel, replaced with a winged avenger wearing an expression of cold determination, a notch-bladed sword extended before her.

"Oh, ho!" Nath said with a fierce grin. "There is our *Revenant* personified. Albion's enemies will learn to fear her approach! Look at how cunningly her face is sculpted, Enid. I would swear I have seen it before!"

Enid noticed a distinct resemblance between the sculptor's work and that of Verity Hicks. The hairstyle was just as she'd worn for the sessions with Verity, down to the marquess's coronet that held it in place. "I believe it is me."

Lieutenant Dalroyd was delighted by her observation. "Indeed, it is, Magister d'Tancreville! I hope you will forgive me taking the liberty of memorializing your part in *Redemption*'s capture in my own way."

"I would have preferred it if you had asked my leave," Enid said coolly. "But I've learned that artists rarely stoop to such niceties when inspiration is upon them. And artist you are, if this is your work, sir."

The lieutenant seemed to have only absorbed the part of her remark praising his artistry and all but blushed. "Thank you, Magister. I can think of no greater compliment than that!"

"Your talents may be squandered in the navy, Lieutenant Dalroyd," Nath said. "If you could work marble as ably as this, the world would be your oyster."

"You are kind, sir," Dalroyd said. "Alas, this is but an extension of the whittling and wood carving I learned as mid. I've never touched a chisel to anything harder than ivory, I fear."

"Well, we were lucky you put your talent to work to our advantage, sir!"

"Thank you, Captain. I assure you my seamanship exceeds my skill with a carver's tools, however. In fact, I have left several affidavits stating as much on your desk. Each written and signed by a thorough tarpaulin sailor of a captain. You should be familiar with most of them, sir."

Nath turned from his close examination of the figurehead to give Dalroyd a searching look. "You wish to leave the yard for service aboard a frigate?"

"Not just any frigate, sir," Dalroyd answered, now standing at attention. "This frigate, under your command, sir. If you will have me."

"Hmmm." Nath tilted his head in a way Enid recognized as a sign that he was intrigued. "Gorwych Yard not to your liking?"

"My work there is valuable, sir, as you can see by the state of *Revenant*, but I believe I'd be more useful at sea."

"How did you come to be assigned to the yard, being such a tarhanded sailor as you say? Did you offend your captain, or gods save you, his admiral?"

"Nothing of the like, sir. The old *Rampant* paid off at the worst imaginable time, after a great number of new ships were assigned their companies. I accepted a commission at the yard to avoid being paupered. Mine is not a family of means, sir."

"I understand, sir," Nath said. "I can make no promises, but I will look at the affidavits you have left me and if they are as glowing as you say, I will request your reassignment—but be forewarned, Admiralty is unlikely to do me any favors."

"Thank you, sir!" Dalroyd said and snapped a salute. "Now, unless you have any further questions, I will gather my crew and leave *Redemption* in your hands, Captain."

Nath, whose face had taken on a stiffer set while he granted Dalroyd's request, was softened by a droll grin. "You won't stay to see if I survive the reading in, Lieutenant?"

"No, sir," Dalroyd said. "If *Revenant* wanted you dead, she would have struck you down before now."

When they had the fo'c'sle to themselves, Nath turned to Enid and asked, "Well?"

"Nothing," Enid said. "Nothing obvious, at least. There is a heaviness about the ship, relieved only by all the activity arising from bringing the crew aboard, the victualing, and so forth. When we all settle into a routine, her wrongness will be more obvious. The gloom will linger. I'd wager my lands on it, if any remained to me."

"Then it is safe for me to proceed with the reading in?"

"I counsel you to wait until tomorrow afternoon," Enid replied after a moment of thought. "That will give me ample time tonight to make preparations to safeguard you as best I may."

"That is a bitterly disappointing delay," Nath scowled. "I'd planned—"

"You may do as you will," Enid interrupted in a most unofficerly way, "but I firmly advise you to follow my counsel."

Nath sighed and nodded. "I would be a fool to ignore the advice of a sorcerer of your accomplishments. I will wait until one hour past noon, but then the formalities must be performed come hell or high winds."

At Nath's request, Enid took an early dinner with him in his dining cabin that afternoon. Compared to the space available on *Alarum*, the captain's rooms were palatial. As they ate a decent meal prepared by Nath's new steward, a tall, lean fellow with a somewhat cadaverous look accentuated by his pale, sunken cheeks and a deep-set right eye. The left was covered by a black patch that concealed its vacant socket but not the scars from the wound that emptied it.

"Fine work, Yarric," Nath said around a mouthful of well-seasoned mutton.

"Thankee, sir. I'm gratified you enjoy it," Yarric said in a deep, strangely hollow voice. "My family are fine restaurateurs, and I was well along in my training before I was pressed into service thanks to a weakness for powerful spirits."

"I saw no marks against your name for drunkenness," Nath said. "I assume you have your weakness strongly in hand now?"

"Yes, sir. I do not require a second scalding to learn the lesson of the first."

Nath smiled. "Well, your family's loss is my gain."

"I'm sure they'd be pleased to know it." Yarric's tone was inscrutable, but Nath frowned after he left the cabin.

"I'm grateful his family were chefs and not poisoners!"

"Sometimes they are one and the same. I assume it's the same in

Albion as Ardainne," Enid said lightly, but continued in a more serious tone. "You insist on sleeping aboard tonight?"

"I must, else the crew will think me fearful."

"How hypocritical of them, considering they have not been subject to *Revenant*'s predation."

Nath shook his head. "No, they have every right to expect their officers to exceed them in courage and diligence, or at least match them. If they must sleep aboard, I shall sleep aboard—and I expect my officers to do the same."

"Save your dour looks for the mids," Enid said with a dismissive wave. "I plan to follow your example regarding lodging tonight."

They drank wine in companionable silence for a time, and then Nath pulled a sheet of paper from within his coat.

"Please present this list to Lieutenant Merryweather. I find that I'm short a few items and I will have no time to see to them myself for some time. I'm sure you have a few similar odds and ends that you should see to before we prepare *Revenant* in earnest." Enid began to demur, but Nath pressed on over her. "I suggest that you both spend one more night ashore and see to the shopping as early tomorrow as possible. I doubt there will be much opportunity to go ashore before we depart on orders."

Enid took the paper and said, "You are most kind, Rue. I will make my preparations tonight and augment them tomorrow with certain components I can purchase ashore."

Nath nodded amiably, but admonished her as she took her leave, "Remember, Enid, I will read myself in an hour past noon, come what may!"

The next morning, Enid and Merryweather untangled themselves from one another and the sheets of their bed in the Best Bower. They parted ways after breakfast, Merry off to her duties aboard *Revenant* and Enid to an armorer's shop that traded in fine swords and pistols for the wealthy. There, at great expense, she purchased a pair of Kreitzer pistols similar in form to those of the Navy pattern for Captain Nath, by way of congratulations for his new command. Her own matched pair of Kreitzers, gifts from her murdered uncle Emile, were among her most prized possessions. She hoped these would serve him well and remind him of her friendship should she ever be carried off by a cannonball or falling spar. Her business there complete, she made her way to a shop specializing in sorcerous ephemera of utility to a ship's magister.

The shop's proprietor was extolling the exhaustive representation of ports in a fine walnut case of carefully labeled soil samples when Dunaughy's thoughts intruded on her own. *Ignore the rascal. He attempts to practice on you. The ship's master maintains a full collection of soil to be used for navigational purposes.There is no reason for a Ship's Magister to duplicate his efforts or expenses!*

Rather than hear his voice within her ears as she had in the past, his thoughts mingled with hers. It was jarring, particularly as she knew explicitly that he found it as disturbing as she. Their thoughts and feelings blended in a manner that exceeded their former relationship, grown to an extent they both found awkward and infinitely disturbing. In that instance, for example, she had a complete understanding of Murchadhan fiduciary philosophy.

And you are a spendthrift who forgets that your opinions are now open to my examination. I am not "cheap," as you think, but merely protective of my silver. I have lived in poverty before and I have no desire to do so again, even vicariously, Dunaughy thought archly.

You have little to fear on that front, short of us being tossed ashore on a desert isle. Between my share of the prize money, the proceeds of Verity's engravings, and the funds secreted away in Albion by my uncle prior to the Theocracy seizing power in Ardainne, I am far removed from poverty.

His approbation was as tangible as if it were her own. *So thought many a person of means before they were crushed beneath the descending Wheel of Fate. At any gate, you have no use for this sharp's questionable dust. You should be well set up now.*

Enid confused the merchant by simultaneously nodding and pushing the soil sample case firmly away.

"I believe I will make do with the master's collection," she told him with a cold glare. "Now, be so kind as to bundle my other purchases quickly, as my time is at a premium."

As the merchant, no doubt cursing himself for pushing this neophyte magister too far in his campaign to extravagantly lighten her purse, Enid engaged with Dunaughy.

I am overjoyed to "hear" you again, Dunaughy! Your long silence left me fearing the worst.

She felt Dunaughy's irritation melt into a fondness of surprising depth. *I would have spoken to you sooner, lass, but I was too weak. In all truth, I'm too weak to spend much time in this conversation, but I was compelled to confirm for you that our workings were a complete success. The process took most of my strength, though, and left me on the very verge of dissipation. I fear it will be some days until I am fully recovered. Until then I must leave you to your own ends and husband my strength like a miser—which, by your estimation of my character, should be easy enough.*

Her lips curled into a mischievous grin that she had never worn before, but suspected it frequented Dunaughy's mien when he lived.

The merchant gave her an odd look. "My lady?"

"It is nothing. A wayward thought," Enid snapped. "I need those parcels before the sun goes out, if it pleases you!"

I must retreat and rest, Dunaughy thought. *Do not be alarmed by my silence. I am well and will rejoin you when I have recovered enough to permit it.*

I have other questions, tarry but a moment and—but she found her mind was entirely her own again.

Outside, the sun was inching toward its zenith over Middlesea's smoke-choked skyline. She stowed her new purchases next to the other parcels, boxes, and bags that filled half the floor space and benches of her hired coach, being careful not to crush the boxes containing an ample supply of the best cigarillos available in Albion.

She found Yeardly on the Steps, overseeing the loading of the wine and victuals for the mids' berth into one of *Revenant*'s boats. He was engaged in conversation with a cox'n as she approached, and she recognized the man from her time aboard the *Alarum*. She returned his smile with a thin version of her own as she approached.

"It's a fine thing to have you with us again, Magister d'Tancreville. We're all cheered by having you aboard, what with your command of the arts and all," the cox'n said. She thanked the fellow and patted his shoulder awkwardly. Before losing her hand, she'd made a pact with Dunaughy to be less distant to the ship's people.

She joined Yeardly and asked, "Has he proclaimed himself captain of the ship yet?"

Yeardly shook his head. "No, he is awaiting your arrival, and good on him for that."

"Indeed," Enid said. "Would you be so kind as to have a couple of your people add the bundles and packages? They'll find them in yon carriage topped by an impatient-looking driver. Bid them have a care if you would. Some of the items are quite delicate."

Within a quarter of an hour, the oarsmen were pulling hard for the *Revenant* where she rocked gently at anchor. The impression she gave of a hulking, malevolent shadow was not relieved by the bright light of the sun, which was reaching its zenith overhead. Enid was reminded again of her first sight of the frigate, then called *Redemption*, and the chill that seized her bones and thickened her blood. The vessel radiated a threatening aura of hatred that was all but palpable. She'd seemed an ill-omened vessel at first sight, but Enid credited that to the fact that she was in enemy hands. Now, here in the hands of her own countrymen, indeed, in the bosom of her motherland, *Revenant* seemed more bitterly bloodthirsty than ever. She was a bride of Woe, and her attendants were Sorrow and Loss.

Yeardly, who noted her fixed stare, asked her in a low voice, "Does she look more menacing today? As if she were provoked?"

Enid nodded but said nothing. Yeardly's innate talent impressed her, but her attention was so captured by the floating ogre before her that she had none to spare. It did look as if it had been provoked to anger by some action of theirs. Was it the preparations she had made? Nath's sleeping through the night in the captain's quarters? Or perhaps it was aware of his intent to read himself in?

"Ahoy the boat!" The shouted challenge from *Revenant's* port-side watch startled Enid. Ordinarily, she would have been embarrassed by her start, but Yeardly's own alarmed jerk was so violent that she doubted he noticed hers at all. The cox'n's answer and hand signals informed the watch that none of the boat's passengers merited a side party. Despite the heat of the day, the battens were icy cold in her grip as she scrambled up the tumble home.

"Have all of my packages tied with green twine delivered to my workspace as soon as may be," she directed Yeardly when they were both on deck. "I have preparations to complete and only a short time to do so. Make haste at what you're doing here and join me below as quick as may be."

Enid dragooned Yeardly into assisting in her final arcane survey of *Revenant* before Nath assumed her command, assuming he survived the attempt. The mid trailed along behind her, bearing a few of her instruments and applicable books while she examined everything above deck minutely. She was not surprised to find nothing save a dolorous undertone to the ship's energies, and it was no more than to be expected from a vessel that had witnessed as much treachery, death, dismemberment, and cruelty as this one. The dark aura was stronger belowdecks, but not alarmingly so, considering *Revenant*'s gloomy history. It was commonly known that all edifices that saw tragedy, slaughter, and sorrow bore their stains, imprinted with the energies of those lamentable episodes long after they occurred. After an hour of clamoring up and down ladders and exploring *Revenant*'s darkest, most malodorous recesses, Enid said, "Well, that is that."

"What are your conclusions?" Yeardly asked.

"What are yours?"

Yeardly chewed his lip thoughtfully for a moment and then spoke slowly. "It seems there is something here."

"Is it malevolent?"

"Perhaps. It is certainly—" Yeardly struggled for the right word.

"Stealthy," Enid suggested.

"Stealthy," Yeardly agreed. "And predatory."

"I agree," Enid said. "Your instincts are keen, Mid Yeardly. It is a shame that your arcane potential is to be wasted on something so mundane as a lieutenancy."

Yeardly bristled. "So, has Captain Nath wasted his potential as an officer in the Royal Navy by your estimation? Or Lieutenant Merryweather?"

"Of course not," Enid said. "They are vastly superior to me in their callings, and I could not match their accomplishments if I were to live three lifetimes. Their gifts are not mine. Your sorcerous potential, however, is another matter. Your ambitions are your own, and I have no doubt that you would make a fine sea officer, but I beg you not to blithely dismiss your uniquely fine talent."

Yeardly heaved a heavy sigh. "I understand, Magister. Still, the question is moot for the nonce. No decision is required until I pass for lieutenant, which will never occur until the captain recommends me to stand before the examination board, a prospect that doesn't seem eminent, as swiftly as he wishes *Revenant* ready to proceed to sea."

Enid made a noncommittal noise, and they made their way out of the stifling orlop toward the open air above.

Nath stood at the break of the quarterdeck with the crew drawn up in an approximation of divisions on the deck below. Enid stood behind him on his left, her eyes staring blankly ahead, ready to protect him however she could if the need should arise. There was a collective intake of breath as he produced his orders from within his coat and unfolded them with unconscious ceremony. She noticed the eyes of the crew nearest her rolled from side to side in search of the instrument of Nath's demise as he began to speak in that strong, vibrant voice that seemed so out of place emanating from such a small frame.

"People of the *Redemption*, I have the honor to present His Majesty's commission, dated the fourteenth of November in this present year, appointing me, Rue Nath, Commander in His Majesty's Royal Navy, to the command of His Majesty's Ship *Revenant*. By the authority vested in me by these orders," he said, pausing to raise those sacred documents above his head for all to see, "I do now assume command, somberly cognizant of the Crown and Admiralty's expectations and the peril of incurring their displeasure at the performance of my duties.

"I expect the utmost from every officer, seaman, and marine in the performance of their duty. I will accept nought but complete commitment to duty, discipline, and conduct befitting the service of our sovereign. As to your expectations of me, you have my word that I will treat fairly with you. You may trust my judgment to be balanced and impartial. The discipline I dole out will fit the nature of the offense and will not be tainted by arbitrary brutality.

"I know many of you and will know all of you by week's end. I trust in your skill and courage, old hand and new, and I give you my word as your captain that I will endeavor, with all diligence and resolve, to guide this ship and her company to honor and victory."

"Now, I am not so in love with my own voice that I will keep you from your duties," he said in a more conversational tone that still carried from *Revenant*'s stern to her stem. "But there I would like to address the deaths of the four captains before me. I admit that they all suffered strange and untimely ends and I have no easy answer for their poor turn of luck.

"I can, however, assure you that *Revenant* is *not* accursed. The *Alarum*s among you will testify that we suffered no hardships on the cruise home. Indeed, we took the barky into battle against a superior enemy and defeated them utterly."

Nath gave the *Alarums* below a moment or two to mutter their assent before raising his hand for silence.

"Now, let us be about our duties," Nath said, gesturing toward the forbidding face of the Admiralty building that brooded behind him. "The gods look down upon us mere mortals. Let us give them an admirable showing."

As he stepped away, Lieutenant Merryweather led the crew in raising three hurrahs before beginning the onerous task of signing them into the ship's log, rating them, and assigning them a watch and division.

She found Nath on the quarterdeck, engaged in amiable conversation with Lieutenant Wilk, an officer she recognized from Nath's reading in. When Nath spotted her and Yeardly, he waved them over with a smile.

"Mid Yeardly, you've already met Lieutenant Wilk," Nath said. "But allow me to introduce you, Magister d'Tancreville. This is Second Lieutenant Wilk; Lieutenant Wilk, this is Magister d'Tancreville."

Lieutenant Wilk took her right hand, still wrapped in a glove in deference to Nath, and said, "Your exploits since joining the Sea Service are well-known and impressive. It will be a great comfort to have a magister of your capabilities aboard, Lady d'Tancreville."

His voice was smooth and warm, but she detected none of that warmth in his eyes, which remained flat and unreadable despite his friendly smile.

"It is an honor to meet you, sir," Enid said as she extricated her hand from his firm, dry grip.

"You should feel more secure with Lieutenant Wilk aboard, Magister," Nath said. "He is a formidable fellow. He was about to share the tale of his last command, so your arrival was well-timed."

He looked formidable indeed. He was a tall man and strongly built. Like Nath, he wore his own hair, which was blond, tied back in the navy man's ubiquitous queue. His features were strong and a bit craggy. The skin of his face was tanned as dark as old leather, a condition that made his pale blue eyes seem to sparkle and flash with an unnatural fire.

"I'm the officer who lost the *Sprite*." Enid arched a brow at the statement, but he smiled and continued, "I'm also the officer that got her back. You may have read about it, sir."

"Enid, you're familiar with the story of Wilk of the *Sprite* brig, of course," Nath said, clapping her on the shoulder. He ignored her blank expression and enthused, "Quite a story and nothing to be ashamed of in it! It could have happened to any of us, and when the opportunity came for you to set things right, you did so in a grand style. I commend your sense of justice, sir!"

"Your approval is a welcome honor, sir," Wilk said with a smile. "It was a terrible adventure and there are some who haven't been so charitable regarding my role in the loss of the *Sprite*."

"What was this terrible adventure, then?" Enid's curiosity was piqued. She produced a cigarillo, which Wilk gladly accepted but plunged into his coat pocket rather than lighting.

"I'll save this for the end of the watch, if you don't mind, Magister. As for my adventure, well, I was Third aboard *Implacable*, 74 guns. We were cruising the Merentian Approaches and snatching up Ardain prizes left and right. One of them was a particularly fine little brig of war—an Ardain privateer. Captain Macheadd put me in her with a prize crew and orders to sail with all haste for Gisbon and return as soon as ever I may upon the next frigate or sloop of war headed for the Merentian."

"This would have been about the time we were bringing *Redemption* home to Albion, Enid," Nath explained. "The Strait would have been thick with Ardain privateers hoping to snatch us up."

"Precisely so, sir," Wilk agreed with a somber nod. "And we were about halfway across when we ran afoul of a powerful Ardain brig, heavily gunned, fast, and full to the brim with boarders."

"What did you do?"

"What else could we do, Magister? We ran!" Wilk smiled emotionlessly. "But we couldn't outfly the *Bon Chance*, for so our privateer was named. She ran us down, and we exchanged fire until *Sprite*'s mainmast was shot away. At that point I struck."

Nath nodded. "What was the butcher's bill to that point?"

"One dead outright, three wounded to various degrees. I went aboard with ten. But the deck was positively shrouded in fallen rigging and we lost way shockingly fast—the winds were variable and light as the hair on a courtesan's"—Wilk remembered his company and cleared his throat—"neck."

"I would call that wisely done. Once you lost the ability to maneuver or work the guns, the battle was over. To fight on would have needlessly jeopardized your men's lives."

"Not that it did the poor devils much good—but I truly appreciate your approval, sir. I know your reputation and feared you might think me shy."

"I judge my officers by their actions under my command," Nath said with a touch of reproach, but a sudden smile warmed his tone. "And in any case, I think the end of the tale puts paid to any doubts about your courage. Now, what happened when the Rats boarded you?"

"The prize crew was apparently frenzied by their losses—our little cannons worked some havoc among their boarders, packed on deck cheek against jowl as they were. They immediately set about beating the men, even the wounded wretches, and for a moment I thought we were all to be slaughtered. Their lieutenant, a ruffian by the name of Jardin, was the worst of the lot. When one of the wounded lads didn't move fast enough to please him, the bastard took to kicking him in his broken leg. When I intervened, he raised his sword to strike me down."

"What saved you?" Enid asked. She knew the type of men who manned Ardain privateers were no better than pirates before the revolution. Now they must be monsters indeed.

"My dog, Otto, actually. A beautiful black and silver Ostmark terrier. He set up such a snarling, barking display that the Rat backed off three steps." Wilk smiled for a moment at the memory and then shook his head sadly. "Cost the loyal brute his life, though. Jardin bashed his head in with a boarding ax and then strutted around as if he'd defeated a lion with his bare hands. Pathetic stuff. Even his own rascals seemed disgusted by it. I need not tell you that I was beside myself with anger. I broke free of one of the fellows holding me and caught Jardin across the jaw with my fist. Then they beat me with belaying pins till I blacked out."

Nath's eyes smoldered, but he remained silent.

These Albions and their dogs, Enid thought with an inward smirk. *Hardly a blink of an eye when a wounded man is abused, but let a dog be mistreated!*

"When I came to, I was tied to a chest in the captain's cabin." Remembered pain twisted Wilk's face into a momentary grimace. "I was on my back and my hands and feet were tied together on either side of the chest. As I lay there, Jardin and his favorites took turns insulting me and beating me. Three of my ribs were stove in during their little games—they've only just healed.

"They kept me bound that way for a day, neither feeding me nor giving me so much as a taste of water. I suspect Jardin planned to liven up his voyage home by watching me die tied to that damned chest. Unfortunately for him, his topmen weren't nearly as attentive to their tasks as he was to me. By the time they spotted *Implacable* bearing down on them, it was too late to flee. Captain Macheadd recognized *Sprite* immediately and put on as much sail as necessary to run her down as swiftly as possible."

Wilk gave a sardonic chuckle. "Jardin came rushing into the cabin and began pleading for his life. I'll never forget his filthy, Rat-accented Albion: 'Please, *mon ami*, Mercy! Mercy on poor Jardin, a right bon homme!' If I never hear that gabble again it will be too soon."

"I'll try to keep my Rat accent to a minimum," Enid drawled.

The lieutenant smiled and waved an apologetic hand. "It is not the same, Magister. It wasn't the man's nationality that made his accent so odious to my ears, it was his character. It was as if a bedbug suddenly learned to walk on its hind legs and talk like a man—repulsive to the eyes and ears."

Enid nodded. "I have no love for his kind, either. How did you answer him?"

Wilk smiled more broadly. "Untie me, I said, and I will see to it that you are given every mercy you deserve. He gestured to one of his men, who cut me loose. I let them help me to my feet. Then, while they were smiling and patting me on the back and breathing their damned garlic breath all over me, I snatched a cutlass from the hands of the one to my left and buried it in his skull. Then there was a merry game of tag around the cabin, I can tell you! Every swing of my cutlass found flesh and bone, packed in as close as we were in that cramped space. The fight had already gone out of the swine, so they didn't put up much of a struggle. Mostly they scrambled, screamed, and begged for mercy. I showed them all the mercy they showed poor Otto, and that was too good for 'em."

"How many were there?" Enid asked, her face pale.

"Jardin and four more."

She couldn't keep the plain horror out of her voice as she asked, "You slaughtered five men for killing a dog?"

Wilk shrugged. "He was a good dog. Besides, when the rest of the Rats surrendered, we discovered Jardin had ordered the wounded men thrown overboard to drown. I believe the Redeemer guided my hand that day. There was a monster there that needed killing."

Enid nodded slowly. She did not doubt that a monster had been aboard *Sprite*—in fact, she imagined monsters were in the majority that day.

"I'm surprised you weren't made Master and Commander after such a display of starch," Nath said. Then, his eyes narrowing, he asked, "Or is there more to this story?"

Wilk nodded and chuckled bitterly. "Indeed there is, sir. It seems First Lord Morrin despises dogs aboard ship—or any other pets, for that matter. He blamed Jardin's behavior on poor Otto. *If your damned dog hadn't infuriated the Rat lieutenant, he wouldn't have behaved so savagely!* Ha! Set aside that if it hadn't been for my damned dog, Jardin would have split my head like a melon! So now I'm in Lord Morrin's bad graces—I understand the First Lord doesn't lose much love for you either, sir?"

Nath drew himself up to his full height, back straight as a plumb line, and said coolly. "It would be unseemly to speak of any personal differences that might exist between myself and any superior officer. Perhaps you should take that to heart yourself."

He softened the reproach by offering the lieutenant his hand. "I congratulate you on avenging your noble dog and murdered men, Lieutenant Wilk. Now, I believe you have a watch to finish, and I have some logs to review."

"Yes, sir—but may I speak to a personal matter before I leave?"

Nath nodded.

"Sir, I have—well, I have another dog. Another Ostmark terrier named Jock. I was hoping you might allow me to keep him on board."

"Jock?" Nath arched a brow. "That's not an Ostmark name."

Wilk smiled nervously. "No, sir, it's not. But he looked like a Jock, so . . ."

Nath nodded again. "Very well. Under the circumstances, I have no objections."

"Thank you, sir!" Wilk made his salute with professional grace and returned briskly to his duties.

When Wilk was out of earshot, Enid said, "Did you observe the lack of passion in his eyes as he delivered his tale? I have only seen that peculiarly flat affect on the faces of certain professional duelists, a monster I saw executed for atrocities against his own family, and the executioner who sent him to his just reward. That man is a killer through and through. War only gives him an excuse to practice his trade: murder."

"Perhaps," Nath said. "But so far he's chosen only the right victims, wouldn't you say?"

"As you will, then," Enid said, pushing down the ire rising in response to Nath's easy dismissal of her observation. She turned to Yeardly and said, "Mid Yeardly, there is a mahogany box on my writing table. If you are not otherwise employed, please fetch it for me."

Yeardly grinned and tugged his forelock before trotting off on his mission.

"While he may have behaved like a wild dog the instance of your meeting, it is clear you have found a faithful hound in Mid Yeardly," Nath observed with a smile. "I hope his devotion has been as beneficial to you as it has been to him. Since frequenting your company, he has become a far more focused and responsible young gentleman. He begins to remind me of the friend he lost in action, Mid Cullen, and that is high praise, indeed."

Enid shrugged. "I have learned most of what I know of the ship's daily operation and the mysteries of naval courtesy from him and Lieutenant Merryweather. So, I suppose our time together has been mutually beneficial. He is a fine young man."

"Why, Enid," Nath said, his eyes glittering with mischief. "Control your effusiveness!"

Her only response was a haughty sniff. They stood in silence for the few minutes required to return the box, which Yeardley presented to Enid with the same deference as he might have shown presenting a crown to a queen.

"My thanks, Mid Yeardly," she said and offered the box to Nath.

"For me?" Nath was clearly pleasantly surprised as he examined the deeply polished mahogany box and ran his fingers across the blank gold plaque centered on its lid.

"I will coax an engraving on to it when you can spare me a moment with it," Enid said, mentally cursing herself for not attending to that minor task *before* handing the box over to Nath.

He nodded as he carefully placed the box on the edge of the binnacle and opened the two gold hasps that held it closed. He lifted the lid and his face transformed from amiable curiosity into shocked pleasure.

"Kreitzers! A pair of them!"

Enid nodded in feigned nonchalance, despite the racing heartbeat engendered by the evident joy her gift produced in Nath. "They are the twin-barreled variety, for which we share a liking. I hope they serve you as well as mine have served me."

"This is damned handsome of you, Enid." Nath grinned, forgetting himself in the moment. "I have long wanted just such a pair—and look, they are decorated with fine engravings of a frigate flying before the wind—but the expense—" He paused a moment and then offered the box back to her. "Enid, this is too grand a gift!"

"It is not nearly grand enough for the service you've granted me," she said, and turned to walk away, leaving Nath to marvel at his wonderful new pistols. Later, as she caught up on her journal at the writing desk in her cabin, she heard a series of sharp cracks from above and knew that Nath was putting his new pistols to use, plinking at bobbing crates and bottles tossed overboard for that purpose. The thought brought a rare, unrestrained smile to her face, which set Dunaughy to chuckling with shared glee.

At Merryweather's behest, Yeardly was on the orlop, inspecting the stores stowed there to ensure they were adequately secured and well distributed when he encountered the old salt. He didn't recognize the fellow, who was apparently one of the new hands. He had a confident air about him that contradicted any idea that he was one of the press gang's lubbers, but his hair and beard were long and shaggy. He knuckled his brow in salute.

"What are you about down here?" Yeardly's voice was firm but not accusatory.

"Much the same as you, I 'spect, sor," the oldster said in a deep and steady voice. "Checkin' the binding and balance o' the stores down here. The work crew was a mixed bag. I'm too old to sink under the waves 'cause some fool don't know his knots."

Yeardly nodded, strangely unnerved by the fellow's relatively innocuous comment. "Good on you for your diligence, Mr.—?"

"Oak, sir."

"Very well, Mr. Oak, you may go. I'll finish down here. You may trust me to keep you above the waves."

"You promise, sor?" The old man's eyes reflected the orb hanging above them like white-hot embers and his voice was deathly serious.

"I promise that I'll do all that I may to keep you and everyone else aboard on the right side of the waves." The moment seemed grave and momentous to Yeardly as he spoke.

"Thankee, sor!" The old salt knuckled his brow in a parting salute, his untamed beard shifting in a way that suggested a smile hidden in its depths.

Yeardly watched Mr. Oak go. The oldster left behind the soft smell of fresh dirt and spoiled meat.

chapter 11

Nath's review of Lieutenant Merryweather's accounting of the hands was not encouraging. While all of *Alarum*'s commission and warrant officers weren't available, as they were far more challenging to protect from reassignment, he was in a bad way along the lines of ship's people. As it stood, half his hands were *Alarum*s whom Emley had abused the Sea Lord's stamp to preserve from being taken up by other captains, while the other half were a mixture of Ainsley Bottom mutineers foisted on him by the Sea Lord and landsmen and a few salts attracted by his recruitment broadsides. Lieutenant Oxley resigned his commission in favor of a position on a privateer partially funded by his prize money, leaving *Revenant* with two lieutenants, other than a young lieutenant the Sea Lord himself assigned, who had yet to present themself. He was even short mids, having only Yeardly, Dinwitty, and Harlech at hand.

As intimidating as the task was, he attacked it with all his energy and attention. He was no Ambrose Aixely. He did not spend the ever-shortening time left to him indulging in the pleasures of the home port. Instead, he poured himself into the tasks at hand, starting each day well before dawn and rarely ceasing his labors until after midnight. He kept his clerk, an old *Alarum* hand, working like the devil to keep up with the flow of official requests, letters to former shipmates in positions to assist him, and his man of business. He spent a few hours ashore each day to engage in personal appeals and meetings with his cabal of supporters to contrive new tactics to address his troubles.

One week after reading himself in, Nath was pleased to have all *Revenant*'s officers, warrants, and mids aboard and settled into their berths. Lieutenant Harcourt and his lobsters were aboard, their numbers slightly enhanced at Harcourt's request, citing *Revenant*'s greater size and the restive nature of her crew. Nath experienced a tinge of shame for being relieved at the windfall, but the mood before the mast was undeniably unsettled.

While the morale of the old hands was bolstered by the victories they had achieved, the prize money in their purses (if any remained), and the efforts Nath had taken to see to their well-being, they were also victims of Admiralty's malicious whims. It was clear to the dullest among them that the Sea Lord did not care a whit how deeply they suffered from his pursuit of a vendetta against their captain. Many of his old hands had a deep empathy for the Ainsley Bottom jacks and were appalled by the treachery they had experienced at the Sea Lord's hands. Their jointly shared grudge against Viscount Morrin was grounds for unity, but it was a perilous, bare-toothed threat to discipline aboard *Revenant*.

"Providing them with a better rallying point is my most pressing and difficult task," Nath said one evening as he and Enid shared a glass of brandy and fine cigarillos, taking in the view of Middlesea's twinkling lights through the dark forest of masts that grew from the myriad vessels anchored in the Basin.

Enid nodded.

"The atmosphere aboard is not as intense as that of the streets of Arden before the storming of the palace, but the sense that a fuse will soon be lit is not dissimilar to the quiet before the revolt consumed Arden."

While walking about to acquaint herself with *Revenant*, she recognized more than a few faces from *Alarum* and shared a smile and decorously cordial greeting with each of them. There were as many strange faces as familiar, though, most of whom confronted her with a mixture of dread and awe. The rest were unapologetically sullen, some bordering on insolent. Enid was empathetic enough to the plight of these wretches, knowing they were effectively enslaved by Admiralty, which worked them until their bodies broke and then discarded them when they were no longer valuable, all the while paying them a pittance of a wage that was typically months in arrears.

"Blood them at the first opportunity, then?" Enid asked. There was no trace of rebuke or condescension in her voice. She had seen how remarkably a victorious skirmish could meld new and old hands on a vessel together as tightly as the folds of a steel in a Malasfandyari sword.

"Perhaps, depending on the nature of our orders," Nath said. "Now that everything is stowed and the barky is in as much sailing trim as she may be while bobbing at the end of a hawser, I believe I will begin mum drills with the great guns and training in the operation of the smashers. I'd prefer to drill with powder and shot as we have an abundance of both, and nothing livens your gun crew like as the almighty bang of the gun and the snap of the restraining lines halting its recoil. I suspect the Master of the Basin would object, though."

"As would the vessels anchored nearby," Enid said. "It goes without saying, I hope, that if I can aid in any way, I am at your full disposal."

"Thankee, Enid," Nath said. "And it does indeed go without saying. At the moment, you can serve *Revenant* best by ensuring the rum-soaked yard magisters didn't flub any of the ship's basic enchantments—and keep a weather eye peeled for signs of curses or what-have-you the Naveroñians may have left for us."

The day was clear and fine, so Enid put it to good use wandering about *Revenant* for no better cause than a desire to admire the spectacle of Middlesea Basin and make her face known to the new hands. She eventually found a spot in the fo'c'sle where she could stand out of the way of the hustle and bustle involved in the final preparations to sail.

As she gazed at the pleasant prospect of wisps of cotton white clouds drifting languorously past the lazy, circular dance of the tops, she became aware of a conspicuous absence from the ship's complement. When she saw a sailor she was familiar with from Yeardly's division, she called out to him.

"If you've a moment, Bolls, where is our lovely mascot, Lady Chum-Chum?"

Bolls knuckled his brow, pleased that Spells recognized him by name. "She is aboard, Magister, but she's havin' a rough time adjustin' to the new barky. She spends most of her time wrapped tight around the mainmast, just where it passes through the main fightin' top."

"Is she ill?" Enid asked. "It would be a shame to lose such a vibrant splash of color from our company. If she requires the aid of a veterinarian, bring her to me and I will see to her care from my own purse!"

"I don't think it will come to that," Bolls said with a wide smile. "She is certainly not off her feed, the great greedy girl. I will pass the word around to have her delivered to you if she needs a visit to an animal surgeon, though, and good on you for carin' so for our dear lady."

Enid treated him to one of the rare slight upward curls at the corners of her lips that served her as a smile. "Ladies of quality must support one another, Mr. Bolls. Especially if they both value time spent alone and their meals delivered by their admirers."

"I reckon you're right, milady, and besides, my mum taught me never to argue with a lady!" Bolls laughed cheerfully and saluted her again before leaving.

Enid was in her cabin when Merryweather found her with Nath's "invitation" to join him at dinner.

"The full complement of officers are aboard," Merryweather said. "Including our mysterious new Third Luff, courtesy of the Sea Lord."

"Even so? What did you make of them?"

"He came aboard while I was settling in the new mids, so I had no opportunity to form an opinion on anything but his provenance, which I know you share."

"What are your thoughts on our fresh mids, then?"

"They are older on the main and should be well-enough seasoned to help Yeardly get the lubber into a useful state. We're awash with 'em from the captain's recruiting broadside."

"Volunteers eager for action with our good captain should help balance out the sullen recalcitrance of the Ainsley people."

"From your lips to the Redeemer's ears."

"The Ainsley folk aside, Nath is far more fortunate in the quantity of sailors and provisions on this cruise than he enjoyed aboard *Alarum*."

"I believe he's intent on demonstrating the wealth of his larder at tonight's dinner, so prepare to tuck in with vigor," Merryweather said with a smile and a wink. "You may want to wear one of your looser uniforms."

Enid arrived for dinner early, as was her habit, but found Nath's dining cabin already crowded with officers seated elbow-to-elbow around the table. A vacant seat was set aside for her next to Merryweather and across from Captain Nath. Dr. Rondelle was there, looking as pinched and irascible as ever, as was the equally familiar and far more attractive person of Marine Lieutenant Harcourt. His new Second Lieutenant, a severe-looking, dark-skinned woman with close-cropped hair, sat next to him, back straight and hands folded in her lap. There was an empty seat on the opposite side of the table that Enid assumed was reserved for Nath's infamous new Third Lieutenant. Nath had banished Maubin and Marbury from the gathering, knowing from experience that sea officers, nearly to a soul, were easy marks for the pleading eyes and whining protestations of starvation from plump-bellied pups.

Nath checked his new pocket watch, an elegant device of silver and gold, and was about to speak when the marine sentry outside the door stamped his feet and opened the dining cabin door.

Nath put away his watch and said, "Ah! Here is our last hold-out, Lieutenant Leonid Bascombe. Here, sir, we've saved a spot for you."

Bascombe made his courtesies and smiled a chilly but civil smile. "I'm obliged to you, sir. I apologize for my tardiness."

Nath waved the apology aside. "You were on watch, Lieutenant. Watch duty takes precedent over vittles, even those served at your captain's table."

Enid schooled her features into a courtier's blank mask. She was surprised she had not foreseen this eventuality. Who would be better for that snake Morrin to place on *Revenant* than Harde's fellow asp? The Sea Lord was a fool if he expected her to rise to such obvious bait.

As Yarric passed around the table and deftly filled their glasses with a decent Velascin vintage, Nath began the introductions.

"Some of you are old shipmates and know each other passing well, but there are many new faces at the table, so I think it best to acquaint you all with one another. I believe you have all met First Lieutenant Merryweather by now?"

Nods rippled around the table, so Nath pointed at Wilk and said, "And here is my Second Lieutenant, Ample Wilk. You may have read about his recent action in the *Naval Times*. Take a lesson from the story and do not abuse his dog!"

He waited for the amused chuckles and Rondelle's scandalized sniff to subside before continuing. "Here is Lieutenant Leonid Bascombe, our Third Lieutenant. He is a young but eminently capable officer and, judging by my own observation, a gentleman of high standards."

Bascombe muttered his thanks and, to Enid's surprise, blushed.

"Last, but far from least, allow me to present our new Fourth Lieutenant, Lieutenant Bierce Dalroyd, late of the Gorwych Yards and a solid sea record afore that. He brings a deep knowledge of naval engineering and solid seamanship, both of which will serve *Revenant* well."

Dalroyd's broad smile at Nath's praise and the puppy-like joy with which he received the welcome of fellow officers proved that one thing he did not bring with him was the usual "officerly reserve" that turned one into a stone-faced monument to rectitude.

Nath raised his glass to the two marine officers and said, "As for our marine officers, I'm pleased to welcome Lieutenant Amiable Harcourt back as *Revenant*'s Captain of Marines, and introduce his second-in-command, Lieutenant Udrin Gardner. I had the benefit of Lieutenant Harcourt's efficiently drilled marines on my last cruise, and I'm sure that his newer, expanded troop will benefit from his efforts and those of Lieutenant Gardner."

Lieutenant Harcourt raised his glass to those gathered around the table, while Lieutenant Gardner sat stiffly at his side like a vaguely affronted sphinx. *What a cold, distant creature*, Enid thought. *She may have a difficult time in the close confines of what the sailors sometimes called the steep-sided tub.* Enid had no sympathy to spare for her, though. Such folk paved their own paths with ice and had only themselves to blame if they slipped.

"I believe we're all accounted for now, as Master Kaliktiklak has duties that excuse him from our gathering," Nath said. "Now let us put business aside until we've polished off this fine dinner, courtesy of the admirable Mr. Yarric's art."

Art was indeed the right word for Mr. Yarric's viands. While he only presented them with three removes, each was more toothsome than the last. The quality of the food and the perfect choice of accompanying wines produced an effect that Enid had never witnessed at a shipboard dinner: silence. It was only broken when the last of the tureens, bowls, plates, and silver were removed from the table and wineglasses had been exchanged for glasses of a warm, tawny Oporto.

"Be at ease," Nath said and leaned back in his chair to unbutton his vest with obvious relief. "Ashes! Yarric outdid himself. If he persists to feed me like an admiral, I will soon roll around *Revenant* like a great ball of blubber!"

"And have officers who roll about their duties like marbles in a puzzle box," Merryweather said. "You must curb the rascal, sir, before we're all as fat as Maubin and Marbury!"

"Yes," Harcourt agreed with a wide grin. "But perhaps that can wait until we're out to sea or inbound at the end of the cruise."

When the good-natured chuckles and several toasts to Yarric's culinary genius subsided, Nath stood and said, "It is good that we have enjoyed a congenial meal together, for there will be little time for such luxuries in the days to come. The ship has been fully refitted and rearmed. The majority of stores are aboard, and I've secured additional powder, shot, and spars. The ship's roster should be sufficiently filled, perhaps even overfilled, within a few days. Therefore, it is my intent to have *Revenant* prepared to sail in a week's time or less, and I conjure you all to adopt the same fervent ambition."

None of the officers, all of whom had made their own surveys of the ship, or at least their little domains within it, voiced any objections to Nath's goal, but Lieutenant Bascombe did raise his voice in question.

"Your ambition—our ambition—seems reasonable," he said by way of preamble. "Is some urgent mission afoot driving our brisk preparations?"

"Not a bit of it, Lieutenant Bascombe," Nath said. "As our orders stand now, we are only directed to take to sea as soon as possible to patrol the Merentian approaches. The sooner we are on station, the sooner we can begin to visit confusion upon the Rats."

"Then this is an independent cruise?" Lieutenant Wilk asked.

"It is," Nath answered.

The room was lit by the sudden flash of smiles on every face at the table save those of Enid and Lieutenant Gardner. Even the somewhat reserved Lieutenant Bascombe spared a pleased grin. Puzzled by the sudden outbreak of good cheer, Enid asked Nath, "What is the significance of this 'independent cruise' that so enthralls your officers?"

"The significance?" Wilk asked with a laugh. "Why, prize money, of course! Rather than dallying about some dismal blockade station, we'll be actively cruising for blockade runners and Ardain warships—both of which make for fat, juicy prizes!"

Enid glanced at Nath, who nodded his agreement with Wilk's words.

"What a venal lot, you Albions," Enid said without thinking.

"We Albions, you mean," Nath said with a laugh. "Remember, you swore your allegiance to the King when you signed your warrant!"

"Well, then," Enid answered with the trace of a smile. "Let us fill our hold with loot with same ecstatic zeal as the Albionic reaver kings of old."

Her words elicited a cheer that was enthusiastically taken up by everyone at the table but Lieutenants Gardner and Bascombe.

At Nath's signal, Enid remained behind after the other officers dispersed to pursue their duties or take their ease. They smoked another cigarillo and drank another glass of Oporto as Yarric cleared away the ruins of the meal with quiet efficiency, his every step literally dogged by the ever-hopeful Marbury and Maubin.

"We should speak of *Revenant*'s young gentles," Nath said, knocking ash from his smoke into a salver reserved for that purpose. "You are acquainted with Yeardly, of course, and Harlech and Dinwitty. We'll have a full complement of mids for this cruise, six in all. You will meet them over the next few days, and I'll leave you to form your own opinions of them."

"I look forward to it. I assume your tradition of readings from classical plays will follow us from *Alarum*?"

"It shall, but not until we're underway and have shaken the crew out a bit. The needs of the service come first, of course."

"Of course." Enid stared at the smoke rising from her cigarillo for a moment before cautiously venturing, "Should we discuss Lieutenant Bascombe?"

Nath sighed. "We may as well. We have both had personal experiences with him and know where his loyalties apparently lie. That said, he has been respectful in all ways since coming aboard."

"That makes him more dangerous than if he were outright impudent," Enid said. "Do not allow yourself to be drawn in by his subterfuge. We saw the hatred he holds for both of us displayed during my affair of honor ashore."

"I'm as wary of him as a lee shore," Nath said. "Fear not in that regard. Still, he was very decent in remaining behind to search for your lost hand and was undeniably disgusted by Harde's murderous behavior."

"Well, perhaps he's one of those lucky few who can set aside their bias when it is outweighed by observable truths," Enid said.

Nath touched his lips and pointed heavenward. "From your lips to the ears of Providence."

"I could not help but notice that Lieutenant Gardner seemed out of sorts. Or is truculent superiority her habitual mien?"

"She seems a sour one, don't she?" Nath chuckled. "Quite the contrast to Lieutenant Harcourt's easy smile and gentle words, eh?"

"Indeed."

Nath shrugged. "I know little of her other than her service record, which is spotless. I suspect she may have a mean disposition by nature."

"Which reminds me of a character I have just encountered in a play by your beloved Marbury, a comedy I was unfamiliar with entitled *The Tempered Blade*."

"I know it well," Nath said.

"You should suggest she read it, then," Enid said. "She could learn from the tale's moral, which is wise despite the clumsiness of its presentation: arrogance and exaggerated self-esteem injure one's chances of attaining love and loyalty from one's comrades."

"Yes, I'm sure she would benefit from the tale's lesson," Nath said, a sublimated smile twinkling in his eyes.

"She should take a lesson from me," Enid continued. "I find myself in a position far below my ambitions and in the company of folks whose social status wouldn't have met the bare requirements to dine with me, let alone cohabitate in the tight confines of a tiny ship. But am I resentful of my fate or hateful to my relatively debased comrades? No. I assume this setback will provide me with an opportunity to greater glories and I treat those around me with a respect and dignity that far exceeds what is owed."

"Indeed," Nath said with a grin. "You are the very figure of enlightened aristocracy and personal restraint. But I fear we must continue this conversation later. I must review today's progress reports and determine where improvements can be made. I trust you have made yourself comfortable in your cabin?"

Enid nodded and fought down an inclination to be irked by his dismissal.

"I have, thank you. I will take me there now. Thank you for a fine dinner, Rue."

"The pleasure was mine, Enid."

Although the light discipline of a home port allowed her many orbs, all as bright as she desired, Enid satisfied herself with a single soft globe suspended over her right shoulder. A book lay open before her to give the impression she was reading if someone should burst into her cabin unexpectedly. Her right hand, sans glove, lay on the cover of Dunaughy's personal journal. She reached out to him and was instantly rewarded by the powerful odor of licorice.

I pray your investigations have been more fruitful than mine, Dunaughy? I've uncovered precious little myself.

Little more than I discovered on the voyage from Gisbon to Middlesea, I'm afraid. There is something unnatural aboard this ship, of that I have no doubt. It is something that smacks of restless spirits, a powerful, tortured phantom or . . . something else.

What?

Something old and powerful. I have the impression of the odors of fresh sawdust, ancient loam, and putrefied flesh.

A strange and frankly off-putting combination of scents. Enid frowned. *A curse placed by the Naveroñians and triggered upon* Redemption's *return to Middlesea?*

Perhaps. Or when she fell out of their control. Recall, whatever it is, it made its enmity clear to me on the voyage from Gisbon and effectively interfered with our ability to communicate until—

The gleaming fingers of her right hand drummed of their own accord upon the cover of Dunaughy's journal as she nodded. *My hand.*

If I were to guess, it is concealing itself until the moment of its choosing, Dunaughy said.

That is my fear as well, Enid said. *And we have no recourse but to wait for it to show* its *hand.*

The days flew by, propelled by Nath's energetic encouragement and the support of his officers and warrants. The fast pace encouraged some friction between "the Captain's People" and the "Newcomers," as the hard bargains from Ainsley Bottom and a few of the new recruits were called collectively, friction that occasionally produced flames. Such flare-ups usually took the form of harsh words or minor altercations involving an exchange of shoves or pushes. These atrocities resulted in stopped rum rations for all parties involved, a punishment that, while odious, earned Nath a reputation for fairness and mercy. Despite these regrettable lapses of discipline, *Revenant* was ready to sail a day or so before the date desired by Nath. When Nath ordered the signal flags raised to announce her preparedness, however, they were instantly answered by the signal for "hold station" from Admiralty.

"Why are we to delay?" Enid asked. She stood next to Nath on the larboard side of the quarterdeck.

"Changes to my orders, no doubt." He chewed his lip thoughtfully. "I'll wager our independent cruise has just transformed into blockade or convoy duty—I should have known the Sea Lord only lifted our spirits to crush them under his heel at the last moment."

"What are we to do, then?"

Nath closed his come-hither glass and sighed. "Await the emissary from the gods bearing word of our doom."

It was a brief wait, which Enid believed confirmed Nath's suspicions. Surely, the orders were already committed to paper and held in reserve by Morrin well in advance of *Revenant*'s readiness. Enid leaned on the port rail of the waist when Merryweather ushered a strange lieutenant with a leather message bag slung over her shoulder into Nath's quarters. She rejoined Enid at the rail a scant few moments later. She answered Enid's inquisitive gaze with a shake of her head.

"That woman's face is carved from basalt, else she knows nothing of the orders she carries. Either way, we must wait to see how the captain—ah, here's Lieutenant Stoneface already. There was no time for her to brief the captain in any meaningful way, so she must be as ignorant of his orders as we."

Enid straightened from the rail and took a step toward Nath's cabin, but Merryweather stopped her, saying, "No, Enid. He will call us when he has read the orders. If they're as bad as I suspect, he'll want a moment or two in private before sharing the dismal news."

"You believe the orders will be so dire?"

"Indeed," Merryweather said grimly. "The Sea Lord has played a cruel game with Captain Nath. I've no doubt of it."

Less than half an hour passed before Nath's steward, Yarric, appeared on deck and spoke to Harlech and Dinwitty, who were on watch. Dinwitty scurried up to Enid and Merryweather and saluted quickly before announcing the captain wished to see them in his day cabin. There, they gathered with Lieutenants Bascombe, Wilk, Dalroyd, and Harcourt. They all stood uneasily and shared grim looks as they awaited Nath's arrival. Only Bascombe seemed untroubled by the prospect of the new orders, which lent further weight to Enid's belief that he was privy to the Sea Lord's plot against Nath and his people.

Nath emerged from his sleeping cabin with his stock loosened and vest partially unbuttoned. Marbury and Maubin trailed behind him, somehow contriving to look as grave as their master. He took in the expressions of his gathered officers and nodded gravely for them to sit.

"I will not waste any more of your time than necessary, as we sail on the morning tide. This afternoon we will take another ten marines aboard." Nath sat down behind his miniature desk and squirmed on its hard seat for a moment. "I truly miss the chair I took off the *Marie*. Enid, do you recall the one? Now Lord Aixely has it, damn my luck."

"Extra marines?" Lieutenant Harcourt asked with one of his patient smiles. "Ten, you say, sir?"

"Yes, along with extra powder, shot, and grenados. I'm afraid your lobsters may be a little cheek and jowl, but Lieutenant Bascombe will assist you in accommodating them as best we can."

Bascombe gave Harcourt a friendly nod. *No matter how odious the viper, Amiable Harcourt's affable aura will have its effect,* Enid thought.

"Our orders have not changed substantially." Nath paused for the sighs of relief to pass and continued, "We are to sail to a point near the Merentian Approach, there to unseal private orders from Admiralty."

Speculative glances were exchanged around the room by all but Lieutenant Bascombe, who chose that moment to adjust the buckle on one of his shoes. Enid fixed him with a narrow-eyed stare when he straightened but was only rewarded with feigned obliviousness.

"Do not raise your hopes too high. For all we know, the orders are to escort a convoy to the colonies and back home to Albion laden with mast timber," Nath cautioned them, but relented a bit at their downcast expressions. "That is unlikely, though. I suspect we have been given an errand of some great import. Each of you is to impart the importance of having *Revenant* in the uttermost state of readiness by morn to your divisions. Get at it now and let the morning tide lift us to glory!"

Let the tide lift us to glory? Saccharine stuff even for such a devotee of Marbury as Nath, Enid thought. Still, he seemed to strike just the right note with his officers. Even Bascombe managed a credible huzzah.

As the senior mid, Yeardly strove to imitate his dear, late friend Cullen, who held the post back aboard *Alarum*. He saw the newcomers settled in, organized the berth's victualing fund—and augmented it a bit with extra purchases courtesy of his prize money. He worked with Lieutenant Merryweather to see them assigned to watches that suited their abilities. The older mids, Arlice and Weard, seemed competent and had experience at sea. This would be Hunig's first cruise, despite his relatively mature age of fifteen. He seemed a bright, decent fellow, though, and was apparently unfazed by Dinwitty and Harlech being his senior in rank. Indeed, Yeardly paired him with Dinwitty, hoping that the experience of mentoring a lubberly young gentle would bolster his self-confidence, while Hunig's noncompetitive maturity might blunt some of his more childish tendencies.

Now, surrounded by his fellow mids gathered for their evening meal in the mid's Berth, Yeardly basked in the satisfaction of his accomplishments. His fellow young gentles dug into their vittles with a gusto that bordered on savagery, and he smiled encouragingly when Arlice put her hand on Dinwitty's shoulder and warned patiently against feeding so roughly lest he ruin his new uniform coat. He was equally heartened when Weard carefully explained the watch bells to Hunig, who accepted her instruction gratefully between mouthfuls of freshly boiled beef and vegetables. He noticed Harlech's open admiration for Hunig and thought Lady d'Tancreville's glory might soon be eclipsed by a satellite with a nearer orbit.

He interrupted the conversations and said, "Mid Arlice and Mid Weard, the three of us must take extra efforts with the gun crews. Captain Nath expects three broadsides in five minutes."

Weard smiled and drawled, "He and every other captain in the King's service."

Yeardly didn't care for her tone but chose to ignore it in the instant. "Yes, but unlike every other captain, he will bring us into grips with the enemy at every opportunity, so a quick rate of fire is desirable for us all."

"It is said that he is a fire-eater," Arlice said.

"He is," Yeardly agreed. "But he is not rash. You may count upon being enriched under Captain Nath and will most likely see command of a prize."

"That is passing good to hear," she said. "I was transferred from *Warrior*, 50, and expected to spend the entire war on blockade duty without so much as a glimpse at a prize."

Harlech beamed at Arlice and piped in with "You're a frigate hand now!"

"And thankful to be one." Arlice smiled. "It's as great a promotion as from lieutenant to Post."

"She's a fine ship for taking prizes, too," Weard said. "Nearly as long as one of the new forties and only a touch under their throw weight, what with these spanking new twenty-eight-pounders and a full complement of smashers."

"Our *Revenant*is fast, hard-hitting," Yeardly said with a grin, "and, I pray, weatherly."

"Do you find her a bit *spooky*, though?" Hunig asked in a lowered voice.

"Spooky?" Arlice regarded Hunig with an expression of patient amusement. "How so?"

"It's hard to describe. Everywhere I go, I feel like there are eyes boring into my back."

Weard laughed and punched Hunig playfully in the arm. "That's just the crew. You will get used to it. They watch us like hawks to take our measure and determine how much mischief they can get up to without punishment."

"And to gather news," Arlice added. "Your Rat spy has nothing on an Albion sailor. They can put together a word or two overheard from two or three officers and uncover Admiralty's entire strategy for the war. Never underestimate how clever they are! Many would be admirals, if not for the misfortune of their birth."

Hunig nodded but chewed his lip. "I'm sure you're right, but the odd thing is that the sensation is at its worst when fewer ship's people are about. I was down on the orlop, fetching the Magister's coat for, her and the place seemed . . . alive. I felt—no, never mind. It is nothing."

Yeardly ignored the chuckles around the table and Hunig's embarrassed half smile, and pressed him, "You felt what?"

"I don't know," Hunig said reluctantly. "Eyes on me, like I said, and a sense that I was not welcome there. And there was a smell I became more aware of the longer I searched for the magister's coat."

"What smell?"

"It was like dried leaves and mold, but with a sweet tang, like meat gone bad."

Yeardly noticed that Harlech's eyes had gone wide and Dinwitty's fingers were crossed to ward off the evil eye and other curses. Even Arlice and Weard looked worried by the conversation's dark turn.

"Well, that explains it," he said with false cheerfulness. "The magister has doubtless placed wards upon her workspace to prevent or detect unwanted intrusions by curious sailors and that is what you felt. As to the smell, Providence alone knows what sort of oddities and ingredients she stores there to aid in her sendings and formulations."

Hunig seemed relieved by Yeardly's pronouncement, as did the other mids.

"Don't worry," Yeardly said, refilling Hunig's glass from the ceramic wine decanter on the table between them. "Even I have trepidations when I enter our magister's lair—but I fear her far less than reporting for duty late or looking as if I just rolled out of my hammock when Captain Nath is intent on departing on the morning tide. Rest as best you may!"

The sailors of the waist division were sharing rougher viands around the bench that served as their table. They were seated on their sea chests and packing away salt beef that could still be identified as genuine meat and washing it down with measured sips of watered-down rum. Their meal didn't compare in quality to that of the ship's officers or even the young gentles, but it was a vast improvement over the fare they were accustomed to on other, less fortunate ships.

"Give Rue-Naught this," said Arlough, an able sailor brought out of hiding and into service by the prize money promised by one of Nath's broadsides. "He sees to his folks' vittles!"

"Aye," agreed Jepsum, an old *Alarum* hand. "Cap'n Nath dipped into his own prize money to stock our larder proper-like. He's a pusser's nightmare, too. You won't find any condemned vittles on his barky!"

"Officers is officers," a hard-faced woman named Grimes sneered. She was one of the bargains from the Ainsley Bottom mutineers *Revenant* was saddled with by the "generosity" of the Sea Lord. "Some'll fatten you up afore feeding you to into the meat grinder to make themself richer, but you're still just sheep in the slaughter pen to 'em. The less of ye they come home with, the bigger their share. Fuckin' bandits is all they is, buying country estates while our wives and wee ones starve with our pay three years in arrears."

"That's enough of that!" Silence settled over the table at Rolliers's bark. She was one of the maintop captains; the brawny, ruddy-faced woman had a reputation for brooking no foolishness. "I sailed as foretop-hand under Cap'n Nath and he did all he could to see to us and our families when we were marooned in Middlesea. I won't hear 'im slandered by you, Grimes!"

"I don't give a fig what you will or won't," Grimes snarled. "You can play your games in front of your masters whose boots you lick, but down here you'll learn not to top it so high."

Rolliers surged forward, seized Grimes by the collars, and half dragged her from her seat. "That's the onliest mistake ye get with me, gallows bait. You'll keep a respectful tongue in your gob or pay the devil for it! And you show that pigsticker you're fumblin' with above the table and I'll break your sodding neck!"

Grimes took in Rolliers's, Jepsum's, and Arlough's grim expressions and raised both hands over her head.

"Easy, mates! I didn't aim to offend. You lot know the cap'n and I don't. Let bygones be bygones, and we'll finish our vittles peaceful-like!"

Rolliers released her hold, and they finished their meal in silence. She made a point not to stare at Grimes, but noticed she shared a dark glance with one of the Ainsley hands at another table. She marked the fellow, a tall, lanky man, his pale skin already burned red by sun and wind. His fingers were remarkably deft and precise as he ate. *A pickpocket or card sharp,* Rolliers thought, *and a bad penny to be polished or else tossed overboard, and his mate Grimes with him.*

PART THREE

chapter 12

Enid was up well before dawn to witness *Revenant*'s departure from Middlesea. She was not alone, either aboard the ship or ashore. The steps were lined with a crowd as large or larger than the one that had greeted *Redemption*'s arrival. When the multitude saw the capstans manned to raise the anchor, a deafening cheer arose from the Stairs. Nath smiled at the sound and raised his hat over his head, a gesture that redoubled the uproar. He turned to Merryweather, and his smile widened.

"Lieutenant Merryweather, I would be most gratified if you and Master Kaliktiklak would take us out in a manner that exemplifies *Revenant*'s vigor and readiness for war."

Merryweather snapped a salute with a glint in her eyes and called for the Master. Orders soon echoed from one end of the ship to another as the old hands, all of whom had been called to duty for the performance, fell to their work with a will. The winds being in their favor, the ship swiftly made strong but sedate headway. Enid was surprised by the deep thrill that seized her as the ship came to life under her feet and all about her. The excited bustle of motion, the men and women throwing themselves into their work with an excess of energy that escaped through their wide smiles and bright eyes, were as a tonic to her. She wondered if this was due to her entanglement with Dunaughy's spirit or represented a literal sea change in her own character. She allowed herself to smile with them and joined Nath at the rail, where he watched the operation of the ship and the activities ashore with equal avidity.

"Ah, Magister! I see the old *Alarum*'s mood is infectious! Mark the difference twixt them and Harde and Aixely's loyalists." He gestured with his chin toward a vessel to starboard that Enid only recognized as they slid past it. It was *Alarum*. Under Lord Ambrose's command the little frigate had lost all its snap and vigor. Her masts stood at angles that were near the opposite of those at which Nath had set them to achieve her best speed, and her standing rigging hung too limply even to Enid's uninformed eye. The slump-shouldered sailors aboard her worked lethargically despite the threat of the mates' starters. The officers and warrants stood in small groups, watching the wretches under their command with gazes which were at once menacing and fearful. It was the very image of misery before the mast that Enid believed to be the typical lot of sailors before witnessing it aboard *Alarum* under Nath's command. She knew that Aixely the younger was in port with *Alarum*, but this was her first sighting of the unfortunate ship.

"That is what you mean when you say a ship is unhappy," Enid said. "How can a crew be so obviously abused by a martinet like Aixely and his ilk under the very eyes of Admiralty? How has he not been removed and replaced with a more humane overlord? A flesh-eating ghoul, perhaps, or a blood-drinking vampire?"

"It is a fair question, Enid," Nath said. "And one that must be answered sooner rather than later. Your average sailor is a habitual complainer at the best of times, but many of their complaints are valid. It is not unusual for their pay to be years in arrears, leaving their families to starve ashore despite their loyal service to the Crown—one of the prime complaints of the Ainsley Bottoms mutineers, you may recall. Not all captains are as diligent in assuring that their pursers secure wholesome victuals or durable slops for them to wear. Progressive members of Parliament and the nobility at large are struggling to relieve these hardships, but reform is difficult in wartime."

"This situation predates the ogre that currently occupies Admiralty's throne?"

"It predates his grandparents and their grandparents. This has been the plight of Albion's sailors for generations stacked as high as a First Rate's mainmast is tall."

"How has your navy risen to such prominence?"

"Sailors love the sea," Nath said with a shrug. "And Albion's treatment of sailors is actually kinder than they'd see in your homeland, Naveroña, or the Malasfandyari Empire."

"I would accuse you of a partisan bias," Enid said after a moment. "But I trust your assessment of nautical matters such as these."

"Thank you, Magister," Nath said, watching the working of the ship. "Albion has the finest sailors; Ardainne designs the best ships. If the two kingdoms should ever be one, their rule of the seas would be unassailable. As it is, Albion has the advantage. Ardain salts will never serve their country with the same vigor as Albion's, but Ardain ships can be captured, their designs copied, improved upon, and sent back to visit havoc on their birthland. Like our *Revenant*, here, for example."

"*Revenant* is based on one of our—an Ardain ship?"

Nath nodded and patted the rail before him. "Yes. The fine lines and graceful curves speak to her origin. Your Albion frigate is a bit more bluff and somewhat broader in the beam. Ardain frigates reflect the folk that design them: long, lean, and elegant. Sadly, they are also rougher handling at sea, so changes were made to *Revenant*'s plans to make her a more stolid, drier lady."

Enid considered making a throw at a jest concerning dry, stolid ladies, but her dignity had not eroded enough in the company of coarse sea-folk to be comfortable with such a gross fling.

"I tell you plainly, Enid, I'm impressed by how well Merryweather and Master Kaliktiklak work the ship together. They have no need for my supervision. I will miss Merryweather, for I have no doubt that she'll have a command of her own at the end of this cruise."

"I will miss her, too," Enid said, her smile dimming. It had not fully occurred to her that their little family must eventually be broken up by advancement and the needs of the Navy, no matter how fortunate they might be in avoiding injury in battle. Indeed, the more fortunate they were at war, the sooner they would be separated.

"Well done, *Revenants*! Our bow is pointed at our prizes and our stern toward our creditors! You made an admirable showing taking us out of port!" Nath called out. The sailors laughed along with Nath and his officers, some elbowing those they thought too slow to catch on in the ribs. "An extra tot of rum for all hands with the evening meal!"

Three huzzahs for Rue-Naught rattled the spars overhead. When the last floated back to Middlesea, whose smoke-wreathed prominences shrank rapidly behind them, Enid watched it recede with relief tinged with regret for not wishing Verity Hicks farewell in person. She hoped she would not be offended by the letter she posted yestermorn, along with Nath's quick note to his cousin and a longer missive to Emley Holyoke.

"Here, Enid," Nath said. "Eyes ahead. Never watch the land sink behind you lest you find it gone when you return. Here's something to occupy your mind: Mark Mr. Kaliktiklak and the remarkable patience he shows in teaching those landsmen their ropes. There's a good Master for you."

Enid had not yet had the pleasure of meeting Master Kaliktiklak, so she followed Nath's pointed finger. She stiffened slightly when she saw the person in question. Mr. Kaliktiklak was a Bogaraet, one of the inhuman natives of the Shards and Spice Islands. Unwholesomely thin, he towered more than seven feet above the deck, so that he must bend at the waist to converse with the nervous landsmen he instructed, like an adult looming over a child. His skin, visible beneath his working slops, gleamed like a polished shell. It was midnight blue mottled with a green that bordered on black. Not a hair stood out on his body.

As she looked upon him, he turned his head by chance and met her gaze with tiny red eyes that floated in his moon-shaped face. He smiled and nodded in her direction, and it was all she could do not to recoil from the sight of his myriad teeth, all gleaming white and of the same general shape as a sailmaker's curved needle. The diabolical impression of his countenance was underlined by the small sprouts of gnarled horns that protruded from his brow.

Nath, noting her distaste at the sight of the Bogaraet, put a hand on her forearm and spoke quietly but firmly. "Enid! Recall that you are an officer and a lady of standing, not some gawping yokel at a penny-horror show! Have you never seen a Bogaraet?"

Enid took a deep breath and returned the Bogaraet's smile with a thin specimen of her own. His red, ember-like eyes held hers for a moment before he nodded to her and returned to the instruction of the lubbers.

"I have seen them scattered in crowds," Enid said in a low voice. "But never so close as this creature."

"That creature is our ship's master and a respected member of our crew. He is qualified to stand a watch, can navigate as well or better than I. He is called Mr. Kaliktiklak and should be treated with all due respect."

"I understand," Enid said. "I was only—surprised. I will treat him as I would any other *Revenant* from henceforth."

Nath nodded. "I'm sure you will."

"Still," Enid said, "don't you find their appearance troubling? Their eerie resemblance to the Darghaur?"

"Not in the least. They hate and fear the Darghaur with an intensity that is a bonfire next to the candle of our enmity. They were created by the Darghaur to serve as their slaves. Generations of their kin were slain in the ancient war between the Darghaur and the Fey."

"How did they break free of their bondage?"

"I don't know, but they did." Nath shrugged. After a moment of thoughtful silence, he continued, "Did you know a Bogaraet inherits the knowledge of previous generations, Enid?"

She averred she did not.

"Well, they do. Master Kaliktiklak there recalls everything that occurred to his folk, back to the time the first of them was pulled from some vat of foul Darghaur alchemy. Bear that in mind, Enid: Make a friend of one of them, and you have a friend in them all. Betray one, or treat him foul, and you have earned the antipathy of an entire people."

"That is a fearsome prospect."

"Indeed," Nath agreed. "So you agree that he would make a far better friend than a foe?"

"There is no need to be patronizing," Enid said. "But yes, I take your point."

"You'll be happy to have him aboard on a crossing of the Albion Sea at this time of year. The Bogaraet are good luck in a blow."

"A blow? But the weather has been exceedingly fair for this time of year! If you are japing upon my distaste for storms, you should be—"

"Not in the least, Enid," Nath said with a wry grin. "I must remind you that there are barometers throughout the barky that you might find profitable to observe."

Enid, following Nath's suggestion, was studying the barometer that hung above the gun room companionway. She understood the basic principle of the device, which provided warning of approaching storms by measuring the relative density of energized sylphs compared with that of similarly energized undines. The barometer reading would lower if sylphs were superior in number, as air is obviously lighter than water. If undines held the advantage, the barometer would rise. A lowering barometer indicated a storm was brewing, and the more rapid the fall, the more violent the tempest would be. Fair weather, in most instances, was heralded by a rising barometer. This much Enid understood, but she was woefully ignorant of the instrument's operation and interpretation.

"How stands the glass, Magister d'Tancreville?" Lieutenant Dalroyd asked upon entering the gun room.

"Vertically, above the companionway." Enid shrugged. "I'm afraid I lack the expertise to say much more with confidence."

He joined her and tapped the demarcations in the device's base-plate. "These fine lines are marked off in fractions of an inch. If we know how far the red bar there has dropped within a given amount of time, we can predict the severity of the approaching storm."

Enid frowned. "And how would one know that?"

"By this small gray line, which can be moved separately from the red line through the rotation of this small wheel. It has fallen over half an inch since this watch began two hours ago. That is a quick fall and most likely indicates a hard blow."

"Is Captain Nath aware?"

Her concerned expression amused Dalroyd immensely, but his own remained one of cordial respect. He knew her well enough to avoid chancing her ire. He wasn't afraid of her, despite the best efforts of some of his former messmates, who sent him off to *Revenant* with tales of her ungovernable wrath, of which, they maintained, Harde's decapitation was but a mild example. Rather, he saw no more benefit in rankling her pride than in prodding a sleeping bear. Personal interest of a less mortal stripe also bore consideration. Enid d'Tancreville fascinated him, and he frequently mused on her character in his journal. These entries were in no way akin to those of a smitten youngster, though. Rather than meditations on the pale, unmarred beauty of her skin or the startling brightness of her green eyes, his thoughts dwelt on the keenness of her mind, her cultured aesthetic tastes, and her effortless and unfailing comfort in her own skin. He was determined to be accepted into Captain Nath's inner circle, embodied in the persons of Magister d'Tancreville, Lieutenant Merryweather, and, oddly, Mid Yeardly. This ambition was only partially rooted in the natural desire to further his career. Its true appeal was the opportunity to forge a lasting friendship with Enid d'Tancreville.

"Indeed he is, Magister. He has passed his orders for preparing *Revenant* for a blow to Master Kaliktiklak, though there was little need to do so. Mr. Kaliktiklak is a diligent and proactive master and was already in the process of enacting the common precautions."

"Hmm. Well," Enid said and tapped the glass tube of the barometer lightly with a carefully buffed nail. “The volatility of weather at sea is daunting, is it not?”

“It can be,” Dalroyd agreed. “But there’s also a certain wild beauty to the elements in an ungovernable state, perilous though that beauty may be. I’m surprised its changeable state merits your notice, though. I assumed the sylphs and undines bombard you with moment-to-moment reports on the state of the sea and sky for leagues around us.”

She ignored Dunaughy’s chuckle at the back of her mind, as well as his teasing remark that another admirer had fallen into her orbit and answered Dalroyd frankly. “At times they do. At other times the conflicting gabble of contesting elementals could portend a sunny day and smooth seas or the mother of all gales and waves as tall as mountains.”

One of Dalroyd’s eyebrows arched in interest. “What do you do on such occasions?”

“I usually dismiss them all and ask Captain Nath or Lieutenant Merryweather for their opinion of the weather.”

Dalroyd smiled at this, impressed by her easy admission that she was not all-knowing, and said, “And now you can study the glass just as they do.”

“So I can,” Enid said, allowing herself a slight return smile. “Thank you for your kind tutelage, Lieutenant Dalroyd.”

“If it is not too intrusive, perhaps you can shed some light on a mystery that plagues me?”

“I cannot answer this question until you ask the next,” Enid said, a gleam of amusement in her bottle green eyes.

“Of course,” Dalroyd said. His self-deprecating grin replaced by a frown as he asked, “By the light of your formidable esoteric knowledge, do you believe *Redemption* to be haunted? Many of the foremast tars, even some who crewed this vessel from Gisbon to Middlesea, are consumed by the idea, which I fear will degrade ship’s discipline.”

“Is their dread based on the captains who died before they could read themselves in? Or are there more recent events behind it?”

“Their deaths figure strongly in their conceptions, of course. But there have also been reports of spectral forms belowdecks, accompanied by an earth odor and, some say, the scent of putrefaction."

Enid's nod was solemn. "Please share such reports with me as you receive them, sir, and, if you would be so kind, ask your fellow lieutenants to do the same."

"I shall do so," Dalroyd assured her, his question for her still crouching inquisitively in his eyes.

"The proscriptions of my role forbid me from speaking to your curiosity. Such reports are for the captain's ears alone. I judge you to be an honorable person, though, and I'll share my opinion with you with the understanding it will go no further."

"My word 'pon it," Dalroyd assured her.

"There is something amiss with *Revenant.* I am, as you might say, 'all at sea' regarding its nature and severity. I am working diligently to that end, however."

"Passing strange," Dalroyd said, and shook his head. "When she was in the yard, there were no complaints of strange or eerie events. Everyone involved in her refit was aware of her dark history—the gruesome mutiny, the murders of Captain Ourey and his crew, and her shameful sale to Neveroña—but not a soul reported anything out of the ordinary aboard her."

Enid nodded. "It is passing strange."

"I will pass any reports from the people that don't reek of spirits found in a bottle to you with all dispatch. If there is aught else I can do to assist you in your task, I am your devoted, and discreet, servant."

"Thank you, Mr. Dalroyd. I shall."

"I must be about my duties, Magister. You might consider resting while you can. Sleep will be hard to find later, I fear."

Enid took his felicitous advice to heart, and once her cuddy door was closed behind her, Lieutenant Dalroyd joined the rest of the current watch on deck to lend a hand in making *Revenant* ready for nature's rough handling.

chapter 13

Two hours later, Enid stood with Nath on *Revenant*'s quarterdeck and marveled at the approaching storm in horrified awe. It was a thing out of her nightmares—a gargantuan mushroom composed of wind, rain, and other barely restrained cataclysmic forces. Its towering base had barely crossed the distant line of the horizon, but it moved so swiftly its progress was plain to the eye. It drove a wall of misty froth before it, stirred up by the winds and vicious, uneven chop that heralded its approach. The upper reaches of the behemoth would soon be directly over *Revenant*, its approach announced by rolling thunder, forks of lightning, and a fearsome darkness upon the waters. She felt the chill of a cold northwest wind scour her high angular cheekbones and the tip of her narrow, sculpted nose and was seized by a banal sense of relief that she'd left her hat on her little writing desk.

"Is it an oceanic snowstorm?" she asked Nath. "A maritime blizzard or some such? The winds driving it are nearly cold enough to burn the skin."

"No," he answered. "It is a typical mistral-fed storm for the season. No gentle wafts of snow for us, Enid, but rather a gale of wind and rain. Perhaps a hailstone or two to admonish us for daring the passage in such an inopportune month."

"It seems the very king of storms," Enid said. "Surely even a stout man-of-war such as *Revenant* must founder under the shadow of such a tempest!"

"I assure you I've prepared *Revenant* thoroughly against just such a happenstance," Nath said with a comforting smile. "Or I should say Master Kaliktiklak has. He had the hands pulling down the courses and t'gallants reefing the topsails before I'd issued a single order! Your Bogaraets have wondrous fine noses for weather!"

"Which is surprising, considering the rudimentary nature of the organ."

"You are quite droll today, Enid. They are an ancient maritime people with a shared memory as old as, well, nearly as old as the world. They are like to have seen every sort of weather imaginable and read storm signs as easily as we read a book."

That may be part of it. Dunaughy's thoughts were a somber murmur in her mind. *But I do not believe that is the entirety of the truth.*

Enid let Dunaughy's observation lie for the moment and glanced doubtfully up at the masts and found there were no hands aloft—nor very much in the article of sails, just the topsails, she believed. "Is so little sail wise?"

"The scraps of sail aloft will be more than enough, I'm sure. Mr. Kaliktiklak believes we may need nothing but bare masts and spars before all is said and done."

She shot him a doubtful glance. "Do we not risk being—I am not sure I recall the correct term, and the one that comes to mind is quite profane, but the meaning I intend is to be flooded from behind."

"Pooped," Nath said with a speculative look at Enid. "No, we are in no danger of being pooped. But I must admit I'm with child to know the word you thought to use."

"I cannot say it. I will not be pressed to say it." The word in question was *buggered.* She was not too prim to utter the word, but she suspected the jocose display it would trigger in Rue would be more than her dignity could weather without satisfaction. "So we are constrained to fly like geese before the winds."

"Oh, no," Nath said. "There are other options available, but I hope to take advantage of nature's beneficence to the confusion of our enemies."

"Beneficence? I would say murderous wrath instead."

"It may seem so to you," Nath said, his tone more patronizing than she cared for. In her mind, Dunaughy silently opined that if she resented being spoken to like a lubber, she should invest a small amount of time in the study of basic ship handling. She didn't find the remark productive at that moment, though, and ignored it.

"But to one who is familiar with the winds that funnel through the Approaches and the northern coast of the Merentian, the advantages are clear. If we run before this storm rather than heaving to, the gale will bear us swiftly into proximity with Tancre without the risk of detection by Rat patrols or semaphore stations. We'll stand in strike like a thunderbolt from the blue."

Enid cocked an eyebrow at the notion of interpreting being driven before a gale as an *advantage*, but the craft of a mariner was not her own, and she would no more gainsay Nath regarding the frigate's course than he would question her choice of sylphs for a spell. She glanced speculatively at the storm just as the forward edge of its upper layer slid over *Redemption* and transformed a bright winter afternoon into a dim dusk. A spatter of icy, nearly horizontal rain slashed across her face and hands, followed an instant later by a gust of frigid wind that forced her back a step. Nath turned and shouted a salvo of orders, a few of which she was proud to find she understood without Dunaughy's interpretation. Then, for a time, the world was all roaring noise, air laden with spume and spray, and the rough texture of the lifeline clutched in her white-knuckled hands. Within the chaos of physical sensations, she was surprised by an almost imperceptible probing of her habitual arcane protections. She instantly reinforced the most formidable of her personal wards, certain that she was about to suffer a sorcerous assault. When no aggressive sendings materialized, Enid attempted to wipe the wind-driven rain from her eyes and consulted with Dunaughy.

You felt that too?

I did and—clap a hand on the lifeline, Enid, before we are both swept from the deck! When she did so, he continued, *I did. It was clearly an attempt to take the measure of the strength and sophistication of your defenses. As you bolstered your words, I engaged myself in finding the source of the feint but met with negligible success. Something inimical to humanity dwells within the barky. As I struggled with it, I gained some insight into its nature. It is no ghost, nor is it a sorcerous, incorporeal automaton driven by a curse. The tactics he—for I had a strong impression of masculine energy—employed were too grounded in the living world for a specter and too immediately and intelligently responsive to be those of a spiritual homunculus that sprung forth to enforce a curse. No, this was something more than either a ghost or a curse.*

Enid nodded grimly and set a nearby sylph to work keeping as much of the spray from her face as possible. *That is far more than we had before, Dunaughy. I commend you for your effort! Knowing what our foe is* not *is nearly as useful as knowing what he* is. *The fences I have erected about Rue's cabin to repel ghosts can be taken down, which will put an end to the admittedly minor strain it placed upon my magical reserves, and we can cease our attempts to banish unknown curses. We must pool our knowledge of entities that might—*

The lifeline in her hand writhed suddenly, like a powerful, wet snake intent on shaking loose her grip. Its serpentine contortions, timed to coordinate with *Redemption*'s sudden lurch in response to the rising, chaotic chop of the sea, met with admirable success. She found herself falling backward, her long, slender fingers grasping fruitlessly to seize the lifeline, which now snapped like a whip in the fierce wind. The pitch of the deck was so acute that the frigate was all but on her beam ends, and Enid plummeted toward the foam-drowned rail, her arms flailing and mouth wide with surprise and fear. She reached out desperately for an undine to catch her and return her to the deck. Before she could wrestle one into her service, a strong hand seized her wrist in a bruising grip and yanked her away from the watery abyss just as *Revenant* pitched to aft, raising her bow until nothing but stormy sky was visible beyond her bare bowsprit. She and her rescuer stumbled aft, lost their footing, and fell heavily to the slanting deck.

"Beg pardon for the familiarity, Spells." The face of the man lying atop her was a scant few inches from her face. His grin was full of strong white teeth, broken only by a single gold replacement. She recognized him as Boyne, a sailor who joined *Redemption* before she made sail for Middlesea. She gave him a weak smile of gratitude as he levered himself onto one knee and offered his hand to help her sit up as well. He opened his mouth to say something else but was struck in the temple by a flying block that trailed a bit of line behind it.

The crack of the small block against Boyne's skull was clearly audible above the shrieking wind, and Enid saw his mouth form a surprised O as the light of intelligence was instantly extinguished from his kind gray eyes. He tumbled sideways onto the deck, which was now steeply tilted to starboard, and his limp form began to roll down its slope. Enid's fingers clutched spasmodically at the hem of Boyne's pant leg. The rough fabric scraped through her nails, and she watched in horror as his body—she refused to think of it as a corpse—picked up speed as it bounced and slid before hitting the starboard bulwarks. Her eyes widened in horror as some unseen force seized the waistband of the sailor's dungarees and rolled him over the safety rail and into the greedy green waters of the sea.

Verlinherrinar is mad or senile if she reckons you a threat to me. A voice of dry leaves underfoot and branches groaning under the weight of the hangman's bounty sounded clearly in her mind. *I will add your soul to the legions who came before you.*

Enid's nostrils filled with the stench of damp earth and rotting flesh, and she collapsed to the streaming deck. All that prevented her from following Boyne into the sea was a loop of lifeline in the hard, metallic clutch of her silver hand.

When the worst of the squall line passed, Yeardly saw Enid rolling about the desk, her uniform and hair thoroughly sodden and her hat and one shoe missing. She was near enough that he could see her blank eyes rolling in their sockets. He clapped a hand on the shoulder of a sturdily built woman from the afterguard and shouted, "Bear a hand, Fitch! We must see the magister into Dr. Rondelle's care!"

Fitch glanced over her shoulder, saw the Ardain lady who served as the barky's Spells, and gave her a brisk nod. Within moments, they had miraculously borne Enid's unconscious form safely down the companionways to the orlop, where the cockpit acted as Dr. Rondelle's sick bay. When a pair of loblolly boys appeared to take Enid into custody, Yeardly thanked Fitch and dismissed her to return to her duties on deck.

After tugging her forelock in acceptance of her orders, she turned and stopped in her tracks, her mouth open in amazement. There, but a few feet outside the cockpit's door, stood a young girl. Fisk took her for Harlech at first, but realized the lass was the mid's senior by a year or two and her hair was a cascade of gleaming spun gold that hung to her knees, rather than Harlech's shorter coif, which was the color of sun-bleached hay in comparison. She wore a perfectly dry shift-dress, the hem of which was stained with dirt and muck. A dead osprey was cradled in her arms, and her brow was crowned with a circlet of woven grass strands from which depended the skeletal claws, heads, and beaks of several dead birds.

Fitch made to take a step backward, but the girl raised her hand and froze her in place. The landsman heard a voice within her head and knew it emanated from the strange girl, despite the immobility of her lips.

Do not speak of me to anyone if you wish to enjoy my friendship rather than suffering my wrath. You understand, Eidie Fitch?

Fitch's nod was jerky. *How does she know my name, this solemn waif of a girl?*

I know your mind, Eidie. Do not trouble yourself about it, dear child. Loyal child. Your mother and father pushed you too far, and you should feel no guilt for setting off on your own. Who are they to say whether you should have sold your young body, and if you did, why should they share in the profits of it?

The girl didn't wait for the sailor's reply, but pressed on, saying, *You are a girl I would be proud to call my own, Eidie Fitch. Even though you are now a woman grown, it is never too late to bask in a mother's love and approval, is it, sweet girl, sweet Fisk?*

Eidie shook her head, a tear pooling in the corner of her left eye.

Good. You are now a daughter of Verlinherrinar. You have my love and protection. All I ask in return is that you watch over your older sister there, sad little Enid. Grave little Enid. The flowers wilt in her hands, and the dead nestle in her heart. Watch over her and keep her safe! Though she is older than you, she is far less wise.

Eidie nodded again, still silent, and the voice cooed in her head, *Do not fear the hazards of the storm above, Eidie, for I am at your side, and no wind or wave will take you while I am.*

"All hands to reef topsails!"

Captain Nath's voice cut through the storm like a knife through butter and brought a grin to Aster Cashton's face. *Redeemer love him,* she thought, *he has the voice of a thirty-two-pounder in the barrel of a nine-pound chase gun!* A glance up at the main topsail proved his order was well-founded. It was bellied out so taut that it might shred at any moment, and then they would surely be pooped.

She and her fellow foretopmen swarmed up the foremast before Lieutenant Merryweather's equally powerful voice called out, "Stand by to reef the foretopsail!"

Despite the violent, jerky rotation of the masts and the gale's efforts to pluck them from the ratlines, she and the other tops were in position at the foretopsail yard while the landsmen of the afterguard were still being herded into place to assist in hauling on the buntlines, clew lines, reef-tackles, and braces. She exchanged a tight smile with Wainwright, who leaned over the yard to her left. She mimed a violent shiver, for there was no talking allowed while awaiting orders, and he nodded fervently in agreement. The storm had brought an uncommon cold wind with it.

"Helm a-lee!" Nath's voice rang out again, and the helmsman, an old hand from *Alarum,* brought *Redemption* close-hauled and held her there, where she shuddered against the fierce, disorganized chop. She nodded in satisfaction when she saw the maneuver had the desired effect of reducing the wind's pressure against the sail to make working it more manageable.

"Clap on to the clew lines and buntlines!" Lieutenant Merryweather's voice rang out from below. "Haul taut!"

Cashton saw the topsail's belly deflate further as its corners and foot were raised by the men hauling on the lines. She heard a disturbance below, but ignored it and boomed out, "Haul up the topsail! Haul out the reef tackles!"

The order given, she and the topmen waited patiently for the sail to be hauled up by the pulley-hauley crew below. When she was satisfied that it was snugged up as much as possible, she barked out, "Lay out and tie the reef!"

She leaned over the yard to lean her belly against it, as did the men and women to either side of her, and pushed hard against the foot lines to stabilize her position as much as possible. Then, in conjunction with her fellows, she grabbed the reef points and passed them through the reef cringles and tied them around the yard. It was hard, dangerous work, rendered more perilous by the wild oscillation of the masts and the bucking of the ship, but she was proud to do it. It took a special breed of sailor to rate a position in the tops, and doubly special to be appointed Captain of the Tops. Over the last two years she had gained the tops, rated Captain of the Mizzentops, and was now Captain of the Foretops. When Rollings moved up the ladder, as she certainly would, Cashton would ascend to the post she most admired, Captain of the Maintops!

"Light up and aloft! Lay in!" the bosun shouted, and the foretop hands inched their way back along the spar toward the mast. Cashton glanced quickly over her shoulder to wink broadly at Wainwright, who was new to the foretops, but was shaping up to be a good 'un. She was confused for a moment when she saw the space next to her was vacant, and her heart sank. He'd fallen without her hearing! The poor devil! An out-of-place movement caught her attention, and she glanced aft and into Wainwright's fear-widened eyes. His hand reached out beseechingly to her as he hung in midair just out of her reach. She tried to scream for help, but the wind forced her words back down her throat and left her coughing and gagging with the awful taste of rotting meat in her mouth. The mast spiraled around, now leaning far out to starboard, and nothing but wind-harried waves were visible beneath her feet. She knew what was coming and leaned as far out toward Wainwright as she could, stretching her arm until she felt pops and tearing pain in her shoulder.

And then he disappeared. The splash of his body hitting water feetfirst was instantly scrubbed away by the rough seas. He was gone without a trace, lost to something unseen and unknown.

Muscle memory alone brought her through the rest of the evolution of reefing the main topsail. Later, she would have no memory of anything between Wainwright's demise and the coffee with a dollop of rum served to her and the other foretopmen at Captain Nath's orders. She could not even recall reporting Wainwright's death to the captain, though her second, Bell, assured her that she had done so, saying that he must have slipped on the footline, for he was there one moment and gone the next.

As the foretopmen sprinted up the ratlines in a death-defying feat of agility and sangfroid, Odric Orlin, a volunteer landsman, struggled to find the courage to cross the deck to one of the ship's innumerable and unintelligibly named ropes. He reckoned that ten thousand miles of cordage was deployed about the *Revenant*, some depending from the towering masts and spars, others connecting the same in a complex array that would leave a globe spider blushing with envy, and still more that passed through gaskets, holes, grates, and what-have-you to disappear belowdecks. He had the devil's own time telling his clew lines from his buntlines. Indeed, the prospect of dealing with them left his mouth dry and his palms damp, and now, staggering against a wind the like of which he'd never known and gasping for air through mouthfuls of breath composed of equal parts air and salt spray, he found himself terrified. He feared each step across the gyrating deck would send him sailing, arms flailing, over the rail to feed the sharks, or be burned to charcoal by a bolt of the lightning that crowded the sky and battered his eardrums with an endless, thunderous roar. Or that a mountainous wave would crash down on *Redemption*, smash her to flinders, and drown every mother's son or daughter within her.

When he finally groped his way down the lifeline to the rope on which he was to haul, he found that he was the last to clap on to it and groaned. He had not learned much in the last few weeks, but he did know that this was the worst place one could find themselves in a pulley-hauley line. He was the anchor, and it was his responsibility to ensure not an inch of progress was surrendered if one or more of his fellow lubbers lost their grip on the line.

"Avast moping about there, ye damned lubber," Dundel, a bosun's mate, shouted, and laid his starter, the butt end of a stout rope, lightly across Orlin's back. "D'ye want to see us pooped! Clap on and haul with a will, damn your eyes!"

Orlin did not, indeed, wish to see the ship pooped, a catastrophe whose details were a mystery to him, but was clearly best to avoid. He grabbed onto the last section of rope and was about to heave on it for all he was worth when he felt it writhe in his hands. He looked down at the end of the rope in his hands and found himself blinking into the cold, ophidian eyes of a great snake. He screamed and attempted to throw the writhing creature away from him. It would not be disposed of that easily, though.

Each time he attempted to fling it away, it sank cruel, curved fangs into his hands and arms. His screams became frantic as his veins burned with venom, and Dundel, to whom it appeared Orlin was engaged in lunatic antics, seized him by the shoulders and gave him a vigorous shake.

"Here now! Cut your capers and clap on to the line or I'll—"

"Snake! Snake!" Orlin turned and displayed his shredded arms, which bled freely upon the deck, where it was instantly diluted by streams of rain. "The line is a snake!"

Dundel gaped at the sight of a half dozen or more wounds, which might have been dealt by a straight razor. He seized the fellow by the elbow and pulled him away from the tail of the clew lines and shouted, "Ashes! You've done yourself a mischief! Step away from the line!" His humane concern for the lubber was clear even through the gale.

He herded the weeping, gibbering wretch toward the hatch and below to the sick bay, pausing only to ask Mid Weard to watch over the hands at the clew lines.

Nath gave the hands a few moments to catch their breath once the topsails were reefed. There would be hot grog for them later, once the next evolution was complete, and he was content with *Revenant*'s course and saw how she behaved before the wind with the bit in her teeth, so to speak. He leaned close to Merryweather and shouted in her ear, "Best put the word out for the magister. We may require her art to weather this with as little harm to flesh and timber as we may."

Merry called out to pass the word for the magister and in a few moments a bedraggled Yeardly appeared, a tarpaulin hat knotted tightly under his chin and his loose, straw-colored hair trailing behind him, shedding great drops of water wrung from it by the wind. His face was solemn as he tugged the brim of his hat and reported to Nath.

"The magister has suffered some mischance and is unconscious. She is in the sick bay now, and Dr. Rondelle has examined her. He reports that she has no injuries requiring his attention, and it is his opinion that the best course is to give her a whiff of the salts if she hasn't come to herself within an hour or so."

"I'm relieved to hear she has taken no serious hurt," Nath said earnestly. "How does the cockpit look? Not too crowded, I hope?"

Yeardly shook his head vigorously, partially in answer to Nath's question and partially to clear the rain from his eyes. "A broken arm, and a broken leg, I believe. One lubber who copped it by contriving to hang himself in the ratlines."

"What in the Redeemer's name was he doing in the ratlines?" Nath demanded.

"None can say, sir. One moment he was jostling about with his division; the next he was gone. His body was noticed by one of the lifeguards stationed at the lee rail, who raised the alarm."

"Strange way to die, but the poor devil isn't the first to spend his whole life looking for a remarkable demise." Nath shrugged the mystery away and focused on more immediate conundrums. "We can certainly weather this storm without a magister's assistance, but damme if I wouldn't feel better with a little magic to even the odds twixt us and old Mother Gwenolc."

"Well, sir, perhaps," Yeardly managed to shout and mumble simultaneously. "I mean, I have, with the magister as a mentor, of course—"

"Yes, yes, Yeardly. I'm aware of your advanced studies with Lady d'Tancreville. If you truly believe you could be of help with what you've learned, then pray, do what you can. Do not overextend yourself or bite off more than you can chew, though, you hear me?"

"Yes, sir! I'm very aware of the limits of my abilities and have no desire to endanger the ship or myself by exceeding them!" The bright grin with which he spoke gave Nath some cause to doubt his earnestness, but he dismissed Yeardly with an outwardly confident nod.

As Yeardly took his place near the binnacle, the same spot Enid usually stood unless Nath called her to his side, Nath ordered the helm to come hard to starboard to bear off on a course that had the wind and, to a lesser extent, the waves quartering to *Revenant*'s stern. She settled quickly into the new course and was soon scudding over the waves at a breathtaking speed. Nath felt the sting of sleet mixed in with the icy range and prayed it didn't accumulate on the masts and spars.

Nath summoned Merryweather and Kaliktiklak to join him near the mizzenmast, where they stood together with their heads bowed like three tarpaulined monks at prayer.

"I believe we are good as we are, Master Kaliktiklak," he shouted over the rush of the wind. "I leave the barky in your and Lieutenant Merryweather's capable hands. See to it that the hands receive a hot tot of rum to reward their efforts. They did a fine job, salts and lubbers alike!"

Lieutenant Merryweather responded with an exaggerated nod and bellowed back, "If the wind continues to rise—"

"It will." Kaliktiklak's strange voice sliced through the gale like a scythe through dry grass.

"—We'll get her down to her bare poles and a slip of storm sail."

"Yeardly has volunteered to use the art he's learned from the magister's private tutoring." Nath's face, stiff with cold, contorted his grin into a grimace. "Put him to whatever use seems best as you judge it."

"Where is the magister?" Merryweather's immediate look of concern was obvious, even through eyes pricked by ice-cold needles of rain.

"She took a slight knock to the head early on," he answered. "Mr. Yeardly had her into the cockpit practically before she hit the ground. No real harm done."

He gave them each a comradely squeeze before going below to look in on Enid and the other injured *Redemption*s.

chapter 14

Revenant ran before the storm through the night and into the next day, racing across the broken chop under bare poles and a lightning-riven sky. The repeated broadsides of thunder eventually roused Enid to consciousness. She found herself in a strange hammock that jerked in random, truncated arcs and occasionally floated in mid-air as if the earth's magnetism had loosed its hold on her. She heard a growling snore nearby, someone moaning a bit farther away, and finally the brassy voice of Dr. Rondelle warning someone not to continue picking at their bandages "lest you pick away the scrap of skin on your wrist that is all that stands betwixt you and rapid exsanguination."

I am in the sick bay, she thought muzzily. *How did I come to be here?*

Our hidden foe has made himself felt. Dunaughy's voice in her skull sounded as bleary and strained as her own. He picked up on her observation and snapped, *And well it might! We were not struck with a physical blow alone, but also by a blade of hatred and resentment, honed to a razor's edge after many years of carefully husbanded spite. We were both lain low with negligible ease.*

We must be better prepared next time, Enid thought gravely.

Indeed, we must, Dunaughy replied. *For there will be not be a third chance afterward.*

She lay quietly in her cot for a time, gathering her thoughts behind a wall of privacy. She and Dunaughy agreed to set aside a portion of their selves as inviolable strongholds in which they could preserve their private thoughts, fears, and dreams. She kept her conversations with Old Herry there, safe from view, along with certain familial lore, and her more lascivious personal recollections. In the privacy of her own thoughts alone, she considered the words that trespassed in her mind shortly before her intellectual lights were extinguished: *Verlinherrinar is mad or senile if she reckons you a threat to me.*

She wondered from whom those words emanated and the troubling after-memory of the scent of death it left in her mind. *Our hidden nemesis, of course. But who or what is he? He gave naught away save confirming his gender, assuming he—it—did not hide even this crumb of a clue to his nature with magic.*

There is little to pursue there, she thought. *But who is this "Verlinherrinar"?* His pronunciation of the name—*Vair-lin-HAIR-een-yar*—left her convinced he referred to the fey being that haunted the dueling ground where she lost her right hand, the very Old Herry who returned her hand to her, clamped in the jaws of one of Rue's awful little dogs. *The entire affair begins to reek of the Ylfar. Perhaps our anonymous malefactor is one of them as well. I must consult with Dunaughy, as the Murchadhans are said to retain more of the old lore than other folk. Ah! Merry!*

"Ah! Merry!" Enid's spoken words failed to convey the deep affection of her thoughts, so she added a wide, if somewhat worn smile, to punctuate them. She swiveled into a seated position, her long legs dangling so far below the hammock that she was able to steady herself with her heels. Conscious of the keen hearing of even an injured or dazed sailor, she restricted her conversation to officerly topics and inquired, "How long have I been *caulking*, as your salt might say? And how fares *Revenant*? I gather by her easier, though still unpredictably variable, motion that we have weathered the worst of the hurricane?"

Though amused, Merry's return smile was clearly laden with

relief. “Nigh on two days, I fear. We are riding the fading vigor of the blow, which you should know is but a speck on the force of a true hurricane, a species of storm completely unheard of in these waters, thank the Dear. Captain Nath has been on deck almost every hour since the blow hit to eke as much speed and seaway as the barky could make without losing her sticks. And we have made a most remarkable seaway, *Magister*.”

The admonition in Merry’s emphasis on her title was not lost on Enid, who, refraining from calling her “Merry” again instead said, “I am pleased to hear it, Lieutenant. How severely was our dear vessel savaged by the storm?”

“We took a bruising only, thanks to Master Kaliktiklak’s preparations and the captain’s seamanship,” Merry replied. “It was instructional to see their methods, the recollection of which will benefit my future commands!”

“I am pleased to see you are on your feet, Magister,” Rondelle interrupted in his brassy, disapproving voice. “Though I would be far more pleased if you had consulted with me before leaving your bed. Seeing that you are erect, mobile, and capable of human speech, perhaps you would lend your expertise to aid me in the assessment of a special case?”

Before awaiting an answer, Dr. Rondelle led them through the few occupied hammocks of the sick bay to a small table the doctor currently employed as a breakfast table. A man dressed in slops stood from the table as they approached and tugged at his forelock in salute to Merryweather.

“Lieutenant Merryweather, Magister d’Tancreville, allow me to introduce Odric Orlin, a landsman of the Afterguard. During the blow, Landsman Orlin had to be subdued by a bosun’s mate. He refused to assist in hauling on the clew lines, claiming they transformed into snakes in his hands. He could not be shaken from this claim despite the application of the mate’s starter.”

“Is that how you came to be hurt? By the bosun mate’s brutality?”

Enid asked Orlin, rather than speaking as if he were not relevant to the conversation centered upon him. Orlin opened his mouth to answer, but Rondelle spoke over him.

"It is not. It is best you see them for yourself." Rondelle took the man's left hand and carefully unwrapped the bandages that swathed his forearm. The process complete, he held the arm up for Enid's examination as if it were completely disconnected from the rest of Orlin's body. "What do you make of them?"

Enid took a quick glance at the proferred arm and arched a brow. "Snake bites?"

Rondelle nodded grimly. "Snake bites. Have you any theories for how my patient acquired them?"

Enid had no inkling of how Orlin contrived to have his forearms and right cheek repeatedly struck by snakes. She shrugged and said, "Were some aggressive sea serpents swept onto the ship by a wave?"

Rondelle snorted, and Enid began to bristle, but her irritation passed as the doctor said, "We are of a mind, Magister, as we so often are. That was my first thought as well, but Master Kaliktiklak assures me the waters of the approaches are too cold to support your venomous sea serpents. He assisted me in searching the ship to ensure none of the sailors smuggled any snakes aboard. We found a prodigious feathered reptile, the size of a frying hen, but no snakes."

"Then these are not snake bites?"

"They certainly are," Rondelle said. "And Landsman Orlin would have died of them if he had not been borne here so quickly for aid. Indeed, my antivenom cantrip was pressed to the limits by the quantity and virulence of the poison coursing through his veins."

"It was the ropes," Enid said, glancing sharply at Orlin.

Orlin nodded, meeting her eyes and matching her steady gaze. "It *was* the ropes, Magister. They twisted into snakes and bit me repeatedly until I threw them from me."

"What happened after that?" Merryweather asked. "To the ropes, I mean. Did they slither off into the scuppers, or . . . ?"

"Once I released them, they were merely ropes again," Orlin said. "And they remained ropes unless I made to touch them, when they become snakes and strike at me with terrible speed and strength."

Merry glanced at Enid, who shrugged and said, "I see no reason to gainsay him. The wounds are not self-inflicted, after all."

"Is it a permanent affliction?" Merry asked. "It will be damned difficult to find a way to employ a sailor for whom ropes and cables are a mortal hazard."

Enid shrugged again. "I will work with Dr. Rondelle and attempt to determine the limits of this . . . malady."

As best as Enid and Rondelle could ascertain, the ropes were likely to remain anathema to Orlin for the foreseeable future. Fortunately, the young man could read Albionic and write in a bold, clean hand. After accepting his oath that he would not reveal the true cause of his change in status to anyone, his name was removed from the landsman column of the log and entered as a volunteer clerk in Nath's service, seconded to Enid should she require his services.

"It is damnably disheartening, Enid, damnably disheartening. The officers carried out their duties as if they'd served together for years and were intimately familiar with each other's habitual methods, and the crew, bless 'em, even the landsmen and Ainsley Bottoms hands came together and made up for any lack of experience by giving full attention to their officers' and warrants' instructions and following them with all their heart and energy! There are crack frigates who would not have done so well, on that you have my oath."

"Then what has you so low, Rue?" Enid asked as she absently blew a stream of smoke that coalesced into the form of intertwined serpents before it was shredded by the brisk, cold breeze that flowed past a window left ajar in the stern gallery.

"That, for one," Nath snapped and pointed at the wispy forms of the smoke snakes before they were devastated by the cold draft. "This poor Orlin was set upon by lines transformed into asps by what? A fey trickster, straight from the faerie tales our youth?"

"Perhaps. It has yet to be confirmed, but it seems likely."

"I thought the Ylfar were a purely notional threat," Nath groused.

"They are mentioned in Admiralty Board documents and in both *Herbstrom's* and the *Instructions for a Magister of the Royal Navy*."

"Sure, and so is the Kraken, but no officer of the combined fleets has ever faced one," Nath scoffed.

"Or at least never done so and lived to tell the tale," Enid said, tapping ash into a salver for the purpose.

"Your levity is rarely displayed, Enid, and when it is, it may be counted on to be inappropriate to the moment." Enid was pleased to see Nath's disapprobation was quite exploded by the amused glint in his eye. "You look well, Enid. You are fully recovered from your fall?"

"I believe so," she replied. The wind-driven rain limited visibility in the opening moments of the gale, so there were no living witnesses to the events that left her stretched senseless on the deck, so it was assumed she'd taken a fall. Enid saw no reason to disabuse them of their misapprehension and kept her peace on the matter. "I've resumed my duties, at any gate."

Nath nodded, and a grin grew slowly on his face. At last, he chuckled and said, "You took my admonishment to clap on to the lifeline and keep your hold on it no matter what may come quite seriously! The line could not be coaxed from your . . . your hand. Fisk was forced to cut the line on either side of it in order to get you below."

Enid arched a brow at this revelation. "How odd. Dr. Rondelle must have cut it free, for it was not in my hand when I awoke."

"That is another odd part of the story. As soon as you were laid in a hammock, your grip relaxed and the scrap of line fell to the deck."

Dunaughy?

I had no hand in the matter. Enid heard the specter's amusement with his own fling and struggled to avoid rolling her eyes, a gesture that would surely be misinterpreted by Nath as he was in the midst of an animated description of the events she missed over the last couple of days as she lay unconscious in the sick bay.

No call for a glare, Enid, Dunaughy said. *It is strange that your hand would cling to the safety line until you were laid out safely below. Does your hand have some degree of autonomy?*

Not that I'm aware of—and I pray not!

"So," Nath sighed airily. "You are probably curious as to our position and how far out it puts us from Not Toulon. Well, I'm happy to say that we have gained one or two days of easting, perhaps more if the post gale winds continue to drive hard on the current quarter. This little gale may have cut as much as a week from the time required to cross the line, which permits me, at last, to open the Sea Lord's orders and understand whether he has sentenced us to blockade duty and no opportunity to excel or sent us into the jaws of a basilisk."

He chased a deep drag of cigarillo smoke with a long sip of wine and shrugged. "Master Kaliktiklak, a replacement for any dozen barometers, assures me we will have fine, if brisk, weather for a week or more, so there's a blessing. You may rest and study at your leisure and Guns and I will see to training the new crews to serve their guns accurately and lively."

chapter 15

The next few days were not the period of restful study Rue promised her. Instead, the storm was followed by an irritatingly noisy trial for Enid. Each day began with the usual racket involved in cleaning *Redemption*'s deck and seeing to her daily maintenance, not to mention the shrill skirling of the bosun's pipes calling the various divisions to breakfast. No sooner was that complete than the marine drummer would beat out the tattoo to clear the decks for battle and Enid would be forced to seek asylum in her workspace on the orlop to avoid being trampled by scurrying *Revenant*s rushing to pull down false walls and stow or secure anything that might get underfoot or be transformed into lethal splinters during an engagement. Then came the mummery of the powderless gun drills, with the air ringing with shouted orders, the dull rumble of feet stampeding back and forth across the deck as the gun crews went through the motions of loading, firing, swabbing, loading, firing, swabbing . . .

It is enough to drive me mad, Enid thought. *When will this nonsensical play-acting cease?*

When our captain is certain that the gun crews have their tasks down to rote. Then things will become wondrously louder as he allows them to actually fire the guns. She sensed rather than saw Dunaughy's smile and had to consciously resist allowing her own face to be drawn into his expression.

Her next thought was driven from her head by a titanic roar and the ship rocked beneath her. Dust sifted down through the planking overhead, and her nostrils filled with the unmistakable odor of burnt alchemical powder.

Well, the larboard watch earned his trust, Dunaughy chuckled in her mind. *The starboard watch seems to lag behind.*

It did. The larboard guns fired twice more times before the starboard side finally blasted away. For the rest of the day, the guns fired at once and their crews raced to see which watch would be ready to fire the next volley first. By the end of the day, both watches were averaging roughly three-and-a-half broadsides in five minutes. There were, however, some few guns on both sides that lagged noticeably behind the other crews'. By that time, Enid had abandoned her workshop to watch the great guns fire. She stood next to Yeardly as the gun crews competed against one another within their watches. The rivalry was intense, as the fastest team on each watch would receive an extra tot of rum. As she watched, the captain of one of the gun crews, a sturdy-looking young woman with pale skin and short-cropped red hair, approached them, hurriedly knuckling her forehead as she came.

"Yer pardon, Mister Yeardly, but I was hoping the magister might take a look at the lock on Number Four. It seems t'be hangin' fire."

Before Yeardly could speak, Enid nodded briskly and said, "Let us have a look at this troublesome device."

She knelt by the gun and examined the lock. The gun's crew gathered around her and practically hopped from foot to foot, so charged were they with eagerness to rejoin the contest. Rather than find their enthusiasm distracting, Enid was infected with it. Her gloves interfered with the precision of her touch, so she stripped them off and tossed them aside. Within a moment, she had the lock recalibrated and recharged besides. She stood and slapped her hands together to shake off the minute traces of the dweomer's charging agent and grinned at the redheaded gun captain.

"There you are! Right as rain!"

Instead of the expected chorus of thanks, she was met with a silent stare of suspicion and no small amount of dread. It took her a moment to realize that the gazes of the Number 4 gun crew were fixed on her right hand, which, by chance, caught a ray of sunshine that threaded the rigging and set its silver to shining like a flare.

She raised the hand in a conciliatory gesture and said, "There's nothing to be alarmed by here. I lost my hand by mischance and was able to restore it by combining my flesh with a specially prepared concoction of—"

Nath called for the larboard watch to fire on the up roll, which set all the gun crews, including the wide-eyed tenders of gun 4, into frenetic action. She retreated quickly to Yeardly's side. He shook his head and said, "Well, the news of your hand will have spread from stem to stern and keel to maintop before the end of the watch."

Enid nodded and a great weight settled on her shoulders and into her gut. "It was clumsily done. I must find a way to set it right."

When the thunder of the guns receded, Yeardly said, "My advice is to avoid trying to explain it. They are likely to misunderstand and anything they don't understand, they will fear. Simply act as if such things are commonplace in Ardainne."

Enid nodded and clenched her right hand into a fist and reflexively hid it behind her back.

"I believe you may misjudge the common person's ability to grasp the unusual, but I will do as you suggest."

After the dinner hour had passed, Captain Nath sent mid Harlech to summon Enid to his cabin with his compliments. She found him in his day room, a map, navigational tools, and a small stack of papers on the table. Marbury and Maubin slept on a wadded blanket on the floor near his feet.

"I'm told the cat is out of the bag," he said, leaning over the table.

"It is, and judging by the dark looks of some of the crew, it may be used to flog me."

"The ship's people are a superstitious lot, but they're also mercurial with their attention," he said and tapped the stack of papers. "Hopefully, these orders from Admiralty will seize their imagination and distract them to your benefit. At the very least, you'll have an opportunity to prove you are of greater value to their welfare than a threat."

"You've read the secret orders?"

"Indeed. We passed through the coordinates at which I was to open them shortly after the noon bells."

"Well, what are they?"

Nath grinned like a schoolboy with an unshared secret and circled an area on the map with the tip of his finger.

"I believe you might recognize the locale, Enid?"

She studied the map for a moment and the landmarks clicked into place in her mind.

"I know it well. It is part of the coastal region of the Duchy of Archinaux and represents the coastal section of the March of Tancreville. Indeed, here is the village that gives the March and my title their name."

Nath pointed to a spot on the map. "And this rocky promontory, marked with a fortification? You are aware of it?"

"Of course," she said. "It is the des Fantômes. A royal holding and not part of my family's demesne. The old castle there serves as a prison for enemies of the Crown—or did, before the revolution."

"Do you have any knowledge of its interior?"

Enid shook her head. "Few save the warden and their guards have walked within the place and breathed free air again. What is your interest in the place?"

"Lieutenant Cierina Bascombe is held there. We are tasked with her rescue."

"Her brother's presence aboard is explained, then."

Nath nodded. "Indeed. And our receipt of these orders was predicated upon *your* presence aboard *Revenant*. It is hoped that your familiarity with the area will be of great value and, beyond that, it is

Admiralty's hope that you can organize some of the locals into an ad hoc militia to hold the bridge to the castle so that the full force of our marines can be thrown into Cierina's rescue. What do you think of the merits of the idea?"

Enid frowned. "I relied on a proxy to see to my demesne, so my sudden appearance to beg them to risk their lives for a foreign officer may not be as inspiring as you might hope."

"Are you hated there, then? Or vigorously disliked?"

"I should think not. I instructed my proxy to take a light hand with them and demand no more taxes than required to meet my obligations to the king. The folk of Tancreville and its environs were left to their own ends for the most part."

"Then the gambit is worth a venture, I suppose," Nath said and retrieved the chart. "Our intelligence indicates that your people are resistant to Theocratic rule, encouraged by royalist holdouts in Arleonne."

"Hmm." Enid did not savor the prospect of risking the lives of the people who once looked to her for protection to rescue a single Albion officer whom she'd never met. "What is the probability that the bridge will be attacked?"

"Fairly high, I'd say. There is a camp of the People's Legion down the coast from the Château des Fantomes. They will likely be alerted by the garrison at the castle when we attack. Providence willing, we might be in and out with Cierina Bascombe before the Rats are alerted, but it is no sure thing."

Enid sighed. The people of Ardainne must eventually rise up, fight, and some must die before Theocratic rule could be overturned. She'd seen Albion spend enough blood in the cause that she could not refuse to risk that of her own people with a good conscience.

"I will do whatever is in my power to win the local militia leader's support for Bascombe's rescue."

"I can ask no more and expected no less," Nath said. "Come, let me lay out my plans so that you can point out any errors based on your superior knowledge of the ground. After we have settled on our stratagem, I will share it with the other officers for their input."

Revenant's other officers arrived in less time than it took Enid and Nath to finish a cigarillo while watching Yaric silently herd the two terrier puppies, both stumbling on unsteady, sleepy legs, into the captain's sleeping room.Once the other lieutenants and other key warrants presented themselves to Nath, they all crowded around his desk and the charts showing the Ardainne coast at varying levels of detail. She noticed Merryweather and Wilk surreptitiously squinting to recognize any clues to *Revenant*'s destination the maps might hold without actually studying them.

Nath noticed too, and said, "Do not strain your eyes so. We are bound for this place, the Château des Fantomes, which stands atop a promontory on the coast of the Duchy of Archinaux. It was used as a prison for unfortunate wretches that the king determined to be too politically dangerous to be free, but too important to execute. Those who were sent there became living ghosts, never to be seen again. The Rats have put it to the same use. Our goal is to rescue Lieutenant Cierina Bascombe from her captivity there."

The gathered officers muttered enthusiastically about the mission, and Lieutenant Leonid Bascombe was the beneficiary of many "give you joy" claps on the back, to which he responded with a tight-lipped smile.

"As it happens, we were selected for this honor due to Magister d'Tancreville, as the château is located within her former holdings. Admiralty hopes that she will be able to gain the support of local royalist resistance members to assist us in our task."

"And hence the extra marines," Harcourt said as he rubbed his chin. "Between a band of militia, my marines, and any sailors sent ashore, we shall have a formidable force, as long as the place isn't home to a regiment or bristling with cannons."

"It is neither," Enid said. "It was formidable in its day, but the methods of war have changed greatly. Now it is a middling strongpoint at best. As a prison, though, it is nearly without peer. The characteristics that once made it a nearly impenetrable fortress now make it an inescapable gaol."

Seeing expressions darken around her, Enid continued briskly, saying, "But stratagems employed to keep prisoners trapped within the château's walls will be of negligible value in keeping us out."

Nath nodded. "Enid has a solid grasp on what will be required for us to enter the château. Once inside, we will locate Cierina Bascombe, release her from her cell, and escort her safely aboard *Revenant.* Then we will make all speed for Gisbon, where she will be handed over to Admiral Weymouth, who will see to her transport home, much to Bascombe the younger's relief!"

Leonid Bascombe returned Nath's smile and accepted another round of handshakes, backslaps, and shoulder punches with patience.

"Master-at-arms Shea will busy herself and her mates in training the landsmen to fight with cutlass, pistol, and boarding axe as well as honing the skills of the rest of the crew. I expect each of you to monitor this training closely and identify any weak links who might slow us down or fail to pull their weight as we assault the château."

Greeted with a unanimous muttering of acknowledgment, Nath said, "That is all, then. Return to your duties!"

chapter 16

Enid was rattled out of bed by drums beating to quarters and bosuns' pipes shrieking from one end of *Revenant* to the other. Damn Nath and his incessant gun drills! She donned her uniform quickly, her mood unimproved by Dunaughy's amusement in the back of her head. She pushed her way through the bustle of sailors running this way and that in controlled chaos and made her way to the quarterdeck. There, she found Nath studying the set of the sails and shouting the occasional order, which was diligently echoed down the length of the vessel. When he saw her approach, he graced her with an easy smile and said, "Well, Enid! It seems there will be a race today!"

"A race? Between gun crews? How is that different from yesterday or the day before?"

Nath laughed. "No, not between gun crews, but between *Revenant* and the Ardain frigate yonder."

Enid glanced in the direction he indicated and gave a slight start. There indeed was an Ardain frigate bearing down on them, the black flag of a Confessor streaming from its mainmast.

"Ashes! How did she come to be so close upon us?"

"There is a magister of some capability aboard her that swaddled her in night shadow until she came close enough that the mainmast watch saw through the glamour and gave the alarm."

"There will be a fight, then?"

Nath chuckled. "You sound as eager as a hound to be after a fox. Alas, we are not the hounds today, but rather the fox. We shall do all in our power to avoid a fight. Indeed, we are under orders to avoid battle until Bascombe is released or while she is aboard."

"I see," Enid said. "That is disappointing."

"Now, let us see how fast our *Revenant* can fly!"

Enid watched the chase from the quarterdeck with Nath's leave. She found the experience too like the agonizing day spent in flight aboard the little merchantman *Marie* to be as sanguine about the affair as Nath seemed to be. Once the ship was on the heading he desired and the sails set just so, he forgot himself and clapped her on the shoulder.

"Now that we are showing them our heels, we may as well bare our teeth as well," he said and called for the chase guns to be manned. Those cannons, which faced directly to the stern, were as different from the hulking smashers that lined the quarterdeck's port and starboard sides as rifles were from a blunderbuss. The smashers were squat and black with gaping maws, while the polished brass chase guns were works of art, long-barreled and elegantly tapered. Nath had enthused about these "long nines" previously and regaled her with tales of his heroic struggles with the Ordnance Board to retain them when *Revenant* was fitted with her massive new smashers.

"We are nearly at the limit of these beauties' range," Nath said as their crews readied them to fire. "So, we'll take a potshot or two before leaving that Rat plodder behind."

And so they did, with Nath moving from one gun to the other to aim and fire it. The crew cheered when an L-shaped hole appeared in the enemy frigate's forecourse sail and Nath grinned like a schoolboy. After two rapid volleys, the chase guns being manned entirely by handpicked *Alarum*s, Nath stood back and shared a look of grave concern with Enid.

"What's our speed?"

One of the *Revenant*s bawled out, "Nine knots!"

"*Nine knots?*" Nath hissed to Enid. "We should be doing eleven at least, based on the trials we've put her through. What in the devil is slowing our speed? Magic?"

Enid let her awareness run free, driven by her will to discover if some unnatural force held *Revenant* in its grip. Already loosened from her mortal bonds to react to any nonsense from the Ardain frigate's magister, her consciousness swarmed over the ship, ascending to the heights of its masts and descending to probe the inky shadows of its lowest, sun-starved decks. Whatever slowed *Redemption*'s pace, it was rooted there, in the dark recesses of her belly.

She snapped back to her body with a minute jerk. Before Nath could question her, she said, "There may be trouble in the hold. May I bring Mid Yeardly to aid me there?"

"Of course! Mid Yeardly! Pray assist Magister d'Tancreville in her duties as she requires!"

Yeardly saluted and passed the command of his division to a master's mate before sprinting to join Enid. Together they rapidly descended from the clean air and bright skies of the upper deck into the thick, foul air and dark gloom of the hold.

"My instructions for you are simple," Enid told him in a low, firm voice. "Stand your ground until I retreat. If I should fall, do all in your power to drag me out of this place, lest I be lost. Do you understand?"

"Lost?"

"Do you understand?" Her voice was sharp and strained.

Yeardly nodded. "I understand."

"Good, now stand here beside me and we shall see what we shall see."

She held her right hand aloft and performed the mental formulations required to coax its silver to glow like the brightest of lanterns. Rats fled from their feet as a circle of darkness around them was banished by sharp, white light. The shadows that inhabited the darkness beyond undulated and writhed in a way that forced Yeardly to grit his teeth to stop their chattering.

It threatens us directly. Dunaughy's warning held an edge of savage pleasure.

We must force him to confront us, Enid agreed. *Or to flee recklessly so we can track it back to its sanctum.*

"What we seek lies forward," Enid said, after taking a few more steps. Her voice echoed tinnily as if the half globe of light centered upon Yeardly and herself was the physical limit of their space and her words careened from one curve of the globe to another before reaching Yeardly's ears. He resolutely followed Enid into the darkness despite the cold sweat that ran in rivulets between his shoulder blades and trickled down his spine.

She came to a halt in the forward hold, before the great curved timbers that described the bluff curve that formed *Revenant*'s bow. The heavy oak's rough surface bore the mark of hatchet and adz, as well as the carved initials of the men who wielded them. She felt she was near the source of the evil sending reined in *Revenant*'s natural swiftness. And then the offending magic ceased.

He has vanished! Dunaughy snapped. *As if he stepped through a door that closed behind him! How can we corner something that can step into another world with no more effort than we expend to step over a deck seam?*

Enid pushed Dunaughy's internal dialog to the back of her mind as it devolved into a caustic but lyrical stream of Murchadhan oaths.

"It slipped free of my grasp," Enid sighed and leaned against the wall, her forehead pressed against the rough timber. The wood was surprisingly cold and soothed her aching head remarkably. The effort to achieve even his unhappy result had been significant, even with Dunaughy's otherworldly assistance.

"Is there aught we can do to refine our search?" Yeardly asked. "I would have sworn on my soul that we were nearly upon it."

"I would have done the same," Enid sighed. "Still, our effort wasn't completely unsuccessful. We came near enough to it that it ceased its efforts to slow *Revenant* for fear of being discovered. And we are now apprised of its general location. Let us get above and inform Captain Nath."

Back on deck, Enid found that the Ardain frigate was still some distance away, but it had closed slightly with *Revenant*. She was now answering *Revenant*'s cannons with fire from her own chase guns, albeit at a slower pace. She joined Nath on the quarterdeck and, at his curious glance, leaned forward and said in a voice too low to carry, "I believe I've found the rough locality of the source of our troubles, but there is nothing I can do about it now without leaving us all but unprotected from the magister yonder. I believe they are the more urgent threat?"

"Tomorrow's problems for tomorrow, today's on the instant. For now, mark that frigate. Does she look familiar to you?"

"No. Honestly, I see little to differentiate between one ship and another, aside from their hulls being painted in some startling color or that bristle with more masts than the norm. They are all one and the same to me."

"Well, if that one yonder ain't our old friend *Artagny*, I'm the Emperor of Malasfandyar. She has had a different pattern of paint applied and they made some changes to her during repairs, but that is her."

"Can we outrun her?"

"She has a fraction of a knot on us, so without we gain our speed, or she loses hers, she'll catch us up sometime tonight."

Enid frowned. "And there's nothing we can do but fire at her with your elegant but ineffectual guns?"

Nath smiled darkly. "These were forged in the Venable armory and are anything but ineffective. Perhaps with a little assistance from you, we can prove that to this thrice-damned Confessor."

She sighed and shrugged. "I will do what I can. At the very least I should be able to counter any wards my counterpart throws up against us."

And so she bent her will toward clearing a path for the Venable guns' nine-pound balls, punching holes in wards and redirecting sylphs meant to divert them from their aimed course. The *Artagny*'s magister made several well-timed and admirably formulated sendings, which Enid was more than capable of thwarting—for the moment. This Magister would be a formidable foe if they survived a few battles and applied themselves to the close study of their art. The effort required by these occupations was slight at first, but as the day wore down to sunset, the hours began to take their toll on her.

Nath, on the other hand, seemed tireless. He jumped from gun to gun to make minute corrections in aim before yanking their lanyard and hurling yet another messenger of death toward his enemy. Her activities lacked his vigor, though, and she became so single-minded in her efforts to guide one of his shots to its mark that she failed to notice when the boom of the larboard chase gun was followed a moment later by a distant but distinct *crack!* The cheers of the crew drew her attention back to the corporeal world in time to see *Artagny*'s foremast shudder under the impact of a ball from one of Nath's beloved chase guns. For a moment it seemed no real harm was done, but then, under the pressure of yards and yards of billowing sails, the wounded mast gave way. It pivoted on its splintered base and, prevented from collapsing forward by sturdy rigging, it toppled in a long curve before plunging its tops and most of its mainsail into the waves on the frigate's larboard bow. The whole ship shivered violently as it suddenly lost most of its way with the loss of a third of her sails and the massive sheet anchor that was once her foremast and foresails.

"Ha!" Nath threw his hat in the air, where the wind caught it and bore it away down into the waist. "Let that be a lesson to you, you Rat bastards!"

"Shall we come around to close?" Merryweather asked, her face split in a wide, predatory grin.

"No," Nath shouted back. "Hold our course and set some of the people to repairing any rigging or sails that have been cut up by enemy fire."

A group of landsmen in the waist who had cheered at Merryweather's suggestion fell into silence and regarded Nath with a combination of disappointment and sullen disapproval. One sour-faced woman at their fore had the nerve to loudly boo his command. Nath's jollity evaporated in an instant. He pointed a finger at her and shouted, "Mid Weard! Take that woman's name! Her rum is to be stopped for a week!"

"Damn the temerity of that woman," Nath growled, pacing back and forth before the windows of the stern gallery. "How dare she boo one of my commands? A less amiable captain would have the grate rigged and see her whipped half to death! It is her good fortune that *Revenant* is not a flogging ship."

"Judging by her woeful expression, I believe your punishment to be more torturous than a mere flogging."

"I saw my Aunt Dolorous put a sailor on bread and water for a week for *frowning* at one of her orders." Nath flopped down onto the couch before the stern gallery and waved a dismissive hand. "She is a lubber. The ink of her mark in *Avarice*'s log was barely dry when the Ainsley Bottom mutiny broke out. Still, her behavior cannot be ignored. Her fellow landsmen and the other poor devils caught up by the press will benefit from her lesson."

Nath sighed and said, "We shall set that aside now. Sit and tell me what you found below. Is *Revenant* cursed?"

"Not in the sense you mean," Enid said. "She has not been invested with a lingering malefic formulation. She may, however, be haunted, perhaps by the malcontents who died during the mutiny, or even the officers who were slain and have been warped by resentment at their ill treatment."

"So, she is not cursed, she is accursed," Nath sighed. "I fear I find little comfort in that distinction."

"Nor should you. Countering a curse can be time-consuming and tedious, but the effort is almost always rewarded with success.

Banishing hostile spirits is far more difficult and, in truth, there is no guarantee that it can be accomplished, nor that the accomplishment will be permanent."

"I trust you will find a way. If you fail, well, it is not worth considering." Nath stared side-wise out the stern gallery for a long moment and then continued, "Captain Ourey, who commanded this ship when the mutiny occurred, was a friend of Admiral Weymouth, who swears by his character. He believed the crew was enthralled by a bad apple and not driven to uprising by a brutal command. Do you think that the crew or officers could have been driven to savagery by this spirit or spirits?"

"It is quite possible," Enid said. "There is historical precedent to support the theory."

"Then I lay this additional duty upon you as both my friend and an officer under my command: See to it that I am relieved of command if you believe that I am no longer acting of my own accord. Your word on it as a gentle, please."

"You have my word."

"Rue-Naught, mine ass," Grimes muttered to her friend and former partner in crime as they carried fresh canvas from the sailmaker's stores that would be used to patch several holes in the mizzen topsail and main course. "We run at the first sight of a Rat and keep runnin' even after she were crippled!"

Ogilvy grunted his agreement and made a show of struggling with the canvas roll. In truth, it wasn't particularly heavy, but he made it a habit of appearing weaker than he was.

"I should sneak over the side, slip in them big windows in back, and slit the little bastard's throat," Grimes hissed. "I could come back the same way and none'd be the wiser."

"Calm your teats, or you'll get us both kilt," Ogilvy hissed back. "Half these sailors are brown to the neck for Rue-Naught. Keep your trap snapped till we make a few more friends."

"Yer right," Grimes sniffed. "We'll put together a crew of our own an' things will be different."

"Here now! What are you two muttering about?" The two startled at Yeardly's sharp words so near at hand.

"Nuffink, sor," Ogilvy simpered, "Just talkin' about old times."

"You were friends ashore, then?"

"More of passin' acquaintances, as you might say. Sharin' gossip makes a fellow a mite less homesick, but we don't want to look like chatterin' fools, so we were keepin' it down."

"Well, there's no need to whisper unless you've got secrets to keep. *Revenant* isn't a silent ship. Talk in a normal tone and keep it civil and no officer will think the less of you. Now, get back to your duties before the sailmaker decides to fix the sails with a patch of your skin."

The bosun piped all hands on deck prior to the evening meal. The *Revenant*s made a credible showing of forming up and toeing their lines, although there was still a bit of fumbling about by the landsmen. Once the divisions were in their place, Nath addressed them from the quarterdeck.

"I know abandoning a plump prize in our wake, rather than snatching her up, confounds you," Nath said. "I assure you, none of you were more pained by leaving that Rat frigate behind than me. Alas, neither you nor I had any choice in the matter."

Nath waved the oilskin orders pouch over his head and said, "We are under special orders from the Lords of Admiralty to undertake a mission of the utmost import and, in order to ensure we are in fit condition to carry those orders out, we are forbidden from engaging in combat until such a time as our mission is complete.

"I'm sure you're all eager to hear the nature of the mission, but I cannot share it with you until the moment of its execution is at hand. Should we fall into enemy hands, the fewer of us aware of the particulars of our endeavor the better. I give you my oath that it is an important undertaking that will cover us all in glory and stick a stout Albion thumb up to the knuckle in the Rat's eye!"

The cheer that followed was more or less spontaneous, though the Afterguard and Waisters required a bit of prodding by their officers.

It was the best I could hope for, Nath thought as he dismissed the crew. He spoke honestly when he said no one had endured so great a pang for letting a fat prize slip from their grasp than he, unless it was Merryweather. The command of a prodigiously fine prize like *Artagny* would certainly have paved the way to a command of her own. He didn't like the way the newcomers to his command moped off with their shoulders slumped, either. The promise of prize money was their only solace for being dragooned from their comfortable lives ashore or reassigned to the ill-rumored *Revenant.* The sight filled him with a superstitious dread the ship's history of blood-soaked mutiny might repeat itself.

He joined Merryweather, whose watch it was, on the windward side of the quarterdeck and motioned for Wilk and Bascombe to join them. Enid drifted over as well, as was her practice. Nath was pleased to see her and asked if she could deaden their voices so that nobody outside the circle of officers could be privy to their conversation. Enid smirked in response and made a few subtle passes with her hands.

"There," she said. "Anyone further than a foot or so away will only discern a rushing of wind if they seek to eavesdrop on our conversation."

"Good," Nath said. "Normally I wouldn't think of taking such a precaution aboard my own command, but these are extraordinary circumstances."

Without waiting for a response, he plunged on. "I expected some dissatisfaction at abandoning a prize, but not the level we just witnessed. The newcomers, particularly the Ainsley Bottom hands, seemed unacceptably restive despite learning my actions were constrained by orders from Admiralty. I conjure each of you to work closely with the mids and master's mates in your watches and divisions to deter the spread of this ill mood. Mind that you show no favoritism to the old *Alarums*, neither, as that could easily engender a resentment that will be far more difficult to eradicate."

The lieutenants pledged to do as he bade and returned to their duties with a spring in their step. Alone with Enid, Nath said, "I need not say that dealing with whatever lurks in the hold is your primary concern. Please see to it as quickly as you may."

Enid nodded.

"I will consult with *Dun—*" She corrected herself quickly by naming a nonsense author. "*—Dunalthin's Primer,* which focuses on such matters. This matter has my full and unwavering attention."

Nath nodded and gave Enid a grim smile. "You have my full confidence, Enid. If there is anyone in the fleet who can put quits to this nonsense, it is you."

You are truly distraught, Dunaughy thought as she took leave of Nath, who had correspondence to finish and send ashore before *Revenant* departed Middlesea. *And there is ample cause it. How are we to defeat something we cannot locate or identify? The only certainties associated with the threat are that it exists, and it means no good.*

Enid's only response was a slight deepening in the frown lines at the corners of her lips.

Nath sat at his compact writing desk and scrawled a quick note to Muirean advising her that he would send her the first of his journals once he'd filled it with his thoughts on whatever boons or banes he encountered in the future. He took longer to complete a letter to Emley, out of concern that she would be hurt he resorted to a writing his farewells rather than making them in the flesh. She'd been a sea officer and was not the sort of lover to be confounded by the idea of responsibility trumping romance, but trepidation still produced a quiver in his hand as he put the first word of many on the blank page before him.

Dear Emley,

I have received a sealed packet accompanied by orders to depart on the morning's flood tide. My instructions do not hint at the nature of my task or destination. All will be revealed when I reach the designated coordinates and open the packet and acquaint myself with its content. Until then, I must do what I can to forge the various metals of which my crew is composed—a goodly number of old Alarums and Redemptions, while the remaining half to two-thirds populated by landsmen, volunteers, and mutineers from Ainsley Bottom, into good fighting steel.

While I may not know for certain whence I'm bound or to what purpose, I freely confess I am filled with such elation to be in command again that dread can find no hold on me. The rumors we spoke of in private can go hang, as long as I have a ship and a crew to work her. As Marbury puts in the mouth of Olwen Goldenhair when she is faced with the treachery of her uncle Turlough of Ten Ships, "Let the Old Gods do their worst, for they have yet to see my best!"

The die is cast and there's naught for it but to wait until it rolls to a stop. It will favor me, or it will not, but I will face chance with a bold heart, an easy mind, and good friends at my side. Should the pips prove spiteful, my only regret will be the nature of my departure made a final embrace between us impossible. If the roll is in my favor, though, and I emerge alive and victorious, I will compensate you many times over for the unavoidable omission.

There. I have spoken bravely as honor requires. Now I will share the truth with you, as is the practice between us. I am duty bound to plunge headlong into whatever lies ahead. If I do not return to you, the diligence of my effort to do so will not be to blame. The fault will be with the frailty of the human frame, no matter how passionately it is inspired to overcome adversity. If my final moment comes in the darkness of defeat, my mind will be so focused on the memory of your impish smile and wild laugh that my nerves will refuse to recognize any physical pain.

I will write you daily, the rigors of command permitting, and send my letters to you at every opportunity. Pray keep me apprised of the political climate in Middlesea and, if you would grant me a boyish boon, send me a lock of your hair to place under my pillow and dream upon.

Your devoted servant,
Rue Morgan Nath
Aboard HMS Revenant
Middlesea Basin, 30 Ralifrimon, 1798

The wind freshened in the night and quartered such that *Revenant* could run before it under full sail. When Enid took her morning exercise on the deck, they were tearing along at a tremendous rate, the ship heeled over at a steep angle and the deck lashed with refreshing sheets of spray. She made her way cautiously to the fo'c'sle where Nath stood on the rail, his elbow crooked around the ratlines, and his hat nowhere in evidence.

"Eleven knots! Can you credit it, Enid?"

"That is swift, is it?" Enid had to shout over the waters rushing along the hull and the wind whistling through the rigging. "It seems that we are flying!"

"It is swift, indeed," Nath shouted back.

She wasn't sure if he was repeating her or had heard nothing she said at all. I must work on projecting my voice, she thought, *if I'm to overcome the racket natural to the mariner's environment.*

Nath leapt lightly down onto the deck, landing nimbly despite the deck's angle. He ran a hand through his wet hair and grinned like a happy retriever who just dropped a fat fowl at its master's feet. "Eleven knots! Fleet as a stag, is our *Revenant* with her bottom clean and with wind enough to fill her sails. I am mortal certain that I can squeeze an extra knot or two from her by adjusting her rake and trim. By the old gods! Can you imagine that? Eleven and a half knots or I'll eat my hat!"

"Speaking of hats," Enid said, gesturing toward her own.

"Hah! Harlech caught mine and bore it back to my cabin. I'll reclaim it now if you will accompany me."

"Happily," Enid said, falling into step behind him.

They passed Mr. Kaliktiklak on their way, and he knuckled his smooth, unlined brow as they passed. Enid paused long enough to return his salute and take his hand in hers. His flesh was supple but oddly cool and smooth. *Like marble,* she thought, *more unnatural to the touch than my own silver hand.*

"Mr. Kaliktiklak," she said, leaning close to where his ear would be, if he had one, "I have not had the pleasure of meeting you yet. Captain Nath speaks highly of your abilities! I look forward to getting to know you better."

The Bogaraet's minuscule red eyes locked with hers for a moment, its expression utterly unreadable because of its lack of human musculature or the slightest sign of eyebrows. Then, in a surprisingly dulcet voice sprinkled with odd clicking sounds, he said, "I am happy to meet you, Magister. I hope we can be friends and you are not as dangerous a demon as you seem."

Enid's eyes went round and then she stammered, "I am not a—I assure you I am no—"

Mr. Kaliktiklak squeezed her hand and smiled his smile of wickedly curved needles and said, "We will see, Magister. We will see."

Enid watched his tall, willowy form practically flow across the deck, shouting orders in his golden voice, her hand still in the position it held when he released it.

"Are you coming, Magister?" Nath's friendly call brought her back to herself, and she rushed to catch him up.

They paused on the quarterdeck long enough for Nath to give Lieutenant Bascombe his orders, which consisted primarily of a command to "keep as much speed on her as you can for as long as you can while on this bearing." Then they descended to his day room.

"It is good to see you in such high spirits again, Rue. The sea air fundamentally improves your cheer."

"You are simply not a good judge of humor," Nath said. "As your distaste for Marbury's comedies proves—oh, and look, the master's namesake has joined us!"

Marbury's small white snout protruded from beneath the lid of a large basket tucked between a chair and the hull to sniff vigorously at the air. A moment later Maubin's nose appeared and followed suit.

"Ashes. The ship is infested," Enid sighed. "Lieutenant Wilk's creature barked at me as I passed through the wardroom this morning."

"Dogs are wondrous fine judges of character," Nath jibed.

"They are, truly. And fine companions and workmates. But these creatures that you and Wilk gravitate to are not dogs. They are too small to be of any practical use, outside the horrid ritual of foxhunting, which aberration is peculiar to Albion."

"Do not listen to the magister," Nath told his dogs in the voice that all humanity uses to address the portion of the canine race they have domesticated. "Her aristocratic blood is too thin to be warmed by a good little dog."

Enid snorted smoke and was about to speak when there was a rap at the door.

"The Young Gentleman Hunig to see the captain," the marine sentry's muffled voice announced.

"Let him in," Nath answered.

A young man who looked to be only twelve or thirteen entered and doffed his hat to Nath. "I've come for the pups, sir!"

"Ah. Magister d'Tancreville, allow me to introduce you to Mid Hunig, one of our new young gentles."

Enid gave the young man a cordial nod. "I look forward to becoming better acquainted with you during sorcery instruction, Mid Hunig."

"Thank you, Magister." Hunig's smile was open and genuine, and Enid was filled with an instantaneous affection for him. *What is it with these mids,* she thought, *that brings out a maternal instinct in me, of which there has been no evidence until setting foot on* Alarum*?*

"Here are the boys," Nath said, pressing the squirming basket into Hunig's hands. "Their collars are on 'em and their leads in the basket. Take a couple of idlers with you to clean the deck after they've done their duty, so to speak."

"Aye, sir!"

The young man departed, struggling under the weight of the writhing, yapping basket of dogs in his arms.

"He is the nephew of a friend of Merryweather's," Nath said after he departed. "A scion of a noble house. His sponsor insists that his social rank be kept a secret until he attains captaincy, so please keep the fact to yourself. It's ridiculous to think it won't come out before the end of the cruise, let alone before he makes post, but there's no harm in playing along with the games of our social betters, eh, Enid?"

"Not if they're harmless, at least."

chapter 17

Enid was drinking coffee in the wardroom mess when Mid Weard burst in like a bombshell and shouted, "Dr. Rondelle! Lieutenant Wilk's compliments and would you join him on the orlop? There's been a stabbing!"

"How serious a stabbing?" Rondelle asked without stirring an inch in his seat. "A mere pinking, or an actual bowel-piercing impalement?"

"There's a lot of blood and Rolliers is choking on it most piteously." Her face was pale, apparently from what she'd seen.

"Well," Rondelle sighed, taking up his bag and standing. "That sounds serious indeed. Lead the way, Mid Weard."

Enid trailed Rondelle as he all but ran to the orlop, the way before them opened by Weard's harsh cries of "Clear the way!"

They found poor Rolliers lying on her side to ease her breathing. The deck under her head was covered with a pink and red froth and bright red blood pooled under her chest. Her left hand clutched at a dagger protruding from her ribs, just below her right breast. Her eyes stared blankly skyward.

Rondelle knelt and gently placed two fingers on Rolliers's throat. After a long moment, he looked up at Lieutenant Wilk and shook his head.

"She is dead," he said in a voice laden with genuine regret. He reached for the dagger that transfixed her, but Enid placed her hand on his shoulder to stop him.

"Do we know who stabbed her?" Enid asked.

"No, Magister," Lieutenant Wilk answered in a respectful tone. "Her body was discovered by the young gentle that cares for my dog and those of the captain. The killer was long gone by then."

"She said nothing before she expired?"

Lieutenant Wilk shook his head. "She could not draw enough breath to speak."

"Dr. Rondelle," Enid said, "since there is no danger of worsening her physical condition, would you consent to allow me to take things from here?"

"By all means," Rondelle said. "And any assistance you might require from me, I shall provide with pleasure and vigor. I cannot abide a murderer!"

The vehemence with which he spoke those words struck Enid. She doubted that Rondelle would demonstrate his signature gentleness should he be called upon to treat Rolliers' killer. She drew the knife from the sailor's corpse and was surprised to find it to be a long, slim blade with a triangular cross section. A weapon with no utility for a sailor, but ideally suited for an assassin.

She held it up and asked if anyone recognized it. Blank stares met her from the small group of sailors Wilk had brought below to assist him if Rolliers's attacker was near at hand.

"Not surprising," Enid said. "I doubt its owner displayed it openly. I'm surprised they abandoned it with their victim."

"Perhaps the cowardly wretch was startled by the approach of Hunig and the dogs," Dr. Rondelle sneered.

"Most likely you are right," Enid said, nodding. "For now, though, I conjure you all to hold your tongues while I work a formulation to guide us directly to the killer."

The silence that followed seemed to deepen the darkness and reduce the orb overhead into a dull, hazy gleam. Despite their best efforts, Enid's observers gasped when a small jet of blood leapt from the blade to splash against the open wound in Rolliers's chest.

"I have sent the victim's blood back to her," Enid explained. "I'd hoped the killer cut themselves while performing their butchery, but alas, they have not. We must rely on a close emotional connection between the murderer and their dagger."

"Such a connection seems likely," Wilk said. "That is a murderer's weapon, and murderers develop a deep affection for their chosen tools."

Enid glanced at the lieutenant and found his slate-gray eyes devoid of emotion. "I will take your word for that, Lieutenant Wilk. Now, follow along behind me if you please."

Enid worked a similar formulation and was rewarded by a slight tug, as if someone had grasped the point of the dagger between their fingertips and pulled it upward. She held the blade before her and let it guide her where it would: up from *Revenant*'s shadowy interior and onto the upper deck. There, the little knot of observers behind her followed her to the waist and toward a group of Ainsley Bottom mutineers who sat sharing a smoke after assisting with the lines. Mid Weard called out for crew members to step aside, but her orders were purely performative. Nobody wanted to be in front of Enid as she strode purposefully across the deck with a strange knife thrust out before her and eyes rolled back sightlessly into her head.

Enid came to a halt before a short, petulant-looking woman and lunged forward to press the dagger tip against the hollow of her throat until the skin dimpled.

"Here is Rolliers's murderer," she said, her eyes snapping down out of her skull.

"Grimes," Lieutenant Wilk said as he drew his pistol and aimed it at the sailor's chest. "I'm not surprised in the least by this revelation. She's been trouble since coming aboard. Mid Weard, my compliments to the master-at-arms and she is needed to take this assassin into custody!"

"Here now," Grimes complained, moving not a muscle save her lips and tongue. "What proof d'ye got?"

"The overwhelming resonance between you and the murder weapon," Enid said. "You shouldn't have left it behind—although I believe Rolliers' blood would have led us to the weapon, and from it to you."

"That's all? The word of a snail-eatin' tart is enough t'take me up in chains? I demand to see the cap'n!"

"See him you shall, Grimes," Wilk's tone was matter-of-fact. He nodded at the master-at-arms and her mates. "Mr. Shea, please take this rogue in hand and lock her up. She's a killer, so take no chances with her. If she resists, bash her in the head till she stops."

"And may you rot in whatever hell will have you," Rondelle snarled with such ferocity that Grimes, whose pugnacious mien had heretofore been set in stone, winced and staggered a step back from the doctor's wrathful face.

"What a disaster," Nath groused as he drained a small glass of Oporto.

"How so?" Enid asked, lighting them a pair of cigarillos. "I thought the killer's quick arrest would comfort the honest sailors and discourage any other would-be murderers."

"And you are right, for the most part, but Grimes's punishment will certainly place a pall over all our people."

"Can we not detour to Gisbon and let Admiral Weymouth deal with her? It would cost time, but would also save the crew from witnessing her execution."

"I fear it is much too far out of our way, and even if it were not, we'd be held there specifically to let Grimes' end be an example to our people."

Enid sighed. "You are a stubborn people when it comes to your executions."

Nath arched a brow at her. "And yet we need not resort to Roget's Device because there isn't enough rope in the realm for all the condemned."

"A fair touch, sir," Enid said with a sad smile. "A fair touch, indeed. Still, it's not as if you'll be drawing and quartering the woman. Hanging is a fairly swift way to part the veil. I saw my first when I was not yet a decade old and, though it troubled my dreams for a while and still intrudes on them from time to time, I do not believe I was traumatized."

"Yes, but your executioners use quick-drop gallows, just as we do ashore. That is not how business is done in the Royal Navy. Grimes will be hoisted from the deck with a rope slung over a yard arm, there to strangle slowly. She'll be left there for an hour to ensure she's truly dead."

"That is barbaric," Enid whispered.

Nath nodded. "Some believe that such harsh measures are required to keep the peace upon his majesty's ships, and since it has worked up to this point, they see no reason to fix what don't require mending. I'd hoped never to resort to it, but a murder demands justice, swift and sure."

He sighed and refilled their glasses with Oporto.

"The best I can do is relieve her of as much dread as possible. We'll undertake the court-martial tomorrow morning and hang her at sunset so that she need not spend another night in the brig, dreading the morning."

"Then there is no chance that her trial might result in a lighter judgment?"

Nath shook his head. "Magic of the sort you used to assess blame is unassailable. She is a murderer, and she must hang from the yardarm for her crime. My hands are bound by the law."

"Well, there's an end to it, then."

"From your lips to the ears of Providence," Nath said. "I've asked the mids, master's mates, and the lieutenants for their opinions on Grimes. They all agreed that she looked perfectly gallows from the moment she was carried aboard too drunk to walk. They were also of the opinion that she and her friend, an equally unwholesome fellow named Ogilvy, have made themselves very popular among the sailors from Ainsley Bottom."

Enid arched a brow. "How so? She hardly seemed likely to be popular with anyone save the hangman."

"She and this Ogilvy are said to be skilled agitators for the leveling, anti-crown cant that is gaining a foothold among your common laborers," Nath said. "They were fearlessly energetic in proselytizing among other sailors ashore in Ainsley Bottom. The resulting mass mutiny speaks to their skill, I fear."

"Ashes," Enid said. "Tomorrow may see a murderer die and a martyr born, all at the end of the same rope."

They sat and smoked together in silence for a time, watching the *Revenant*'s faint phosphorescent wake trail off toward the sable, star-speckled horizon.

"Nature is oblivious to our petty dramas," Enid said. "Unlike a play, the backdrop doesn't change to reflect the story's mood. Some of history's most portentous events have unfolded under just the sort of sun-soaked, cloudless day we can expect tomorrow, if today is any indication of the weather."

Nath gave an amused snort.

"What humor do you find in my observation? Is it flawed in some way?"

"Not in the least, Enid," Nath said. "It only occurred to me that if Nature is oblivious to us, you return the favor in equal kind."

"How so?" she asked, an irked edge to her words.

"You may have noticed the barometers scattered about the ship? Indeed, there is one right there, in plain sight by the stern gallery windows."

"What of them?"

"They have been falling steadily throughout the day," Nath said. "I will be surprised if we don't see at least half a blow by tomorrow night."

The inquest, such as it was, proved to be no more than a pro forma ritual. Once the charges were read, Enid gave her testimony and

Grimes's defense was presented and dismissed. Nath read the verdict with the same dispassion he would order the helm to change course. Enid was appalled by the process, which she assumed was a more subdued version of the mockeries of justice that fed Roget's Device a constant stream of noble heads to sever.

She knew the blackguard was guilty of killing a well-liked and loyal member of the old *Alarum*'s crew as sure as she knew the basic laws of magic, but this procedure was a sham. No attempt was made to argue for a lesser charge and Grimes did herself no favors by staring in baleful silence at her interrogators when they made a weak fling at establishing her motive in the killing. Indeed, after giving her full name at the beginning of the trial, the only words she spoke were to proclaim that Rolliers "had it coming."

Nath announced the outcome of the court-martial from the quarterdeck and ordered the Master-at-arms Shea to arrange for the sentence, and by extension, Grimes herself to be executed at dusk. The *Revenant*s gathered on the upper deck received the grim proclamation with a mixture of resigned solemnity and shock. Some of the waisters wore tight expressions and there were more than a few clenched fists hanging at their sides. After the master's mates saw the men back to their duties, Nath turned to address the officers formed up behind him.

"Executions under sail are never good for the people's morale and take the greatest toll on landsmen and newcomers who believe they are most vulnerable to the ship's justice. Take care to reassure your people and, if need be, take them firmly in hand to avoid the caustic effect of fear and resentment on the ship's discipline."

"Lieutenant Harcourt, have your marines ready to respond at a moment's notice, but do not make a show of it. Marines lining the rails and bristling with bayonets will fan the flames rather than quenching them."

"Aye, sir," Harcourt said gravely. "My men will be ready at your signal."

A sudden gust of wind blew a thin sheet of rain across the sunwashed deck. Nath shot a significant glance at Enid, who frowned in return, and said, "I believe the weather will worsen as the day goes on. Master Kaliktiklak, do you concur?"

The master nodded his round head energetically. "Strong storm building, sir. We'll see it get increasingly rough after dusk."

Nath nodded with satisfaction. "Good! That will keep the people busy and their minds off the execution. Conversely, their moods should lift as the storm subsides."

"I had wondered about the timing of the punishment," Lieutenant Bascombe said. "Your stratagem is impressive, sir."

"Thankee, Mr. Bascombe, I do my best." Nath's smile was melancholy, but good humored. "Be on your toes, all of you. I don't want to hang more of our people because some damned fool agitates them into mutiny."

Lieutenant Wilks paused at the break of the quarterdeck to fill and light his pipe. As his hands went through the motions of the task without the necessity of so much as a stray thought to guide them, he gazed upward. The *Revenant*'s mastheads traced complex patterns against the thin shreds of cloud that raced above them. They left him with the impression of gaunt trees animated by an ungovernable desire to savage the eyes of heaven. He shrugged and sheltered the bowl of his pipe with one hand while he lit it with the other. After three forceful puffs, he whistled for Jock, who ceased his half-hearted attempt to rouse *Revenant*'s nanny goat into a game of chase and bolted toward his master with his ears lain back, eyes wide, and tongue lolling despite the chill. Wilks knelt to scratch behind the dog's ears and tousle his head from side to side.

Wilks had the sense of being watched and looked up. There were two of the mids, the one called Hunig and the other named Weard? Whatever her name, her face was set in the most unofficerly display of sentimental appreciation of what must look like the popular engraving *His Master Home from the Sea*, which depicted an old salt squatting to present an even older dog with a handful of ship's biscuit. Hunig's expression was nearly as saccharine. Wilks smiled and waved at the two younkers, thinking, *You'd soil yourself if you saw some of the things my hounds have fed on while I was ashore to provide for them with my hunts, you harebrained simpletons. You're safe enough, though, you don't have the sense to know you're in danger. I never hunt prey I've shipped with, no matter how much they deserve it.*

He straightened and leaned backward from the waist until something in the center of his chest audibly popped. The sensation always took him unawares, but left him feeling looser and more limber. Enid stepped into sight from behind the ship's boats, currently stacked neatly on the great, curved beams that arched over the open gun deck below. He didn't look directly at her, and instead watched her from the left corners of his eyes. The precaution was wasted though, as the tall Ardainne queen, for she clearly thought herself a queen, locked her eyes upon him. He saw her right hand, the silver one, brush the hilts of the long, narrow-bladed dagger that hung from her right hip. She regarded him for a heartbeat or two, her expression could not be called hostile, nor friendly. He knew the detached, unconcerned mien she wore intimately. It was the same he wore when he prowled the trash-filled, thief-haunted alleyways of any city in the world. Hers was the face of a wary hunter that takes advantage of every opportunity to observe the habits of her prey.

He might make an exception for her. She had magic, after all, and was murderously accomplished with the small sword, hanger, and, he didn't doubt, the ridiculously long rapiers of the last century.

She would be a challenge, a test he might well fail. For all he knew, she might serve his choicest pieces to Lady Chum-Chum, who had taken to circling far above her head whenever she was on deck. Of course, she might just as well fall to his knife, which was swifter than the passing of a mayfly. The thought cheered him, even though he had no cause to wish her ill, other than her obvious suspicions. Suspicions born entirely of her own prejudice, for he'd given her no cause to believe he might bring her harm.

For the moment, he set aside thoughts of dismembering such a noble specimen of a gentle lady and withdrew below for a caulk before assuming command of *Revenant* for his watch. As he and Jock sauntered toward the companionway, a foremast jack jostled him. Wilk turned a sharp glare on the fellow, who looked to be one of the oldest seamen aboard. Before he could voice a warning about having a care so near the quarterdeck, the oldster spoke up in a surprisingly strong, warm voice. "Beg pardon, Lieutenant Wilks. I ain't too steady on my feet and staggered into you all accidental like."

"Never you mind, old fellow. I ain't too steady on my own pins these days, so I'm the last to judge you on that account."

"Thankee, Lieutenant," the old man said. "Most kind of you, sir. Most kind!"

Wilk felt the old man's eyes on his back even after he went below, which set his skin to crawling. *You'll be flinching away from Nath's noisy little ratters, next,* he thought. *This fucking ship is a man-killer, though. Something ain't right about her.*

The old man, Mr. Oak, watched Wilk go and thought, *There's a monster beside whom I might pale. I thought I might ride him for a spell, but one touch of his skin dispelled that erroneous thought. He lacks my power, of course, or even that of the lady magister, but I have no desire to wrestle with a monster in the blood-drenched halls of their own twisted mind! Better to wait for a less perilous mortal to wear until their flesh rots and falls from me like leaves from an oak in the fall.*

The weather worsened steadily as the day passed on. Fast-moving clouds blocked out the sun and irregular gusts of wind lifted spray off the choppy waves by midday. The clouds overhead darkened to blue-black as the storm piled higher into the heavens and the fatal hour approached. By the time all hands were piped up to witness punishment, it was nearly dark as night and dull peals of thunder rolled in from the west, trailed by flickering lightning that lit the horizon in intermittent, flashing forks.

The crew gathered in their divisions at the foot of the mainmast. Most were clad in oilskin capes and coats, but all clutched their hats to their chests out of respect for unavoidable mortality, if not for the wretch about to meet hers. Enid chose to witness the ordeal at Lieutenant Harcourt's side, in case his marines required her assistance in maintaining order in what seemed to her a ritualistic celebration of chaos.

"An ugly business," Harcourt said. "Although apparently predestined."

"How so?"

"One of my marines is from the Low Warrens, the neighborhood our guest called home until swept up by a press gang; claims Grimes had such a grim reputation for murder, mayhem, and riot she was betrayed into the hands of the Royal Navy. Her mate, that cadaverous fellow over there in Yeardly's division, was caught up with her."

Enid studied the man Harcourt nodded toward. He was skeletally thin and taller even than her. His eyes drooped lazily as he watched his friend manhandled into position, a hood forced over her head and a noose fastened about her neck. Grimes responded more violently. She kicked her feet as much as her manacles would permit and voiced an inarticulate howl of rage and defiance.

"She is allowed no last words, then?"

Harcourt gave his head a sad shake. "She's had nothing to say but a stream of the foulest vitriol imaginable, so profane that even the sailors and marines within earshot blanched and blushed. Master-at-arms Shea had her gagged, as it was clear she has nothing sensible to say."

Enid frowned. "If a soul wishes to depart the world in a storm of curses and blasphemy, who has the authority to deny them their last act of defiance in the face of death, earned by villainy or not?"

Harcourt shrugged. "The master-at-arms, apparently."

Enid frowned. For once Amiable Harcourt's good humor and wit rasped against her sensibilities. She was about to admonish him to respect the gravity of the event but was interrupted by Nath's shout to heave away.

And heave away the master-at-arms mates did. The first pull, a bit reluctant and unsure, lifted Grimes to her toes. The second pulled her feet clean off the deck and she began to kick and spin like a deranged marionette. Pull after pull lofted her higher until her black-hooded head was a mere foot or two below the mainsail's spar. She continued to kick, jerk, and rotate.

"Ashes," Enid said. "How long does it take?"

"A few minutes," Harcourt said, all traces of humor gone from his voice. "Hanging in this manner is a terrible way to die and a terrible death to watch—but we owe the poor creature that much, do we not?"

"It is a horror to see her life cut short, no matter the method."

"And yet hers was not cut so short as poor Rolliers's, eh?"

Enid said nothing, but her mind began to pick at the idea that a society of laws should not stoop to the murderous behavior of criminals.

When Grimes's struggles ceased entirely, Nath dismissed the crew. Those not on watch scurried quickly belowdecks to rid themselves of their wet oilskins as the rain had begun to come down in earnest. The rest rushed to their duties, none of which seemed to include lowering the late murderer to the deck.

"How long will be she be left to swing there?" Enid asked, staring fixedly at the body, which traced increasingly long ellipses over the deck thanks to the ship's roll. It was occasionally backlit by nearby lightning strikes, and she could clearly see the details of Grimes's shoe soles.

"An hour at least," Harcourt said, watching Grimes as well. "To ensure she's truly departed."

"Or arrived," Dr. Rondelle said as he joined them. "Welcomed with the burning embraces and tearing claws of the most sadistic devils hell has to offer, I pray."

Enid arched a brow at the doctor and asked, "Was Grimes a particular adversary of yours, sir?"

"No, but I reserve my most concentrated spite for murderers.

When I was young, my wife was slain by gutter-scum like that. Her throat slit over her wedding ring, which she didn't surrender with sufficient alacrity. It was shortly thereafter that I took to sea."

Rondelle stared up at the corpse, which swung in increasingly eccentric orbits as the sea's surface became confused by the storm's ever-quartering winds.

"My only regret is that this villainous killer will be shriven before she's tossed overboard like the bag of offal she is. Now I must wish you both a good night, as it seems that young Podinger has ruptured himself like a fool."

Enid and Harcourt watched Rondelle's back as he strode off to see to the unfortunate Podinger.

"I must say that I'm surprised by the depth to which his wife's passing affects him to this day," Enid said.

"I'm surprised that he was ever young," Harcourt said, and Enid chuckled despite herself.

"See 'em up there?" Ogilvy said to a group of waisters standing ready to lend their backs to the handling of the ship in the face of the worsening storm. "That Rat bitch having a laugh with the boss lobster? Right proud of hangin' Grimes to shut her up."

"Seems like they hung her for killing Rolliers," Durand said. He was a fellow that had voluntarily taken the king's shilling after his apprenticeship and hopes for the future died with the master mason he served.

"And with no more evidence than Lady Rat's accusation! They couldn't even be arsed to look for witnesses!"

"Thank Providence for that," said a pale-skinned young woman listed in the ship's roll as Prettyflower, Sweet.

Ogilvy shot her a murderous glance and pressed on: "Where is the justice in it, I ask? Any of us could be hung for whatever crime it pleases that Rat bitch to lay against us!"

"Well, it's pretty clear Grimes did kill Rolliers," Durand said with an apologetic shrug.

"Which don't signify," Ogilvy snapped. "Get it through that thick skull of yours it don't matter if you're guilty or not. They can hang anyone they want if the Rat bitch jabs her devil's finger at 'em."

"Well, she's a mage," Durand said. "And a treble-shotted one by all accounts so her spells is pretty hard to argue—"

"How do you know the Rat bitch cast any spell?" Ogilvy hissed. "Because she says so? Because you're some officer who dines on roast beef while we grind our teeth on biscuits laid in afore we were born?"

Durand held up his hands and nodded. "Aye, I take your point. I was just saying—"

"Well, stop saying it," Ogilvy snarled. "There ain't no room for playin' a devil's advocate here. We gotta stick together if we don't want to join poor Grimes, hangin' like a hare from a game pole!"

"What can we do?" Prettyflower asked. "They has all the power, yeah?"

"For now," Ogilvy said, glaring at Enid from beneath the brim of his tarpaulin hat. "For now they do."

Enid remained on the quarterdeck for Merryweather's watch, while Nath repaired below with instructions to summon him the instant that the storm took a turn for the worse. By then, *Revenant* was running before the wind under light sails, rising, falling, and yawing this way and that in a manner that Merryweather characterized as "weatherly." Enid saw less to admire about the ship's bucking and gyration, though. Her stomach roiled and threatened to rebel, but she seemed to have absorbed some of Dunaughy's maritime constitution from their intimate connection.

And you are gaining your sea legs at last, even after so long ashore, she "heard" him say in the depths of her mind. *Be grateful for it, too! Some admirals have gone their entire careers beset by seasickness.*

"I would abandon nautical life altogether, were that the case!"

Merryweather shot her a puzzled look. "What was that, Magister?"

"Nothing," Enid extemporized. "I was simply saying that I would abandon life at sea if storms like this were more frequent."

"Hah! This is nothing more than the previous storm's little sister come to have a run at us. There will be thunder, lightning, and enough wind to keep our *Revenant*s' minds off the night's lesson on the swift, unambiguous justice of the Sea Service. I tell you, Enid—Magister, rather—that I will never see enough hangings so that the next won't leave me half sick and woefully downhearted."

"How many have you seen?"

"Grimes was the third. I admire her for going out game, for all she was a black-hearted bitch for knifing poor Rolliers. Ten of her wouldn't account for a tenth of him." Merryweather glanced up at the dark silhouette of the murderess's dangling corpse and took in her drooping shoulders. The loose, boneless sag of her body was completely at odds with the nervous energy that galvanized it in life. At that moment, a triple fork of lightning danced across the waves and revealed a gnarled figure crouching on the spar directly above Grimes's head. Whatever it was, the thing was a horror and its sleep-slaying image was practically etched in her mind by the brilliant flash in which it was revealed.

She found her voice at last and locked Enid's upper arm in a bruising grip with her left hand and pointed up with her right. "Did you see that, Enid? Did you?"

Enid peered into the tangle of ropes, spars, and canvas that snapped and popped under the freshening wind. "I see nothing out of the ordinary, other than that poor woman's body."

Merry stared at the spot where she'd seen the stranger and shook her head, mystified. "I don't see him now, either."

"Who was it? Did you see?"

"It looked like a tall wraith of a fellow, with arms and legs bent like oak branches under the wind. It was misshapen in body and limb. Its face was shrouded in shadow, the lightning flash being behind it, but its eyes glowed like the corpse-lights I've seen in the salt marshes near my home. It squatted on its haunches like a hunter examining tracks—or those statuettes of demons that decorate Ardain churches."

"Gargoyles," Enid said. "Whatever you saw is long gone, though. My eyes now see with the nighttime acuity of an owl, and I see nothing in the rigging other than Lady Chum-Chum who is taking her rest coiled about one of ropes supporting the fighting tops."

Merryweather nodded, still scanning the tops through narrowed eyes. Her attention was drawn back to the moment by the sharp ring of the ship's bell marking the hour. Reminded of her duty, she shouted for Harlech, who was supervising several members of the Afterguard as they ensured the great guns were still snugged up tight against the grasp of the winds and rains. The little mid rushed to answer, her cherub's face still set in the firm expression she wore when dealing with the hands.

"Harlech," Merryweather said in the same officerly tone she would use for any other officer under her command, "Cut out a few of the waisters to lower Grimes's corpse from the yard. Take care to ensure she don't get loose and drop into the sea."

"I'd never!" Harlech protested without thinking. "Not even a lubberly killer deserves to sink without a shroud!"

"Of course not," Merryweather agreed. "Now, be about it if you please."

Harlech sketched a salute and scurried off, leaving Enid and Merryweather to the relative privacy of the windward side of the quarterdeck.

"How bad is it?" Merryweather asked. When Enid only arched a brow in response, she clarified, "The unnatural situation? Perhaps what I saw is a part of it?"

"It's difficult to say. It is certain that something is attached to the ship, but as to what it is and why it plagues us—" Enid shrugged.

"How much danger does it pose to us?" Merryweather asked. "Is it more prone to mischief or mayhem?"

"Alas, I cannot say. Its past actions reveal the level of malevolence to which it can sink, however. The deaths of the officers sent to command her are a long step beyond mischief. I believe the sooner we are rid of it, the better. It strikes me as a wound that will fester quickly. Still, I must know more of its nature before I dare attempt a banishment."

"It doesn't bear saying that I will assist you however I can, should you require it."

Enid smiled warmly, her back turned to the crew to conceal her emotion. "It does not, dear Merry. It does not. I know—"

A hair-raising scream forestalled any further professions from Enid. The shriek sent her and Merry sprinting toward the sound, which originated from the waist. From the break of the quarterdeck they saw the gun deck below was filled with rushing, aimless action. Enid followed Merryweather down the ladder to the gun deck.

"Make way!" Merry boomed. "Cut your lubberly capers somewhere else and make way for us to pass or I'll have all your names on the captain's desk and we'll discover together if this is a flogging ship or no!"

The mob of stricken landsmen from the Afterguard, leavened with a few able sailors who were caught up in the flash of panic parted like waves under *Revenant*'s bluff bows. Enid and Merryweather found themselves on the verge of a compact huddle of sailors halfway between the mainmast and the larboard rail. One of their number cried out in anguish, "The rope broke, I swear on it! We didn't let it loose! Oh, gods, does the poor tyke live yet or no?"

When the knot of sailors parted for Merryweather, Enid saw Harlech lying half under Grimes's boneless sprawl. Ogilvy cradled the mid's head in his lap and brushed his skeletal fingers across her lids to close her sightless, crystalline eyes. He looked up at Enid wearing a woeful expression that did not touch his flat, stony eyes.

"She has passed," he said in a surprisingly basso voice. "Poor thing. Shame on her parents for sending their child alone into a sea of peril."

Enid instinctively reached for the small sword on her hip, but Merryweather placed a hand on her wrist and said, "That will be enough, Ogilvy. Be along with you to fetch the surgeon, quick as you may."

"Aye, sir," Ogilvy said, and gently lowered Harlech's small head to the deck before he unfolded to his full height and loped off to summon Dr. Rondelle.

Enid fell to her knees next to Harlech and tossed Grimes's body off her with an effortless flick of her silver hand, raising a murmur from the onlookers. She placed her hands on either side of the girl's clearly broken neck and plunged into the most powerful healing formulation she knew. It availed her not. The damage to Harlech's neck was too severe and the bright butterfly of her soul had departed for whatever afterlife awaited beautiful young girls that loved ships and the sea.

Dunaughy's turmoil within her nearly overcame her. His thoughts were all inarticulate violence and sorrow. He had known Harlech far longer than she, after all. She had a momentary flash of his memories and saw the girl come aboard *Alarum* in a mid's uniform that drooped off her shoulders as if she were playing dress-up in her older brother's clothes and a smile as bright as a knife's edge to Enid's heart.

"Here now," Merryweather whispered, and helped Enid to her feet. "Save your tears for your cuddy, Enid. It is unofficerly to weep so in front of the ship's people."

Her composure was largely intact when Rondelle arrived, looking as stricken as she'd ever seen him. Nath was on his heels and, through dint of hours passed in company, she saw that he only maintained a collected expression only with the greatest effort.

"What happened here?" Nath barked as he sank to his knees by Enid.

"Rogue wave," Master Kaliktiklak said gravely. "The rope parted near Grimes's neck as the ship bucked. Our folk's grip on the rope never failed, but the rope failed them."

Nath examined the frayed end. "No one tampered with this?"

Kaliktiklak shook his round head, which glistened like glass in the rain. "No, sir. And I inspected the rope myself before releasing it for Master-at-arms Shea's use."

"Enid," Nath said close to her ear. When she didn't respond, he nudged her with his shoulder and said, "Enid, I need you here now. There will be time to grieve later. Look at this rope end and tell me what you make of it?"

She shook the rain and tears from her eyes and studied the stub of rope just above the loop around Grimes's mottled throat. "It has been cut. Obviously cut."

"Say nothing more. We shall discuss it in your study," Nath said, and stood. "Master Kaliktiklak, please bear poor Harlech to the magister's workspace on the orlop. The magister and I will join you there shortly. Lieutenant Merryweather, please take the crew in hand and get them back to their duties before we find ourselves on our beam ends. Have the rest of the hangman's rope brought to me on the Orlop if you please."

He helped Enid to her feet and together they went below, followed by the ship's master, who bore his small burden as lightly as a bundle of flowers.

Kaliktiklak placed Harlech's body with infinite care upon Enid's worktable and stepped away, his head bowed in apparent prayer.

"I did not know her long," he said quietly. "But I will remember her fondly forever."

"I've brought the rope," Rondelle said in his normal brassy, condescending tone. He placed the short length that had formed the loop around Grimes's throat on the table next to Harlech and allowed the rest of the rope, which was in a coil over his right shoulder, to drop to the deck at its feet.

Nath nodded. "Did the crew have an opportunity to examine it?"

Rondelle gave his head a single sharp shake. "I assumed you'd want as few of the crew clapping eyes on it as possible, Captain."

"Your wits were about you as always, Doctor," Nath said. "I assume you have drawn an opinion about the rope ends yourself?"

"Cut by a sharp knife," Rondelle said with a sniff. "But how that was done twenty feet above the deck in the midst of a blow and in plain sight of every officer and hand on deck? That, I cannot say."

Nath nodded, satisfied with the answer. "What else could do such a thing? For I'll stake my word it was no dereliction by the Master-at-arms, even without Master Kaliktiklak's assurance the hanging rope was serviceable and stout."

Kaliktiklak nodded. "Mr. Shea is diligent to her very bones."

"Then what could have done this?" Nath glanced at Enid and asked, "Sorcery? Some hedge-warlock's work? They've been picked up by the press before."

"I would have noticed. A charm to dry one's feet or deaden a sore tooth might slip by me, but to slice a rope of such thickness requires enough, well, let us call it energy, which I would have perceived just as surely as you would a change in the wind." Enid cast a furtive glance at Merry, before continuing, "But . . ."

Nath's eyes narrowed as he studied each of their faces in turn. "But?"

Merry described what she'd seen, her account uninterrupted by any questions from Nath. He stood next to the table upon which Harlech's limp body lay, her face covered by her own tarpaulin hat. *She would laugh suddenly and throw away the hat to reveal her glittering eyes and bright smile if the gods had built any justice into the world they created for us,* he thought. *But they were too busy squabbling among themselves and pitting us against one another to waste time on such a trivial ingredient.*

Enid could deduce from her lover's taut face that she expected a harsh rebuke from Nath, but when he finally spoke, his tone was flat, even, and unfaltering. "Enid, what did Lieutenant Merryweather see? A presentiment of tragedy? Or its author?"

Before Enid could form her thoughts into an answer, Kaliktiklak spoke in a voice couched in the doom-laden chorus of lost heroes.

"She saw an evil spirit. Either a being from beyond the veil that has anchored itself to our ship or the tormented soul of a mortal who died here and, driven by a deep sense of retribution or fearful of the just end that awaits them in the afterworld, refuses to leave. She saw the bane that overshadows *Revenant*."

Nath glanced sharply at Enid, his right eyebrow crooked.

"My thoughts as well, in the main," Enid said.

He nodded and then, in the same forced, level tone announced he must return to the quarterdeck to be on hand should the morale of the ship's people falter. As he passed Enid, he paused and leaned in and spoke quietly in her ear, saying: "Find Harlech's murderer and kill it. You have a full remit to send it to hell, however you may."

"They weep when it's one of their own," Ogilvy said to a group of four other waisters who knelt together belowdecks. They pantomimed a game of cards as they spoke to avoid the attention of any warrants or officers that might pass by on a routine examination. "But when poor Grimes choked out her life kicking on the end of a rope, they couldn't muster a single tear."

"Stood around 'n looked bored," Balis said. He was a short fellow, but stout and heavily muscled. The glowing tattoos of cannons on his left and right forearms stood out starkly against his dark skin. He'd been a bare-knuckles fighter before being nabbed by the press and his face reflected his former occupation with a flattened nose, scarred brows, and mashed ears.

"Aye," hissed Sweet Prettyflower. "Same as when they hang some wretch ashore. Your nobs and toffs all gather 'round to watch and turn up their noses. It was the same when my mother was hanged."

"What'd the string 'er up for?" Balis asked.

"Corpse desecratin'."

"They hung her for that?" one of the other waisters asked.

"Well," Prettyflower said with a sly grin. "He weren't dead when she started the desecratin'."

Ogilvy let the grim chuckles die down before saying, "They'll be putting both Grimes and that worthless little baby officer in the sea tomorrow. I hope they grasp the lesson: Take one of ours and we take one of yours."

So saying, he returned to his assigned labor of securing any loose items on the deck, a task so familiar from the previous storm that it required very little of his attention, allowing his thoughts to wander back to the strange events earlier in the evening. Not the death of that little squeaker "Harlot," as Prettyflower called Harlech, nor even all the officers' suspicious capering about afterwords, but rather his own actions. When he saw Grimes's body hurtling toward Harlech, he dashed forward, knocking other foremast hands aside to reach the mid before anyone else. Her eyes widened when she saw him rushing toward her and, caught by the magnitude of their innocence and kindness, he nearly shoved her out of harm's way. He had time to do it, he was certain, though he would have suffered her fate as a reward for his selflessness. But his heart went cold and stayed his hand at the fatal moment in which it would have done the most good.

He immediately dropped down next to her and took her head in his lap. He brushed the hair from her forehead and surreptitiously traced strange symbols there in the process. The prayers he appeared to mutter over her were not prayers at all, or if they were, they were not directed at the Redeemer. Instead, they were short verses of some sort, uttered in a language he neither recognized nor understood. He felt strangely *distant* as these events transpired, as if he observed them from some vantage far remote from his body.

A hand gripped Ogilvy's shoulder softly, and he jerked violently.

"My apologies for taking you unawares, Ogilvy," Mid Yeardly said softly. "I did not mean to startle you. I noticed that you looked troubled and thought it might comfort you to know that your actions during the tragedy did not go unnoticed. The instant you saw poor Harlech's peril, you acted to deliver her from harm at the risk of your own body. You did more to save her than anyone else on deck, and when Providence denied you success, you held her in her final moment and prayed for her redemption. You have my undying thanks for that, Mr. Ogilvy."

Yeardly offered Ogilvy his hand, who stared at it for a moment, as dumbfounded by the gesture as he was at the tears coursing down the mid's cheeks. When he took the young man's hand, he was surprised to feel the icy tracks his own tears left on his face in the cold air.

"Thankee, sir," he choked.

"Thank you, Mr. Ogilvy," Yeardly said and quickly took his leave.

The mid's gratitude and respect were so genuine that Ogilvy's faith in the idea that all officers were evil and should be overthrown wavered a moment. He considered ceasing his campaign to use the ship's fractious nature of *Redemption*'s crew to incite a mutiny, but it was but a moment's fantasy. He was mortally certain that his opportunity to change the course of his life and the fate of the *Revenant* passed when he stood by and allowed Harlech to die before his eyes.

I am too far down the track to turn back now, he thought, *The mark of the child slayer is on me now. I am branded a monster, and monster I will be.*

chapter 18

Enid was awakened from her fitful, grief-haunted sleep by a strange noise in the night. The fact that she could distinguish between a strange sound and the plethora of random racket that accompanied the running of a ship under sail spoke volumes to how much her grasp of shipboard life had improved since she first set foot on *Marie.* The reflexes born from living as an aristocrat during the dawning of the Revolution had not dimmed yet, though, so she only opened her tear-swollen eyes a slit and lay quietly in her cot, waiting for the out-of-place sound that roused her to repeat itself.

There it was! The strange thump and slither against her thin cabin door made Enid's flesh crawl. The sound was utterly alien to her and seemed both furtive and demanding. Horror and regret for the loss of Harlech combined momentarily to derange her thoughts to the degree that she considered letting whatever was behind her door have both barrels of the Kreitzer pistol she'd taken to keeping beneath her pillow as she slept. Reason prevailed, though, and she stepped to the floor as quietly as her damnable hanging cot would allow. She withdrew the dagger that counterweighted her small sword on her sword belt, which was secured to her cabin bulkhead within easy reach of her bed. So armed, she approached the lathe and canvas door on the pads of her bare feet, the dagger poised for a quick underhand thrust.

Hard by the door, the offending sound was even more disturbing. In addition to the soft impacts and slithering sound, she heard a low chuckling that never left the mouth of a sane human. *Perhaps this is the beginning of a mutiny,* she thought. *I'll burn this ship to the waterline before I allow my friends to be tortured and killed by the sweepings from Middlesea's foulest gutters!* The thought had barely passed her mind before she bust through the door.

Something varicolored and softly glowing rushed at her face and she flung herself to the side with desperate speed. This was no mutineer. Perhaps the blight on *Revenant* had finally chosen to show itself. She raised several wards about herself with a brief thought and struggled to trace the intruder's glowing chromatic path about the confined space of the cubby. She began to draw strength for whatever magical duel would follow.

It's Lady Chum-Chum, Dunaughy thought. *And she's terribly distressed about something. I suggest you close the door, put away your dagger, and try to calm the poor thing.*

Enid rubbed away the sleep and tear-salt that gummed her eyes and squinted at the rapidly flitting phantom. Her clearer vision confirmed Dunaughy's observation. Lady Chum-Chum had come to call.

Half an hour later, with coaching from Dunaughy, who had taken a close interest in Umoki in his younger days, Lady Chum-Chum was much calmer and relaxed. She was coiled around one of the lines that supported Enid's cot, cooing softly while her feathers cycled slowly through the colors of the spectrum. Her large, grass-green eyes followed Enid's every movement, but displayed no sign of wariness or concern. She accepted sweet treats from Enid's hand with obvious pleasure and gusto, seeming to produce more crumbs than could have constituted the biscuit thus reduced. Enid's thin coverlet was covered with crumbs, but she was not concerned. Clearly, no further sleep was in the offing.

Why do you think she came here? Enid thought at Dunaughy out of idle curiosity.

She was clearly in extreme distress, so I would imagine she fled here to escape some threat.

Perhaps an osprey or some other predatory bird?

That is doubtful. The Umoki keeps its legs so tightly pressed to its sides that they are nearly invisible. At the terminus of each of those legs can be found a three-toed talon with claws that can, and have, puncture a steel cap. No Osprey would dare to challenge a healthy Umoki like our dear Lady, here.

The next day dawned calm. Thin, gray clouds raced east on the tail of the gales of wind that put *Revenant* and her crew to the test yestereve. They left washed-out blue skies behind. The deck was still damp in patches from the rain and sea spray when the pipes summoned the crew on deck to observe the rites for Sailor Rolliers, Sailor Grimes, and Mid Harlech. All three were sewn up in shrouds of sailcloth, with the last stitch run through their nose to ensure they were truly dead and not simply in the grasp of a torpor. Enid found the practice savage and unnecessary, but no old salt would send their mate to their last reward without observing the awful practice. A round of shot from one of the great guns rested at the feet of each unfortunate to speed them swiftly away from the sun, wind, and waves of the living world into the unfathomable depths and the silent halls the seas provided for their dead.

Revenant had no chaplain aboard, for Nath was no tract-reading captain. He read the verses recommended for burials under sail himself, intoning the familiar words smoothly and with affecting gravity. There was no lack for sniffling noses and red eyes among even the hardest old *Alarum*s. The Ainsley hands and some of the afterguard looked on with set expressions that spoke more of resentment than grief. Occasionally one or another of them would glance directly at Enid and she would return their frosty glare with a cold, ophidian stare.

Eventually, the service ended and the boards at the rail were tilted upward to allow the corpses of the three women to slide feetfirst into the sea. Enid was mortally sure that one of them would land in the cold hell reserved for child-killers, another in whatever reward awaits a steadfast sailorwoman, while the third would ascend to a paradise of fast ships, fair winds, and plum puddings.

As the pipes sounded, releasing the crew to a "make and mend" day, Enid and Merryweather walked away together and reserved a spot for themselves by the rail, forward of the foremast. Merryweather leaned on the rail and smoked her pipe while Enid sat on the carriage of one of the ship's big twenty-four-pound cannons. The easterly breeze was warm and, for reasons she could not fathom, smelled of land. Enid looked up at Merryweather and found her expression difficult to read.

"It is a terrible thing to lose a friend in battle," Merry said at last. "To lose one to a senseless murder is nearly unbearable. I would that we were ashore, Enid. This charade of polite distance is as difficult as it is necessary."

Enid studied the deck between her feet while the warm breeze tickled the short tendrils of hair that escaped from beneath her hat to dangle down the back of her neck.

"It is difficult indeed. Last night was . . . well, it was terrible." Enid took a deep draw on her cigarillo to distract herself from further tears. "I tell you, Merry, I wept more for Harlech than I did for my uncle, and far more than for my father."

"You are close with all the mids," Merry said. "And we all doted on Harlech. While it may have seemed so, you did not weep alone last night."

Enid gave a perfunctory nod and stared up at the sky to cool her eyes.

Harlech's death cast a pall over *Revenant*. The mids were particularly stricken. Having berthed with her for over a year, her absence from their mess was a negative space that sucked the joy from their previously convivial community. Dinwitty's eyes were perpetually red from privately shed tears and Yeardly's features took on a grim set that rarely softened into anything less somber than a sad smile. As senior mid, his gloom was contagious. Weard, Arlice, and Hunig lost much of the energetic enthusiasm they exhibited previously and went about their duties with joyless, if resolute, efficiency. Even Hunig's time with Maubin and Marbury was more perfunctory, although the little dogs' mischievous energy couldn't fail to brighten his mood a little.

Worse, her death created a division between the old *Alarum*s, for whom Harlech was a beloved mascot, and the Ainsley hands, whom they saw as indirect accomplices in her death. The tension between the two groups served to divide both the afterguard and the experienced sailors drawn aboard by Nath's broadsides, which promised a happy ship and rich prizes, neither of which were in the offing as far as they could see. When Rondelle, in a moment of ill-thought multiloquence, let slip that Harlech's death might have been deliberate, the tension aboard ship became tangible. Petty bickering and profanity between the *Alarum*s and the Newcomers, as the factions began to identify themselves, led to three sailors having their rum stopped. Enid didn't need Dunaughy's counsel to know that the grate would soon be rigged for its secondary brutal function if the crew's complaisance could not be restored.

Nath was anything but oblivious to the situation, the seriousness of which was underlined one afternoon shortly after *Revenant* entered the Merentian Sea on her final leg to the Château des Fantomes. Enid witnessed the atrocity when he invited her to dine at his table, as he did two or three nights a week. She found Nath with Maubin in his arms and a pool of sick at his feet.

"Enid, do you know? Can dogs become seasick? If I didn't know better, I'd say Maubin is."

"He's not seasick. He's been poisoned." The smell of something chemical mixed with the noxious odor of the dog's most recent meal.

"Poisoned? Do you think he will live?"

"Judging by the state of your cabin floor, I'd say he has purged himself thoroughly enough to survive a dozen poisonings."

Nath was visibly relieved.

"I'll have Rondelle mix him some sort of curative draft!"

"You might, but then again, you might spare the poor fellow two poisonings in one day. Here, I will perform a formulation that will set his bowels at ease and neutralize whatever insidious agent might be left in his belly—not that I think there can be much left. Your steward, I would say, deserves an extra tot of rum for the duties ahead of him tonight. You might also sequester Marbury there. He appears to be intent on poisoning himself secondhand."

Nath shooed Marbury away from the mess with the toe of his shoe.

"I must speak to Hunig about this. I warned him not to allow these rascals to forage about deck. *Revenant* is a clean ship, but there is tar and varnish to be licked. I feared an accidental poisoning such as this."

"As to that," Enid said as she finished her formulation and scratched Maubin behind his ears despite herself. "You would be better served by warning him not to allow the crewmen to offer your dogs treats. This was no accidental poisoning."

"What? Are you certain?"

"As certain as mortality. Did you note the overwhelmingly offensive odor of Maubin's vomit? I believe the beast was fed a morsel of rotten meat, perhaps soaked in filth from the bilge. Just the sort of thing a little savage like he would view as a delicacy."

Nath frowned.

"Some sailors put mothballs in their sea chests, so it could be an accident. Considering the circumstances, though, it's best to assume this was a personal attack. Still, I will treat it as a mishap for the moment and caution Hunig against allowing the dogs to accept food from any of the hands on some pretense of a special diet or some such nonsense. The last thing the people need is an inquisition over a poisoned dog."

Enid nodded. "The mood among them is not good."

"I have never seen a crew become so divided in such a short time," Nath said. "The hanging was not arbitrary, nor were any of the other punishments. The people seem hell-bent on some sort of confrontation with me and my officers, else with one another. I don't want to resort to flogging, but I am precious short of other options."

"Something unnatural is at work here. Locating its source and eliminating it is my only priority."

"Good. Report anything you uncover to me," Nath sighed. "Now, let us try to enjoy this fine meal. The stores won't support such feasts indefinitely."

They left Yarric to his unpleasant task and withdrew to the small meal he'd laid out for them on a bench before the stern gallery. Nath wasted no time getting to the matter nearest to his heart.

"I must do something about the people's morale, Enid. If it continues to dwindle apace, we shall awake one night to the rumble of loose shot rolling about the deck!"

"Perhaps you could be freer with the spirits? The sailors do love their grog."

"No," Nath said. "Grog would simply add fuel to the flames. It is my experience that it increases the joviality of a happy crew, but only deepens the dissatisfaction of one that is troubled."

Enid nodded. Her reservoir of advice was depleted.

Nath stared down at his hands and said, "I have had the most disturbing dreams the last two nights. In them, I'm up on deck and observe some sailor who should know better showing disrespect to you or one of the lieutenants. I overreact with senseless cruelty and order the wretch to receive two hundred lashes, a certain death penalty. For some few hours after I awake, I'm smitten with the idea of making a brutal example of a few of them to silence the baseless complaints of the rest. The idea hangs with me until I come to myself later in the day."

As they were in private, she reached across the table and lay her hand on his. He flinched slightly at the touch of the warm silver but did not pull away.

"You would do nothing of the sort," Enid assured him. "I know you too well. You are not a monstrous martinet like Lord Ambrose of

Aixely. You are a good-hearted and honorable man who would never dream of committing such an atrocity."

"And yet I have dreamt of it," Nath said, and Enid had no answer for him.

Ogilvy found himself without a trusted lieutenant and efficient throat-slitter. None of the Ainsley folk he'd gathered to his cause were suitable, being either too simple, too naïve, or too touched by cheap gin's wormwood fairy. That aside, his plot would come to naught without a few seasoned mariners to steer the ship once the deed was done. Toward that end, he set his sights on Weems.

Ogilvy recognized Topman Weems the moment he set eyes on her, but he knew her as Daline Clumber, a pickpocket and occasional cutthroat with a solid reputation as an upright crook in the Downside. He assumed she fell afoul of the press gang and no opportunity to run presented itself yet. It didn't surprise him to find her working in the tops, where her nimble fingers and natural agility served her well. He approached her one day as she dropped lithely to the deck and whispered as he passed, "Good to see you, Clumber. Meet me in the hold to jaw privately about old times—assuming you want to keep them old times private, that is."

Weems/Clumber joined him in the bowels of the frigate in less time than it took him to smoke a skimpy bowl of cheap, fast-burning tobacco.

"I'm surprised it took you so long to try to blackmail me," Weems said. "But I got bad news for you. Ain't no water in this well and even if there was, the King's Navy ain't gonna send a top hand to gaol over pickin' a few pockets."

"Blackmail?" Ogilvy said. "That's the furthest thing from my mind! Even if I could wring a few pennies out of you, where would I spend 'em, stuck in this bucket as I am?"

"Then what did you want to chaw over? And don't tell me old times, because we didn't cross paths much, and by design, too. You were born with a noose around your neck."

"Closer to the truth than you know." Ogilvy chuckled. "I was born with my cord wrapped around my neck. Tell me, how happy are you with our good captain, who promises prizes and the sails off leaving a defenseless mark behind?"

"I don't like losing the prize money, but he had his reasons. I trust him."

"Do you trust that Ardain strumpet that he dines with—or on, more likely—every other night? Because you can bet she's the one pulling the captain's strings!"

"Don't matter if I do or don't, so long as the cap'n do. Besides, you didn't see her when we took *Redemption* or blew that bloody Rat frigate to hell."

"Right ye are, but I was there when she played her mummer's game to finger poor Grimes for killing of one of the captain's people. And I was there to see Grimes swing without so much as a kiss-my-hand to a trial or hearing. If the witch wants you dead, you die."

Ogilvy saw a flicker of doubt in Weems's eyes and pressed on in earnest, "And more the fool you are if you think you're safe just because you're an old hand. We know her type from on old, don't we? How many friends did you see swing because some toff thought they knew too much about their goings on in the Downside?"

Weems's frown deepened. "Too many."

"And those was just wealthy merchants or hardscrabble barons. How much more a marchioness whose face is on posters all over the city for her part in stealing this tub from the Naveroñians? Even a topman is just human coin to be spent however pleases our 'betters' best."

"I take your meaning. But what can be done about it?"

"Well, if the Naveroñians bought this floating hell during peacetime, how much do you suppose the Rats would pay for her now?"

"There it is, laid out in simple words," Weems snarled. "Mutiny and treason! I knew you'd say it plain if I kept you talking. You love your own voice too much, you traitorous dog."

Ogilvy backed away as contempt contorted Weems's face and he reached for the knife in his belt. "Here now, what is all this about?"

"It's good news for you," Weems said. "You'll be reunited with Grimes soon, either at the end of a rope when I report you to Captain Nath or at the point of my knife if you pull yours on me. Decide your fate now: Either go above deck peaceably or bare your blade so I can gut you now and save us all some time."

"I'm no match for you with a knife," Ogilvy said. "I'll take my chances with the captain."

Ogilvy turned as if to leave but drew his knife in a smooth motion as he made a full revolution and charged at Weems. His eyes widened as he found Weems awaiting him on the balls of her feet. Her hands moved with swift assurance. One of her palms struck the inside of his right wrist and the other slapped into the back of his hand. His knife leapt from his grip as if plucked by a magical force. As he stared after it in stunned wonder, she drew her own knife and buried it under his rib cage. He collapsed to the ground gasping for breath through the great gushes of blood that filled his throat. Experience told him he was dead, so he cursed Weems for betraying her own kind with his last cogent thoughts.

When Ogilvy's eyes dimmed and his bleeding was no longer timed to the last desperate beats of his heart, Weems knelt and wiped her knife on his shirt.

"You'd have been better off begging Nath for mercy," she said. "Not that you deserved any."

"No, it's much better this way," said the old salt who stepped out of the shadows.

Weems instinctively brought her knife up. "Who are you?"

"Mr. Oak, they call me." The old fellow smiled to reveal a mouth full of irregularly sized brown teeth.

"I don't know you. What's your watch?"

Mr. Oak ignored the question. "That was a bloody business, eh?"

"A bit. You saw the whole thing?"

"Aye. You gave him a chance, I saw it. He could'a gave himself up to the captain, but he pulled a knife on you instead. His blade landed over here." Mr. Oak pointed at the base of a stack of crates. "You'll want that to prove he was armed."

"Wise thinking," Weems said. "Thankee, Oak."

As she knelt to pick the knife up, the ropes securing the crates against the ship's motion writhed loose. Weems noticed the slithering sound and looked up just in time to be buried beneath an avalanche of heavy wooden boxes as *Revenant* lurched over a wave. Her scream was muffled and cut short by the staccato sound of bones cracking.

"Think nothing of it," Mr. Oak said.

The old man sauntered over to Ogilvy's corpse and knelt by it. After a brief examination, he gave a satisfied nod. At a motion of his hands, all the blood surrounding the body soaked rapidly into the deck's wood. The dark stain it made was inconspicuous among all the other stains that gave the deck its mottled appearance. Satisfied with his efforts, he knelt and whispered into Ogilvy's dead ear.

"Let's see how fine a puppet you'll make for old Mr. Oak!"

Ogilvy's eyes snapped open and winked alternately and then blinked in unison. His mouth writhed from a frown to a smile and then through every other expression it could form. A moment later, his eyebrows performed the same exercise, and then his head swiveled to all possible positions upon his neck. The head's antics complete, the corpse lurched to its feet and shook out its limbs like a loose-jointed marionette.

"You fit like a glove," Mr. Oak said and slowly dissipated into the shadows that crowded the hull.

"Now let us visit hell upon these insects who tore me from my home, from my very self," the late Ogilvy muttered as he turned to climb the ladder leading to the deck above.

No sooner had Enid sat at her workbench and begun arranging the various instruments and diagrams before her to attempt an experiment regarding the use of the semblance between one sort of element and another, such as the fluid way in which flames moved, as a source of affinity when there were three sharp knocks on the door to her workroom. She had just heard the bells chime out the watch, so she knew it was not Yeardly arriving for his lessons, so rather than simply shout for him to enter, she rose and stomped over to the door and flung it open. A bitter imprecation was forming in her throat before her hand had so much brushed against the door, but it died there when she saw one of the new mids, Weard, she thought, standing before it, her eyes already wide with the surprisingly abrupt way Enid revealed herself.

Enid swallowed her annoyance and, in a strained but adequately companionable tone, asked Weard what brought her to her door after the dinner hour.

"Lieutenant Merryweather sent me to fetch you, with her compliments, Magister."

"I see," Enid said. "She is on the quarterdeck, I take it?"

"No, Magister. She is in the hold, not so far from where we stand. She bids you make all haste."

Only then did Enid realize that the fearful timber of the mid's voice was not rooted in the alarming way she'd been greeted. "What has happened?"

"Weems, one of the captains of the tops, failed to appear for her watch, so the Lieutenant Merryweather sent Mid Dinwitty and me to look for her. When we could find no sign of her anywhere else, we searched the hold, thinking she may have slipped down there for a caulk and not heard the bells of her watch. We found her, but she was not sleeping. She was crushed to death beneath a pile of crates that broke loose and fell upon her. We only found her by the gleam of our orbs on the blood seeping from beneath them."

"Let me fetch my sword and pistol and we'll be on our way, then."

When she arrived in the hold, she found several waisters under Merryweather's supervision clearing the boxes that formed poor Weems's impromptu sepulcher. Enid stepped to her side and was treated to a clear view of the top captain's head, which had been crushed nearly flat. Nothing she'd witnessed during the excesses of the Theocratic purge or in the recent sea battles in which she'd participated had prepared her for the horror of the sight. As more bloodstained crates were shifted off the corpse, it was evident that Weems had literally been flattened beneath them.

"What was in those crates?" Enid asked, looking away from Weems's horribly destroyed form. "Lead ingots for the casting of spelllock balls?"

"No. And that is why I asked you to join us, Magister," Merryweather answered. "These crates were filled with slop cloth. They are heavy enough to have injured Weems, or even to have killed her if she were abandoned by fortune entire, but certainly not so heavy to have caused such devastating damage to her entire body."

The cold clutch of dread tightened around Enid's heart. The atrocity visited upon Weems was beyond the means of a simple ghost or vengeful spirit. *What hellish force haunts* Revenant*? And will there be aught I can do against it if it ever deigns to show itself?* She kept her horror from her face, though, and gave Merryweather a curt nod.

"I will survey the area for signs of sorcery," she said, and opened her senses to the unseen world. There were echoes of strange magic here, but so faint that it was impossible for her to trace back to its source. This was troubling, for it doubtless indicated that smashing poor Weems to paste with those crates had constituted a minimal effort on the part of her killer. When she turned her attention to the top captain's corpse she noticed a bloodred string of affinity stretching from her ruins to an object tucked beneath a stack of nearby barrels. She followed it and found a sailor's knife there, its blade slightly notched but sharp as a cat's claws. Examining it closely, she saw there was freshly dried blood in the crevices between the handguard and the blade.

She held the knife up and focused the light from the orb Merryweather had summoned upon it. "Can any of you say for certain whose knife this is?"

The waisters offered no answer but a glum gaze by way of answer, but Weard raised her hand and said, "Aye, Magister, that is—was—Weems's knife. I saw her using it as recently as this afternoon!"

Merryweather nodded. "I've seen it in her hand or on her belt many times every day since she first came aboard *Alarum*. Why would it be all the way over there?"

"Perhaps it fell there during a struggle," Enid suggested. "It has fresh blood crusted on the guard and hilts, so it has drawn blood recently, probably that of the same villain that slew her. Shall I follow the blade to the person whose blood it spilled?"

At Merryweather's nod, Enid began to sort through the various objects that harbored an affinity for it, from frayed rope ends that it had been used to square off, to Weems's plain tin plate, which the blade had scored over the course of a multitude of meals. The mental image of the plate, no different from any of its fellows owned by every other sailor aboard, filled her with a sudden abject woe. It would never feel the scrape of Weems's knife again, nor hold a hot meal for her after she spent a cold night aloft in the tops. It would almost certainly be put to use again, but never by Weems. It astounded her that the thought of a cheap, plain plate could force her to swallow tears when the wreckage of its owner only inspired a vague sense of her own mortality.

She gave her head a shake and allowed the knife to draw her through the ship for the second and, she prayed, last time. It pulled her back on to the gun deck and, from there, to the fo'c'sle where it drew a straight line to the back of a tall, cadaverous man who stood laughing with a couple of waisters as they passed a pipe around in a brief moment of leisure. The knife fairly throbbed in her hand, as if it longed to sink into the wight's flesh once again and to better effect.

"It is his blood," Enid pronounced, only recognizing the man as Ogilvy when he turned at the sound of the voice.

"What is this?" Ogilvy exclaimed. "Here now, I've done nothing to you, Magister! Why do you wave that knife at me like an assassin? Here, Lieutenant Merryweather, sir, why are you and young Mid Weard giving me such evil looks? How've I offended ye?"

Enid lowered the knife as Merryweather said, "We have just come from the hold, where we found Weems crushed to death beneath a mysteriously unstable stack of crates."

"Poor Weems," Ogilvy said in a woeful tone as he removed his hat and clutched it to his breast. The two fellows he'd been smoking with mimicked his action. "But it sounds as if it were a, what do you call it? A mishap, hey? So why is the magister waving that knife at me like as she did when she accused Grimes of being a murtherer?"

"Weems' knife lay near her corpse, blooded," Merryweather said, staring icily into Ogilvy's large, hollow eyes. "It appears there was a struggle before she died and she drew her assailant's blood before the 'mishap' claimed her life."

Ogilvy shook his head and sighed mournfully. "Poor Cap'n Nath's luck has fled altogether, ain't it? The poor gentleman stuck with such an unhappy vessel as *Revenant*. A hangin', accidental deaths, and roughhousing what ends in a prime hand losing their number. It is a shame, sure as I stand here, but I still don't understand why, respectfully, ye all have rounded on me"—he turned his hangdog face on Enid and said—"unless it's because of my friendship with Grimes. Do you have a grudge against me, Magister? Is that why you torment me?"

Enid sniffed disdainfully and fixed Ogilvy with a frozen glare down the length of her nose. "I do not *torment* you. We are here because this knife drew us to you, and it did so because it has recently tasted your blood."

"Here now, you're mistaken, Magister! I ain't had so much as a nick from my razor, let alone been cut with a knife as thirsty as that one appears!"

"Come now, Ogilvy," Merryweather barked. "Show you have some decency about you and reveal the wound Weems dealt you and let us be done with this charade!"

"I have never received a scratch from the blade of any man or woman on this ship. I swear it 'pon my brother's grave!"

Merryweather sighed. "Must I call for a pair of lobsters to strip you to the skin to reveal the damning wound? Are so desirous to be completely shed of your dignity?"

"You needn't call anyone," Ogilvy said with a sad shake of his head. He then shed his clothes swiftly and shamelessly until he stood before them, stark naked. He raised his arms and turned a pirouette before them.

There was no wound of any sort on his body.

Merryweather cast a worried sidelong look at Enid, and the small crowd of waisters and lubbers that had gathered around them muttered among themselves and eyed Enid suspiciously.

"Well, what have to say that, Magister? Your little tricks don't work on a man who's willing to stand and proclaim his innocence, do they? Is this the same mummery you used on poor Grimes? Would she'd the same gumption as I, but she was overawed by your magical powers. Beware, though, there are other full-blooded Albions aboard who'll make you do your own dirty work, rather than letting the hangman's noose do it for you!"

"That is enough," Merryweather barked. "One more seditious remark from your beak and I'll have your wings clipped! You'll find paying the devil all the harder with shackles and a ball clapped about your ankles!"

Enid's blood was like fire in her veins and her face felt as if she were pressing it into the open maw of a bread oven. She turned to Merryweather and said, "With your permission, Lieutenant, I will take my leave to return to my workspace to unravel what has occurred here."

Merryweather gave her a curt nod and Enid departed, her fists clenched at her side.

Nath rapped on her workroom door less than an hour later, his face clouded with a combination of professional worry and personal sympathy. Enid ushered him into her new workroom and gestured to one of the stools hanging from the bulkhead that were normally used to seat the mids while they were at their lessons. As he plucked one down, she produced a bottle and two glasses from a cabinet. The glasses were plain and serviceable, while the bottle's label was marked with sinister-looking script, a skull and crossbones, and a horribly evocative image of the rotting corpse of a rat.

Nath noticed the forbidding appearance of the label and said, "Come, Enid. It is not as bad as all that. Let us save the shared cup of poison for a more climactic scene, shall we?"

Enid did her best to return his grin of amusement at his own wit and replied, "This is not a grand vintage, but it is far from poison. I mark the bottle thus to discourage any hand that might find themselves alone in my workroom to save them from being drunk on watch."

"It is quite palatable, indeed," Nath said after taking a generous taste of the stuff. "Far more so than recent events. I have heard Merryweather's report, would you share yours now?"

They sat and sipped wine as Enid did just that, and, when the trajectory of her tale brought her back to the very space in which they sat, Nath glanced around the room and asked, "Is it safe to smoke here, Enid?"

"It is," she said with a companionable shake of her head at Nath's round-about request for one of her cigarillos. She secured one for each of them from a box near her elbow. She lit them both with a snap of her fingers and handed one to Nath, who accepted it with a grateful nod and filled his lungs with a deep draw of comforting smoke.

"I do not criticize Lieutenant Merryweather's judgment in the matter," Nath said, exhaling twin streams of smoke from his nostrils. "But had I been in her place, Ogilvy would have found himself in chains before he'd said half as much against you. Still, I understand the outburst caught you both unawares, yes?"

Enid nodded. "We should have expected it from the unctuous snake."

"So, have you arrived at a theory to explain the apparent failure of your magic?"

"I have none," Enid said. "The sorcerous operation itself was successful. There can be no doubt that the blood on Weems' knife came from Ogilvy. The sympathetic bond between it and the man are so powerful that they leave no doubt as to whose veins it was spilled, yet Ogilvy had not so much as a nick on his entire person."

"Then how could it be his?"

"The only explanation that makes any sense to me is that the wound or wounds he received from Weems were healed completely between the time he received them and our confrontation with him on the fo'c'sle, which is, of course, impossible. Rondelle and I working together could not make even a minor slash vanish without a trace within less than a day."

Nath frowned. He answered her as if he were trying to work a sticky puzzle out by talking his way through it. "If you say your spell worked, I am mortally certain it did. So, if it is impossible for you and Rondelle to heal a wound completely in the same day it is struck, who or what *could*?"

Enid shrugged and, at the completion of the operation, her shoulders remained a little slumped. "I am at a loss, Rue. I truly am. An archimage specialized in the art of healing magic, perhaps, but I can confidently assert neither Ogilvy nor any of his friends are archimages."

"Tell me, Enid, might an archimage who specialized in maritime and naval war magic be called a *barkymage*?"

"It is good you are so skilled at your trade," Enid said, pitting her disapproving frown against his smug smirk. "For as a humorist, you make a fine eulogist."

Nath's smirk widened into a grin. "It is just such wry comments that confirm my suspicion that you refuse to acknowledge that you secretly find flings amusing.

"But back to the matter at hand: The damage Ogilvy wished to do is done. Even if you were to find a way to prove he and Weems did fight, those in the crew that are disposed to believe ill of you will only say your evidence is but another sorcerous trick."

"So, there are folk aboard who believe that I am at best a liar, and worst a murderer?"

"There are," Nath said with a dismissive shrug. "And some believe all my decisions are influenced by the flash of your green eyes or the delectable arc of your neck, but they are all fools. Do not be troubled by the opinions of fools. Some will come around as they know you better. Others will find themselves dismissed at the end of the cruise whether I shift commands or not."

"So, I should ignore their gibes?"

"Not in the least. If one of them flies out at you in such a wise again, take their name for punishment, or, if their affront is truly egregious, have the lobsters take them up in the moment to secure them in the brig until such a time as I can hear what they say for themselves and pass judgment upon them."

Enid chewed her lip a moment, and then asked, "But won't such actions confirm their low opinion of me? Will they not accuse me of turning martinet, now that the hangman's rope is denied to me?"

"Some will, but being seen as being shy regarding discipline would do even more harm. Use your native wits to know when to take a name and when to let a minor infraction slip by. You are blessed with more than enough of it for the purpose."

"I pray you are right," Enid said, refilling their glasses. "I cannot boast of much in familiarity with the culture of the baseborn, but I will do my utmost to behave as you suggest."

"Thank you, Enid," Nath said. "I know you will do your best. I'm grateful to have the undivided support of my officers and warrants, for that quality is far from universal among the foremast hands. I would only confide this in you, Enid, but I fear Sea Lord Morrin's 'gift' of the Ainsley Bottoms hands may have been the winning card in his hand. The temperament of the crew is sullen and divided. My efforts to bring them together have failed completely, and now this."

Enid stared down at her hands, unable to meet Nath's eyes. *Why must I always be so precipitously rash? The blood on that knife would have maintained its sympathy for Ogilvy long enough to fetch Rue. Instead, I rushed forward to the detriment of us all.*

"Here now," Nath said, seeing her downcast eyes. "I meant no criticism of you or Merryweather. Even if Ogilvy hadn't braced you in front of the hands, he would have poured his poison into any ear willing to receive it."

Enid nodded silently, unconvinced.

"The important thing now is to continue to treat all the hands equally and allow no difference in the way we treat an old *Alarum* or hand from Ainsley Bottoms. Nothing is more likely to ignite the fuse to the powder keg Ogilvy is filling, one scurrilous scoop at a time."

"I will bear that in the forefront of my mind at all times."

Nath smiled and stood. "Well, I will leave you to the privacy of your sanctum, barkymage. I intend to bunk down early tonight after drinking the foul-smelling potion Dr. Rondelle forced upon me. I have not slept well for several nights, and it is taking its toll."

"I wish you a peaceful slumber, Rue." Enid stood and walked him the short three steps to the door. "And if Rondelle's herbal concoctions do not serve, send word for me and I will work a minor formulation to ease your sleep."

There were no more dramatic incidents in the few days that passed as *Revenant* ran down the miles that separated her from the Château des Fantômes. They forged through the crosscurrent that marked the mouth of the Merentian without mishap and now Gisbon, a faint spot of lighter sky on the larboard horizon, would be left in her wake. Nath and the other officers kept a wary eye on the bad bargains from Ainsley Bottoms and Enid redoubled her efforts to determine the nature of *Revenant*'stormentor. The ship's people wore uniformly guarded expressions and went about their duties with one eye on their task and the other on the nearest member of their opposing faction.

Nath kept the crew busy, alternating drills on the great guns with training at small arms with Master-at-arms Shea and Marine Lieutenant Gardner. Harcourt drilled the rest of the marines regularly to fuse the new lobsterbacks with the old. Enid was certain that the constant activity was productive, and they would all be glad of it when the time for action came at the Château d'Phantômes, but she found the noise quite irritating.

"Magister d'Tancreville!" Harcourt called out from where he was leading sword drills with the mids. "Leave the rail and join us to practice some swordsmanship!"

"I believe my time in the salle will serve me well," Enid called back.

"Then let these Young Gentles benefit from your experience. Let us play at swords a bit and introduce them to some of the finer points of the art!"

Enid damned Harcourt's winning ways and joined him in the area of the upper deck set aside for the purpose of such practice.

Harcourt turned to the mids and said, "Mark the Magister's footing, grip, and movements. The Ardain style is less direct but, in many ways, more deadly than ours. It is good to understand it, even practice it if you can. This is the sort of swordplay you can expect from an Ardain officer intent on holding onto their ship."

He turned then and greeted Enid with a warm, boyish smile. "Well, milady, shall we?"

Enid nodded, and they touched the tips of their swords. There was a bit of wary circling and then steel flashed in as much earnestness as could be supported where lives were not at stake. Enid was surprised by Harcourt's style. While he adhered to the Albion manner of fighting in the main, she saw shifts of technique that indicated a more than passing familiarity with the art as practiced by the Ardain, Naverroñans, and Velascins. It soon became clear that his thrusts and parries were designed to allow her to show the Ardain style at its most effective.

As they lunged, stamped, and virtually danced around the central point formed by their blades' crossing, Harcourt kept up an easy, instructional description of each Ardain technique and Albion's answer to it. Enid was awed by his wind, as she was already beginning to huff and puff a bit while Harcourt's voice sounded like that of a dispassionate observer rather than a participant in the exercise. He dropped the tip of his blade to the deck just as Enid was on the verge of gasping for breath.

"Thank you for the demonstration, Magister," he said. "It has been edifying to practice with such a fine swordswoman."

As the practice broke up and the mids scattered to their various duties, Harcourt offered her a silver flask. When she looked at it askance, he said, "It is light stuff, Magister. Barely more than fruit punch. Still, I think you will find it refreshing."

She did and thanked him for the drink. She was about to take her leave when he said, "You should dragoon Lieutenant Merryweather into practicing with you if you are to continue dueling ashore, Magister. You would benefit from learning more about Albionic swordplay and she is my best student. Captain Nath would be better, but his time is dearer than Merryweather's."

"I have no desire to fight another duel," Enid said.

"Desire it or not, you should prepare for the possibility. Isembarde Harde is far from the only bigot in Albion who will dismiss your deeds to hate you for your birthplace."

His expression was friendly and concerned as he spoke, but she found no trace of humor in it. He touched the brim of his hat and sauntered off to assist the master-at-arms in teaching the cutlass drill to a knot of landsmen.

"Ogilvy" stood among a knot of panting Newcomers gathered around the scuttlebutt awaiting their turn to drink coolish water from the tin cup that hung from it by a braided cord. One of the Ainslee tars leaned close to him and muttered, "They save the fancy fightin' tricks for the officers. For us, it's just a waste of time and sweat, eh? Just more of the same old stamp and slash."

Ogilvy grunted noncommittally, distracted by the final moments of the Rat magister and lobster captain.

Since donning Ogilvy, Mr. Oak finally had the opportunity to behold his foe through mortal eyes. She was as tall as some of the warrior queens whose souls he bound to his cantle so he might ever be delighted by the music of their sorrowful wailing. The mortal woman wore the champion's mark of an Elthaur in place of her right hand, though the sigil that circled it like a self-illuminating ribbon of black and gold was enchanted to defy recognition without its owner's leave. She was outmatched at the sword by the pleasant-featured marine officer, he reckoned, but she was deadly. He was gratified to see no sign of recognition in her eyes as they swept over him. In his reduced state, this mortal would require care. No clumsily crafted effigy of divinity would ever be a genuine danger to him, but an exceptional moppet such as this could prove tiresome if she were not treated with care. Besides, the ordinary mortals had proved to be so entertainingly delicious thus far. It would be a sin to rush through such a pleasant and diverting meal.

chapter 19

Enid was awoken in the wee hours of the mornings by a soft but frantic knocking on her door. She heard a hushed voice say, “Magister! The captain wishes to see you in his cabin at once!”

The voice was unfamiliar but filled with such concern that it banished all traces of sleep from her eyes. “I hear you. I will join you shortly.”

She dressed quickly and donned her sword belt. She thrust her two Kreitzer pistols into her belt as well, in case Nath’s urgent summons was due to a crisis of loyalty among the crew.

When she emerged from her cuddy, a nervous-looking marine awaited her. “Thank you, Magister! Please step along as quickly as you may. The captain is in a terrible state. I heard him cry out several times in his sleep before he fairly shrieked for me to bring you to him at once! I fear he may be the victim of black magic!”

They ran to the door to the captain’s quarters, and the marine did not come to a halt before announcing her arrival in a booming voice, and Nath answered with equal volume, “Enid! Thank the Gods! Enter!”

She found him seated at his desk, still clad in his nightclothes. His face was moist with sweat, and he fairly sparked from nervous energy. Marbury and Maubin sat on either side of him, gazing up at their master with such obvious concern that Enid's fondness for them increased threefold.

"The marine said you required my immediate attention." She took a seat on the narrow chair next to his desk and asked, "What is amiss?"

"I have had a visitation and you must needs be apprised of what I learned from it immediately!"

"A visitation?" Enid arched a brow. "By whom—or what?"

"I will tell it from the beginning. It happened thus: I was awakened by a nightmare of poor Harlech. In my dream, it was dark as pitch and I could barely discern her. She was entangled in the roots of a great oak tree that loomed formlessly above me. Her eyes glowed faintly in the dark, limning the tears that overflowed them in pale blue light. I knelt before her and struggled to free her from the great roots, but to no avail.

"She began wailing, 'Don't let him get you, Captain! Don't let him get you, it is terrible here!'

"*Who? Who is trying to get me?,* I asked, and she cried out 'Mr. Oak! Beware Mr. Oak.'

"At that moment, there was a sharp pain in my knee and when I looked for the source of it, I found that I knelt on Grimes, her decomposing body half-submerged in the mud and muck at the base of the tree. She worried my knee with her teeth, her eyes wild and devoid any hint of reason. I reeled over backward to escape her maw, and as I did, I saw the shape of the oak in whose roots poor Harlech was trapped. It brooded down at me, its form clearly outlined by the roiling, luminescent purple sky above. The sight chilled me with inexplicable terror and I awoke with a start, drenched in cold sweat."

"Do you recall the form of the tree well enough to sketch its semblance?"

"I shall never forget it. I found it terribly familiar, but strange at the same time. Here, pass me your pencil and paper."

When Nath finished a crude sketch of the tree, Enid took back the paper and pencil and asked, "And after you awoke?"

"It was so dark in my little bed closet that I could not see my hand before my face, but I knew I was not alone . . ."

"Could you have been dreaming yet?"

"No, no. I was awake. You have my word on't."

"I believe you," Enid said, and she did. "What did you do?"

"I whispered the globe to life and lit the room. He stood hard by my hanging bed staring down at me with a mixture of fearful pity and agonizing pain. I recognized him immediately, despite the deep slashes that disfigured his face. I'd seen engravings of it often enough in the papers and *Navy Journal*."

"Who was it?"

"Captain Ourey, may Redeemer have mercy on him."

"*Redemption*'s last captain?"

"The very one."

"Did he speak to you?"

"Not in words, but he filled my mind with images. Enid, I pray you never see the like of the horrors he revealed to me! I saw the atrocities visited upon him, his officers, and the crewmen who remained loyal to him—like me, he had a core of hands from his previous command, but the new hands outnumbered them. Worse yet, the mutineers were aided by a monster of some sort."

"A monster?" Enid asked. The hairs at the back of her neck stood to attention as a powerful chill passed them to run down the length of her spine. "Can you describe it?"

"Only vaguely, as I only saw it in brief snatches. It had the general shape of a man, but it was larger by far. Its proportions were unnatural, and it left me with the impression of a predatory insect, or a sickly tree come to life.

"The longer he shared these images with me the more frantic his expression became. His eyes rolled wildly and his savagely mutilated face contorted in fear. The last sight he presented me was that of the tree from my dream, drawing life and power from a towering mound of corpses held together by the tangle of its repulsive, writhing roots.

"Then his mouth flew open in a silent howl and his body twisted as if he were suddenly wrenched in all directions by some unseen force. Then he vanished."

"You were right to summon me immediately," Enid said. "I believe this is the first useful information to come to light regarding our unseen adversary. It tears at my heart to think of Harlech's sweet spirit in the clutches of such a monster, though."

"As it does mine, but if we can find a way to put down her captor, we can surely contrive a way to free her as well," Nath said. With most of his manic energy spent in telling his tale, he appeared wan and tired.

"She may well be freed the moment we end this thing's hateful existence," Enid said. "But for now, it is obvious you need your rest. I can perform a brief formulation to ease you off into a restful slumber, devoid of any troubling nightmares."

"Will it be possible to rouse me easily if I'm needed?"

"It would be no more difficult to wake you than if you slept naturally, I assure you."

"Then pray, let us be about it," Nath said. He rose to his feet and walked tiredly toward his sleeping closet. "These drafts of Rondelles taste foul and are only marginally effective."

As she closed the door to Nath's sleeping chamber, she perceived Dunaughy's conversational thoughts mixing with her own. *Ask Kaliktiklak for his counsel. The Bogaraets have a deep knowledge of spirits and ghosts that would serve you well.*

Although her shiver of dread was purely mental, it was tangible to Dunaughy, who thought, *Come! Are you a child? Kaliktiklak looks different from you. Has he given you any other cause to fear or distrust him?*

It is not that he looks different from me, but rather that he resembles the Darghaur, which does not foster my trust.

And yet Nath trusts him with much of the sailing and most of the navigation.

It is different. I have no reason to doubt Kaliktiklak's nautical skills—but I distrust him in more arcane pursuits. How can I be certain he has our best interests at heart and isn't yet a servant of the Old Enemy?

Did you learn nothing of Pre-Diasporic History in your vaunted Institut? *Without the help of the Bogaraet, humanity would never have escaped Darghaur bondage. They taught our heroes to resist the* Taking, *and those heroes passed the knowledge on to their boon companions, and so on until we were able to rise up with the Bogaraets and escape the Fastness. The treatment they received from the Darghaur, their very creators, was so vile that they hate them more than we do—and they all remember, in their bones, how we fought side by side with them so that we could all be free. You can trust Kaliktiklak.*

He named me a demon, Enid said. *And prayed I was not as evil as I seemed.*

So, he mistrusts you as much as you him. You have a common ground to work from. Do not be fearful of a friend. Seek his aid! So saying, he faded into obdurate silence.

She found Master Kaliktiklak in the wardroom, congenially conversing with Dr. Rondelle and the purser, a bitter-looking wight named Perrin with whom she'd had no cause to interact with thus far. They were all smoking pipes, even the lipless Bogaraet who drew on his with great, hissing intakes of breath. As much smoke escaped between his needle-sharp teeth as he pulled into his lungs. He eschewed a chair and sat with oddly boneless ease on the floor next to the wardroom table. Enid noted that he was still eye-to-eye with the men seated in chairs around it.

"Your pardon, Dr. Rondelle and Mr. Belvine," Enid said. "With your permission, I should like to impose on Mr. Kaliktiklak's patience for an hour or so."

Rondelle and Belvine smiled, muttered nothings, and waved with their pipes as Master Kaliktiklak followed her out of the wardroom. Outside, the Bogaraet asked, "How may I help you, Magister?"

Enid was once again struck by the butter-and-honey smoothness of his voice. Even with the subtle clickings behind each word, it was by far the most melodious speaking voice that ever graced her ears. It was difficult to believe it emerged from such a nightmarish visage.

"I'm told that your people are deeply erudite in matters of the spiritual plane. Ghosts, haunts, vengeful spirits, and so forth." She left the question implied.

"We are, Magister. We have a peculiar bond with such entities—you would call it a sympathetic attachment—because we are, ourselves, ghosts."

Enid regarded him silently for a moment and then said, "Perhaps we should discuss this in my workroom, below."

Once there, with the lathe door closed and small formulations set to alert her of eavesdroppers, Enid asked, "You are a ghost?"

"It is likely that I am several," the Master said with a fluid shrug. "We Bogaraet are vessels for ancient lost souls."

"Vessels?"

Master Kaliktiklak nodded, his minute eyes red sparks against the glistening dark moon of his face. "After the Dissolution War, the world was filled with wandering spirits of slain Darghaur and Ellethaur—the beings you call the Fey or Ylfar. The Darghaur were greatly reduced by the war, and it would be centuries before they recovered a fraction of their former numbers. Though the Ellethaur had left the war, the Darghaur feared they might return at any time. As a hedge against this fear, they created diminished versions of themselves to bolster their legions. These were my ancestors, the first Bogaraet.

"The Bogaraet were created as inert, lifeless vessels to avoid breaking the Darghaur's implacable laws against creating new forms of life or souls. To animate us, they gathered the spirits of the slain Darghaur and Ellethaur and combined them in a titanic brass vat. The souls were rendered down, and the molten spirits were poured into the Bogaraet. When we awoke, we found we were all fundamentally connected, as we were a distillation of an uncountable number of souls. In our tongue, 'Bogaraet' means 'Ghost of All.' We share memories and experiences even today."

"Does your memory extend to the time before the Dissolution War?" Enid asked.

"Of course, but we prefer not to discuss those days," Kaliktiklak said. "Now, how may I assist you, Magister?"

Enid shared Nath's description of his nightmare and the uncanny visitation that followed. She answered Kaliktiklak's few questions as well as she could. When he was satisfied he grasped the events as fully as possible, he shook his head and sat on his heels next to her worktable.

"What do you make of our captain's dreams and visions?" Kaliktiklak asked.

"I believe that Harlech and Captain Ourey sought to warn Nath of the danger he faces. Harlech named our foe 'Mr. Oak,' and I believe the visions Ourey shared with him indicate that Mr. Oak's power is drawn from the souls of those he has slain. I do not grasp the importance of the tree, I fear, unless the fact that it was an oak and our adversary is its namesake."

Kaliktiklak bobbled his head in a nod. "We agree on the first two points, Magister. I wish we knew more of this darksome tree, for I believe it is more significant than a clue to our enemy's name."

"Nath drew a crude representation of it," Enid said. She pulled her sheet of notes from her jacket pocket and smoothed it out on the table before Kaliktiklak. The Bogaraet studied it for less than a heartbeat and then met Enid's eyes.

"This is a compass oak, a tree that either by chance or careful manipulation grows into shapes ideally suited for some of a vessel's most critical timbers. It is far stronger than anything that can be turned out by a carpenter and their tools," Kaliktiklak said.

"So, its *axis mundi* is in a piece of this compass wood?"

"Not just any piece. The tree in Nath's scrawl is perfect for the great span of oak that forms the center of a ship's bow. His *axis mundi* is in the bow compass wood. Harlech and Ourey tried to tell Captain Nath, but his mind was too addled by Dr. Rondelle's sleeping draughts to perceive the shape of it in the tree they showed him."

"How do we confirm it?"

Kaliktiklak looked around Enid's workroom and said, "Allow me to take a few pinches of this and that from your stock of herbs and minerals. I have most of what I need here"—he held up the large leather satchel at his hip—"but there are a few items I lack."

"Please, be free with my provisions. Take what you need with my blessing!"

When Kaliktiklak was satisfied that he had all the materials required for whatever he planned to do, they descended from the orlop to the hold. There, Kaliktiklak located the compass wood as surely as rain finds the ground. He touched it with his forefinger, which reminded Enid of nothing so much as a spider's leg.

"His sanctum is well warded," Kaliktiklak said softly. "I am mortally certain his center of power is here, but I can find nothing to prove it."

Enid stamped her foot in frustration. "I dearly yearn to confront this devil. If I cannot make him pay for Harlech's death, I will at least drive him out of *Revenant* or be damned in the attempt!"

Kaliktiklak studied her for a moment, and said, "I did not say that nothing can be done, I only said I cannot find proof this is the devil's abode. There is a ritual I can perform that will allow you to enter this Mr. Oak's fastness. If our theory is correct, your wish might be granted. If we are wrong, we will simply have wasted our time and a few of our magical ingredients."

"Then let us be at it!"

"No," Kaliktiklak said. "I will not aid a demon for fear of making it stronger, even if it means suffering the predations of this unknown evil."

"I've told you before, sir, I am no demon."

"And yet, like them, you have adorned yourself with a limb of precious metal and trapped within it the soul of a human man."

"I don't know about your people's demonic lore, but it obviously differs from mine." Enid held up her silver hand slowly, palm open toward him. "As for this, it is no more than a prosthesis augmented by my art. The soul within it is not trapped there—he is my friend and mentor, Magister Dunaughy. He volunteered to dwell within my hand so long as I lived, both to provide it with the arcane energy it requires to function as my natural hand and continue my education as a naval magician."

Kaliktiklak's pinprick eyes bore into hers for a long moment. Then he stood as upright as the confines of the hold would allow and gave a single, brisk nod. "I believe you. You are no demon. Let us be about our business, then."

Enid sat in the center of a complex circle of Bogaraet glyphs, traced on the deck with a combination of sea salt and a powdered resin from a tree native to Kaliktiklak's home island. He loomed over her left shoulder, kneeling into the circle while keeping his body outside its perimeter. In his hand was one of Enid's silver salvers upon which burned a pile of aromatic herbs that he brushed toward Enid's nose with a raven's wing from his seemingly bottomless satchel. The fumes had a harsh initial taste, and a faint finish of tart, equatorial fruit when Enid drew it into her lungs. It oozed warmly from her lungs and seep into her brain, where it settled in a pool of red so dark it appeared black. She stood nude and unashamed in the pool, slicked from the collarbones down by its incarnadine fluid.

Dunaughy stood next to her, equally unfettered by modesty and noticeably bereft of bullet wounds. He looked from his hands to her, a puzzled look on his face. She shrugged.

Kaliktiklak's voice floated between them, interrupting any further interaction. His words glowed pale green and hung in the air like physical representations of his speech.

"I see you take to the smoke well," his words said, each annunciating itself and then vanishing with a faint pop. "Are you well grounded? Are you confident or fearful?"

"Confident but confused," Enid said. "Dunaughy is here."

"Of course, he is. His soul is bound to yours. Where you go, so must he."

Enid looked at her right hand and found it to be made of ordinary flesh and bone. "But the silver hand is not here."

"Why should it be? If you had a wooden leg, it would be just as absent. Your form in the spiritual realm is always your perfect self, as you perceive it to be."

"So I see," Enid said, after a glance at Dunaughy, who appeared twenty years younger than the apparition he presented on her first night aboard the *Alarum* and the gunshot wound that slew him was nowhere in evidence on his somewhat stocky but well-formed body. "Is there a tendency to self-delusion in how people imagine their best selves?"

"There must be," Dunaughy drawled. "For I reckon you are half a foot shorter than your flesh and bone form."

Enid translated a series of staccato clicks ricocheted around her as Kaliktiklak's laughter.

Dunaughy stepped up next to her and grasped her arm gently just above the elbow. It was the first time she had ever experienced his actual, physical touch.

"We must make haste, Enid. Our time is limited. We must uncover as much as we can about this villain from his lodgings."

"It is clear that he is bloody-minded," Enid said, lifting one of her feet from the pool of the stuff they stood in. "Other than that, I see nothing but a featureless orb."

"The place will unfold as you venture forth," Kaliktiklak's disembodied voice assured her. "Dunaughy is correct. He will recognize your intrusion into his realm soon and come to drive you out."

Enid nodded and walked forward. The edge of the red pool presented itself, blank and featureless, but when she stepped onto it, it was transformed. Blood thinned, and the color drained from it until it was cool, transparent water. The shore on which she stood was smooth gray-brown mud, compacted to a firm but giving surface beneath her bare feet. The texture transported her back to her childhood, playing along the mud beach under the warm sun, with the Merentian Sea before her and the gaunt shadow of the Château des Fantomes looming to the west. There were children there with her. A boy and a girl. Commoners. Their names were at the tip of her tongue when someone shook her arm.

"Enid!" Dunaughy barked. "Stay focused! You could literally become lost in your thoughts there."

She shook her head to clear it and looked around. The ground sloped up before them to form a domelike hill. An enormous oak tree stood at its crown and its long branches seemed to strain toward them. The sky behind it was whirled with glowing shades of purple and black, pricked with stars of brilliant violet and sickening green. The air smelled of wood chips underlain with the faint scent of dry leaves, foul excrescence, and rotting flesh.

"This is where he lives, if you can call it that." Enid began trudging up the hill but Dunaughy stopped her with a word.

"Wait! There is something in the underbrush at the pool's edge."

Enid joined him there as he knelt and spread the branches of a bush rooted by the pool. She stepped back with a gasp as she recognized Harlech's face staring sightlessly at the varicolored heavens above. Her nose was pinched into a lopsided shape by the coarse thread that passed through both of her nostrils. She lay at the top of a shelf composed of dozens of child corpses of both sexes, all in various states of decomposition.

"These are all his handiwork," she said, forcing herself to look at the horrors before her. "His trophies. He keeps them here so that he can gaze down on them from on high, in the shade of that great patriarch of an oak."

"He is a devil," Dunaughy said.

"There are no devils, so he cannot be one," Kaliktiklak corrected. "But it also seems less likely that he is a ghost."

"Whatever he is," Enid said. "I will make him regret harming Harlech."

They labored up the hill toward the great oak. Ribs crunched beneath their feet, the sickening crack occasionally accompanied by a faint moan of pain. The hill seemed to grow steeper with each step they took, despite its apparently gentle slope. When Enid looked up at the tree, she saw that its branches were now adorned with hung men and a few hung women, all dangling from its sturdy branches like overripe fruit, complete with swarms of buzzing flies.

Dunaughy studied the tree and its human burden carefully. "This is a gallows tree, but mark you the shape and dimensions of its branches."

"Compass wood."

Dunaughy nodded.

"Was Harlech's killer a hangman, or a hanged man?"

"He is no man," answered the corpse dangling nearest to her, its voice was raspy as it stared at her over the bony rise of its chest. A faint wind blew through the limbs as he spoke, resulting in a rattling of bones that seemed to echo his words, "He was the tree. He was part of a forest."

"He was never a man?" Enid asked.

"Never," the corpse rasped. The surrounding bones rattled again, this time sounding for all the world like a host of people clucking in disapproval.

"How was he called?"

"We cannot say his true name, but he calls himself Mr. Oak." An ossuary rattle followed the words.

"What is his grievance with us? He allowed us to return to Middlesea without interfering with our officers or crew."

"He feared you," the dead man said. The sound of raucously rattling bones rose to a deafening crescendo and then went silent in an instant. "He fears you more now."

"Why?" She took the soft rustle of bones that answered her to mean they could not say or would not say.

"Where is Mr. Oak now?"

"Outside, hunting."

"What prey does he seek?"

"Souls."

Enid and Dunaughy shared a dismayed look.

"To what end?"

"He is severed from his self. Without the power he draws from us, he would fade away." The rattle of the bones rose to an earsplitting crescendo and then faded back to the occasional rattle in the corruption-laden breeze.

"Why are you so free with this information," Dunaughy interrupted. "And why should we believe it?"

The spokesman for the dead rotated slowly on their rope until they faced the Murchadhen mage. Its eyes glowed with a yellow fire. "If you were I, a brave hero reduced to *this*, would you not take any opportunity to see the author of your tragic tale take hurt, however minor?"

Dunaughy nodded grimly. "Indeed, I would, sir. What is your name so that we can recall you to your descendants for gallantry that breached the walls of death?"

"I have forgotten my name, with much else. I know only that I was once king of a place named Orrithania and that I died fighting in the ruins of its capital city when the dog who holds my soul switched allegiance and betrayed us to our enemies."

"I will find your name and remember it," Dunaughy said.

Kaliktiklak's words appeared in the air before them and popped with each word that reached their ears. "Time is short. If you do not wish to stay there, you must depart soon."

"I understand," Enid said. She made to turn back down the hill, but, seized by a sudden inspiration, she turned on her heel and reached out to touch the tree.

"Enid!" Dunaughy cried out in alarm. "What are you—"

She ignored him and placed her right hand against the trunk of the tree and sought power where she could. Her mind was instantly caught in a crashing cataract of death, death distilled. The strength of it was exhilarating. With such power she could strike half the world dead. But that is not what she sought. She strengthened her intent and forced her mind past the wall of death and into—someplace else, tendrils of deathly power clinging to her. The place she'd glimpsed as a student and recoiled from in fear and awe. The place that glittered and gloomed at the edge of her awareness as she forged her right hand. It was a realm of unbound potential, and she seized it.

The skin of her right hand began to sear, as if the bare wood under her palm was the white-hot surface of a foundry furnace. She returned to herself enough to see the flesh of her hand char away in ashy flakes to reveal the silver that lay beneath. Ignoring the pain, she focused her will, strengthened by her longing for vengeance, and, in this small place at least, forged her intent into a tangible force of nature. She continued to fold the force of her intentions in the same manner a master swordsmith folds layers of steel to double and redouble its strength until the world went black around her.

When she came to herself, she stood with her right hand pressed against the compass wood that Mr. Oak called home. Tendrils of white smoke curled between her fingers as she withdrew her hand to find its charred imprint on the wood beneath. When she turned to face Kaliktiklak, she was mildly surprised that a naked Dunaughy didn't stand beside him.

"What have you done?" Kaliktiklak asked.

"I have deprived Mr. Oak access to the power stored in his *axis mundi*. Nor may he enter it until I remove my mark. He is trapped among us now, and we will make him wish he'd never left his little corner of hell."

You did well, Dunaughy thought, *But I saw the method of your magic and it is fearsome. I pray you, Enid, my friend, do not expose yourself to such power without great need. I fear it may change you as much as it allows you to change the world around you.*

You need not fear on that account, Enid said. *I do not believe I can perform such feats at will. I theorize that it was only possible for me today because I was outside the physical world.*

That is just as well, I think.

Master Kaliktiklak interrupted their exchange, saying, "We should report this to Captain Nath, but I am at a loss as to what we should tell him. We know little more than we did before. We know the enemy's name, but not his purpose. We have barred him from his haven, but he still walks unknown among us."

Enid sighed. "I think it might be best not to burden his mind with unnecessary worries. The task set to him by Admiralty is burdensome enough. Let us shoulder this responsibility and leave the mundane aspects of our cruise to him."

"I see the sense in your suggestion, Magister," Kaliktiklak said. "But I advise you to apprise the captain of the situation in broad terms, if not in detail."

"Of course, we mustn't leave him completely in the dark."

Enid found Nath at his desk, the top of which was littered with charts and measuring devices. He looked up from them as she entered and smiled a smile that would not have been out of place on the face of a merry wolf.

"Enid! You may be pleased to learn that we will make the Tancreville coast tonight! Tomorrow we'll ghost in for a quick reconnaissance and, depending on what we see, we will put you ashore to contact the militia the same night."

She returned a pale shadow of his smile and took the seat by his desk. As she settled herself into the narrow, uncomfortable wretch of a chair, he filled a glass for each of them with a sweet, herbal concoction that tasted strongly of elderflowers.

"I tell you, Enid," Nath said, unceremoniously wiping his lower lip with the back of his hand, "I was dead certain that we'd run afoul of a great Ardain ship-of-the-line and be captured or killed long before now. I would not have put it past our rascal of a Sea Lord to leak our course to an Ardain spy, all by accident, of course. My relief at arriving within striking distance of the château is inexpressible! Now, what news do you have for me, Enid?"

"More good tidings, I believe," Enid said, choosing her words carefully. "We were able to locate the source of the power that has bedeviled us, thanks to the implications of the dream and vision you described to me.

"With Master Kaliktiklak's indispensable aid, I have sealed that source and denied the entity entrance or egress from it until I can arrive at a more permanent solution."

"Good tidings, indeed!" Nath topped off her glass and leaned back in his chair. "So it should make no trouble while we are ashore?"

"I do not believe so," Enid said. "Or at least no serious trouble."

Nath drained his glass and smiled unreservedly. "Ashes, it is good to have another worry behind me, if only for a while. I begin to hope we will survive the Seal Lord's little jaunt in the park! Now, come, a few final questions have occurred to me as I compared your map to this chart of the coast and I hope you can settle them for me."

PART
FOUR

chapter 20

"As most of you know, we raised the coast of Ardainne and the Château des Fantomes yestereve," Nath said. The officers and warrants gathered in his dayroom hunched like starving vultures over the map he unrolled on the table.

"I'm sure you've all committed the coastline and waters to your memory, so we will dispense with reviewing the navigational charts and focus on this, a detailed map of the area around the Château des Fantomes. Enid has drawn it from her memory."

"As you can see, the château stands at the seaward end of this promontory. Here, a little over an hour's ride from the château, is the town of Tancreville. It was the seat of our Magister's fief until the Theocratic revolution. Here, on the northeast edge of the town, is a keep whose grounds were once the Magister d'Tancreville's home. Now she suspects that it may now be home to a unit of Theocratic Militia, as it was to a cavalry squadron during her rule."

"Then reinforcements for the château garrison are but an hour away?" Lieutenant Harcourt asked.

"Or less," Nath said. "There is also an encampment of Rat troops further up the coast. They can make the château as well, though it would take them longer than the troops in Tancreville."

Nath ignored the frowns and concerned expressions of his officers and pressed on. "But there is a narrow point on the promontory here. A small force positioned here can hold off a superior force for some time. Long enough for us to retrieve Cieran Bascombe and withdraw to our landing point here. The rearguard will be under the command of Lieutenant Gardner of marines and supported by Magister d'Tancreville and Mid Yeardly. They will be in command of a combined force of Marines and *Revenants*."

"What of the rearguard if they are engaged by reinforcements? Are they to be sacrificial pawns, left to die in place while we withdraw?"

"Lieutenant Gardner!"

"Do not scold her, Lieutenant Harcourt," Nath said. "The question reveals an admirable sympathy for the men and women my orders put in harm's way. The rearguard's retreat will be covered by the local militia, under Magister d'Tancreville's command if necessary. Once our folk are safely in their boats, the militia will withdraw."

Lieutenant Gardner nodded her approval, and Lieutenant Harcourt shook his head.

"I shall lead the assault," Nath continued. "With the support of Lieutenant Merryweather and Lieutenant Harcourt."

"Excuse me, sir," Lieutenant Bascombe interjected. "Am I not to be included in the assault to free my sister?" The silence that settled over the room was so dense that Nath's response seemed muted.

"You are not, sir." Nath's voice was gentle, but firm. "You will remain aboard to ensure that the ship is secure and ready to sail at a moment's notice."

"I see, sir," Bascombe said and produced a folded document from his coat. "The Sea Lord bade me to present this to you if I were not included in the rescue party."

The patient, sympathetic expression on Nath's face rearranged into something cold and flatly emotionless. He accepted the paper and read it through twice before thrusting it into his own coat pocket.

"Very well," Nath said, never removing his eyes from Bascombe, who returned his gaze with a steady, neutral stare of his own.

"Lieutenant Merryweather will remain aboard *Revenant* and Lieutenant Bascombe will accompany me on the assault on the château. Our force will comprise the bulk of the Marines and a force of veteran sailors. We will include an armorer capable of planting explosive charges to blast doors and gates as required. Dr. Rondelle, you will accompany us. You will be left in as safe and near a location to the château as is practicable to render medical aid to Lieutenant Bascombe when we deliver her from her prison."

Nath waited until everyone nodded their understanding, and continued, "Once Lieutenant Cierina Bascombe is in our hands, we will withdraw to the boats. When we are under way, a flare will be launched to alert the Rear Guard to make their retreat. The flare will also be *Revenant*'s signal to stand in to pick up the boats and use her batteries to discourage assaults on the landing site.

"So there you have it, gentles, save for the timeline of events. Magister d'Tancreville and Mid Yeardly will make a landing after full-dark tonight to seek out her contacts and, Providence willing, convince the local resistance to assist in our efforts. If she fails, she will fire a flare to warn us off. Assuming she is successful, the raiding party will land after dark tomorrow night and will be back aboard *Redemption* with Lieutenant Cieran Bascombe in our care before dawn."

Cries of "Hear, hear!" rang out around the table. When they receded, Nath spent the remainder of the war council answering his people's questions about the particulars of their roles and, with Enid's help, describing the ground as fully as possible. He maintained a chilly civility with Bascombe, but only with great effort. When all the key points were covered, he dismissed everyone but Merryweather and Enid. He called for Yarric to pour them each a glass of brandy and turn in for the night. Once they were alone, he handed Bascombe's letter to Merryweather without saying a word.

"Have you ever heard of such a thing?" Merryweather said. "And why weren't these directions included with your orders to rescue Cierina Bascombe?"

"I cannot say," Nath said. "But I thought you should know that my hand was forced."

"What does it say?" Enid asked. Nath offered her the paper, but she refused to take it. "A precis is enough. Your admiralty's impenetrable prose holds no attraction for me."

Nath waved the paper in disgust and said, "These are supplementary orders in the Sea Lord's own hand requiring me to include Lieutenant Leonid Bascombe in the main effort to rescue his sister, only to be presented to me after I announced otherwise to *Revenant*'s officers."

"What a spiteful and obvious ploy," Enid said. "He reminds you that you serve at his will and then places you in a position in which you will be damned if Leonid Bascombe comes to a bad end and reduced if he performs a signal act of valor. Your Sea Lord is a venomous scrub."

Merryweather and Nath flinched as one at Enid's plain speech.

"Forgive me, I forgot the cultic awe in which you hold the Sea Lord even while suffering under his childish rancor."

Merryweather chuckled despite herself.

"Be that as it may, my hands are tied," Nath said. "And in truth, this may be the hand of Providence at work. While there have been no signs of outright disobedience from the Newcomers in the crew, they have not yet had enough time to come around from the ill treatment they received from Admiralty or Grimes' hanging. I worry that without the calming effect of the Marines in their full numbers, the hard bargains that are left behind may become restive."

Merryweather nodded. "I share your concern, sir. I was relieved to see that you did not draw the assault force exclusively from the loyal *Alarum*s. I believe I can maintain discipline with the *Alarum*s and marines left to me. Particularly if I place marine sharpshooters in the fighting tops to keep watch for the approach of enemy boats."

Nath grinned in approval. "And keep an eye on things on deck at the same time. A fine idea, Lieutenant! I'm confident that you are equal to any challenge that might arrive while the raid is under way."

After Nath summarized his instructions to Merryweather and reiterated some key guidelines for Enid, they shared a drink and smoke before retiring for the night. Outside his quarters, Enid said, "Lieutenant Merryweather, I have something for you in my workshop that may prove useful to you tomorrow, if your duties will permit you to join me there?"

"I will meet you there presently, Magister," Merryweather replied. "I wish to check the mids on watch at the moment."

"I will await you below, then."

Enid's formulations to guarantee privacy and warn of an intruder's approach were in effect when Merryweather arrived, but the workspace looked no different from usual, other than a bottle of fine Ardain wine and two glasses on prominent display in the center of her workbench. When Merryweather entered the room, she looked both relieved and disappointed.

"I feared I might find the place adorned with silks and strewn with flowers," Merryweather said, only half jesting.

Enid smiled sadly. "Would that I could have made it so, but alas, we have both sworn an oath to Rue."

Merryweather nodded and sat on one of the stools by the workbench. She picked up the bottle of wine and arched an appreciative brow. "Shall I pour for us?"

"Please do," Enid said and took the opposite stool.

"Both your integrity and choice of wines are commendable," Merryweather said after taking a sip of the stuff. "I am sorry we have not had the freedom to spend more time in private, if only to deplete your store of this vintage and share a quiet conversation."

"I must admit to my fault in that, Merry," Enid said. "Truth be told, I feared I lacked the resoluteness to be true to both my word and my heart."

"I understand. It is much the same with me. It is difficult to be so near and yet, in practice, so far apart."

They drank in silence for a moment, and then Enid suddenly turned and seized up a bundle of cloth bound by a string. She placed it on the table between them and said, "I made this for you, to protect you from hurt. Its dweomers will blunt the force of swords, axes, and even bullets that strike you. It is similar to the jacket that I made for Rue and the one I wear myself if fighting seems likely."

Merryweather picked the bundle up by the strings and said, "It seems quite light."

"It should be. It is a silk shirt I purchased for you in Middlesea, in accordance with Dr. Rondelle's advice. It is sheer enough that you can wear it beneath your uniform and not be discomfited in any way."

"How sheer is it?" Merryweather asked, and carefully untied the knot holding the bundle closed. She held the garment between them and could see Enid's vague outline between the front and back layers of silk.

"Passing sheer," Enid said.

"And how did you know my proportions?"

Enid coughed. "From familiarity."

"Ah. Estimated, then?"

Enid nodded.

"Then I should try it on. Please, turn your back."

Enid did as she was told and was rewarded by the sound of Merry shrugging off her heavy officer's coat, removing her stock, and unfastening her uniform blouse. A moment of silence followed, in which Enid had a distractingly clear vision of her bare to the waist and standing enticingly nearby. She was on the verge of turning when she heard the soft slither of silk on skin.

"Hmm. The fit seems a little loose. What are your thoughts on it?"

Enid turned and found that the gauzy image of Merry's body through the clinging silk was more provocative than reason and self-discipline could support. She was unaware of the low growl in the back of her throat as she rose from the stool, or of rising, either. Her next conscious perception was Merry's warm skin under her palm through the cool, diaphanous silk.

Merry caught the hair at the back of Enid's head and pulled her mouth from her neck to look her in the eyes.

"What of our oath?" Merry asked, mischief gleaming in her eyes.

"It was less an oath than an acknowledgment of regulations," Enid said. "And I have never been one to be bound by foolish rules."

Later, when both women were fully dressed and recomposed, Merry said, "Judging by your reaction to this purely utilitarian garment, perhaps we should visit a certain shop I'm acquainted with back in Middlesea. It specializes in nightclothes you might admire."

"I'm sure I would, if you were modeling them for me," Enid said with a relaxed smile.

Enid took Merryweather in her arms and kissed the face that looked up at her. "Be mindful after the landing parties depart," she said when their lips parted. "Ogilvy is a snake. It requires no prophetic powers to predict he might attempt to take advantage of Rue's absence ashore, forced as he is to take most of the steady hands with him. Should he lead a jacquerie against you, spare him and his rascals he leads no mercy!"

"I will be the very incarnation of wariness," Merry said. "Step carefully when you are ashore. The land may have changed since the last you set foot on it."

Enid nodded. "Of that, there can be no doubt."

They embraced and afterwards Merryweather made to depart. Enid delayed her by clasping her wrist. "Hold a moment more, Merry. I have one more gift for you before we part."

Merry watched with open curiosity as Enid opened a drawer in her workbench and produced a small pouch of royal blue satin with draw-gilded drawstrings. Enid placed it in Merry's open palm and said, "I had this made for you in Middlesea at the same time my hand was forged. It is not currently enchanted, though I plan to add some protective dweomers to it when I return, but it does carry a piece of me within it, which I hope you'll find a comfort when we're apart, however briefly."

The little bag contained a silver ring contrived to display the hands of two women clasped as if they walked hand-in-hand. The craftsmanship was exquisite, despite the simplicity of the metal of which it was composed. As if compelled, Merry instantly slid it onto her ring finger and admired it through tear-misted eyes.

"I have seen these rings on the hands of Murchadhan betrothed," Merry said softly. "Does this mean—"

Enid took Merry's upraised hand in her own and locked eyes with her. "This means anything and everything you wish it to. We will discuss it more fully upon my return."

With that and a lingering farewell embrace, Merryweather took her leave, the bundle tucked under her arm and the ring glinting on her finger. Enid finished the last swallow of wine in the bottle and began preparing for her homecoming.

Nath stood on the main t'gallant spar, his arm wrapped around the mast to steady himself and the powerful come-hither glass pressed to his eye. The Château d'Phantomes dominated his view. The place didn't appear materially different from any of the hundreds of old castles he'd seen at home in Albion or scattered along the coast of the continent, but even from such a great distance it emanated an aura of lonesome dread. He supposed that had more to do with the place's reputation than its architecture but didn't discount the possibility that the place was visibly haunted by the awful use to which it was put for the last century or so.

When they gained the shallow harbor formed by the promontory, it was empty of anything more threatening than a few skiffs pulled up above the tide line, which was reassuring. He'd half-expected to find a Rat frigate or two loitering at anchor just offshore. He lifted his glass a fraction and adjusted it to view the hills inland of the château. The smoke from Tancreville, which lay just beyond them, rose in slightly darker wisps against the evening sky. Satisfied, he slid effortlessly down the lines, where he joined Enid at the base of the mainmast,

Lady Chum-Chum chasing her own tail a few feet over her head. This became a common sight since the Umoki shifted its nest from the main fighting top to Enid's cuddy.

"It all looks as you described," Nath said. "And there are no signs of anything untoward."

"Good."

"Are you certain that Yeardly alone is all the escort you require?"

"If I require more, the undertaking will be over before it began."

Nath nodded and then, in a booming voice, he directed Lieutenant Wilk to stand off and take *Revenant* out of sight over the horizon until after nightfall.

Enid stood in the shade of the tree line that brooded over the pebble-strewn beach while the sailors and marines commanded by Yeardly and Lieutenant Gardner secured the landing party's boats. She breathed in the familiar odor of loam, sea-wet stones, holm oak, and pine and was seized by a shiver born simply of being home. She had played on this very beach when she was a child, heedlessly bruising her feet on the wave-rounded stones that littered it. Even though it was well past dark, she could somehow feel the warmth of that day's sun baking her skin and turning her lustrous black hair into a headdress of silken heat. She remembered she was tended to by two older common children and was certain that they had enjoyed one another's company, but she could not recall their names or appearance, only that they were the children of M. Dardot's, the man who oversaw her estate until she was old enough to take it in hand herself. She distinctly recalled her little dog Friponne, however, and the belled collar she wore around her fluffy neck. She thought that observation explained her homeland's current state with eloquent brevity.

Yeardly approached quietly and said, "Well, will I pass muster, my lady?"

He was dressed in baggy trousers knocked up from the ship's slops, one of his own shirts, and a waist-length jacket borrowed from one of the ship's folk. Atop his head was a shapeless wool cap. He presented an image that would pass for a laborer or poor crafter and had the calloused hands to support the look. Enid wore her old buff hunting jacket and trousers. Her blouse was of fine cotton cloth but was stained in several places and she went hatless, with her hair hanging free.

Enid nodded with satisfaction. "I believe we will pass as a bourgeois merchant and her helper. Simply take pains not to speak. Your Albion accent would reveal you instantly."

Yeardly nodded. "I'll be mute as a stone!"

Lieutenant Gardner joined them, her usual sour expression replaced by a look of barely concealed excitement.

"Well, Magister," she said. "Lead on and my lobsters and I will follow!"

And so she did. A cautious walk of less than an hour brought them to a low hill on the promontory's narrowest point. Just below it ran the road that connected Château d'Phantomes to Tancreville.

"I do not mean to tell you your business," Enid said to Lieutenant Gardner. "But unless they bring cannons along, you should be able to hold the road from here with your sharpshooters and musketeers."

Lieutenant Gardner nodded emphatically. "Indeed. Your judgment in selecting this point is inarguable."

"I am relieved to hear it," Enid said with a genuine smile. "I'm no military tactician. Now, I'll visit some friends in Tancreville and see if I can find you a few more muskets and perhaps even a cannon or two for the job."

Lieutenant Gardner took her hand in both of hers and said, "Providence watch over you, Magister. Do not expose yourself to unnecessary danger."

Then, grinning widely, the lieutenant turned to her marines and said, "Let's get about it, you scarlet amphibians! Sharpshooters, find positions among the trees! The rest of you, begin a quick trench work from here to there."

Enid turned to Yeardly and said, "Let us see if the people here remember me fondly or not. If they make to seize me up, run back here as swiftly as you may, or our heads will share the same basket."

Yeardly chuckled gamely and fell into step behind her.

Candlelight still gleamed through the sitting-room windows when Enid and Yeardly arrived at the estate of M. Dardot, Enid's chatelaine for the small keep that loomed over Tancreville from a hill on its east side. His home stood on the opposite side of the village from the keep, which, as Enid assumed, now served as the barracks for a Theocratic cavalry troop tasked with keeping the peace in the region.

Enid rapped three times on Dardot's door, which opened a few moments later to reveal the worried face of an older woman. Enid stepped into the pool of light that flooded through the door and laid her fleshy hand on the woman's shoulder.

"Elianna," she said, "it is Enid. May my friend and I enter?"

The woman sucked in a deep breath and then stepped out to scan the darkness behind them in all directions. Satisfied nobody was lurking nearby, she shoved them bodily into the home's foyer.

Once inside, she seized Enid in a hug. The little woman was forced to stand on her toe-tips to lay her head on Enid's shoulder, where she sobbed freely.

"Oh, Enid! We thought you dead, drowned when the ship you fled in was overtaken by a Confessor!"

"Now, now," Enid said, patting the woman on the shoulders. "You know I'm too disagreeable to die so easily. I am well, as I pray you and Lucan are."

"I am well," came a gravel-laden voice from the door to the sitting room. The speaker was a lean man of much the same height as Enid. His graying brown hair was pulled into a loose tail and his face was clean-shaven. The man's eyes gleamed with happy tears that could not be contained by his lashes as he gestured for Enid and Yeardly to join him in the sitting room. “Please let us sit, and we can speak as much as we may. I assume you will not be able to stay long?”

“We cannot,” Enid said as she sank into a settee beside Yeardly. “I am here to ask a favor of you, dear Lucan.”

“I am at your command, Lady d’Tancreville.”

“No.” Enid smiled warmly. “You are not. The world has changed around us, Lucan, and we must move with it whether we would or no.”

“Be that as it may,” Elianna said, standing at her husband’s side, “we shall serve you however we can.”

Enid nodded and leaned forward to ask, “Do you know any royalist sympathizers in the area? Is it true that there is a militia here?”

Elianna and Lucan shared a look before Lucan said, “It is true. I am its captain.”

Enid’s face was stricken for a moment, but pressed on, “Can you summon a dozen or so men and a cannon or two to the point where the road narrows as it approaches Château des Fantomes?”

Lucan nodded grimly. “I can have thirty men and four cannons there well before dawn.”

“Can you do it without incriminating yourself?”

“I can or I can’t.” Lucan shrugged. “I will do my best not to, of course, but I have made peace with dying, so long as I have done my part to oppose the Theocracy. As I believe you have, no?”

Enid frowned but, after a long moment, nodded.

“I take your point, sir.”

“May I ask what is afoot?” Elianna asked.

Enid shrugged. “I cannot speak as plainly as I would like but suffice it to say that there will be a great disturbance at the Château d’Phantomes tomorrow night and it is critical that reinforcements from the keep here in Tancreville do not arrive there before the crisis has resolved itself.”

The woman nodded.

“A rescue, then,” Lucan said. “All I ask is that you let as many of the wretches there free as you can. This disturbance will begin in the dead of night tomorrow, then?"

"Indeed," Enid said. "Ideally, your troop would join a party of Albion marines at the road to Château des Fantômes where it bisects the narrow neck of the promontory shortly after dusk, there to repel any reinforcements until an hour or so before dawn. Is this within your means?"

"It is," Lucan said, "and it will be done just as you say. Will you be there as well?"

"I shall be," Enid said, and then struck by an afterthought, asked, "What are the names of your son and daughter? Those a few years my senior?"

"Fulcher and Isoulte, my lady," Lucan answered. "Why do you ask?"

"I thought of them recently and could not remember their names."

"Ah! They still speak of you and the joy they had as your playmates and guardians. They are safe in Arleonne, for the nonce at least."

"I am glad to hear it," Enid said and stood. "Now we must rejoin the marines outside the Château des Fantomes. Providence willing, we will reunite there tomorrow evening."

She embraced Lucan and Eliana in turn before slipping back into the night with Yeardly. The pair walked in silence until they were well out of Tancreville, when Yeardly spoke quietly.

"I command enough of your language to know that went well." When she nodded, he continued, clearly amused, "Your playmates? It is difficult to imagine a young Enid d'Tancreville at play with her sitters."

Enid didn't reply, and the darkness cloaked her wan expression.

Enid passed a sleepless but oddly restful night lying on her cloak on a patch of cool grass and watching the stars play hide-and-seek behind wisps of fast-moving clouds. She found the view bucolic and restorative, but Yeardly was less enchanted, claiming that some bones that he'd broken in his left hand while skylarking pained him, a sure sign of a falling barometer. He was certain of another blow and spoke to Enid about something called an *outre-montagne*, which blew with terrific force from the central mountain ranges in the north to sweep south across the Merentian Sea. He seemed to believe that this wind might jeopardize their mission, but Enid didn't spare him much attention—her awareness was primarily focused to the north, where the road curved westward behind a tangled copse of oak, pine, and volunteer cork trees.

Twice patrols in the ragged uniform of the Theocratic army sauntered east down the road toward the château and twice decided there was no point in drawing any nearer to the dismal pile. As the sun set, she recognized riders moving furtively down narrow forest trails as members of Captain Lucan Dardot's militia. When they arrived with four small galloper guns in tow, she relaxed her vigil enough to introduce Captain Lucan Dardot to Lieutenant Gardner. Together with Dardot and Yeardly, Gardner disposed of the militia cavalry and their little cannons, placing them where they would do the most good.

As the sun dropped fully beneath the horizon, Nath, Harcourt, Bascombe, and Master Kaliktiklak arrived at the head of the bulk of *Revenant*'s Marines and a force of armed sailors. Harcourt and Nath conferred with Lieutenant Gardner and joined Enid a short time later. Both men practically glowed with their desire to get into action.

"Superb work, Enid," Nath said, beaming at her. "You have accomplished all I hoped and more! Four guns, even little four-pounders like those, will go a long way toward holding the road should things go awry. And some veteran Ardain cavalry troopers are never out of place when blood is in the air!"

"Do not thank me," Enid said. "Thank Lucan Dardot, the Royalist militia captain. These are his guns and chasseurs."

"Thank him I shall," Nath said. "He is a brave fellow to put himself and his rebels at risk. I will not forget his courage."

Enid nodded. Nath's word was as good as his bond.

"I made a survey of the château last night," she said. "And most of its sorcerous defenses are focused on repelling artillery attacks from the sea and detecting escapes. The warden of the château is clearly no longer an accomplished mage but rather a Theocratic appointee."

Nath clapped his hands and rubbed them together like a gourmand presented with a luxurious feast. Lieutenant Harcourt stood at his side, a handsome, confident smile on his face.

"We'll make swift work of this and be back aboard *Revenant* quicker than you can say knife," Nath said. "And a good thing, too, what with the weather looking like an *outre-montagne* is upon us."

"Again, with this famous *outre-montagne*," Enid sighed. "You sailors and your superstitious glorification of naturally occurring winds!"

Nath stared at her in disbelief for a moment, and then asked, "Do you recall the story of the destruction of Luagh's great fleet before it could reach Almery to relieve the crusaders there?"

Enid nodded.

"His fleet was broken against the southern shore of the Merentian Sea, driven onto the rocks there by the *outre-montagne*."

"I see," Enid said. "But if the wind blows south, it should help us in our escape from the château, should it not?"

Nath chuckled and shook his head. "It should, but it may make it difficult to claw our way out of the Merentian basin. Setting that aside, though, I have decided on a change of plans."

"How so?" Enid asked.

"Master Kaliktiklak will take command here, while you join us in the assault on the château."

"Do you think that wise? I have a personal connection with Dardot and many of his troopers and I can support them should a mage accompany any reinforcements from Tancreville."

Nath shook his head firmly. "No. You will come with us. We may require your art if the cells or their locks prove to be ensorcelled. They will certainly come in handy during the assault itself. It is highly unlikely that a backwood Theocratic post will have a magister in their service."

Enid glanced in the direction of Kaliktiklak, whose inhuman form was clearly recognizable among the *Revenant*s whom he directed to the positions specified by Lieutenant Harcourt and Captain Dardot. He seemed to be the shadow of a shadow in the darkness.

"I hesitate to say it," Enid ventured. "But it is improbable that the locals have ever encountered anyone of Kaliktiklak's race, and they are likely to view him with suspicion and distrust, if not outright fear."

"Introduce him to Captain Dardot and vouch for him, then."

Enid started to raise another objection, but Bascombe doffed his hat and said, "I know that I have given you no cause to love me, but I would take it as a particular favor if you helped us more directly in my sister's rescue."

Any further objections she might have voiced evaporated under the man's eyes, which were feverish in his desire to see his sister safely home.

She laid her hand on Bascombe's shoulder and said, "It is no favor, sir. It is my duty, and a pleasant duty at that."

Nath was still beaming at them both as she left to acquaint Captain Dardot with Master Kaliktiklak. The captain's immediate reaction to Master Kaliktiklak was to take a step backward and snap his fingers to ward off evil spirits. Kaliktiklak evinced no offense and stood silently by as Enid made the introductions. After she explained who and what Kaliktiklak was and vouchsafed for his character and reliability, Dardot removed his glove and offered his hand to the fearsome-looking master.

"Master Kaliktiklak and I will work together well, I'm sure," he said, shaking the master's hand with far more sangfroid than Enid had evinced the first time she had done so. "Do not fret for us, Enid. We shall get along famously and bloody the noses of any Theocratic dogs that come sniffing around. May Providence look over you, ward you, and usher you to success."

"And you as well," Enid said.

"Good fortune, Magister," Kaliktiklak said.

"And to you, sir," Enid said. "And confusion to our foes."

Two *Revenants*, one a poacher and the other a former game warden, were sent to scout the way ahead. Upon their return, they reported that there were no sentries along the road to the château and only a pair of sleeping guards at a post near the château's main entrance. They would never have to explain their dereliction of duty, judging by the dark stains on the sailors' tunics. Lieutenant Harcourt was scandalized by the lackadaisical attitude to security, but Enid only shrugged. The Château d'Phantomes was not a place that people tried to break into, even to assist an inmate's escape. The place's name was illustrative of its nature—those imprisoned there vanished from society without notice or warning. They were transformed into living ghosts, their fate and location unknown and eventually forgotten by all but the most powerful and merciless of government ministers.

The same two scouts led the raiding party forward. Enid sensed no sign of magical defenses until they reached the castle's heavy gate, where they split into two groups, one to the left of the portal and the other to the right. The gate was pierced by a double door large enough to admit four people abreast or a pair of riders. It was sealed by a mechanical spell, similar to the artifice that allowed a spell-lock to fire even if its bearer possessed no art. She imagined there was a lever of some sort inside that, when manipulated, would create a tight sympathetic bond between the postern doors and the massive gate.

"Can you counter the dweomer?" Nath whispered.

"Certainly, but it will take time we may not have. I suggest a more direct approach."

Nath nodded and waved over the gunner's mate he'd included in the raiding party for just such an eventuality. "Mr. Thayer, pray set a charge to blow that postern door off its hinges!"

Thayer knuckled his forehead and rushed off with a gleam in his eye. In short order a small keg of alchemical powder was packed against the doors. Enid watched him cock a spell-lock attached to the keg and rigged it with a slow fuse that would trip the lock once it burned out. The gunner's mate lit the fuse and then scrambled back to flatten himself against the château's massive wall with the rest of Nath's party.

The boom that followed rolled across the promontory and echoed back from the hills that sheltered Tancreville from the sea. The echo barely reached their ears before Nath led the howling *Redemption*s into the dark maw of the Château d'Phantomes. They immediately encountered a half-dozen guards who rushed to meet them, staggered from the unexpected explosion or, more likely, strong drink and sleep. The clash of steel and occasional pistol shot ceased before Enid had time to do more than draw her sword. She saw Nath grab one guard who sought to crawl away, his leg bleeding prodigiously from a cutlass wound.

"Where is the Albion officer called Bascombe kept?" he shouted into the wretch's face as he shook him by the collar.

"*Je ne parle pas Albion!*" the guard pled as he struggled to cover his face against the blows he expected to receive at any moment.

"Fortunately, I speak Ardain quite well," Enid interjected, and repeated Nath's question. When the fellow's pathetic gabbling ceased, she handed him into the care of a marine who bound his hands and wound roughly but efficiently.

"She is held in a tower room with a dangerous Ardain prisoner, some fellow named Epolytte, which is surely a nom de guerre as that is the name of an ancient demigod known for his beauty and warlike prowess."

"Dangerous to whom?" Bascombe asked. "Is he some madman who may have hurt Cierina while they were confined together?"

"Dangerous to the Theocracy, of course," Enid answered. "As to the other, I cannot say."

"Then let us not waste another moment," Bascombe said and dashed toward a broad set of stairs that led to the gatekeeper's upper floors.

"Lieutenant Bascombe," Nath barked. "Govern yourself, sir! You saw this place as we stood in to release the boats. It is a massive pile with several buildings and towers. It is unlikely that those stairs, situated here, hard by the entrance to the castle, will lead to its most secure cell, don't you agree."

"Aye, sir," Bascombe said, returning to the group. He jabbed the tip of his hanger in the direction of the fellow Enid had just interrogated and said, "Perhaps he can show us the way."

"Now you are thinking coolly again," Nath said in a softer tone. "See to it that you continue to do so. Enid, please instruct that pitiful fellow to show us to the cell of which he spoke."

Within moments Enid and the Theocratic guard, who named himself Firman, were leading the way to Cierina Bascombe's cell with a pair of marines posted in front of them to protect them from any sudden attacks as they wended their way through the mazelike château. They entered a central courtyard at the very moment that a Theocratic officer was forming a dozen or more guards into a firing line. Nath ordered an immediate attack, which the marines prosecuted with energy and élan, followed closely by the bloodthirsty *Revenant*s. Enid was always astonished by the tars' enthusiasm for bloodshed. A common trait of the Albion sailor seemed to be an unmoderated bloodlust when released from the rigorous social restrictions of life aboard ship and unleashed on an "enemy of the Crown." The fracas was disposed of with a savage rapidity that left Enid's ward pale and shaking for reasons totally unrelated to blood loss.

"They are devils!" he said in rustic Ardain. "Please protect me from them, milady!"

"They are angels," Enid replied in her elegant *cité d'Arden* accent. "And they are a far greater danger to a lickspittle to evil such as you than any demon fresh from the pit."

Spell-lock balls spattered around them as the quaking Theocratic soldier led them across the courtyard toward the base of a tall tower that looked out over the Merentian Sea. Enid bent her will toward deflecting the balls by thickening and agitating the air between them and the sharpshooters, but several still found their mark. The sailors and marines dragged their wounded after them to the base of the tower, where the musketeers in the tower could not fire down on them without exposing themselves. Enid left her prisoner sprawled in the courtyard, the upper portion of his skull carried away by the fire of his compatriots above. She saw Bascombe's shocked expression and shrugged.

"There's no need for concern," she said as the fire from the tower abated. "I think we can safely assume this is the tower your sister is held in."

"No, not that," Bascombe said. "There is—on your face—"

Enid brushed her cheek, and her hand came away wet with blood and splinters of bone.

"Oh, that is not mine." She grinned. "All is well!"

"Stand back," Gunner's mate Thayer cried out as he scrambled back from setting a smaller charge against the tower's stout doors.

Smoke, fire, and splinters of wood and stone blasted across the courtyard. Some of it was still in the air when Enid, infected by the wrathful spirit of the *Revenant*s, leapt through the smoking portal and discharged both of her Kreitzer pistols into the ragged mob of Theocratic soldiers that awaited her. Deafened by Thayer's powder charge, she was unaware of the dull bangs that accompanied the muzzle flashes of the smoke-belching muskets before her or the sharper crack of her own pistols. She saw a man and a woman in Theocratic uniform collapse at the impact of her rounds and felt dull thuds as her charmed hunting jacket deflected three balls to some degree. Without thinking, she shoved the pistol in her right hand into her belt and drew her sword. She blooded it twice before she dimly perceived other *Revenant*s at her side laying into the Theocrats with cutlass, boarding axe, and bayonet. The cries in Ardain quickly shifted from brave challenges to pleas for mercy and declarations of surrender.

Half a dozen marines tended the wounded Rats and, along with a like number of *Revenant*s, took up positions in the room to repel any more who were drawn to the sounds of battle. The rest of the raiders followed their officers up the tower's central stairs. Their ascent was uncontested, but not untroubled.

A miasma of long-unbathed bodies hung over the place, along with the sweeter tang of decomposing flesh. Enid was mortal certain that some of the cells on each floor were now sepulchers of those who passed their final days within them. Worse, once the din of battle had passed the frightened prisoners began to cry out plaintively, begging to know if they were to be executed or if the Theocracy had fallen. When Enid answered that they would assist them shortly, most of the voices went silent, but a few shouted their names weakly and implored her to tell their families of their fate.

"It must boil your blood to see the depth of the Rat's cruelty," Nath said at her side. "Particularly so close to the town from which your title is derived."

"This tower stood here centuries before the rise of the Theocratic Republic," Enid said in a flat voice. "And served the same purpose. I played on the shore in the shadows of this monstrosity and never spared a thought to the horrors within."

"I'm sure you did not know—" Nath ventured, but Enid spoke before he could finish.

"I knew, Rue. We all knew. We simply didn't care."

A narrow finger of the tower reached upward from its peak, rising another thirty or forty feet into the air. Within, a narrow stair wound along the circumference of its inner wall. Its uppermost floor was given over to a large room, sealed off by a stout, iron-bound door secured with a well-cared-for lock. After giving the door a preliminary rattle to ensure it was locked, Nath called out, "Clear the way for Larkin and make haste!"

A moment later a young woman appeared at the top of the stairs and knuckled her brow at the gathered officers. Enid admired her hair, which was dyed a brilliant Emer that contrasted wonderfully with her dark complexion.

"Cap'n," she said, acknowledging Nath.

"Larkin! We have here a locked door. I would admire it if you were to put the talents of your former life to good use and save us from blowing the officer we're here to rescue to paste by mischance."

"Aye, sir," Larkin said, a gleam in her eyes.

The sailor knelt by the lock and gave it a short examination before producing a leather roll-up from her belt pouch. She gave it a practiced flip that revealed a set of odd tools that Enid assumed were lockpicks. The sailor selected two and inserted them into the lock's keyhole.

"There," she said and stepped back with a bow. "It is open, sir."

Leonid Bascombe lunged forward and burst into the room before Nath could react. He was greeted by the bang of a spell-lock and staggered back, clutching his chest. Enid caught the lieutenant as he fell and quickly dragged him away from the door. He looked up at her, his eyes wide with shock as blood pulsed strongly between his fingers.

"I have more pistols at hand," a voice called out from within the room. "As you can see from your comrade, I am a fine shot, and I will kill anyone I see in the door. Should you rush in en masse, my fellows here will slit these prisoners' throats."

Lieutenant Bascombe coughed blood and said, "He is alone. My sister and the other prisoner are bound in chairs in front of him. He hides behind them like a—"

His words were cut off by harsh coughs that spattered Enid's face with more blood.

"Quiet," she said. She concentrated on a formulation to staunch Bascombe's bleeding and slowed it considerably. When she was certain that he was not in danger of expiring on the instant, she bade Larkin care for him and keep steady pressure on the wound in his chest.

"Rue," she called out, military courtesy lost in the heat of the moment. "You recall the light when we boarded *Redemption*? It is about to shine again."

Nath nodded; his expression was fierce. "Cover your eyes," he hissed at the Albions behind him and shielded his own in the crook of his elbow by way of example.

The hall and room beyond visibly dimmed as Enid drew the luminous energy of various preternatural forces near at hand and concentrated them through force of will. When the light was sufficiently distilled to its purest form, she unleashed it in the cell and shouted, "Have at them!"

Nath was through the door before she finished speaking, with Harcourt hard on his heels. Enid stepped into the room just in time to see Nath leap over two hooded prisoners bound to crude but sturdily made chairs. His sword was thrust out before him and found the heart of the well-dressed man who stood behind them, rubbing his eyes with the heels of his hands, each of which clutched a blunt-barreled pistol. The little captain landed astride the fallen Theocrat and plunged his sword into his heart twice more with a rapidity Enid's eyes could barely follow.

"Who is there?" a muffled, female voice asked.

Nath rushed over and removed the hood from the woman's head and recognized her face with obvious relief. "Lieutenant Bascombe! We have come for you!"

"Captain Nath!" Cierina Bascombe exclaimed. "I despaired of ever seeing your or any other Albion's face again! I feared I'd be forgotten here."

"Never forgotten," Nath said, freeing her from her bonds. "Lost for a bit, but never forgotten."

Enid and Harcourt went about freeing the other prisoner, a tall, handsome man who greeted them with a startlingly bright smile as soon as he was freed of his hood.

"Thank you," he said in thick Ardain-accented Albion. "I am in your debt forever."

"You are Epolytte, I take it?" Enid asked in Ardain.

"I am," the fellow confirmed, standing and chafing his wrists to restore sensation to his swollen fingers. "You have heard of me?"

"No. Are you fit to walk?"

"Indeed, I am! Cierina and I contrived to capture gulls to augment our meager diet and made a practice of exercising our bodies to maintain the strength and flexibility of our muscles in case an opportunity for escape presented itself. In fact, we—"

"That is all very good and fine, but we must make haste if we are to have the pair of you whisked to safety before more Theocrats arrive." She turned to Harcourt and said, "I will leave Monsieur Epolytte in your hands while I ensure my rushed work was sufficient for the severity of Lieutenant Bascombe's wound."

Cierina Bascombe who stood near at hand said, "I've received no hurt."

Nath put a hand on Cierina's hand and said, "But your brother has. I fear he is sorely wounded."

"My brother? What in the name of all the powers is my brother doing here?"

Lieutenant Bascombe was sorely wounded indeed. Enid hoped her magic would prevent his condition from worsening until Dr. Rondelle could apply his life-saving craft. He was too hurt to walk or ride, so they commandeered a light, narrow wagon from the château and loaded him into it. Enid rode beside him to monitor his condition while his sister sat opposite her and stroked his hand gently, maintaining a steady stream of quiet, reassuring words. The other injured *Revenant*s were thankfully still mobile. Before the raiding party departed, Enid and several of the marines opened the cells of the healthiest prisoners they could find and pressed into their hands the keys they'd found on the corpse of the fellow who had shot Lieutenant Bascombe and bade them release as many of their fellows as they could. Enid doubted any would remain free more than a day at most and, further, that any of them would live to return to incarceration. Still, she reasoned, it was better to die free than starve by increments in a dank, foul-smelling cell.

Dr. Rondelle and his two loblolly boys awaited them in a charcoaler's hut that squatted in a knot of trees some distance from the château. As he tended the wounded Bascombe, the distant crackle of musketry accompanied by the deeper boom of the galloper guns passed their ears on the way to echo off the château's walls. The rear guard was engaged. The volume and rapidity of the spell-lock fire increased noticeably by the time Rondelle finished changing Bascombe's bandage and coaxed him to quaff a medicinal draft. Enid craned her head over her shoulder to peer in the direction of the choke point. Nath saw and, reading her mind, said, "No, Enid. You must stay with us. Your involvement in direct conflict is at an end for the day, unless we find Rats crawling over our boats."

Enid opened her mouth to speak, but Nath shook his head. "I'll brook no argument on this, Enid. Master Kaliktiklak and Lieutenant Gardner have my full faith."

Enid swallowed her objections and turned her attention to offering Dr. Rondelle whatever assistance she could provide.

Cierina held her brother's hand and continuously wiped perspiration from his forehead. When Nath departed to take his place in the van of their little column, Cierina asked Enid, "What was Captain Nath thinking to bring Leonid on the raid? Surely he knew he would act rashly if he found me in danger! We could have both been killed by this 'kindness' he did my brother!"

The woman's rising anger toward Rue was palpable as she spoke, so Enid said, "I fear the decision was not in Captain Nath's hands. I assure you he had no desire to include Lieutenant Bascombe—Leonid—on the raid for that very reason."

"A captain is the king of his wooden-walled castle!"

"Even kings must answer to a higher power. But I will let Captain Nath explain himself. He does not require my defense."

Nath's poacher led the assault force stealthily through the woods that crowned the last low rise before gaining the shoreline. The ragged trees they threaded were all hunched southward under the force of the rising wind that whistled and moaned through their branches.

Enid was relieved to see the boats were not, in fact, crawling with Theocratic soldiers. She helped Lieutenant Bascombe and Rondelle's loblolly boys bear her brother Leonid to one of the boats, into which Rondelle saw him tucked safely. The pain-easing philter the doctor poured down the young officer's throat in the shade of a rustic shack was insufficient to the task demanded of it, and Leonid, his reason and dignity overruled by his hurt, began to moan and grit his teeth spasmodically. There was no trace of consciousness in his tortured features or tear-streaming eyes.

"Is there anything within your art to ease this poor lad's suffering?" Dr. Rondelle asked Enid. "Another dose of my medicine might sedate him so strongly he never awakens and the art available to me will do little more than dull his agony."

"There is." She took Leonid's hand in hers and muttered something soothing under her breath. After a moment, his breathing deepened and became more even. "There. He is in a deep sleep. He will not awaken for several hours at least, despite any rough handling he might suffer. He knows no pain as he dreams."

Cierina gave her a grateful look and began to speak, but Nath's approach silenced her.

"Look," he said, pointing out over the water. "*Revenant* rounds the point exactly as scheduled. Lieutenant Merryweather can always be counted on for punctuality!"

They watched the frigate coast sedately into the sheltered cove until the thunder of hoofbeats descending the hill behind them drew their attention. Enid turned and recognized Captain Dardot and several of his chasseurs approaching at speed. Dardot brought his mount to a mud-spraying halt a few feet away from their little group and doffed his hat in an admirable display of horsemanship and personal grace.

"Captain Nath," he said, "your rear guard will arrive shortly. They are being pursued by Theocratic soldiers from a camp farther up the coast. They are all afoot, save an officer or two and in poor order. I have given the command to my little troop of cavalry to harass them and draw them away from your men. I suggest you make haste to your ship, for I fear we will not distract them for long."

"Thank you for the warning, Captain Dardot," Nath said, doffing his own hat in salute. "You and your fellows are as gallant as any that rode with Achard I and the world will know of your bravery. Risk your life and that of your men no more than you must, sir, I implore you. Our retreat to *Redemption* will soon be covered by her guns. I pray you live to fight another day and inspire other true patriots of Ardainne to do the same."

"I would we had more time to know one another, Captain Nath," Dardot said. "I believe we would be great friends owing to your open heart. For now, though, I must bid you adieu. Come, Lady d'Tancreville, let me kiss your hand before I go. It has been an honor to fight in the name of a Tancre again!"

And after kissing her proffered hand, he produced a locket and chain from his coat pocket and pressed it into her hand.

"To better remember us when you are gone, Marquise d'Tancreville!" With that, he spun his mount and waved his hat over his head as he and his fellows galloped up the hill toward the distant sound of sporadic spell-lock fire.

Enid opened the locket and found that it was carefully made to display four enchanted images: M. and Mme. Dardot and their children, Fulcher and Isoulte. As her eyes settled on each image, it would shift from profile to three-quarter view.

"I would that I had more time to know him, too," Enid said as she snapped the locket closed and settled it around her neck.

Nath arched a brow. "I thought he served you since you were a little girl?"

Enid nodded; her face set with barely concealed regret. "Indeed, he did. But I never bothered *knowing* my servants. They either served well and were rewarded, or poorly and were discarded. I can describe the lands I held in minute detail, but the folk who live on it are mostly faces without names or names with naught behind them but an occupation. Like the characters in a play whose only purpose is to arrive and say, 'There is a strange knight at the gate, milady,' before exiting stage right. What opportunities did I miss, I wonder? What wisdom slipped past me unknown? What pleasant recollections died stillborn?"

"Enid," Nath said, "I have noticed that you are prone to morose revery after a victory. You should—"

He was cut short by the crackling of spell-locks across the water. He and Enid whirled in time to see puffs of smoke rising from several locations across the length of *Revenant*'s deck, followed shortly thereafter by the faint sound of steel clamoring against steel.

"Mutiny," Nath hissed, and then he turned his head and shouted, "To the boats, *Revenant*s! To the boats! Our shipmates need us aboard!"

chapter 21

The *Revenants* with Nath rushed to their boats with alacrity, spurred on by the sound of combat from the frigate they called home. The Newcomers in the group took note of the grim determination on the old *Alarums*' faces and, having witnessed their handiwork at the château, adopted their zealous attitude. Within moments, a small armada of blooded and bloodthirsty salts was pulling hard toward *Redemption* to put paid to the mutinous affront to her honor.

"What of Wilk and the Marines?" Enid asked as Nath helped her climb into his boat as his cox'n and the oarsmen shoved it out into the surf, which became choppier by the moment under strengthening winds from the north. "The Theocratic troops will surely return here as soon as they realize they cannot keep up with Dardot and his chasseurs!"

"Their boats await them, so they can make their escape if time permits," Nath said as he took his place beside her. "If not, I believe we can trust Lieutenant Gardner and Master Kaliktiklak to perform admirably if slaughter is required. I'm more concerned with them crossing safely to the ship in this damned wind. The *outre-montagne* approaches quickly, but this one seems to come on at an uncanny pace!"

Uncanny indeed, Dunaughy agreed. *It is spurred on by* Revenant's *malefactor. The tentacles by which it pulls the winds down upon us are as thick as a first rate's mainmast and black as a Darghaur's heart! Look and you will see!*

Enid did as he bade and saw the night-dark vines of will emerging from *Revenant* to grapple with the great sylphs that formed the *outre-montagne*. There was no coaxing or comingling of intent on display, only raw force of will that subdued the desired elements and demanded their immediate and utter obedience. Enid was left overawed by the sight. Her very thoughts seemed to tremble as she asked Dunaughy, *What has such power and how can we hope to defeat it?*

Whatever it is, it is afraid of you, he said. *Otherwise, it would not have waited for you to be ashore to attempt to seize* Redemption *or exert so much of its power to prevent you from returning to challenge it. It seeks to drown you because it fears to face you.*

Enid focused her attention on the natural world and found the little flotilla of boats pulling toward *Revenant*, fighting against increasingly violent waves. The wind had risen to a howl that drove stinging spray into her face and forced her to shout to be heard by Nath, who sat hard by her side. "We must make better speed! The evil in *Revenant* has revealed itself and is bent on destroying you and those loyal to you!"

"This is as best a way as we can make in these waters," Nath shouted back, his mouth inches from her ear. "The folk at the oars are already flagging. Can you ease the way for us with your art?"

Enid remembered the huge, grasping branches that sprouted from the frigate and despaired at the thought of wresting such gargantuan sylphs away from them. Elementals of such power would challenge her ability under the best of conditions. As things stood, they would be unmanageable even if she were able to free them from the strands of power that currently choked them into obedience.

Reluctantly, she shook her head.

"We must find a way, Enid," Nath yelled, his hand squeezing her shoulder to emphasize his words. "We cannot hope to go back to shore against this gale and we will never reach the barky before we're capsized at this rate. Our fate is in your hands, Magister!"

Enid nodded silently and retreated into herself to escape the distraction of wind, spray, and impending death. Soon the only sound she heard was her own breathing and the indescribable thrum of Dunaughy in her mind and, faintly, on the very edge of her awareness, the gasping pants of someone strenuously exerting themself. It could not be Nath, no matter how close he sat to her. It could only be someone with an arcane connection that allowed them to—*Merryweather! The ring I gave her is cast from the same silver as my hand. I did not think it would—*

Never mind what you thought, Dunaughy snapped. *Can you converse with her?*

Enid tried to do so. She called out to Merry, focusing closely on the image of her face, the smell of her hair, the touch of her lips on hers.

Enid? Merry's "voice" was faint but distinct. *Have I lost my mind? I could swear I* hear *you in my head.*

You have not and you do, Enid said. *It is a property of the ring I gave you. We can speak across the distance. There's no time to explain how, though. We know you are facing a mutiny. What are your prospects of victory?*

In a fair fight? Absolutely assured. Facing Ogilvy's magic? We will hold out as long as we can, but without your help we have no hope to win the day.

Ogilvy? Dunaughy said in disbelief. *If he has an ounce of art, I'm the Archimage of old Eressa!*

I am *mad*, Merry said. *Now I hear old Dunaughy's voice in my head as well.*

You are not mad, Enid assured her. *Dunaughy is here with me. I will explain all of this later, on my oath, but it must wait. I'm going to attempt to steal a glance through your eyes. It won't interfere with whatever you're doing.*

Good. I'm fighting for my life. Any further distraction will leave you with no one on the other side of your ring.

Enid concentrated on the tenuous link between her and Merryweather and allowed a portion of her consciousness to follow it across the rabid, foam-flinging waves until she found her way into her lover's mind. She was instantly bombarded with images and emotions that she had no right to perceive and, blindering herself as best she could, found herself looking through Merry's pale blue eyes.

She saw one of the Newcomers before her, hacking at Merryweather with a boarding axe. Her view tilted sickeningly as Merryweather leaned to one side to avoid a swipe of the axe and then lunged forward to open his throat as he lifted the axe to strike again. As Merry straightened and regained a balanced fighting stance, Enid caught sight of Ogilvy forcing his way onto the quarterdeck. The shock of what she saw broke the conduit between her and Merry.

Ogilvy was a walking corpse. He didn't appear so to those around him, of course, but the glamour he had maintained for some time, based on the progress of his decay, had been weakened by his efforts to dominate the *outre-montagne* sylphs and was no longer sufficient to conceal his nature from Enid.

Worse yet, a creature out of nightmare hulked over him like an obscene puppet master. The thing's form was vaguely humanoid, though its arms and legs were unnaturally long and its torso was little more than a barrel. Its skin suggested the diseased meat of a tree stripped of its bark. There was a wreath of gnarled branches in a halo around its round face, which resembled that of a "green man" such as Murchadhans peasants carved to appease the old gods in hopes of a bountiful harvest. Instead of hair and a beard of verdant leaves, though, this abomination was all thorny vines and choking weeds.

A rope noose hung around its neck and smaller nooses of twine adorned each of the branches that framed its face. The corpse of a tiny woodland creature dangled at the end of each noose, as if the unforgiving hand of justice had fallen fatally on a vicious tribe of field mice, voles, and hedgehogs.

That is no ghost, Dunaughy muttered as she shared the memory of what she'd seen with him. *Nor an unruly spirit. It reeks of ancient power and art that knew no limits.*

Enid nodded. It was growing harder to ignore the boat's frenetic bucking and the cold slap of water in her face. If she did not do something soon, she would die, as would Nath and Merry shortly thereafter. The spectacle of the creature granted her the seed of a plan that would save them all if Merry would consent to it.

Augusta, she said, using Merry's given name to underscore the importance of her request. *I cannot defeat Ogilvy unless I am in his presence, and I will not live long enough to do so if he is free to assail the boat that bears me with preternatural winds and waves. Do you understand?*

Yes, Merry grunted tersely, and Enid knew she was once again locked in combat. *What can we do?*

If you will permit me to take control of your body, I can face him as you and give the boats a fighting chance to bear my body there. Then I will return to it and return control of your corporeal shell to you. But I must have your unreserved permission, for I will not allow Ogilvy and the thing that pulls his strings to force me to become a monster, too.

Possess my—ugh. Merry's grunt of pain was unmistakable, and Enid's heart nearly froze in dread. But then Merry continued, saying, *You have my permission. Save us if you can, dearest.*

She returned to the mundane world long enough to grasp Nath by the arm and shout through the sheets of green water that doused them in the trough between each wave. "I have found a way! I may appear unconscious or even dead for a time, but I will live. Make for the *Revenant* with all speed and bear my body to her deck on the instant you reach her. All depends on my body reaching *Revenant*'s deck! Do you understand me?"

Nath nodded grimly and shouted back, "Race to the barky, bear you to the deck immediately. All depends on it."

Enid nodded and gave his arm a reassuring squeeze before sinking back into herself. Her eyes clenched closed in concentration as she forcibly propelled her full consciousness into Merry through the silver string that connected them. Merry resisted Enid's invasion for a moment out of an animal instinct to survive and then relented completely. The razor edges of sharp memories and emotions threatened to flay her, but she pushed them aside and refused to allow them purchase in her own mind. However this impromptu experiment ended, she would leave the sanctity of Merry's inner thoughts and recollections intact.

The solid deck was shifting below her feet, its motion far more placid than the boat in which her physical form now slouched nervelessly in Nath's arms, and she opened her eyes just as a huge bruiser among the Newcomers rammed a boarding pike past her faltering guard. She felt the impact blunted by the combined thickness of Merry's uniform coat and vest and was certain the enchanted silk undergarment beneath them would absorb the blow's remaining force. Instead, the silk parted as silk is wont to do and the pike's head pierced her abdomen just right of center and a little below her ribs. The impact stole the breath from her, and she doubled over, her left hand clutching the haft of the pike to prevent the Newcomer from twisting it or tearing it free to strike her again.

"There is the mortal mage who thought she could face me like a champion of old," a booming voice pronounced with a laugh. "The world is much reduced since those days, Lady d'Tancreville, but I am not of this world. Your pitiful enchantments will not protect you from wounds dealt in my name!"

Her whole world was reduced to the sight of Merry's blood as it spattered on the off-white planks between her feet. Enid would survive if the darkness that gathered on the edge of her vision closed in. Her consciousness would snap back to her own body to die a slower, more agonizing death as the water in which she swam as a child filled her lungs as a woman grown and poor Merry would never rise from the blood-slick deck again. Worst of all, Harlech would never be avenged. Instead, she would spend a miserable eternity as a pitiful trophy in the lair of an aberration against nature and reason.

Enid found the situation intolerable. With an effort that seemed to snap an intangible bone in her being, she pushed the darkness back and dropped Merry's hanger to seize the pike in both hands. The solution to her quandary was simple, she realized. It was a matter of elementary sympathetic magic: if the pike drained the life from Merry, it could be coerced into restoring it. She lifted her head enough look in the face of the Newcomer on the other end of the pike and locked eyes with him from beneath her brows.

Enid/Merryweather's smile was horrible, and her eyes promised worse horrors still. The pikeman made to release his weapon and back away but found his hands could not be budged from the shaft. The man's back arched in agony and his scream was so inchoate and primal that the fighting on the quarterdeck ceased as the Newcomers retreated a step or two in order to determine whether an atrocity had turned the tide in their favor or against them. Even the Ogilvy thing ceased yanking rigging from the mizzenmast to permit it to writhe into nooses by which the loyal *Revenant*s were yanked from the deck to choke out their last agonizing minutes, kicking their legs and clawing at the rope that bit deep into their flesh. Its eyes visibly widened as Enid plucked the pike from Merry's side and gave it a shove that toppled the Newcomer pikeman onto the deck, still clutching the weapon in apparent rigor. His broad chest and massive shoulders now hung loosely from a frame best described as skeletal. The paper-thin skin stretched over his skull in a tooth-baring rictus thatreinforced that impression.

Enid stood to Merry's full height, rolled her shoulders, and shook out arms that were slightly shorter but far stronger than her own. Merry's blood still poured from her wound, but Enid paid it no mind. She plucked the pike from the dead man's hands. Two of his fingers came with it, embedded in splintered grooves as it came free. The combatants on both sides separated and formed into half-circles around their champions, with the Newcomers for'ard on the quarterdeck and the *Revenant*s aft. Ogilvy picked up a pair of boarding axes from the gore-stained deck and stalked forward, his face and that of his puppeteer split by equally ferocious grins. Enid hefted the pike as he came on.

"It has been centuries," Ogilvy snarled as he padded toward her on the balls of his feet. "A millennium and more, in fact, since I dined on the heart and liver of another champion of Elthaur. I thank you in advance for providing a delicacy I feared lost to—"

The rest of the creature's words were lost as the pike Enid threw smashed through Ogilvy's open mouth, severed his spine, and pierced his puppeteer's stump-like body. The abomination threw Ogilvy's limp body aside and gave voice to its agony in a high-pitched shriek that would have served a wounded panther well. It plucked at the pike but could not budge it.

"It's part of you now. Its wood has merged with that of your flesh," Enid said. When she saw the thing raise one of its axes to hack the thing off, she smiled. "Yes. Do that and watch yourself bleed as it grows back. That should be entertaining for all of us."

The thing leaned toward her menacingly and threw its mouth open in a wordless bellow of unbridled rage. Its fetid breath was warm and moist against her skin. She had a clear view of the thing's thorny teeth and the writhing mass of tendrils that served as its tongue. Over its shoulder and over the railing beyond it, she saw the sky to the north lighten and the violence of the waves abate slightly. The sight satisfied her immensely. She was forcing him to divide his attention and, by extension, efficacy between her and the reinforcements in the slowly approaching boats.

Hope sprang in Nath's chest as the wind weakened for a moment, but he fought it down for fear of chasing good fortune away by rushing too eagerly into its arms. He embraced it tightly when the gale's scream sank to a mere howl over which his shout could be heard clearly by the folk in his boat and those nearby.

"Lay into your oars with a will," he cried. "Take advantage of this lull, and we can make the *Revenant*! We can pull together or drown together, but you've proven you're too bloody-minded to die today!"

His boat crew let out a shout that was echoed by the boats within earshot. The little fleet surged forward, their coxswains shouting out a brisk cadence and encouraging the rowers with praise or profanity as needed. *Revenant* was soon near enough that she filled most of his vision. She lay at anchor before them. It was as if she bobbed in the placid waters of another cove altogether, where no *outre-montagne* battered her masts and sails and no waves assaulted her hull.

The situation of *Revenant*'s boats was quite different but much improved. It was still hard going, though. They clawed their way forward, the stinging spray scourging the oarsmen's backs and hampering their breathing. Each yard was gained by dint of superhuman effort, but they were gained. Nath wrapped his cloak more tightly about Enid, whose head lolled back against his chest, and he tightened his arms around her. *Bless you, Enid, whatever you are doing is working. I only pray your success is not purchased at too dear a price!*

"How are you called?" Enid asked in Merry's voice as she and the abomination circled one another warily. She had retrieved Merry's hanger from the deck and now wielded it, as well as a stout dagger in her off hand. "So I know how to address my curses when you die."

The pike staff that now formed a useless limb impeded the movement of the creature's right arm and it moved awkwardly as a result. Its momentary fit of rage had passed, though, and its laughing voice seemed untroubled as it replied, "You may call me Mr. Oak, a name you will surely curse as I add your head to my collection of trophies!"

Its last word still hung in the air as it lunged forward, slashing at her with the axe in its right hand while raising the one in its left hand high for a downward stroke. Enid sidestepped the arching slash and deflected a blow that would have split her head in from its crown to the point of her chin if it had landed. The impact of the axe shaft on her hanger numbed the palm of Merry's hand. Her hanger rebounded harmlessly from Mr. Oak's knee, and she nearly lost her weapon from the jarring impact. She staggered a few steps back with a grunt.

Oak stood his ground and twirled his axes with indolent disdain. His face split into a grin that revealed splinter-like teeth and released a flood of yellow-green sap that ran down over his chin.

"You were fortunate with this." It grasped the pike staff turned flesh and tore it from its body, producing a gout of ichor that smelled strongly of rotting wood and decaying leaves. He tossed the offending growth to the deck, where it writhed in like a beheaded snake. "But now I've taken the measure of your magic, and you will find your childish tricks to be of little avail against me. Please, continue your efforts, though. I have not been so amused in almost a century."

Mr. Oak was not dissembling to dishearten her. While her ability to divide her awareness between the mundane and arcane worlds was greatly reduced by her less-than-complete mastery of Merry's senses, she clearly perceived the natural flow of sorcerous energies had been altered into a strange, unfamiliar pattern that would hinder her workings. It was magic the like of which she'd never seen or heard. In her own body she might be able to counter it. In Merry's, the best she could hope was to survive until Nath arrived. She retreated another few steps, which seemed to serve as a signal for the general melee to resume. The Newcomers let out a ferocious howl and charged the *Revenant*s, who immediately countercharged. The warring groups of sailors split to pass around her and Mr. Oak on either side to come to grips with one another.

Mr. Oak laughed as he stalked forward, his axes spinning with sorcerously enhanced speed so that they were little more than a blur. Were she to come within reach of them, Merry would surely die. With that in mind, Enid continued to back away from the creature. She was already even with the ship's wheel, so her retreat would be curtailed by the aft rail soon. She considered attempting to sidestep Oak and dash forward, but she found that her feet were unsteady beneath her. She looked down to see that the entire front lower half of Merry's coat was black with blood, as were her breeches leg and stocking. With that realization, she was struck by pain of both the physical and emotional variety. The deep wound below her ribs was agonizing and seemed to worsen with each breath she took, but it was far less painful than the realization that, rather than saving Merry, she had contrived to be with her as she died.

Mr. Oak seemed to recognize the nature of the anguish in Enid's eyes and his evil grin widened.

"Oh, have I broken the magister's favorite toy?" it asked in a crooning voice. "Cry as you might, I will break the rest of them and sail out of reach of your captain and his boats. Go to sleep, mortal girl, and sleep eternal. Your day in the sun has passed. Only darkness awaits you now."

Enid thought it may have said more, but she missed it as her grip on Merry became too tenuous to maintain. The gray clouds at the edge of her vision darkened and expanded until they obscured all but a tiny dot of blue gray. When even that was gone, Enid's consciousness diminished until it was reduced to a faint spark, which was borne away on the wind.

Enid jerked suddenly in Nath's arms and feared she was suffering a seizure of some sort. Her cheek, which had been feverishly hot a short time ago, was now cold and clammy beneath his fingertips. When he saw her eyelids flutter, he brought his face near her ear and said her name loudly enough to be heard over the wind but not so loud as to startle her. Her eyes opened with a snap and the top of her head impacted his face as she suddenly sat up straight. He released her and fumbled out a handkerchief to press to his bleeding nose.

Enid looked around frantically for a moment and then seemed to relax a little as her new location became clear to her. She noticed Nath's bloodied nose and grabbed him by the shoulders to say, "You have been hurt! Is the injury serious? Did Oak contrive a way to attack the boats?"

"No," Nath said. "When you came back to yourself—never mind that! How fares Merryweather and *Revenant*?"

"Not well," Enid replied. "Mr. Oak, which is to say the thing that possessed Ogilvy, is powerful. The *Revenant*s are holding out as best they can, but—" She was interrupted by a severed head that thumped and rolled unevenly between their feet and a headless body that splashed into the waves less than a foot from the boat's larboard side.

"I see," Nath said, recognizing the contorted features of the head staring up at him as belonging to Robson, a sailor skilled enough to rate as a master's mate that had been drawn to his death by the *Revenant*'s recruitment posters. *Damme*, Nath thought. *Here is all the fortune and glory the poor wretch found for answering my call for hands. When I face whatever judgment awaits me when death claims me, I will have much to answer for.*

"Rue!" Enid said, shaking him by the shoulder. "Come back to us, dear! You must urge your folk at the oars to greater effort! Merry . . . our only hope is to get me aboard *Revenant* swiftly. In my own body, I may be able best this devil, or at least force it into submission!"

Nath nodded, thinking, *In her own body? What does she mean by that?* He put the question aside for later and half stood in the rocking boat to shout, "One last effort, *Revenant*s! We're less than a hundred yards from home. Our friends need our help, and our enemies need our steel in their guts! Pull! Pull for our mates! Pull for *revenge*!"

Lieutenant Wilk's heart fell with Merryweather's limp body and despair hit him as hard as the deck that rose to meet her. He'd allowed his hope to grow as the first lieutenant revealed she knew more of sorcery than most officers as evidenced by the ease with which she put Ogilvy down. It bloomed when he saw her contest with the monstrosity that the mutineer's leader, obviously a witch, seemed to summon with his dying breath. Her moment of glory was brief, though, and now she lay bleeding on the deck while a monster from the depths of the darkest drunken delirium loomed over her defenseless form, poised to finish her off.

Well, fuck that, Wilk thought. He cast his eyes about the blood-spattered quarterdeck and clapped them on a primed blunderbuss lying near the nerveless hand of a fallen marine. He grabbed it up and raced down the catwalk to the quarterdeck. Any mutineer who made to contest his passage was clubbed to the deck with brutal efficiency. The familiar old blood rage seized him, but, rather than seeing red and gnashing his teeth, the world took on a crystalline clarity in which every detail around him leapt into preternatural resolution. The pace of the world slowed around him while his thoughts sprinted effortlessly ahead of it. He was on the creature in a flash, leaping from the deck to lock his knees around the creature's abbreviated trunk, intending to fire his weapon directly into the back of its skull. Its reflexes proved to be inhumanly swift, though, and it half turned toward him, its hideous mouth agape and the claws of its right hand curled to slash. Wilk grinned fiercely at being able to turn the creature's advantage against it and thrust the barrel of the blunderbuss down its throat.

There was a dull thud when he jerked the spell-lock's trigger and unloaded nearly half a pound of heavy lead shot and shards of iron down its gullet. The thing staggered in a half circle and coughed up a flood of odorous, clinging ichor that drenched Wilk from head to waist. He was blinded by the stuff, so the thing's blow caught him unawares. It swatted him away with the same ease that a gale dislodged autumn leaves. Wilk gasped as his ribs broke and talons sank deep into his side. He lost what little breath was left to him when his flight was brought up short by the mizzenmast. His body lolled like a bag full of broken bones as he slid down the mast to the deck. There, he mustered the strength to wipe the effluvia from his eyes with the hand that would still obey him. He blinked several times to stop the mad gyrations of his vision and was rewarded with a view of the abomination on its hands and knees, gushing gallons of viscous, muddy-green fluid and small human bones on the deck.

Fuck you, he thought, *you ain't dead, but you won't forget Ample Wilk soon, will you? The world won't remember me for a week, but you, you are a fucking monster, you make me look like a damned saint, and you'll remember me as long as you live, won't you!*

Wilk's body shook in a violent palsy, and he coughed up his own, perfectly natural, bright red blood onto the deck. *Any as survive'll be busy with the holystones*, he thought. *Whinge about a little dog shite, will you? Hah! Oh, gods, what'll become of my poor young Jock?*

Then the light left his eyes and all his worries with it.

The *outre-montagne*, which had begun to pick up strength again when Enid came to herself, dropped off again so drastically and suddenly that she thought she'd gone deaf. Everything seemed silent and still in the absence of the gale's constant roar. Nath, on the other hand, turned to her with a ferocious yet boyish smile and said in a louder voice than was necessary, "Prepare yourself, Magister. We'll be boarding before you can say *knife*!"

There was no need for him to shout encouragement to the *Revenant*s at the oars, she saw, as they had let out a shout of their own and were driving their boats forward with exhilarating rapidity. In a blessedly short time, Nath's boat was hull-to-hull with the frigate, whose boarding battens were within easy reach. Nath made to launch himself onto them, but Enid restrained him with a hand on his shoulder.

"No," she said firmly. "I must be the first to ascend."

Nath began to argue the point but, seeing the steel in Enid's eyes, he simply nodded and stood ready to steady her if she had trouble with the battens. She did not, and he scurried up after her when she had progressed far enough up the tumble-home, grim-faced *Revenant*s with daggers and swords in their teeth. Many of these weapons were recently liberated from their late Rat owners and would now be put to use against a different set of oath-breaking rebels.

chapter 22

Enid scrambled over *Revenant*'s rail on deck and nearly ran Lieutenant Dalroyd through with her small sword when she mistook his helping hand for an attempt to shove her overboard. The clangor of battle, muted from below, struck her ears as she accepted the lieutenant's hand and cleared the way for Nath and the others to follow. A quick glance at the gun deck below revealed a roiling melee in which *Revenant* strove against *Revenant.* She saw the scattered bodies of several dead or wounded sailors at the edge of the fray. They gave no indication of the current situation as their supine forms offered no clues to the faction for which they'd wagered their lives and limbs, but she'd learned enough of the way of a ship to know that the loss of each was a bitter blow to *Revenant*'s well-being. She looked forward and saw the quarterdeck was choked with struggling figures, but there was no sign of her prey, Mr. Oak.

"The fighting is still fiercest on the quarterdeck?"

Lieutenant Dalroyd nodded, smearing blood of unknown origin across his forehead with the back of his hand. "Yes, Magister! We have them at a standstill here, but it seems the fight to for'ard will decide the day!"

Enid nodded. "So it would seem, Lieutenant Dalroyd. Is Ogilvy, or rather the thing, the—"

"The monster," Dalroyd filled in for her, and nodded with a baleful glance forward. "I lost sight of it a moment ago. I believe Lieutenant Wilk may have killed it."

"If any of the artless aboard could, it would be him," Enid said with a cold smile. "But the thing still lives."

So saying, she strode toward the quarterdeck, her sword in her left hand and one of her Kreitzers in the other. At that moment, Captain Nath's head appeared at the top of the battens and Dalroyd turned to assist him aboard, this time identifying himself first.

Enid heard Nath call her name behind her, but the meaning of the sound was lost on her. His cry slid off the cold silver shell of her resolve and concentration without leaving so much as an echo. Indeed, to Enid it seemed as if she were striding through a soundless fabulism. She was peripherally aware of fighting in the waist below her, but it didn't signify against her purpose. When she came upon the first of the Newcomers that crowded the aft third of the quarterdeck, she cut through them with a clockwork's efficiency and lack of emotion. Several more fell before she saw her quarry staggering to its feet and scattering everyone around it with great splashes of unnatural gore. It seemed dazed and hurt, and Enid saw no advantage in allowing it to recover before she struck it. She raised the Kreitzer, aimed carefully, and fired the left barrel and then the right.

The bullets struck Mr. Oak in the side, just below its right armpit, one above the other and separated by less than the width of two of her fingers. Green and black ooze fountained from the impacts, and the monster, for Dalroyd had named it correctly, Enid thought, staggered sideways and nearly fell again. She expected an angry howl but heard nothing more than a low groan at so deep a register that it rattled her bones. Gratified by the result, she dropped the Kreitzer, drew its twin, and fired two more heavy bullets into the monster. Her shots did elicit a roar this time, as high-pitched as its groan had been low, and it shuffled unsteadily on its feet to face her. Awful green blood bubbled and flowed over its lower lip. The same unnatural fluid poured from its nostrils, and each breath it took was a harsh, bubbling wheeze.

She dropped the other pistol and marched toward the obviously stricken monster.

"Lieutenant Wilk did you great harm," she observed. "Particularly great when one considers he had no art with which to bolster his attack."

"Hate is enough for some," the thing said in a gurgling voice. "I admire the man. He is the closest any mortal is like to come to being acceptable as my human champion. He was hatred given flesh and a cheerful smile."

"He loved his dogs," Enid said, and ducked a vicious backhand blow before slashing at the tendons below the kneecap of its forward leg. She was gratified to see its flesh part with a splash of weird blood. Half a heartbeat later, the savaged leg buckled under it.

She danced away from another awkward blow and contemplated Oak's ill-considered words. *Hate is sometimes enough*, she thought. *Then hatred combined with art should be doubly potent.*

Dunaughy's agreement flooded her mind and then she heard him think, *He has given you a weapon. Use it!*

Enid flung open the gates of her violent hatred for the monster before her, this murderer of bright-eyed young girls and defiler of the only true community she'd ever known. She thought of the harm it had sought to do against a man to whom she owed her very life, and the hurt it had done to Merry, who might or might not still live. She coupled the surge of emotion with an amorphous mass of violent intent unlike anything she'd ever experienced while preparing a formulation. At that moment, she understood this was no mere formulation. This was an atavistic explosion of power whose utter strangeness filled her with dread even as its inexplicable familiarity welcomed her with the open arms of the Creator itself.

A static charge seemed to enfold her, and her raven hair lifted from her head as she ground her teeth from the effort required to contain the enormous energy that spun like a maelstrom behind her eyes. Her vision expanded, and she was suddenly aware of every movement around her and the details of anything she gazed upon came into such sharp relief that they had the appearance of tiny objects created by a master doll maker. Indeed, the entire world suddenly seemed like a thing of artifice to her, the work of many master artisans whose craftwork complemented one another in the main but was marred in a few places by scars or patches of partially finished work. She realized in that moment that her peculiar globe of vision had expanded to take in ten or twenty miles in all directions.

She saw Captain Dardot and his brave comrades racing at a gallop along a narrow ravine, the entrance of which was concealed by a fallen tree draped with thorny branches. In the distance behind them, a squadron of Theocratic chasseurs did not spare their mounts the spurs as they pursued the counterrevolutionary rebels. Closer at hand, she perceived Master Kaliktiklak and Lieutenant Gardner boarding the last boat beached on the inlet as spell-lock balls kicked up mud and fountains of seawater around them. In the distance, beyond the headland, she saw the mainmast of a ship peek above the horizon, a black pennant fluttering from its masthead. She looked upon *Artagny*'s main topmast.

All this she saw, yet still noticed as Oak's long, vine-like muscles coiled to leap at her, its gaping maw filled with sharp, splintered teeth, repeatedly snapping in its eagerness to taste her blood. She raised her small sword to plunge it into the thing's gullet, but at the last moment, it swatted the blade from her hand. They landed in a pile near the binnacle and Enid found her crushed beneath the surprising weight of the spidery monstrosity. It snapped and slavered at her neck and tore at her body with its clawed hands. She grasped its ropy windpipe with her silver hand and struggled to free a slim-bladed dagger from its belt sheath. As she struggled, the dweomers of her stout hunting jacket shredded along with the leather that bore them. Soon its thorn-like claws would do the same to the flesh over her ribs.

Enid's growl surprised her as she tightened her argent grip about Oak's throat until her fingertips nearly pressed against her thumb. It was an atavistic, blood-hungry sound she would never have imagined emanating from her person and spoke of a level of potential violence that far exceeded the doom she brought down on the heads of her uncle's murderers.

The aberration responded with a snarl of its own and grasped her wrist in one claw while slashing her body with the other. Their faces were so close that its eyes filled her vision like a pair of mad planets swathed in rapidly moving clouds of yellow and scarlet. Its pupils formed twin irregularly shaped obsidian moons, polished to a mirror sheen that reflected her own snarling face. Was that truly her visage? Or, more likely, was she beginning to lose the ability to accurately interpret reality as this savage new magic coursed through her? Surely there was no raven perched on the back of her head, its wings outspread like a primitive headpiece of the ancient Murchadhans, nor could her eyes truly glow lambent green within their sockets?

Oak's body shifted on top of her as it struggled to release itself from the ever-tightening vise of her silver hand, which movement allowed Enid to free her dagger. She drove the blade up, expecting it to rebound from the creature's unnaturally durable skin, but it sank into its body as if it were made of butter. Encouraged by this success, she stabbed the thing rapidly and repeatedly, giving the blade a cruel twist before withdrawing it. Oak's eyes widened, and it heaved itself backward with all the force it could muster. It slammed onto its back with Enid still attached to its throat like an elegant tick. She landed straddling what passed for the abomination's chest and used the leverage her position provided to tighten her relentless grip on the fiend's throat. The monster abandoned mauling Enid with its claws and devoted its full attention to wresting itself free from her enchanted grip. It raked at her wrist and pried at her fingers with its sharp claws, but to no avail. Enid sat astride the thing now and had no intention of allowing it to escape. She held Harlech's image in her mind as she stared into its eyes, attempting to force an image of the bright young girl's smiling face to the forefront of the brute's consciousness through its slowly dilating pupils. She prayed it would be the last image it perceived before the dark closed over its thoughts forever. *Let it know the life it stole that cost it its own*, Enid prayed silently.

Perhaps her effort was successful. Oak's eyes bulged suddenly and the stygian black of its pupils lightened to the gray of rain clouds over a funeral. In her mind, she and Dunaughy heard the arrogant power of its voice reduced to a panicked pleading.

Mercy, Champion! I am only a splinter of great oak, but I love life still! Spare me and I will serve you true! I acknowledge your greatness and will take up my place among the other obedient souls enslaved within your awful, argent hand!

She sensed Dunaughy bristle at being named a slave and vaguely perceived the undertone of his thoughts as he considered whether such cohabitating with the monster might be worth the power it would bring Enid, and by his extension his beloved Albion Navy, but she ignored the distraction and poured the last of her strength, both physical and metaphysical, into closing her fist around the monster's throat.

Will you not speak? Oak's "voice" was strained and frantic. *Why are you so set against me? You've slain children with fire and shadow yourself. The memory of it is paramount within your mind! How are you so different from me? What Eldhaur has made you its assassin? Who—the sigil on your hand! I recognize it now! Whatever Verlinherrinar has promised you, I will—*

Enid silenced the thing with a savage twist of her wrist.

Oak's foul-smelling lifeblood dripped in thick, sticky gobbets from her silver hand and sizzled and smoked where it touched the good, honest wood of *Revenant*'s deck. The monster's obscenely distorted form was already succumbing to corruption, and its progress filled her nostrils with the stench of rotting wood and flesh. She stood there for a moment before she realized that the racket of combat had been replaced with a strange, breathless silence.

She glanced around her and saw that all the fighting on the quarterdeck had ceased. Nath stood a couple of yards away, at the head of the iron-eyed old *Revenant*s with whom he'd forced his way through the mutineers to come to her aid. The mutineers themselves stood wide-eyed and slack-jawed at the nauseating remains of their leader, which now flattened and spread across the deck in a slow, throat-choking tide of greenish-black effluvia. The silence was finally broken by the dull thud of the mutineers' weapons hitting the deck as they surrendered en masse.

Enid met Nath's eyes and saw a mixture of horror and wonder there. She ignored his expression and shouted, "Send for Dr. Rondelle! I fear I have slain Merryweather!"

Enid came back to herself with Yeardly kneeling by her on the deck which rocked and swayed beneath her. The unnatural stillness that had seized *Revenant* had died with its author. Now the frigate bore the full brunt of the *outre-montagne*. She heard Nath and Master Kaliktiklak shouting orders over the wind and could feel the deck vibrate under her from the many sailors' feet pounding to and fro across it to obey them. She looked up at Yeardly, whose face was a mask of worry to rival her own. She had no need to name the source of grief that threatened to crush her heart in its merciless grasp.

"She has been taken below," Yeardly said, and gave her hand of flesh a covert squeeze. "Dr. Rondelle is with her. He is exerting himself to the utmost to see her through the crisis."

"Crisis?" Enid asked, raising herself to a seated position with the mid's assistance. Her voice vibrated with dread.

"She lost a great deal of blood," Yeardly said, "but I heard Rondelle tell the captain that he had a concoction that would charge what she had left with increased vitality and urge her body to crack on to refill her veins with the stuff. She is sore hurt, but she is in good hands. Now, let's get you on your feet so we can get you below until the doctor can see you as well, milady. I cannot lie: the disparity in the size of your pupils troubles me."

"I'm sure it's nothing," Enid gasped as Yeardly and a fellow whose concerned face she recognized as belonging to one of the old *Alarum*s helped her to her feet. She leaned heavily on Yeardly's shoulder, her body complaining in earnest regarding the long trial she had forced it to endure since yestermorn. Her breath came with a wheeze that rattled in her chest. That, coupled with the excruciation accompanying a full inhalation of breath left her mortally certain that one or more of her ribs were broken. Most of the cuts and punctures left by Oak on her arms and shoulders were well within her skill to quickly mend, but the ribs might require the doctor's assistance once he finished tending to Merryweather and the other seriously wounded. Still, a short nap in her hanging cot couldn't hurt—*the Artagny!* Dunaughy's alarmed voice intruded and banished all thoughts of the comforts of her cot from her mind. Enid nodded and dug her heels in to stop the belabored progress she and Yeardly made toward the hatch. "I must warn Captain Nath of an approaching enemy and assist in its dispatch before I retire below."

"An enemy approaches?"

"Yes," Enid snapped, her patience thinned to onionskin by pain, fatigue, the awful things she'd just seen and done, and fear that she might soon slip the reins of consciousness again. "An enemy ship, a frigate flying the black pennant of an Inquisitor, approaches from just beyond the headland. I must warn the captain immediately."

"How do you know?" Yeardly asked. He was staring intently into her eyes, clearly unconvinced that her mismatched pupils were no reason for concern. "What with the wind and blowing spray?"

Enid loved Yeardly for the worry in his own eyes, but she had no time to be coddled. If Dunaughy was correct and the *Artagny* was closing on them, *Revenant* would be caught in such a deplorable state of unreadiness, she had no doubt the outcome would be as lethal to her as any number of burst blood vessels in her brain. "Lay that aside for now and help me to my feet. Rue must be warned of our peril!"

"Are you certain that you are—that your injuries have not—I mean no disrespect, but I've seen a man with eyes such as yours after a fall down the stairs. For days he was mortally certain that he was the true captain of old *Alarum*."

"Ashes! I am not delusional!" Enid groaned as she attempted to stand on her own and found that her legs were too weak to answer. She had sufficient vigor to slap Yeardly's hands away as he attempted to resettle her on the deck. "Help me up, Yeardly! I must speak to Rue immediately!"

"I will send for him straightaway." The conflict between Yeardly's concern for her health and his subordinate's duty to obey her was writ large on his troubled features. "If you will rest a moment, he will be here before you can say—"

"*Knife*!" Yeardly took half a step back at the ferocity with which she exclaimed the word. "There! I have said it! Where is he? He will not rush to your summons or mine while *Revenant* is in such dire straits! Take me to him at once!"

Yeardly saw Mid Weard nearby, assisting in dragging dead mutineers into a pile for summary disposal over the leeward rail. He motioned for her to join him and said, "I will make sure Weard imparts the urgency—"

"Damn Weard and damn your obstinance!" Enid's low snarl was redolent with wrath. "Is it beyond your means to follow a simple order from your superior, *Mid* Yeardly? This is not a request: Take me to Captain Nath immediately!"

She regretted the violent heat of her words the moment she spoke them, and the sight of Yeardly's features transforming from deep concern to affront and hurt only deepened that regret.

"Aye, Magister." His reply was even but cool. She felt his hands tremble with restrained emotion as he helped her to her feet, but his face was as unreadable as a statue's. "Come lean more fully upon my shoulders and I will present you to the captain with all the speed you can muster."

Nath stood on the quarterdeck not far away, hard by the break in the railing at the forward end of the larboard catwalk. Half of his attention was occupied by the maneuvering of *Revenant* into position to receive the rear guard's boats from shore while avoiding the shallows she'd drifted toward when her helm was abandoned during the struggle between the mutineers and loyal *Revenant*s, while the other half was occupied with boats of the rear guard pulling across the cove and the wooded ridge behind them. He glanced over his shoulder as Yeardly announced Enid and himself.

"Enid! It is good to see you on your feet, Magister. Are you well?"

"Well enough," Enid said. "But I must warn you that an Ardain frigate closes with us from around the headland. It flies the black pennant. I fear they may have been notified by the semaphore system ranged along the coast. I have reason to believe she may be the *Artagny*."

Nath was curious as to how she came by her intelligence but accepted it regardless of its provenance. "How long until she rounds the head?"

Her pennant had just topped the horizon, Dunaughy thought. *But the wind is awkward for her. Advise him that she shouldn't arrive here for two hours, barring their ship's sorcerer is able to enhance her speed.*

Enid shared Dunaughy's appraisal and Nath nodded his head once, smiling at the news.

"Excellent!" he enthused. "We should have the rest of our people aboard within half an hour at most. We'll bring *Revenant*'s head around and take advantage of this *outre-montagne* to make our best speed sailing by and large for as long as the masts and spars will bear it."

Nath lay a hand on Enid's shoulder and stared earnestly into her bloodshot eyes. "Now, here are my orders for you: You have clearly exhausted every reserve of energy and you have sustained a number of injuries requiring Dr. Rondelle's attention. Take you to your cuddy and await him there. After he has finished with you, you are to sleep until I, and only I, summon you. Is that clear, Magister?"

Enid began to argue, but Nath's obdurate expression silenced her objections. She nodded tiredly and allowed Yeardly, whose face was still stoney and fixed, to assist her to her room and into the folding chair at her writing desk. Once she was settled, he gave her a curt nod and departed without a word.

There is a hurt I must heal at the first opportunity, Enid thought. She leaned back gingerly in the fragile chair, which relieved some of the aches in her bones but did little for her mind, bruised as it was by the memory of sights that she found increasingly difficult to reconcile with sanity. As for the pangs in her heart, they would not cease until she saw Merry fully recovered. Despite the racket of the of *Revenant*'s devastated crew rushing to set her right enough to sail and the nightmares that would throw themselves upon her the moment she dozed, each passing moment made slumber's embrace more welcoming. She gave her head a shake to clear the fog of fatigue from her head and opened her personal journal to pass the time until Dr. Rondelle arrived.

She was writing a particularly poetic yet accurate account describing the experience of inhabiting Merry's body when she heard the faint rattling of bird bones. A quick glance to her left revealed the tangled hair of a young girl leaning on the corner of her desk and attentively reading her account as she wrote it. She thought it was Harlech for a fleeting moment, but the circlet of dead, dry grass woven through tangled hair disabused her of that notion. Without looking up from her journal, she said, "Verlinherrinar."

"If you prefer," the girl said in a voice that brought visions of leaves swept across a vast plain of menhirs by a cold, autumn wind. "It is far more formal than 'Herry,' which you have my leave to use, but, pray, please yourself, dearest. It is the least reward I could offer since you have served me so well today."

"You are mistaken." Enid continued to write and, in a voice so steady it surprised her, said, "I have never served you, Lady Verlinherrinar. My actions today were entirely motivated by my loyalty to my shipmates and a sincere desire to shed the life's blood of a child murderer. If you benefited from that in any way, it is only by the caprice of Providence."

"Providence? You mortals are too short-lived to notice or

understand the powers that govern the world in which you live, but I will share this with you: neither Providence nor the Redeemer have aught to do with the tides of your life." Verlinherrinar's giggle was the light, flat tinkle produced by a wind chime constructed of tiny hollow bones caressed by the final exhalation of a dying man. "Now, as to whether you served me, be assured that your motives do not signify against the value your deeds hold for me, Loriessenid."

"'Loriessenid'?"

"Your eyes narrow so prettily when you are suspicious! Put yourself at ease, my severe little moppet! It is a pet name for clever girls in the Old Language, nothing more."

Enid's only response was a cool, flat stare.

Verlinherrinar's answering sigh was a gust of wind that stripped the last leaves from a dead tree.

"Never mind, my headstrong girl, I take no offense at your distrust," Harlech said. "I will earn your faith eventually, and your resistance to my efforts will make the attainment that much sweeter. Now, I feel you deserve a reward or boon of your choice. What do you wish for, dear girl?"

"I have but one boon to ask of you," Enid said, her voice as cold as hoarfrost. "Is there aught I can do to repay your covert *favor* and be free of my debt to you?"

"Of course," Verlinherrinar said with a sad moue. "I will mourn your absence at my side in the years to come, but I love you too much to bar you from pursuing your own desires."

Herry stroked Enid's cheek with the back of her soft, child's hand. It took all of Enid's resolve to resist flinching from her touch.

"Return the hand I lent you and, as the mortals say, we will be quit."

"Then you shall have it." Enid's voice crackled with satisfaction. "You will find I repay the loan in silver that exceeds my hand's weight."

"Oh, Enid. You misunderstand me. I do not wish the trinket you wear. I must have the one of flesh and bone that I lent you."

"It was reduced to ash in the making of this hand!"

Verlinherrinar frowned. "That *is* unfortunate, but, because I love you, it does not leave you in an impossible strait. I will remove my mark from your silver hand when you perform a service that merits the gesture."

Enid seethed in instant rage and began gathering power to herself, intent on wiping the Ylfar's false expression of solicitude from its face.

"Ah, sweet one, I have no desire to punish your misguided and fruitless wrath, so I will leave you to consider another boon that actually lies within your reach—perhaps something related to your stalwart lover?"

And so saying, the Ylfar was gone before Enid's shout escaped her lips. She was still howling in rage when Rondelle and one of his loblolly boys burst into her cuddy, their faces stricken with alarmed concern. The efforts of both were required to restrain her, plus the invisible aid of Dunaughy, who, freed from Verlinherrinar's restraints, reasoned with the frothing monster raging about her mind until she was calm enough to relax her magical wards sufficiently to allow Rondelle's calming cantrip to do its work for her.

chapter 23

Enid awoke in her cuddy, alone. Her body ached, and there was a sharp pain in her sides when she drew a deep breath. Her mouth tasted of recent illness and was as dry as a ship's biscuit. Still, she was able to extricate herself from the hanging cot with minimal distress and, after a moment or two of heavy breathing, found she could cross the short expanse of deck to her writing desk and the porcelain jug of water upon it. After several long draws on the jug, she took stock of herself as she dressed.

She ran her hand over the planes of her face and found swelling there, but no plasters or bandages to indicate serious damage. Her vanity satisfied, she continued her survey and found her torso bound with tight bandages from just below her breasts to her navel. The wrappings were stained with blood in places on her sides, and she assumed those spots marked where Mr. Oak was able to penetrate her protective aura with his bare hands—or, more accurately, his *claws*. There were scratches and cuts on her arms and hand, but nothing Rondelle's salves and time wouldn't set right in a day or two. She examined her silver hand out of habit and took in a deep breath of surprise that agonized her sides.

There, inscribed in the silver on the back of her hand, was a strange symbol or sigil, which neither she nor Dunaughy had engraved during her hand's creation.

What is this mark, she thought, *so dreadful and portentous?*

I know not. Even in thought, Dunaughy sounded as if he had taxed himself to the limit and the utterance of each word required a supreme effort. Enid pressed him for information, nonetheless.

What of Merry? And how long was I insensate in my cot?

After a short pause, Dunaughy thought, *Lieutenant Merryweather yet lives but is unconscious. That is all I can see of her. I do not know how long we were in a torpor, though I doubt it was more than a day or so.*

Enid nodded and bade Dunaughy rest, however that was accomplished by the dead, and dressed herself with painstaking care to avoid undoing Dr. Rondelle's neat bandage work. She opened the door and found Lieutenant Dalroyd and Perrin, the purser, huddled over their steaming cups of coffee. They both looked as if their bitter cups were their frayed lifelines to the land of the living. Despite his obvious fatigue, Dalroyd surged to his feet to take her elbow and support her as the ship yawed and threatened to throw her to the deck.

"Magister d'Tancreville! Has the doctor given his leave for you to be abroad so soon? You appear weak as a kitten, m'lady!"

Enid started to jerk away from his grasp and suggest where the doctor and his leave could dwell for eternity but resisted those urges and instead said, "Thank you for your kindness, Lieutenant. I believe I can stand unassisted now. I am seeking the counsel of Dr. Rondelle this instant, in fact. Do you know where I can find him?"

"On the orlop, m'lady, tending to Lieutenant Merryweather and some of the other hands who were sorely hurt."

"Of course," Enid said. "I should have known. He is a very diligent man. Were many injured or killed in the melee with the mutineers?"

"I fear so. Nearly twenty were slain outright in the fighting. Another dozen or so are unlikely to survive their injuries. Nearly twice that have sustained hurts that will interfere or prevent them from doing their duties. It is a sad day when loyal hands suffer more aboard their own ship than a raiding party sent into the enemy's own land," Dalroyd said.

Enid heard the sincere regret in his voice and noticed that while he had loosened his grip on her elbow, he had not released it. *This fellow has an artist's heart*, she thought. *I pray it does not break him.*

"Twenty dead," Enid marveled somberly. "And nearly twice that injured! That is far more than we lost taking this ship, or in any battle since."

"More akin to losses aboard a first rate," Dalroyd said, and gently guided her by her elbow toward the hatch leading below. "Please do me the honor of escorting you to sick bay and Dr. Rondelle. Your refusal would shame me, so please humor my undoubtedly unnecessary effort at gallantry."

Enid nodded and treated Dalroyd to a rare, unguarded smile. "I would not dream of shaming a fine officer such as yourself, sir, and your gallantry is most welcome."

Enid was happy for the lieutenant's assistance. Her current equilibrium was no match for the random and violent gambols of the deck beneath her feet and she would have surely taken a fall if she'd attempted to reach the orlop alone. Dalroyd's supporting hand on her arm was a comfort, as was the gentleman's humorously distracting observations on the differences between an empty vessel in the yards, smelling of fresh wood chips and sawdust, versus an active ship at sea, redolent with the smell of sailors and livestock.

Dalroyd knocked three times sharply on the sick bay door before ushering her into *Revenant*'s version of a hospital. The room was not large and was crowded with narrow box cots that rocked in unison with the ship's movements. Rondelle's loblolly boys moved among them, checking bandages and providing drinks of water to their injured shipmates. Enid was surprised at how gently the fellows treated their injured, stopping to share a friendly word and brushing the fever-damp hair from their eyes. However intimidating their size and musculature might be, they were tender and conscientious caretakers.

The air in the room was close and stale, heavy with the odors of blood, waste, and vomit. Dr. Rondelle finished reattaching a young woman's foot and ankle to her shin with tiny, precise stitches and greeted his unexpected guest.

"Magister Tancreville," he barked as he wiped his bloody hands on the leathern apron about his waist. "What in the name of the most dear are you doing out of bed?"

"Seeking news of Lieutenant Merryweather," she said, and gently extricated her elbow from Dalroyd's hands, who seemed to release it with regret. "Where is she? And why does this room stink like an abattoir? Surely that cannot be healthful for your patients!"

Rondelle's obvious effort to bite back a sour retort surprised her, not in the article of its sourness, but rather that he made the effort at all. Such reticence to offend was alien to his character, in her experience. At last, he found his words and spoke.

"As for the atmosphere within my sick bay, it is my habit to consult with the ship's magister when it is so overtaxed and request a temporary dweomer to stir the air into motion and occasionally exchange it for fresher stuff from above. As my magister lay senseless in her cot, Mid Yeardly was unsure he should attempt such a feat. I could have brought you around with some strong-smelling salts and brought you here to perform the task regardless of how far the healing formulations at work on your shattered ribs had progressed."

"No," Enid said, knowing when she'd "stepped in it," as she'd heard Rue say. "Your actions were perfectly correct. I apologize for my tone—my head still sings from some of the blows to it I received on the quarterdeck."

Rondelle's face lost most of its confrontational set, and in a lower tone he said, "The good lieutenant is here, sequestered from the common sailors as best as the circumstances permit."

Enid followed his gesture to a small, curtained-off area that was only slightly larger than the cot it surrounded.

"May I?"

Rondelle nodded. "You may poke your head in to see her, but do not attempt to awaken her. Not only would the attempt be useless; it would be contrary to her recovery. She requires rest more than anything else we can provide her."

"I only wish to see her," she said and stepped by the doctor.

Enid pulled one of the curtains aside and, as Rondelle suggested, poked her head inside. Merryweather lay on a cot, her body covered from chin to toe by a soft blanket that she suspected had been secured from the lieutenant's cuddy for its familiarity and comfort. Enid choked back a smile at the sight of her paramour's face, which was waxy and pale. There was no trace of the mischief or wry humor that animated her features at better times and her glorious eyes were sunk deeply into their sockets. Her breathing was so shallow that it was barely detectable.

"Oh, Merry," Enid whispered, "what have I done to you, my love?"

It took but a moment for her to press a tiny sylph to dry her eyes and a moment more to swallow her grief. When she withdrew her head from the curtains, her expression was composed.

"How long has she been in this state, Dr. Rondelle?"

"Three days, since the fight to secure *Revenant* from the mutineers," Rondelle answered.

"Three days? She and I have been unconscious for three days?"

"Even so. And I am surprised to see you on your feet after such a short rest. I believed you would be confined to your bed for another week at least. How fare you? Here, step behind this screen so I can examine your bandages."

He clucked over his handiwork, tugged at bandage here and resecured a knot there. When he finished, he gave a brisk nod. "Your recuperative abilities are as remarkable as your capacity for mayhem, Magister. I conjure you to eat lightly for another day or so, and avoid any work that strains your body or mind unnecessarily. Other than that, I am happy to say that you are well enough for light service."

"Thank you, Dr. Rondelle," Enid said with a wan smile. "Since I now have my physician's leave, I will see to freshening the air here and cool it a bit while I'm at it."

Enid parted ways with Dalroyd outside the sick bay, as she was far steadier on her feet. *It is time to see Captain Nath and discover how things stand,* she thought, and dreaded the prospect. With each moment that passed, the memory of her actions of the night before—*no, the nights past*—grew vaguer and more incomplete. She knew she would have much to explain, an imponderable task given the holes in her memory. She paused for a moment to run her fingers along the mysterious new glyph on her hand and cursed silently. *Even this is beyond the pall of my understanding!*

Perhaps Mr. Kaliktiklak can cast some light on this and other conundrums, Dunaughy thought. *Your actions—the capabilities you displayed—are inexplicable to me. Your deeds that night remind me of nothing more than my people's tales of their ancestral heroes.*

He's already called me a demon. I can only pray that what he saw on the quarterdeck didn't confirm his judgment. I suspect I'm no match for him, with weapons or sorcery.

The sea was still active, so she was forced to cling to the rail as she climbed to the quarterdeck to join Nath on the windward side. Before her was a vista of choppy waves dotted with wind-torn detritus, including tree branches still bearing green leaves, shattered crates and barrels, and the occasional broken spar trailing rope and canvas. The blazing orange glare of the sunrise filtering through shreds of fast-moving clouds gave the scene an apocalyptic cast that Enid found disconcerting. Nath noticed her awed expression and said, "We had barely sunk Ardainne behind us when the *outre-montagne* was upon us. The divisions were in chaos after the mutiny. Some were missing hands who were dead or hurt; others were depleted because the mutineers who numbered among them were locked belowdecks in shackles. In our state at that moment, we were doomed."

"What did you do?"

"It was clear we would not survive the blow unless all hands pitched in with a will, so I freed the mutineers. The choice between being shackled in *Revenant*'s hold as she sank or taking a fighting chance to save themselves by saving the ship required no consideration, even from some of the former leaders of the uprising. We survived the gale, but only by the skin of our teeth."

"I regret I was not able to assist you," Enid said. "But I was far too depleted to have done much in any case. Still, I—"

"Stuff and nonsense!" Nath waved a dismissive hand. "Without your efforts we would have all drowned before ever gaining *Revenant*. And in a way, you did help us through the storm, for Mid Yeardly was able to use some of the advanced sorcerous techniques you taught him to bolster the strength of our masts and spars and, in one instance, repair a critical line that was about to part. Without the magic he learned from you, we may not have weathered the *outre-montagne*."

Enid was filled with such a strong pride and fondness for Yeardly that she was robbed of the power of speech, so she restricted herself to an approving smile and nod.

"In the end, the angry winds deposited us here, on the southern shore of the Merentian, within eye shot of ancient Kmet." Nath waved a hand vaguely, taking in the entire larboard horizon. "For a time I was afraid that the winds would not release us until *Revenant* was berthed amid that haunted land's ancient monuments!"

Enid glanced to larboard and saw the faint smudge where the sky met land rather than sea and nodded. Someday she would love to take in the sight of those monuments and make a firsthand record of the glyphs that decorated their bases and the entire length of the towering ebon obelisks that stood guard before them. This was not that day, though, so she asked the question dearest to her heart.

"How long until we reach Gisbon?"

"Longer than I'd like," Nath answered. "Particularly with Merryweather and Lieutenant Bascombe in their current condition." He noticed the shadow of worry on Enid's face deepen and continued, "But we will make the best time possible and will not divert from our direct course unless absolutely compelled."

Enid nodded. "I know you will make all speed, Rue, and any delay will lie at the feet of nature or the enemy."

"Both of whom should be thin upon the waters, thanks to the *outre-montagne.* Any ships in this region of the Merentian will have suffered its wrath just as we have, and perhaps fared worse. Better yet, steady north to nor'-nor'east winds inevitably arise in the aftermath of the *outre-montagne.* That is an advantageous wind for Gisbon."

"Thank Providence for any small favors it can spare," Enid said. "I wish our Lieutenant Bascombe a swift recovery and that his sister's prayers for the same be granted. Truly, I do. But Rue, my blood freezes at the thought of losing our Merry."

Rue gently guided Enid to the taffrail by her shoulder so that they could face nothing but *Revenant*'s wake as they spoke. She allowed it, knowing the sight of her suddenly streaming tears would do the crew's battered morale no good.

"Enid," he said gently, "I have badgered Rondelle so regularly that he could set his watch by my appearances in the sick bay. He initially held only a middling hope that Augusta would survive her surplus of injuries and deficit of blood, but he labored over her tirelessly despite his misgivings. For the past two days he has assured me that she is out of danger and needs no more than rest and further replenishment of her blood and vital humors and she will awaken."

"And will she still be fit enough to serve? She loves the sea service as deeply as you, Rue. It would crush her to be invalided out of it!"

"As to that," Nath said in the same gentle, reassuring voice, "she may limp awhile or favor one arm over the other for a time, but Rondelle does not believe she has suffered any lasting injury, unlike poor Leonid."

At Enid's concerned look, Nath explained, "The ball that struck Lieutenant Bascombe did an inordinate amount of damage to the lung through which it passed. Rondelle believes this was due in part to the short distance between the lieutenant and the warden, but he is also inclined to believe the bullet bore an enchantment to increase the grievousness of the wound it caused to whomever it struck. He fears that poor Leonid's breathing will be hindered for the rest of his days and he will no longer be fit for naval duty."

"I am sorry to hear it," Enid said, and found she truly was. "What of the other officers? Lieutenant Dalroyd was drenched in blood when he handed me aboard."

"Dalroyd took a few nicks, but he is hardy and whole. Lieutenant Wilk, bless him, was slain, but not without doing the enemy some hurt first. I will praise him to the heavens in my report to the admiral, but, sadly, it is too little and too late for the poor fellow. I don't know what will become of his dog."

"Jacques."

"Jock," Nath corrected. "The wretch is very particular regarding his living conditions. He refuses to bed down with the hands before the mast, though they adore him and would fatten him until he burst. No, he must sleep in a cabin, else he makes his complaints heard throughout the night."

"And none of the officers of the gun room will adopt him?"

"Officers of the wardroom," Nath corrected again. "No. I'm sure Merryweather would if she could be consulted."

"I will take him," Enid said.

"You? I thought you disdained small, 'useless' dogs? And you lost no love for Wilk, I think. Besides, you have already extended your hospitality to Lady Chum-Chum. I fear your cuddy was never meant for a menagerie."

"I will take him," Enid said more firmly. "I believe Wilk was a monster of some sort, but he died fighting for his fellows. That deserves some recognition. Besides, whatever his owner's sins, his dog had no hand in them."

"As you will," Nath said. "In any case, a dog might be beneficial to you."

"In what way?" Enid's eyes narrowed in anticipation of one of Nath's incisive japes, but he simply shrugged.

"Who would not benefit from the company of a good dog?"

As they talked, Nath began to pursue a line of questions aimed at hearing her account of her battle with Mr. Oak, a topic she was not yet ready to address. Claiming to be betrayed by her wounds, Enid abandoned Nath's company on the pretext of returning to her cuddy to rest. He encouraged her to do so, for he wished to see her at his table for a dinner that would also be attended by Lieutenant Cierina Bascombe and Monsieur Epolytte. As she descended the stairs to the gun deck, stairs that were little better than a ladder, she lost her footing and her grip proved too weak to save her from falling. With a swiftness that beggared belief, Mr. Kaliktiklak was there to catch her in his thin but powerful arms. He clutched her to his hard, narrow chest and scuttled, bent nearly double under the low ceiling, through the gun room and deposited her with care into her cuddy's lone chair. The entire operation was complete before Enid had time to do much more than gasp in surprise.

"Thank you, Mr. Kaliktiklak," she said. The Bogaraet nodded his head and squatted before her. His legs were so long his knees overtopped his head. This, coupled with his obscenely long arms, gave him the appearance of an otherworldly cricket whose round head was fixed with red pinpoint eyes and a broad mouth full of cruel, needle-thin teeth.

"I have only just heard that you have risen from your stupor, Magister. Are you well enough to speak?"

You need to speak with him sooner or later, it may as well be now, Dunaughy's thought crossed her mind as she considered begging off for the moment. She subdued a sigh and said, "I am, Master. It is fortuitous that you came upon me, not just because you saved me a broken leg or worse, but because it saves me the effort of seeking you out. I fear walking is extremely tiring, particularly with *Revenant* engaging in bucking and sliding as she is."

"I am happy I could be of service," Kaliktiklak said. His voice was mellifluous as ever, but there were more clicks behind it than usual. Enid wondered if she was hearing a tonal clue that she lacked the familiarity necessary to identify. Perhaps he was nervous or, Redeemer forfend, angry. “We need to speak of your deeds against Ogilvy and the power that animated him.”

“We do indeed, for I’m at a loss to understand how I survived the encounter, let alone emerged victorious. I did things I cannot explain and reached levels of awareness that, in remembering them, seem impossible. And then there is this.”

Enid held her silver hand up, its back to Kaliktiklak to present the new glyph there for his examination.

Kaliktiklak’s intake of breath at the sight reminded her of the sound he made when smoking a pipe. He unfolded one of his long hands to trace the symbol with his spider-leg fingers.

“When did this appear?”

“Sometime after Mr. Oak’s defeat. I was in a stupor for days afterward, so I cannot say precisely when.”

He withdrew his hand and stared at her until she thought the bright sparks of his eyes might set her own aflame. At last, she broke the silence and asked, “What is the meaning of this sigil?”

“Does the name Verlinherrinar mean anything to you, Magister?”

Enid shook her head. “I’ve never heard it before you spoke it. Should it be familiar with the name?”

“She is certainly familiar with yours,” Kaliktiklak said, his words a little difficult to understand due to the rapid undercurrent of clicking behind them. “That sigil proclaims to the world that you are her chosen champion.”

Enid frowned. “I have not met any ‘Verlinherrinar.’ I would certainly recall such a tongue-twisting name.”

“You have met her, or some fragment of her; you simply didn’t know it. She would have appeared in a human form, or near enough to human. Her manner of speech would probably be teasing and replete with riddles. You almost certainly met her in a lonely place that sees or has seen the regular spilling of blood.”

“Herry,” Enid said, and her stomach writhed into a cold knot.

She described her meeting with Herry of the Bailey in as much detail as her memory allowed. At Dunaughy's encouragement, she also spoke of the duel, the loss of her hand, and how she and the Murchadhan mage created her silver hand. By the time the telling was completed, her throat was nearly as parched as it was when she awoke from her long sleep.

"And that is the last of it," she said after describing the grisly process of attaching her silver hand.

Kaliktiklak tapped his long fingers together in a gesture that resembled a spider dancing on a mirror before saying, "That was Verlinherrinar, or a fragment she left at the ruined keep for some purpose."

Hearing those words, Enid was seized by an arctic chill and visibly trembled. Lady Chum-Chum noticed her distress and swept down to drape herself like a scarf around Enid's neck. Its befeathered head pressed softly against a spot above her heart and made soft crooning and chuckling sounds.

Calm yourself, Enid, Dunaughy thought soothingly. *Panic will not serve you well in this.*

Enid ignored him and said, "I thought she was just some sort of Fey creature! Had I known, I would have departed and demanded a new location for the duel."

Kaliktiklak made a noise that Enid had learned to interpret as a chuckle or laugh. "What do you think the Fey are, Enid? Most are minor Ellethaur or fragments of major Ellethaur nobles left behind to keep them informed on the state of the world. It is said that some of the greatest among them stayed behind as they were too enamored of their creation to let it go."

Enid gave a shaky nod. "That explains much but lays bare a myriad other questions."

"Most truths do," Kaliktiklak agreed as he rose to as full a height as the confines of her cuddy would allow. "There is nothing to be done now. I must search my deepest memories before I offer further counsel. Limit yourself to familiar magic until we know more about this Ellethaur and the nature of Mr. Oak. I will share anything valuable I learn from the All Ghost."

Enid thanked the Bogaraet for his help and watched as he made his fluid, boneless exit. His movements reminded her of those of an octopus she'd once seen in the Arden Royal Aquarium as it navigated a maze contrived for its entertainment.

She sensed Dunaughy was about to engage her in conversation and thought, *We'll discuss this later tonight or, more likely, tomorrow morning. I must rest a bit before dressing for dinner with our captain.*

Enid arrived fashionably late, but not by design. The combined rapping at her cuddy door and the mental shouts from Dunaughy weren't sufficient to rouse her from what was meant to be a short nap. When the racket finally penetrated the warm wool around her mind, she dressed quickly and practically ran to the captain's door. The lobster stationed there gave her a sympathetic smile before announcing her and throwing open the door for her at the sound of Nath's cry of "Enter!"

She found that Nath and his other guests, Lieutenant Cierina Bascombe and Monsieur Epolytte, were already seated and the first remove had been served. A place had been left for her and someone, most likely Yaric, had filled their wineglass and hers.

"I beg your pardon, sir," Enid said with a bow to Captain Nath. "I fear I may have overexerted myself this morning and could not be roused until a few moments ago."

"There's no call for that, Magister! I'm happy to see you have enough vitality left to join us!" Nath grinned up at her, a twinkle in his eyes that she judged to be engendered by his amusement at her discomfiture or an early start on the wine.

When she was properly seated, Lieutenant Bascombe leaned toward her until they were shoulder to shoulder and said, "Captain Nath has shown me the orders that required him to send Leonid on the raid and explained the machinations of Lord Aixely and the Sea Lord. I have apologized for doubting him and I owe you an apology as well for my sharp tongue ashore."

"Nonsense," Enid said. "You were distraught over your dear brother's injuries. Anything that might have been amiss in your behavior is utterly excused by that simple fact."

"Thank you, Magister," Cierina said. "You are every bit as courteous as our captain said. It is aggravating to know that my capture was used as a weapon against him. The crew didn't rise against us; we were captured by two fast frigates that *Artagny,* beaten about as she was, had no prayer of outrunning, no matter how large or small the prize crew the captain sent aboard her. I will explode that specious lie thoroughly when we make Gisbon!"

"I am pleased to hear it, but act with caution," Enid warned. "Ambrose and Morrin are enemies to any friend of Captain Nath. Speak against them or deny their claims and they will target you just as they have him."

"Let them try," Epolytte interrupted. "I will challenge them one after the other and put them down like the rabid dogs they are!"

Enid began to urge Epolytte to restraint, but Cierina placed her hand on her former cellmate's fist on the table and said, "No number of duels will resolve this problem. It is a political problem that requires finesse."

"Ahh! Political finesse!" the handsome Ardain gentleman said. "You will secure the service of a poisoner, then?"

Enid and Rue both stared at Epolytte while Cierina rolled her eyes and shook her head. The tableau held for a moment and then Epolytte winked at Captain Nath and laughed, which triggered an outburst of answering laughs all around the table.

When the jollity subsided, Epolytte said, "Forgive me for practicing upon your credulity, my friends. It is what passes for my humor, I fear. For some reason, people find it easy to believe that I am stupid as a, what is the word in Albion? Ah, yes, stupid as a post!"

"It is easily explained by the vacuous set of your features," Cierina drawled. "However handsome they might be."

Epolytte pulled a face that contorted his handsome features into a travesty of his regular features and extended his tongue in Cierina's direction. The rest of the meal passed in easy conversation, unbridled by any pretense of naval formality. If half of Enid's heart were not reduced to ashes by the thought of losing Merry to wounds inflicted on her while Enid controlled her body with less regard for her safety than a puppeteer felt for their marionette, it would have been one of the finest nights she'd had since leaving Ardainne.

After dinner, a few glasses of the remaining brandy from the *Tape a'Bord*, and some of Enid's fine tobacco for those who took it, the gathering came to an end. Epolytte and Cierina commended Nath on the quality of his table and his graciousness as a host. As they left, Cierina pulled Enid aside and whispered in her ear, "Dr. Rondelle swears that Leonid would not have survived to reach the beach if it had not been for your efforts to replenish his blood. I owe my brother's life to you, which is a debt that cannot be paid in one lifetime. If I can ever serve you in any way, you have but to ask."

At Nath's signal, Enid hung back after Lieutenant Bascombe and her charming cellmate departed. She and Nath stood together and gazed out the stern gallery and watched as her wake was churned under the waves rushing toward the distant shore of Kmet. The reflection of the red beads of their cigarillos in the glass of the gallery reminded her of Kaliktiklak's eyes.

It was Nath who broke the silence, saying, "Enid, I have given you ample time to approach the subject yourself, but I fear I must press the matter as many of the crew have confided in their seniors that while they did not understand what they saw in the fight for the quarterdeck and are grateful for your intervention there, they are fearful of you now."

Enid lowered her eyes and thought, *How much should I tell him, Dunaughy?*

All of it, he answered immediately. *Save my part in it, or even of my existence.*

Master Kaliktiklak may have informed him of that already.

No, Dunaughy thought. *He will leave it to you to report to the captain as you will. It is your prerogative as the ship's magister. The master will not interfere unless your deceit endangers* Revenant, *her crew, or her officers.*

"Even Yeardly avoided your cuddy while you were *hors de combat*, the same Yeardly that sat by your side every moment he was not on watch when you were incapacitated with seasickness on the old *Alarum*."

"And are you afraid of me, too?" Enid asked.

"No, I am perfectly at ease with you. I must own that I am as wary of the power I saw you wield against Ogilvy as I would be of a hungry panther in my cabin."

"I didn't cast so much as a cantrip at Ogilvy, for he was dead long before the mutiny occurred." So saying, Enid did as Dunaughy suggested and unburdened herself of every detail of her contest with Mr. Oak and the preceding relevant events, save only Dunaughy's condition and involvement in the affair. When she was finished, Nath stared at her for a long moment, obviously aghast.

"You *possessed* Lieutenant Merryweather?" he asked in a tight, strained voice.

"It would be more accurate to say that I borrowed her body, a loan for which I had her leave," Enid said. "I would never take such liberty without her permission."

"You *borrowed* her body? You speak of it as if she loaned you her coat!"

Enid winced at his tone, which bordered on contempt, and fought down a tide of anger-tinged remorse.

"Forgive me if I sound callous, Rue, but it is the only way I can speak of that day without abandoning my dignity altogether to weep at your feet," she said. "I implore your forbearance. I know full well that I placed Merry in peril and that many of her hurts are the direct result of my actions. If she dies, that will be my fault as well—and I doubt that I will be able to shoulder the weight of her loss and my part in it without abandoning my senses or my very life."

Nath regarded her coldly, but the unfamiliar sight of tears glistening in her normally glacial green eyes struck at his heart. In a more normal voice, he asked, "You had no choice in the matter, I take it?"

"None," Enid said, ignoring the heavy tear that escaped her lashes and traced a path down the pale angle of cheek. "If I had not done, our boats would have been dashed beneath the waves, and without our arrival Merryweather and the rest of the officers and loyal *Revenant*s would have died if they were fortunate enough to fall to the mutineers, or else suffered a darker fate at the hands of Mr. Oak. I could not allow that! I could not permit the monster that slew Harlech to rob me of the rest of you."

Nath took a long drag on his cigarillo and exhaled the smoke in a twin stream from his nostrils. When he looked up from the lit end of his smoke, his expression had lost most of the cold contempt it held but a moment ago.

"Set that aside for now," he said. "This Mr. Oak was Fey? One of the Ylfar out of legend?"

"So Mr. Kaliktiklak believes," Enid said. "He was certainly no ghost or spirit, elemental or otherwise. I have never seen the like of him."

Nath shook his head and rolled his cigarillo from one side of his mouth to the other. "And he believes that your silver hand marks you out as the champion to another?"

Enid nodded and held her hand up to Nath to display the sigil that marked it now. "This symbol names her as Verlinherrinar."

He leaned closer and squinted his eyes. He sat back in his chair, his eyebrows raised in bemusement, and said, "I see no marks there, Enid."

"I see it as plain as the anchors on your buttons," Enid said, "as did Master Kaliktiklak. That is passing strange."

"Perhaps one must have a certain amount of sorcerous skill before they are allowed to see it," Nath suggested. "Another mystery for another day, though. A more pressing question is the matter of Mr. Oak's fate. You are certain you have slain him, or banished him?"

Enid nodded. "He is no more. *Revenant* is free of him."

"And the crew is free of any influence he may have had over them?"

Enid nodded again. "Any sway he had over them died with him."

"Good," Nath said. "Perhaps some good can come from all of this, then. Perhaps I can convince Admiralty that the hands who rose up against me did so against their will and are blameless for their part in the mutiny."

"I do not believe that—"

"Now is not the time to begin offering your arcane insights with me, Magister," Nath barked, and stood so suddenly his chair toppled behind him. "That would have been the moment you had any inkling of what was afoot aboard *my* ship rather than treating it as your own demesne and keeping your own counsel like the Duchess of None-Such!"

"I didn't think—"

"No, it is patently clear you did not," Nath interrupted. "Else you would not have left me going about my own merry way without informing me of the threat that loomed over my command. Had I known, I would have taken us farther out to sea and given you and Master Kaliktiklak time to address the problem. Instead, you chose to leave me in the dark! It is only through the kindness of Providence that I did not lose half of my crew and the *Revenant* entire, all for being kept ignorant by the officer I rely upon most for intelligence!"

He stamped back and forth before her as he spoke, his features the very image of anger and disappointment. Enid was reminded of her father, although he had been far taller and solidly built than Nath.

"And what of poor Harlech, Captain Ourey, and the other unfortunate souls suffering in the monster's oubliette of oak? Were they freed upon his destruction?"

"I fear not," Enid admitted, her voice low. "Master Kaliktiklak and I intend to—"

He stopped suddenly, directly before her chair, and hissed, "Ashes! If you have any further secrets you are withholding from me, now is the time to reveal them!"

Do not reveal our arrangement now, Dunaughy thought. *Let his temper subside.*

"What is the significance of that nod, Magister?"

"Only that I understand you, sir."

"That is well," Nath snapped. "I have one last question for you: On your word, are you fully in control of your arts?"

"On my word, I am," Enid said, meeting Nath's eyes and holding them. "I am no danger to you or your command."

Nath held her eyes for a few beats and then shook his head and turned his back on her. "Thank you. You are dismissed, Magister. I suggest you use your spare time to revisit the section of *Herbstrom's* that describes your responsibility to keep your captain apprised of all sorcerous or uncanny threats to the ship or her people."

Shame and rage warred for ascendance in Enid's heart. Shame won, and she stood, saluted Nath, and departed his presence without a word.

Enid found Yeardly giving the sailor at the helm a course correction. She waited until he was finished and then called his name and asked, "Do you have a moment to spare, Mid Yeardly?"

The young man seemed to weigh his words before answering, "As you will, Magister."

She followed him to a spot in the rail between two of *Revenant*'s new "smashers," where a quiet conversation would be inaudible to the hand at the helm.

"Yes, Magister?" Yeardly stood at attention before her, his face devoid of expression.

"I fear I have greatly offended Captain Nath," Enid said quietly. "You have known him far longer than I have. Is his wrath a slow-burning fire or a flash of lightning that strikes and recedes?"

"It would not be appropriate for me to speak of such matters with regard to my commanding officer," Yeardly said flatly. "I am afraid I cannot help you, sir."

"'Sir'?" Enid said. "No such formality has stood between us in our privacy for some time. If this is some sort of jape, I am too forlorn and worn down by the day to detect its humor."

"It is no jape, sir. When last we spoke, you made the difference between our ranks quite clear and reminded me of the courtesy required by the disparity."

Enid's knees went weak, and she steadied herself with a surreptitiously placed hand on the breech of the smasher behind her. "Yeardly, you must believe I meant nothing I said. Pain and fatigue clouded my mind. I beg your pardon, most sincerely!"

"Aye, sir," Yeardly said in the same monotone. "If you say I must, I must."

The young man's blank stare bore into her back as she made her way off the quarterdeck.

As she passed among the *Revenant*s on her way to her cuddy, she noticed for the first time the way they stepped well out of her path as she approached and refused to meet her gaze. Rather than slump her shoulders in disconsolation, she straightened her back and squared them. If they would make a villain of her, she would give them one whose malice was only exceeded by their dignity and noble bearing.

It has been a traumatic time for them all; give them time and they will be more accepting of you and your actions. Dunaughy's thought was a soothing caress against the dolorous surface of her consciousness, but she ignored it.

When she reached her cuddy, she heard the indistinct sound of movement within—the scrape of her chair across the floor, she thought, and perhaps something brushing against one of her sea chests. She froze in alarm. What if Mr. Oak had contrived to return? She had assured Rue that the monster was slain, but what if she was wrong? Would he accept it as a mistake, or brand her a liar? Worse yet, she doubted she had the strength to repeat their contest and emerge victorious.

Cold sweat prickled on her forehead as she slowly opened the door, fully expecting to see the awful form of Mr. Oak crouched in her cabin, slavering for her blood. Instead she was met by the sparkling eyes of Wilk's dog, Jock. A small brown-and-red blanket hung from his jaws, which he gave a slight shake by way of greeting. His docked tail twitched in two rapid circles as it regarded her sagaciously from beneath silver-shot black eyebrows that flirted up and down in synchronicity with its gleaming black eyes.

She closed the door softly behind her and increased the brightness of the orb lamp on her little writing desk with a twitch of her index finger. She spied a note there, next to a couple of parcels. Jock sniffed around her feet and ankles with intense interest as she read the note, which was written in pencil on a scrap of the same coarse brown paper as the parcels. It was from Mid Weard and explained she'd left Jock in Enid's cabin at the captain's direction and that the large parcel contained dried beef for the dog's consumption, while the smaller contained a selection of his favorite bones and strips of an old leather belt that he chewed to occupy himself and clean his teeth. There was also the blanket upon which he slept, the same article he was now engaged in dragging from one end of her cuddy to the other—his transit frequently interrupted by sudden, jerking halts when he trod upon it—and a pair of wooden bowls, one for food and the other for water.

She located the bowls where he had apparently tossed them before her arrival, one beneath her writing desk and the other in the corner formed by the bulkhead and her sea chest. Upon examining them, she found that they were both hand carved, no doubt by Wilk himself. Each had the dog's name carved into the bottom in the intricate script beloved by Albion's sailors.

When Jock noticed her handling his holy of holies, Enid replaced his blanket as the center of his canine universe. The puppy—for Enid now realized the creature was too young to be described accurately as a dog—began to hop hopefully on his hind legs and serenade her with sharp, high-pitched barks as his tail beat the time.

"When is the last time you ate, Monsieur Jock?" Enid asked in the sort of voice all of mankind, regardless of their station or breeding, uses to address dogs and infants. "Not so long ago as that, judging by your plump belly! Still, I suppose it cannot hurt to feed you a little before we retire."

She placed a little of the dried beef in one of the bowls and water from her porcelain jug in the other, and Jock set upon them with enough vigor to challenge that of a starving jackal. He pressed his snout into his food bowl so energetically that it was shoved about in jerky circles as he pursued it. Enid was forced to squat over her heels to hold the bowl steady so the dog could eat without becoming too dizzy to hold his meal down.

Lady Chum-Chum, alerted to the presence of food by her sharp eyes and sharper nose, abandoned the corner in which she had lurked while cautiously surveilling this frenetic little creature that had invaded her haven. She essayed a couple of half-hearted swoops at the pup's head, but the little fellow could not be distracted from the serious business of emptying his bowl. Enid took pity on the Lady and tossed small pieces of pork into the air for her to catch while performing unnecessarily complex feats of aerobatics.

Despite the jolly aerial display before her, she was seized by a sense of absolute desolation. *I find myself as alone as I have been since I was loaded into what amounted to a coffin for my escape from Arden.*

I am with you, Enid, Dunaughy thought.

You are, sir. Her answering thought was loaded with as much contrition as her nature allowed. *And I am ever grateful for your mentorship and company. Truly, I would be lost without your mentorship and, more dear to me still, your affection. I fear my equanimity is as battered and tossed as fiercely as* Revenant *was in the claws of the* outre-montagne.

It is nothing—and, to answer the question that fool Yeardly would not, Captain Nath's ire is of the thunderbolt variety. It shakes the ground but passes in an instant. I'm sure you will find his mood much improved by morning. As for Yeardly, remember he is still but a callow youth, only old enough to stand for lieutenant due to his role in cutting out Redemption. *Like most youths who have yet to exchange their passionate humors with another, his passions are ungovernable. He will come around in time. He admires you with too deep a fervor to resist the gravity of your respect for any significant time.*

I am not as sanguine as you, Enid thought as she lowered herself to sit cross-legged on the deck. Jock fumbled his way into her lap, and she absently scratched behind his ears. Lady Chum-Chum refused to be excluded from Enid's attention and doubled herself up to settle over her shoulders like a feathered stole.

Enid smiled despite herself and picked the yawning, sated pup up and, after rubbing his belly and asking for his opinion on who was a good little fellow, she carefully placed him in the corner of her box cot.

If you allow him to sleep there tonight, that is where he will sleep from henceforth, Dunaughy warned.

That is a risk I'm willing to take for the comfort his company will provide. I'm in mortal fear for Merry. If she passes, I will be to blame, as I shall be if she awakens and hates me for not confiding in her regarding the connection between my hand and you. I would be furious at such a lapse of trust, so I cannot fault her if she holds me in odium for my failed constancy. She climbed into the box cot and, as she reclined, took pains to accommodate her new bedmate, who had already set to snoring with the volume of a hound thrice his size.

Do not borrow troubles for tomorrow before you've dispatched today's, Dunaughy chided.

Enid may or may not have heard this admonition, as the exhaustion of the day's activities and the toll on her emotions dragged her into the warm embrace of the goose down pillow and mattress she'd purchased in Middlesea, and from thence into a deep, dreamless sleep. She lay on her side with her knees crooked, a posture that proved too inviting for Jock to ignore. He was soon curled up in the shelter of her legs, with the dome of his head pressed firmly into the hollow formed by the backs of her knees. Lady Chum-Chum, not to be outdone, wound herself into a tight coil in the angle of her ankles and laid her head along Enid's calf. As they slept, *Revenant* cut a steady and unrelenting course for Gisbon and an uncertain destiny.

Glossary

Aback: Movement of a ship toward its stern, either purposefully by the set of the sails or inadvertently by a shift in the wind.

Abaft: Closer to the stern.

Abeam: Objects to the starboard or larboard of a ship.

Accommodation Ladder: A set of steps by which officers and visitors can board or leave a ship.

Admiralty: The Royal Office that oversees the Navy under the direction of the Sea Lord.

Aft: Toward the rear.

After-Cabin: The cabin reserved for the captain's use, located in the ship's aft.

Afterguard: The ordinary sailors and landsmen responsible for working the aft sails. They are posted to the quarterdeck and poop deck.

Alee: The lee or sheltered side of a ship.

Athwart: Across the ship, from one side to the other.

Amidships: The middle section of a ship.

Barky: Sailor's slang for a happy and/or well-loved ship.

Beam-Ends: A ship "on its beam ends" is laying over so steeply that it is in immediate danger of capsizing.

Before the Mast: Someone berthed forward of the foremast, or, in other words, common sailors.

Belay: To make something fast, such as securing a rope to a cleat, or to cease or disregard something, as in "belay that gabble" or "belay my last command."

Belaying Pins: Iron or wooden pins stored in holes in the pinrail around a mast. They are used to store rope coils and can be pressed into use as a weapon if necessary.

Berth: A sleeping area.

Bilge: Both the lowest-lying area in a ship and the foul liquid that accumulates there.

Binnacle: A small cabinet near the wheel in which the ship's compass is housed to protect it from the weather. At night, the binnacle is often illuminated by a low orb of light.

Blacking: A paste used to protect an object from rust or rot. The polish blackens the item.

Blackstrap: A fortified wine of inferior quality.

Block: A strongly made pulley used to ease the effort of setting rigging or lifting the anchors or other heavy items.

Boarding Net: Nets strung along a ship's rails to discourage and entangle boarders.

Bogaraets: Nonhuman natives of several islands in the Shards. While they have a nasty reputation as man-eaters and pirates, the majority of Bogaraet communities are peaceful fishers, and it is against their religion to consume the flesh of sentient creatures. Unlike humans, they refuse to eat dolphins, whales, or octopi. They will, however, consume Darghaur.

Bosun (Boatswain or Bos'n): A petty officer charged with inspecting the ship's sails and rigging and keeping the officer of the watch apprised of their condition. They were also responsible for overseeing the raising/weighing of anchors, sail handling, and other moment-by-moment actions required to work a ship. Their orders are broadcast to the crew using coded calls from the bosun's silver whistle.

Bosun's Chair: A swing-like chair used by sailors working aloft or to safely hoist lubbers aboard ship.

Bow (Bows): The forward end of a ship or boat.

Brig: A square-rigged, two-masted ship.

Broadside: The total number of guns on one side of a ship or the firing of all such guns in a single volley.

Buffskin or Buff: Leather made from buffalo or ox hide. It is a dull, light yellow in color.

Bulkhead: The partitions that form a ship's cabins. A wall.

Bulwark: The wooden "wall" enclosing a ship's upper deck.

Bumper: A glass filled to the rim with wine or spirits.

Calendar (in Albion):

Month	Meaning	Season	*Terran Month*
Wyrdmon	*Month of Weirds*	Winter	January
Challachmon	*Hearth's Month*	Winter	February
Aliesednesmon	*Redemption Month*	Spring	March
Nefaemon	*Holy Month*	Spring	April
Murchathmon	*Reiver's Month*	Spring	May
Curoanmon	*Month of Crowns*	Summer	June
Lughnaesamon	*Lugh's Festival Month*	Summer	July
Filyehmon	*Month of Returning Reivers*	Summer	August
Ylfeymon	*Month of the Fey*	Autumn	September
Doíradmon	*Month of Offerings*	Autumn	October
Ralifrimon	*Starfall Month*	Autumn	November
Cruachmon	*Cruach's Month*	Winter	December

Capstan: A horizontal wheel on the deck that turns an axle belowdecks. It is used to raise the ship's anchors. As the capstan wheel is turned, a cable is wound up that lifts the anchor. Series of ratchets, or pawls, are engaged as the wheel turns to prevent the cable from unwinding if the capstan is released. The capstan is pierced around its circumference by a series of sockets into which capstan bars can be inserted to give the hands more leverage to turn the wheel.

Captain: The commanding officer aboard a warship. Captains can only be placed in command of post ships. They are commissioned officers and all other officers and ratings aboard a ship are their subordinates.

Carabines: Carabines are muskets with short barrels. This makes them less accurate at long range but very handy for boarding or anti-boarding actions.

Cathead: Sturdy wooden beams projecting from the side of a ship's bow. They are used for hoisting and storing the ship's anchors.

Cat (Cat-o'-nine-tails): A whip used to deliver punishment floggings for violations of the Articles of War. It consisted of nine cords attached to a thick rope handle. The cords, each about a foot-and-a-half long, are each knotted three times along their length. Sailors are usually tied bareback to one of the ship's grates, where their punishment is witnessed by the assembled crew.

Colors: A ship's flag that indicates its nationality.

Commander (Master and Commander): A rank above lieutenant and below captain.

Commission: The orders requiring a captain to take command of a ship.

Commodore: A captain placed in command of a squadron of ships on a particular mission. Also, a rank granted to the commander of a given naval station, such as the commodore of Far Harbor.

Complement: The official number of sailors and officers required to crew a ship. It is a fortunate officer that finds himself with a full complement at the beginning of a cruise, let alone at its end.

Corsair: A pirate or privateer or a ship employed in either pursuit.

Course: The compass point toward which a ship currently sails.

Course: The lowermost sail on a mast. There are three courses, listed from stern to bow: *mizzen course*, *main course*, and *fore course*.

Courses: The sails depending from the lowest spars. There are normally two courses, the forecourse, and the main course.

Coxswain (Cox'n): The sailor assigned to helm one of a ship's boats and supervise its crew. The captain's cox'n is responsible for his boat and attends to him.

Crack On: To carry as much sail as a ship will bear to coax as much speed from her as possible.

Cutting Out: Capturing an enemy at anchor with a surprise attack by boats.

Darghaur: Non-human creatures that inhabit the continent known as the Darghaur Fastness. The Darghaur are inimical to humanity. They are obviously intelligent and possessed of highly advanced magic. They have never communicated directly with humanity, with whom they wage an off-again, on-again genocidal war. They have currently withdrawn into the Fastness and have not launched any major attacks in a century or more.

Deckhead: The "ceiling" of a space belowdecks.

Dophir: A colloquialism for a wealthy merchant who made their riches in the Shards. Derived from a Bogaraet word for "chief."

Dunnage: A sailor's or passenger's baggage.

Ensign: A flag that announces a ship's nationality.

Eressa: The ancient, and likely mythological, continent that was dominated by humans prior to the Cataclysm. Its higher points are said to form the many small islands forming the Shards Archipelago.

"First" or First Lieutenant: A ship's second-in-command and executive officer. Also referred to familiarly as the "first luff."

Flag Officer: An admiral, vice admiral, rear admiral, or commodore.

Fo'c'sle (Forecastle): The deck forward of the foremast is referred to as the forecastle, or fo'c'sle by nautical types.

Fore: Toward the front.

Frigate: A three-masted fifth- or sixth-rate ship built for speed and firepower. Too light to take a place in a line of battle, they are used for patrols or to perform commerce raids, scout for a fleet, or carry out independent cruises.

Gig: One of a ship's boats. A gig is a light, graceful boat that can be propelled by either oars or sails as required. It is usually reserved for the use of the captain.

Grating: The cover for a hatchway. It is composed of a grid of wooden slats. Its secondary use is to secure a sailor for punishment.

Grog: A strong mixture of water and rum that is served to Albion crews twice a day. Other spirits may be substituted if necessary, which is uniformly greeted with displeasure and complaint by the tars.

Hanger: A short, often curved sword worn on one's belt.

Head Money: A reward paid for the prisoners taken from a captured ship.

HMS: "His/Her Majesty's Ship." A ship of the Albion Royal Navy.

Holystone: A soft sandstone roughly the size of a thick holy book. Used to scour a ship's decks.

Jolly Boat: One of a ship's boats. Its bluff bow and wide stern make it an ideal workhorse. It is usually carried suspended from a ship's stern for quick and easy access.

Landsman: A sailor with no naval training, fit only for hauling and pulling on ropes.

Larboard: The left side of the ship, looking forward from the stern.

Launch: The largest of a ship's boats. It can be rigged with a fore-and-aft sail.

Lee: The lee side is the side away from or protected from the wind.

Lieutenant: The lowest commissioned rank in the Navy. They are referred to numerically according to their seniority, with the most senior lieutenant being the first, the next senior the second, and so forth. The number of lieutenants aboard a ship depends on its rating.

Loblolly Boy: An assistant to the ship's surgeon.

Lower Deck: The deck upon which a ship's sailors are berthed, situated above the orlop.

Lubber (Landlubber): A person who is grossly ignorant of life at sea. The term can be extremely derogatory when aimed at a fellow sailor or affectionate when directed at, say, a ship's rather exotic and attractive magister.

Make a Leg: To bow with one leg drawn back and the other bent, normally to the accompaniment of doffing one's hat.

Master: A ship's master is responsible for its navigation and sailing. Masters are appointed by the Navy board. They have the authority of a lieutenant but are subordinate to them as they are not commissioned officers. Also, the commander of a merchant ship.

Master and Commander: A lieutenant who has been approved for the command of small, non-post vessels. It is increasingly common for masters and commanders to be referred to simply as "commanders." A commander's rank is higher than a lieutenant's but subordinate to a post captain. Officers of this rank are only referred to as "commanders" when they are not assigned a command. While in command of a vessel, they are referred to as "captain."

A commander's uniform distinguishes them from lieutenants, most notably by the single epaulet worn on their left shoulder.

Master's Mate: Petty officers subordinate to a ship's master. They are the only ratings allowed to take command of a prize vessel.

Mid: Also referred to as a ship's "young gentles." The Albion Royal Navy requires any person seeking a career as a commissioned officer to serve as a mid until such time as they pass their lieutenant's examination. Mids are accepted from age ten onward. Despite the youth of most mids, they are expected to take responsibility for the supervision of the sailors assigned to their division.

Not all mids are children or teens, however. Unfortunate would-be officers can be stuck as mids for their entire career if they continuously fail their lieutenant's exam, although most find a new line of work rather than suffer the shame of being called a "long-toothed mid."

Mum Drill: Gun drills in which gun crews practice loading, laying, and recovering the guns without firing them. This form of gun drill isn't ideal, but captains resort to it when they lack a surplus of powder and shot or the specie to purchase it.

***Navy List*:** An official quarterly publication printed in Middlesea. It lists the officers of the Navy and their seniority within their rank.

Orlop: The lowest deck on a ship. The space is below the waterline and has areas reserved for use by the ship's surgeon and magister, in addition to providing storage for spare cables.

Petty Officer: A naval rank similar to that of a noncommissioned officer in the Albion army.

Pinnace: A ship's boat, generally used as a light tender.

Post Captain: An Albionic naval rank indicating an officer who has received orders to command a post ship. Once an officer has received this honor, referred to as "making post," they will never be assigned to a non-post ship. If they live long enough, they will eventually rise to the rank of admiral.

Post Ship: A rated ship with no less than twenty guns.

Purser (pusser): The officer responsible for provisioning a ship and keeping its accounts. This position offered many opportunities for profiteering, often at the expense of the common sailors. For this reason, pursers are not well-loved before the mast.

Quarterdeck: The area of deck described by the space between the mainmast and a ship's poop, or, should it lack a poop, its stern.

Rake: The angle of a ship's masts, which can be raked forward or aft. Also, a particularly devastating attack in which a broadside is fired into an enemy's bow or stern, its two weakest sections of hull. The balls from such an attack tend to run the length of the ship's decks, causing terrible destruction and death.

Rue de Sanctuaire: A street in Arden that was declared immune to Canon Law to permit duels to be performed legally despite the ban on the activity by Cardinal Gisboneaux. It retained this freedom until the Theocratic Revolution. The street's pre-Revolution reputation for immodesty—"dressed for Rue de Sanctuaire" meant being naked and ready for sex—was well-deserved.

Scantlings: The breadth of a vessel's planks. The larger the vessel, the stronger the scantlings are and the more resistant they are to iron shot.

Sea Service: The Navy.

Smashers: Smashers are a relatively new form of shipboard artillery. They are lightweight guns that can fire a very heavy ball, but only for a short distance.

Spanker: On a square-rigged ship, a fore-and-aft sail rigged in place of the mizzen course during fair weather. The spanker is sometimes called the *driver.* It can be used to increase the maneuverability or even steer a vessel.

Spell-Lock: Spell-locks are enchanted "locks" used to ignite the alchemical powder used in guns of all types, from pistols to the massive siege cannons. An unenchanted lock will not ignite alchemical powder. They are kept "charged" by the ship's gunner, armorer, mids with the required training and ability, and, if absolutely required, ship's magister.

Starboard: The right side of the ship, looking forward from the stern.

Stern Gallery: An ornately carved and painted balcony built on the stern of the ship. Its glass windows face aft.

Taken: The colloquial name for humans who have been enslaved by the Darghaur.

T'gallants (Topgallants): Pronounced "t'garns'ls." The square sails immediately above topsails.

Topsail: The sail mounted on the topmast immediately above one of the courses. There are three topsails, listed from stern to bow: *mizzen topsail*, *main topsail*, and *foretopsail*. Also referred to as "mizzen top, main top, or fore top."

Wardroom: A mess (dining) area reserved for the use of commissioned and warrant officers of wardroom rank. The gun room serves as the wardroom on smaller vessels, like *Alarum*.

Warrant: A certificate of appointment issued to officers below commission rank.

Wheel: A ship's wheel is located on the quarterdeck. It is attached to a mechanism that allows it to control the rudder and thus steer the ship.

Younker: A youngster.

acknowledgments

I was fortunate in the support I received in bringing *The Silver Hand* into your organic hands. Here are the names of a few of the people who were particularly generous with their time and expertise. Those who don't find their names below have my word that while I have limited space for acknowledgments on these pages, the Hall of Worthies in my heart is limitless. Within it, your portraits hold positions of the highest esteem.

First, and predictably, I thank my family for their enthusiasm and moral support. The enthusiasm shown by my mother, brother, daughters, and sons reenergized me when my batteries ran low. Peggy Carpenter, my wife, showed infinite patience with my authorial personality, which is best described as "like Eeyore, but with less jollity."

Clearly, the alpha reading efforts of my favorite gobbo, Channy Kobalos, require recognition. Their involvement has helped me improve my writing and made *The Silver Hand* a better book. They also introduced me to a wonderful Discord server for writers, ranging from hobbyists, fanfic writers, and traditionally published authors. It's a great community, despite a propensity among its members for licking newcomers.

As always, my agent, Caitlin Blasdell, has proven to be an active, insightful contributor to this book's creative process and a wise and patient advocate for its neophyte author.

Last, but certainly not least, my heartfelt thanks to Joe Monti, of Saga Press, who took a chance on this and the previous volume simply because they struck him as something he would enjoy reading.

Shawn Carpenter
21 April 2026
dscarpenter@gmail.com

Aboard HMS Caliginosity, *standing off and on Pointe de Non-Retour.*